Trusting in Faith

A Medieval Romance

Lisa Shea

Cover design by Debi Gardiner / GardinerDesign.com
Book design by Lisa Shea

Lisa Shea
Visit my website at LisaShea.com

First Printing: October 2012
Minerva Webworks LLC

Print version ISBN-13 978-0-9798377-3-9

Dreams come true
Honor exists
Truth overcomes all –
You just need to believe.

Trusting in Faith

Chapter 1

England, 1191

Patience is a conquering virtue.
The learned say that, if it not desert you,
It vanquishes what force can never reach;
Why answer back at every angry speech?
No, learn forbearance or, I'll tell you what,
You will be taught it, whether you will or not.
--The Canterbury Tales, Chaucer

Sarah stretched low over the neck of her galloping horse, straining to maintain sight of the narrow deer path she traced through the dense, darkening woods. Even in the approaching dusk the stifling summer heat made the air almost liquid. The warmth from her steed washed against her in rolling waves, threatening to suffocate her. She longed to stop, to throw off the heavy black cloak she was wearing and to breathe, if only for a moment.

She knew she could not. Too much depended on her reaching her destination quickly and without being identified.

Sarah's lower back ached with throbbing pain; she pushed the sensation away with practiced discipline. She had been on the road for over three hours, starting off at once when the summons came. Despite the urgency, she had taken all usual precautions to ensure she hadn't been followed. Even so, her body remained at a tense alert. Nothing could guarantee safety from *wolves' heads* – bandits who roamed the shadows, preying on the weak.

The reassuring weight of her longsword on her left hip tugged gently at her; she took in a deep breath. She knew enough to keep herself safe from the casual cutthroat. It was these newcomers who concerned her - the disaffected who were returning from the crusades with a penchant for crime. She understood her odds with realistic sobriety. An encounter with a man of that training would be brutal and short.

Lights flared ahead; she pulled her mount in hard. Her horse skidded forward a few feet with a loud whinny, sliding in the gravel to a rough, panting halt. Almost immediately, she was surrounded by a wall of glinting steel. She threw her hood back in the flickering shadows, shaking loose her long, tawny hair to show herself more fully.

"It is me, Sarah," she called out in a low, urgent voice. "I am alone, I swear it."

The swords were pulled back in an instant, and the crowd of men retreated a step to let her dismount. A tall, reedy, blond-haired man in his early twenties scurried forward to help her down from her steed. He assisted her with the leather bag she removed from the side of the saddle.

Once she was on her feet, he pulled her hurriedly through the crowd. His lanky body easily pressed through the roughly dressed men. They soon moved into the main clearing where a series of tents were set up around a campfire. There were a few simply garbed women and children scattered here and there, but the group was primarily comprised of armed men, suspicious, alert, and watchful.

Numerous pairs of eyes followed her as she ran toward one of the smaller tents.

She pulled open the coarse flap of fabric, took one look inside, and spoke calmly over her shoulder without turning. "Lloyd - go get me a pail of hot water, and some clean rags. Hurry." She took another step forward, letting the cloth fall closed behind her, and moved in to kneel beside her patient.

"Shhhh, Abigail, you are doing fine," she murmured soothingly to the young, willowy woman who lay before her. Sarah tenderly brushed back a few loose strands of blonde hair, and the teen relaxed slightly beneath her touch. Sarah then ran her hand with practiced ease over the large bulge in the woman's stomach, feeling for the position of the baby's head and limbs.

Sarah's face eased into a smile. "Your child is just right. The head is pointing down, and everything feels proper. In a few hours you will be the proud mother of a beautiful son or daughter."

She shook off her heavy cloak and laid it to one side. Even without the extra layer of fabric, the air in the tent was sweltering and close, like the inside of an oven. A surge of pity swept over her for the girl lying before her, drenched in sweat. "You might have chosen a better month to give birth in, though," she added with a light tone.

Abigail attempted to smile at the quip, but another contraction shuddered through her, and she gritted her teeth against the pain. When it faded, she gasped, "I am afraid we were not thinking about a baby at the time ..."

Sarah nodded. "As is often the case," she commented half to herself. "Still, here we are, and you will get through this fine, just as your mother did, and her mother before her. Focus on the thought that this is a short ordeal in exchange for a lifetime of joy." Her eyes twinkled. "If birthing really was that awful, no woman would bear a second child!"

"My mother had three," responded Abigail weakly, leaning back and closing her eyes. Sarah cleared out the floor space of the tent, arranging her bag to one side where it would be within easy reach. "Maybe she was a masochist," the pregnant woman muttered under her breath. "It might explain her temper."

Sarah chuckled. "I help many women who are on their second, third, or fourth child. They say it gets easier each time, and that the memory of the pain fades quickly when you hold your new child in your arms. This will be over soon. Just take it one moment at a time."

She turned her head at a noise. Lloyd had returned dutifully with the cloth and pail and was standing nervously by the entrance.

"Thank you - now wait outside," Sarah instructed him tenderly but firmly. "Stay within calling distance, but let her have her privacy."

Lloyd's face was creased with worry, but he nodded in understanding. He looked past Sarah to the woman lying on the rough blanket. "Abby - I love you," he whispered to the young woman in labor. "I am right here for you." Then another contraction began, and he closed the flap, leaving the women to their work.

Sarah washed and rinsed, then quickly prepared the cloths. She returned to the young woman and first helped her to a sitting position, then to stand. The low tent made them stoop, but they were able to walk small circles around the interior. Sarah moved slowly, helping to bear the woman's weight. Abigail was a coltish girl of sixteen, maybe five-foot-four, awkward with her low belly and the pain spasms rippling through her. Sarah kept up a running commentary of soothing stories and advice, knowing that the teen she half-carried barely heard what she said. The important thing was to keep her body moving and her mind distracted as much as possible so that she would relax into her labor.

The hours passed slowly, with the pair alternating between moving and taking short rests. Even while Sarah spoke and sang, part of her continually evaluated the signs she received from Abigail's body. Sarah had been helping deliver babies for eight years now - since she was fourteen - and had seen a wide variety of situations. She glanced at Abigail's face and thought how common this story was.

"I know we have been meeting for a few months now, but I enjoy hearing the tale. Tell me again how you and Lloyd met," she suggested quietly, looking to draw Abigail's attention away from the pain of the contractions.

Abigail nodded, taking deliberate steps as she spoke. "I have known Lloyd for many years," she explained, her voice rasping. "He cared for the horses in our stables. When he was able to, he would go riding with me to keep me company. He is the kindest, gentlest person I have ever met. He is five years my senior and always watched out for me." Her face softened into a smile. "I suppose our falling in love was inevitable."

She winced as another pain swept through her, and it was a moment or two before she could continue. "My mother caught us kissing behind the stables, and she was furious. She forbade me to see him ever again. It was too late, though – I was already pregnant. When she heard that, she threw me out of the house, saying I had disgraced the family name."

Sarah nodded, encouraging her. "Mothers can be like that. At least you two were not alone – Kyle came with you?"

Abigail focused on putting one foot in front of the other. "Yes, Kyle is like an uncle to me. He was our witness when we married in a nearby church. This group of wanderers was moving through the area, and we joined up with them to have food and shelter while we figured out what we wanted to do. They have been very good to us. They even agreed to find a fixed camp location so that I could give birth in safety. I knew of your reputation for discretion, and sent out a messenger. Now here we are."

Sarah shook her head, moving slowly around the tent with her young charge. Would the mother really still deny the daughter if she could see her now, doubled over in pain, about to deliver a new life into the world? How did it benefit anybody to be so stubborn about who someone fell in love with?

There was a change in Abigail's walking rhythm; Sarah pulled to a stop. She quickly evaluated the position of the baby and broke into an encouraging grin. "You are a lucky woman, Abigail. Your great health has brought your child out in record time!" She looked up into the woman's eyes. "You are doing so well, Abigail; I am quite proud of you. Just a little while more, and your infant will be in your arms."

She helped Abigail move over toward the clean cloths. "Squat down over this area. Spread your feet out to support your weight. There you go. Now, slowly, push. Push down, low and hard."

Sarah knelt before Abigail, and in a moment the girl's thin hands were pressed into her shoulders for support. Sarah moved her own hands beneath Abigail. It was only a short while before she felt the head crown, and then slowly the rest of the body emerged. When the head was out, the baby gave out a lusty cry, and then, over Abigail's moans, Sarah could hear a shout of celebration from outside the tent. Soon the cheers were echoing all around them, and Sarah held the newborn life in her arms. A slicing cut with the dagger she wore at her side, and the baby was free.

Sarah quickly cleaned and bundled up the young child, then helped the exhausted mother move onto the bed. She tenderly placed the infant into her mother's arms; tears welled in her eyes as she saw that first look between parent and child. This moment was always special to Sarah - the ending of a dangerous ordeal, and the beginning of a new family.

She spent some time cleaning and checking on both patients. Many women in surrounding villages died during childbirth due to complications. Sarah prided herself on her attention to detail, checking carefully for tears or injuries. Luckily, there was little need for concern here. The baby was in perfect health, and the mother's bleeding stopped almost immediately.

Worn down, Sarah pushed herself wearily to a standing position and gathered up her cloak and bag. Giving one last look around the tent, she moved to the entrance. Lloyd stood waiting, a wide smile on his face, shaking hands with a boisterous group of grinning men.

His eyes held hers, a flicker of concern showing. "She is fine? My wife?"

"Both your wife and daughter are perfect," replied Sarah warmly. "You can go in and be with them now. Just wash your hands in the water first, please, to keep the baby clean."

Lloyd needed no further encouragement, and was through the tent doors in a flash.

A weathered man in his late forties approached Sarah. "I am not sure if you remember me. My name is Kyle, and I am Lloyd's good friend," he introduced himself. "Come, let me find you a drink. You must be exhausted."

Sarah followed him without a word. He guided her through the tents toward a crackling campfire on the far edge of the clearing. Only a quiet pair of elderly men sat to one side of the glowing embers, their creased faces shadowed, lost in thought. The crowds were beginning to settle down again, and a muted hush drifted over the dark camp. Sarah seated herself with relief on a moss-encrusted log, and soon Kyle brought over a stained pottery mug filled with mead.

Sarah drank the liquid gratefully, noting that the semi-sweet concoction was surprisingly good. She sat back, rolling loose the tension that had built up in her muscles over the past few hours. “This is tasty,” she commented to Kyle, who had found a seat on a nearby rock. “Do you make this here?”

The greying man nodded his head with pleasure. “Indeed, I do. I was a beekeeper at Abby’s estate,” he explained with a wry grin. “When Lloyd said he was leaving, I packed up my supplies and came along with them. I could not in good conscience stay behind when they were out on the road. Lloyd was always the impetuous one, but I keep him out of trouble when I can.”

Kyle took a sip from his own mug, contemplative. “We do have plans for the future. We could build a house a few villages over, once we have earned a bit of money for supplies. Between my skills and his we should be able to make ends meet.” He shrugged, looking around him at the rough collection of tents and people. “Unfortunately we have not built up our reserves yet. Life does not always work things out the way you think it will.”

“That is true,” agreed Sarah, taking another drink. “Life is sometimes more like riding a wild horse and hanging on as best you can. I am sure you will get there soon enough.”

Kyle leant forward, his face serious. “What is intriguing is that months can go by - or years - where it seems like nothing is happening. Nothing is changing. Then - wham - out of the blue comes something urgent, and you have to make a decision in a split second that will affect the rest of your life.”

Sarah's mouth quirked into a smile. "That is why it is so important to make good use of those quiet months," she commented with a chuckle. "If you have prepared yourself, and readied yourself, then when those moments come you can act wisely. Life is all about taking good care of yourself - and training your mind - so you can get through the sharp dips and turns when they do come."

She finished the rest of the mead, then gave a long stretch. "I really need to head back home, or I will not make it before morning," she sighed with a yawn. "Abigail and Lloyd already know how to care for the baby for the first weeks - I have gone over that with them several times, during calmer visits. I know there are other women in the camp who can share their wisdom should they need it. Please remind them that I will be back in two weeks to check on their progress and to answer any questions they might have. If there is any sort of problem in the meantime, send a messenger, and I will come."

Kyle stood as she did, and took both of her hands in his own. "Thank you, for both of them," he offered heartily. "It means the world to them that you came out to help her through this." Kyle turned and waved to a scruffy young boy, who promptly brought the brown stallion over for her. He had been given oats and water, and looked ready for the return trip.

Sarah took a deep breath, then drew her heavy, disguising cloak around her, pulling up the hood. The heat was nearly overwhelming, and sweat immediately poured from her skin. She mounted with an effort and gathered up the reins.

She waved down to Kyle. "Until a fortnight." Then she was heading back down the trail toward home.

The road lightened in front of her as she rode, allowing her to move more easily as the path evolved from wood to clearing to cart trail. Her pace, though quick, was not so frantic as before. Soon she was passing through an isolated village. Sleepy chickens nestled against the small homes in feathered clumps and a lone, mangy dog roamed the dirt street. Although none were awake at this early hour, she stayed at the outskirts of the next, larger village, and then turned south to cover the final miles toward her home.

Relaxed pleasure eased through her as she came over a rise and beheld the structure. The central three-story keep was built of sturdy grey stone, and the collection of smaller buildings were hidden behind the solid curtain walls which encompassed the area. Her parents were sticklers for discipline, and even in this pre-dawn light she could make out the alert, well-groomed guards manning the main gates. The pair had them open for her before she had a chance to call out, and the men waved a friendly greeting as she passed through, relieved to be home.

She rode directly to the two-story wooden stable building, only reining in once she was fully within its walls. She wearily dismounted and handed the reins to Lou, the young red-headed stableboy who stood ready at her side.

He gave her an impish grin. “Another late night, M’Lady?” He looked impossibly fresh and chipper to Sarah’s fatigued eyes.

“That it was, Lou. Please take good care of him, he has earned it,” she added, giving her mount a fond look. She smiled as Lou tenderly ran a hand down the horse’s neck. The lad was meant for the stables and cared for each animal as if it were his own child. Turning, she picked up her worn leather bag and headed slowly into the main keep.

The building was quiet in the pre-dawn light. She nodded in greeting to a guard in the main hall, then made her way up the stairs to her own quarters. By habit, she stopped by her younger sister’s room, poking her head in to check on her. The room was messy by her standards, with ribbons and lace strewn in all corners. The bed itself lay neat and untouched. Sarah shook her head, closing the door softly. Where had her sister gotten off to this night? Was it another tryst with the bard from the next town, or had she acquired a new beau?

Sarah put it out of her mind. What she needed right now was sleep. She moved down the hall to her own room, heaving the heavy door fully open with her shoulder. She hung up her bag, then shut the door solidly before wearily pulling her sweat-stained clothes off and piling them in a heap. A relieved sigh eased through her as she slipped on a light chemise.

She glanced up as the sun peeked over the horizon, sending a golden shaft of light across the floor. She pulled the heavy curtains fully closed over her two large windows. A breeze still curled around the edges, sending a refreshing breath of air into the room. Feeling relatively cool for the first time in many long hours, she climbed into bed and was instantly asleep.

Chapter 2

Sarah was being firmly shaken. Despite her exhaustion, she came awake instantly.

"I am up, what do you need?" she asked in a gravelly voice, struggling to open her eyes. The world slowly came into focus, with only a faint light coming around the edges of her curtains. It was hard to judge the time of day by that slim hint. Had she slept straight through the afternoon? If so, why was she still so tired? "Is it evening already?" she wondered aloud, gaining her bearings.

"Take your time, it is not an emergency," soothed a familiar voice. Polly, Sarah's nanny and maid since she was a toddling child, was moving to the windows to pull the curtains open slightly, bringing only a bit more light into the room. Polly was in her early forties, but to Sarah she seemed as active and alert as she had been when they would chase geese together so many years ago. Polly's light brown hair was braided down her back in one long plait, and she wore a cobalt blue dress over a white chemise.

The woman stepped back to the bed with a cheerful smile, her speech slow and languorous. "Give yourself a moment to awaken. It is your parents who have called for you, not a patient."

Sarah wearily eased herself into a sitting position. She could see now that beyond the bedroom's curtains heavy, dark clouds roiled in the sky. She sighed with pleasure as she took in a deep breath. The stifling heat of yesterday had gone, replaced by a welcome coolness.

Polly brought over a rose-colored dress for Sarah and laid it across the foot of the bed. She then gently helped her charge to stand. "It seems a knight arrived at the keep an hour or two ago; he is downstairs with your sister, Rachel. Your parents have been stalling him, saying they will not talk with him until after they finish lunch. They apparently want you present for some reason. Now lunch is almost over ..."

Sarah sighed and nodded, dressing quickly. Had this knight been insulted by her sister and come to demand recompense? Did he have another point of honor to bring up regarding her? A thought occurred to her, and she smiled. Had her sister gotten pregnant and finally snagged herself a permanent partner?

Her younger sister's impulsive behavior had been relatively harmless in the past, but Sarah had always worried that there would come a day ... she pushed the thought out of her head. It was best to see what the problem actually was before she began imagining the worst.

Polly finished twining her hair into a simple, long braid. "There now, you best get going," she encouraged with a smile.

Sarah nodded her thanks, then moved quickly out the door. She hurried down the long hallway, pulling up short as she reached the edge of the banister. She took a few deep breaths before turning the corner to walk calmly down the stairs and into the hall.

The central room of the keep was the largest in the building, and at the moment it was occupied by a scattering of tables, each holding a few diners. The banners on the wall fluttered in the pre-storm breeze, which was wafting a deliciously cool stream of air through the room. Two maids moved deftly through the area, refilling goblets and clearing away the remnants of meals.

A large, oaken table sat at one end of the expansive grey stone hall, and the remains of a delicious lunch lay spread out across the surface. Sarah's stomach rumbled as she spotted two hens, a plate of turnips, a large loaf of bread, and several other smaller dishes.

Sarah's mother and father were chatting comfortably with each other, and Sarah smiled to see them. She was renewed each time she returned home, especially when she took care of single mothers or women in difficult situations. Her mother and father, after all these years, still adored one another and it showed in every movement. Her mother, her blonde hair fading to grey-white at the edges, radiated a stately beauty and quiet wisdom in her bearing. Her father was reckoned a seasoned fighter by the troops. His short-cropped hair sported the same mix of blond, white, and grey. His lean build had not yet gone to softness.

Beside her father sat her sister. Rachel had inherited the blonde hair and buxom beauty of her mother, and she deftly used it to her advantage. She wore the cross necklace that every family member did, but her choice of material was a sparkling gem-encrusted gold creation which nestled deep within her bosom, drawing the eyes there. She was attired in a ruby red dress, artfully gathered to show off every curve of her body. She nibbled playfully at a piece of pastry, her eyes caught up with the visitor to the table who sat at her other side.

Sarah moved across the room, weaving amongst the tables and occupants. The knight looked up as Sarah approached and immediately stood to face her. Sarah was impressed; her first thought was that he was by far the most well-built man Rachel had ever brought home. She estimated he was just over six feet tall, with thick, raven-black hair curling to his shoulders. His build was sturdy, and she had no doubt from his sure movements that he could use well the sword he wore on his hip. His tunic was white with a red cross in its center.

A templar.

Sarah's mouth quirked, and her estimation of her sister's talents rose even higher. If Rachel could convince a templar to wed her ... but that was yet to be seen.

Her father smiled proudly. "Ah, here she is," he crowed. "Sir Reynald, have the honor of meeting my eldest daughter, Sarah."

Sarah stopped across the table from the foursome and obediently dropped a curtsey, lowering her eyes. "My lord," she greeted him quietly before moving to sit in a chair across from the group. Sally, the flaxen-haired housemaid with the build of a pixie, immediately brought her a wooden trencher and a pewter cup of mead. Sarah drank down the honey wine gratefully, her throat still parched from the previous day's work.

The knight bowed slightly to her, but his eyes showed irritation, not welcome. Sarah's mind skipped through the possibilities. If he was here to present a suit for her sister's hand, he would surely want to endear himself to the family, not be annoyed that a random sibling had come down late for a meal.

Her thoughts were eerily echoed by Reynald. "Your daughter is a late riser," he commented with an edge to his deep voice, "and I am on a timetable. Can we now please get started?"

Sarah's mother quirked an eyebrow at her husband, but said nothing. Sarah's father nodded genially and opened his hands to his visitor. "We are all here now. Please feel free to begin."

Sarah watched as Rachel turned her large, luminous eyes on the guest. Sarah held in a chuckle and sat back, enjoying a mouthful of the freshly baked bread.

Here we go. He loves her, he adores her, he cannot possibly live without her.

"My name is Sir Reynald, and I am a Knight Templar," stated the guest, sitting back in his chair. His eyes met those of Rachel, and his tone became indulgent. "What that means is -"

Rachel's heart-shaped mouth tweaked with mischief. Her voice recited with smooth certainty. "A Knight Templar is a member of the Rosecrutians – the 'The Order of the Rose Cross Veritas'. The order was founded in 1119 by a pair of French knights - Hugues de Payens and Godfrey de Saint-Omer. They had been active during the crusades, and sought to ensure that pilgrims could visit Jerusalem unmolested."

Rachel's eyes sparkled as she looked to her older sister, grinning more widely now. "I believe it was King Baldwin II, ruler of Jerusalem, who gave them initial permission to form? Then, in 1139, Pope Innocent II granted them enough privileges that they became unchecked Gods on Earth …"

Sarah chuckled in response, then glanced over at Reynald to see his reaction. His mouth hung open as if an infant had just spouted gospel. Sarah had lost count of how many men had underestimated her younger sister, assuming that her flirtatious beauty equated with an empty head.

Reynald showed a new alertness as he looked between the two sisters. "You have accurate dates, if a slightly skewed version of the meaning," he agreed finally, his eyes hard. "The Templars are a noble group, and you should be grateful that we exist. I myself have been serving in the Holy Lands for many years. My official duties have only now sent me back here to England."

Rachel leant forward, a mischievous gleam lurking in her eyes. "As I recall, the Templar rules forbid physical contact with any woman … or talking during meals …" Her eyes flickered to the wealth of food spread out at the table, then back to the guest.

Reynald's eyes narrowed in annoyance. "Indeed, we have tenets we swear to uphold when we take on the tunic," he agreed, his tone tight. "However, they are open to interpretation based on the necessity of the situation."

Rachel lounged back in her chair, her eyes bright with delight. "Why, that seems quite convenient," she teased.

The knight pursed his lips, then deliberately moved his gaze to Sarah's father. "Sir Christopher. My purpose in being here is that I seek permission to go house to house through your villages," Reynald continued without further preamble. "I seek a midwife. She is rumored to have information I need for the mission I am currently on. I need to learn everything she knows about recent births – names, dates, and locations. If you could provide me a list of women to start with, it would help me greatly on my task."

Sarah automatically steeled her expression to hold no emotion. Now this was a surprise she had not expected! She realized with a jolt just why her father had wanted her to come down for this discussion.

She kept her gaze on her bread, eating it with studied nonchalance. Inside, her mind roiled. As if she would give up privileged information to this arrogant knight! She promised each woman she worked with complete privacy. She'd be damned if some interloper would stride in and demand she break those confidences. For this she had been dragged out of bed?

Her sister cried out with enthusiastic glee. "Why, then, you can begin with us!"

Sarah willed herself not to turn, and took in a deep breath. Surely Rachel was not so swept up by him as to -

Rachel turned the full force of her cherubic gaze on the man at her side. "My sister, Sarah! She is easily the best midwife in the area. Everybody says so." She purred with pleasure, pressing herself against Reynald's arm as she spoke.

Sarah bit back a curse. She loved her sister dearly, but there were times ... she focused on cutting free a piece of the chicken on her trencher, and felt rather than saw Reynald's gaze swivel slowly to look at her.

Against her will, she brought her own eyes up to meet his amber ones. She watched cautiously as his look changed from dismissive disinterest to careful focus.

"So it was not simple laziness which kept you in bed, after all," he mused consideringly. Sarah's cheeks flushed at the implied insult, but she held her tongue. If that self-important knight thought he could prod her into speaking up, he was sorely mistaken.

Reynald kept his eyes on hers, and his gaze sharpened. Suddenly his question burst from him with startling directness.

"Were you with the local wanderers last night?"

Sarah had not prepared herself for such an immediate and accurate attack, and despite her best intentions, her face showed her shock. She had never been skilled at lying, and had always prided herself on her honesty and honor. She considered the irony that her virtue could be used against her by this knight.

Reynald saw at once that his guess had been accurate, and he stood in triumph. "My investigations have done me well," he congratulated himself with pride. "Well then, we shall set off at once."

Sarah blanched at the thought of causing trouble for her parents, but she held her seat with a stiff posture. “I have not said where I was, and I shall not leave this keep today unless I am called for by a patient,” she insisted with quiet deliberation. She reached forward to pick up another piece of bread, buttering it with patient care.

Reynald’s head swiveled automatically to her father. “Sir Christopher, I insist you force her to tell me if she has seen the wanderers, and to take me to them if she has.”

Sarah’s father sat back, considering. When he spoke, his voice was inflectionless and steady. “Here is the issue. You see, sir, she is of course an adult in her own right. That is item one. Item two is her profession. From the moment she started her training as a midwife, we have had an agreement - with the whole family - that the business she conducted was completely private. Surely you can imagine the types of situations she finds herself in. If the women she dealt with thought that their location and situation might be revealed, they would not call for her - and they could die.”

Reynald’s eyes moved to Sarah’s mother, but found her stare to be equally firm. Her voice was smooth but resolute. “Now, if you are considering extracting the information from our daughter by force ...” she purred, her voice deceptively pleasant.

Reynald’s eyes sparked in anger. “God’s teeth, no!” he snapped. His face became steely. “However, this is a riddle I must figure out, with or without your help.” His face showed the effort of his struggle to remain calm and poised.

He took a deep breath. “Your daughter is not the only midwife in the region. Sir Christopher, do I have your permission to talk with the other women in your villages, to discover what *they* are willing to tell me?” The internal conflict showed on his face, and after a moment he bit out, “of their own volition, of course?”

Christopher nodded his head complacently. “Certainly, every person in our lands is free to speak or not speak as they wish, and you are free to talk with them, to see what their decision is.”

His voice gained an edge. "However, sir, if I hear from one person that you have used pressure to extract what you wish to know ..." Sarah saw the flare of her father's honor and strength in his eyes, and pride welled in her chest at his statement.

Reynald nodded in agreement. "That is quite fair," he replied, his voice only conceding temporary defeat. "I shall seek lodging in one of your towns -"

Sarah's mother spoke up immediately. "That would not be necessary," she stated with a smile. "We have ample quarters here to see to your needs, and our stables will take fine care of your horse."

Reynald bowed slightly at this. "It would be an honor to share in your hospitality," he agreed more gently. "I have already found your food to be quite commendable."

Sarah sighed. With Reynald skulking around the keep, any follow up visits to the gypsy camp would become hard to manage. Her gaze sharpened as she realized this was undoubtedly his aim. She would not allow this meddlesome knight to interfere with her responsibilities.

A wave of dizziness hit her, and she remembered suddenly how little sleep she had gotten. She needed to get clear of Reynald before her tongue slipped and she said something she regretted.

Taking one last bite, she stood slowly, her body steeped in exhaustion. "If that is all the news for now, I have tasks to attend to." She glanced briefly across the table, her eyes stopping as they met with Reynald's. His eyes seemed so sharp and clear, she felt as if he could see within her. She quickly dropped her eyes, then turned and went out the rear door. Three short steps led her down into the fragrantly verdant herb garden, spread out in decorative grids behind the main keep.

Sarah spent the next few hours in a daze. She still ached from the lack of sleep and barely knew which plots she was weeding or tending. She did not want to go to sleep for fear that it would prolong her off-cycle rhythm. If she could just stay awake until evening, she would be back on course.

She worked her way wearily through the herbs, moving further and further from the keep's towering height, back towards the circular gazebo which sat alongside their small pond.

She knelt down in the deep, rich dirt next to a large patch of dill, admiring the circular head of yellow flowers. So many uses for dill. For example, she simply adored pickles ...

The next thing she knew, her face was pressed against the rich soil, she was soaking wet, and a heavy rain was drumming incessantly against her skull.. A pair of strong arms was gathering her up, hoisting her against a solid chest. Her eyes struggled to open; a horrific flash of lightning lit the sky, immediately corresponding with a thunderous peal. Then they were running …

Within a few moments her rescuer came to a neat stop, and the rain was suddenly shielded from her, although the tumult was all around her. She looked up and saw he had carried her into the gazebo. A curtain of water surrounded them, isolating them from the world.

She looked up at him and was caught by the tenderness in his eyes. He stood easily, showing no strain in holding her in his arms. She found she was comfortable, almost safe, cradled against his body, her head against his shoulder. His wet tunic was redolent of musk and cedar. It was almost intoxicating.

Blushing, she forced herself to speak.

"You can put me down now, Reynald. I am awake."

The knight gently lowered her to the stone bench which sat to one side. She brushed a few strands of wet hair away from her cheek as she settled herself. He leant against a support of the gazebo, watching her.

"You must have fallen asleep tending the herbs," he explained. "I was watching the storm approach out the back window and spotted you lying there, unmoving. I am only sorry that I did not reach you in time."

Sarah chuckled softly, self-consciously smoothing out her dress. "Over the years I have experienced far worse than a little soaking," she consoled him with a grin. "I will not melt. In any case, I suppose my hopes of staying awake until the evening were far flung, given how little sleep I had last night."

Sarah regretted her words immediately; she saw in a glance how Reynald's mind was reminded of his task, and how his look became cold and calculating again.

"Was it a long ride you made, on this errand of yours?" he asked with casual smoothness.

"Long enough," Sarah replied shortly, turning her head to gaze out at the falling rain.

"Do your errands normally involve assisting those outside the law?" he further queried, his voice gaining a slight edge.

Sarah bit back a curse. *Patience*. "Just what information do you have about the wanderers who live in this area, that they have broken any law?" she asked with forced lightness.

Reynald's eyes shuttered. "You are not in a position to question me," he replied shortly. "What they have done is my business. You need to tell me everything you know, to help me find them."

Sarah's eyes snapped. "I do not *need* to say anything to you," she reminded him.

Reynald took a step closer to her, and she could hear his increasing frustration in the clipped tone of his voice. "I cannot stress enough the importance of my mission," he stated coldly. "It is your duty, as a loyal Christian, to aid me in my task. Would you go against the will of God, as conveyed by me, his sworn knight?"

Sarah's shoulders tightened. That this soldier felt he could walk into her home and instruct her on her Christian duties! She stood suddenly and walked to face the sheets of rain descending from the sky. She stared through the deluge at the sturdy building beyond. She could sense Reynald's presence a few steps behind her, silent but potent.

She spun to look back at him, her face taut with anger. A hundred retorts sprang to her lips, but she fought them back with an effort. He was a guest in her home, and a man of power. It would not do to deliberately antagonize him. She forced herself to remain calm.

"Well?" he pressed, his voice low.

A jagged blast of lightning lit the sky, and Sarah made her decision. Retreat was the safest option. She pitched her voice so it was low and without emotion.

"We are done talking, my Lord."

She looked up again at the roiling, dark clouds, and the stone path drenched with buckets falling from above. Then, taking a deep breath, she took the first step into the downpour.

"My lady, please wait here," Reynald immediately called after her in consternation. He seemed shaken that things had gone so far. "Stay, if only for a short while. I am sure the torrents will abate soon."

Sarah glanced back at him, her eyes firm, standing in what felt to be a powerful waterfall. "It is but water. The walk is a mere hundred yards." She held his gaze for a long moment. Pique made her add, "After our talk, I feel I am in need of a bath."

Turning, she strode out into the near-dark afternoon, walking with a slow, measured step through the deluge. She considered herself a martyr for her cause, and held her head up high as she moved.

She felt less sure of her proud actions a half hour later after she had left a river of rain between the entry door and her room, which the poor servants were attempting to soak up with rags. She was shaky and weak, although whether due to her lack of sleep, her lack of food, or her to-the-bone soaking she could not tell for sure. Once she had been toweled off, Polly tucked her in to bed, and she fell immediately asleep.

The next day passed in a haze of noise and darkness. Her conscious moments were tormented with shivers and heat. Polly sat by her side, passing wet cloths across her head and pressing her to drink soup and mead when she was able.

She was beginning to feel better on Sunday morning. Despite Polly's protestations, she insisted on dressing for church. She wore her best dress, russet colored with short sleeves over the long white chemise. Her outfit was topped with the traditional white headdress, held fast with a vine-design bronze circlet. On her chest she wore her simple but beautifully carved wooden cross, a present she had earned many years ago from a woodcarver whose wife she had helped through a difficult birth.

She came down to the main hall to find her mother and father waiting, both dressed in richly embroidered violet clothing. They came over to her as one when she entered the room.

Her mother's eyes held concern. "Are you sure you are all right to attend, my dear?" she asked solicitously. "You know well that Father Smythe would not mind coming up to you afterwards, if you wished."

Sarah shook her head. "I am quite fine to sit through his sermon," she insisted. "The worst of the fever has passed."

She turned as more footsteps sounded. Reynald entered the hall, freshly shaven and groomed, wearing a somber, dark blue tunic. At his heels followed Rachel in an outfit Sarah found less than appropriate for Sunday worship. The dress was sunshine yellow, cut in a revealing manner. Her headdress was more of a see-through lace mesh of yellow gold than an actual covering. She wore a circlet of gold on her head, decorated with laughing cherubs.

Sarah's mother and father exchanged glances, but said nothing. Together they turned, leading the small group out to the stone chapel which lay to one side of the keep's entry stairs.

Sarah was not surprised when Rachel maneuvered herself to follow Reynald into the quiet stone chapel, sliding down the polished wood pew to kneel at his side. Chuckling to herself, Sarah took an empty pew two rows back. She sat back to relax, letting the soothing sounds of the Latin mass wash over her. She knew much of the litany by heart, and found the experience comforting.

Her mind wandered; she found herself silently praying for the strength to stand by her convictions, to protect the women she helped from the interference of others.

The minutes eased along in gentle rhythm. Without meaning to, she found that her eyes strayed to the strong, jet-black-haired man who sat solemnly two rows before her. Why was he after bandits – and why was he sure that they were part of the group she had worked with? He had refused to give her further details. If they truly were law breakers, wouldn't he have shared the charges, both with her family and with the local sheriff?

From everything Sarah had seen during her visits to the camp, the group was made up of tinkers and craftsmen, not of cutthroats. If they were armed, it was only to protect themselves from the wolves' heads who regularly roamed the area.

Sarah shook her head. In the end, it did not matter why Reynald wanted access to the wanderers. She knew that if rumors circulated that she revealed the secrets of those she helped, women would no longer believe in her or her word. She would not betray that trust.

Father Smythe's gentle voice came to the end of his sermon, and he offered one final "Amen," which Sarah echoed with heartfelt sincerity. She crossed herself and slowly stood, giving her weary head time to adjust to the movement. She was able to hold onto the pew back until she moved to the end of the aisle, then paused for another moment as her father and mother moved on ahead down the path.

A low voice sounded at her shoulder. "Would you appreciate an arm, M'Lady?" Sarah looked up in surprise to see Reynald standing there, quietly offering his support. "Your face is a bit white," he added more softly by way of explanation, gazing in concern at her eyes.

Rachel piped up from his other side, her voice sounding piqued. "Sarah is fine," she insisted. Her voice dropped down an octave. "However, I would love an escort, sir Knight," she added with a husky quality.

Sarah took a step back, clearing the aisle for the couple. "I will be fine; please, go on ahead. I just need a little air," she explained with a forced smile.

Reynald's face creased with concern, but he nodded in acceptance, moving forward with Rachel. Sarah waited until the two were well ahead of her, then took a deep breath. She eased slowly down the stone floor of the aisle, placing her feet carefully to support her.

To her surprise, she found the two lingering by the entrance when she reached the arched doorway. Reynald was staring up at the top of the chapel, and Rachel was eagerly explaining the history of the cross on the top to him. His eyes flickered briefly to Sarah's face before nodding to Rachel.

"I think I understand now, thank you so much for describing the details," he responded to the blonde with a nod. "I believe I am ready to head in to lunch now." Rachel enthusiastically pulled him inside, and he allowed himself to be led, although at a slow pace which Sarah found easy to keep up with.

The group settled themselves around the main table, with the smaller tables filling up with various members of the household staff. Sarah sat beside her father while Rachel and Reynald took seats on the opposite side of the large wooden table. The conversation swirled around Sarah at a dizzying speed while she wearily sipped at her mead, taking small bites of her cheese pie. She barely noticed as Sally flitted in to refill her cup or take away her trencher.

Her father nudged her on the elbow. "Sarah, are you sure you are feeling fine?" he asked in a worried tone. Sarah realized everyone at the table was looking in her direction, and she blushed. Apparently she had missed something important.

Her mother leant over. "Reynald was asking who the other midwives in the area were, so he could visit with them later today," she prodded, her voice rich with concern.

"Oh, of course," replied Sarah listlessly, her mind struggling to focus. It would be churlish of her to refuse him even this most basic information. She listed off the names of the other four midwives in the area, giving details for each on where they lived. Reynald listened intently, committing the information to memory.

A wave of weariness washed over her. She stood slowly, and her father and Reynald rose with her.

"I am sorry, but I think I should return to my room," she apologized to the four. "Some more sleep would do me good."

She nodded to the group, then turned and headed toward the stairs.

A tripping set of footsteps sounded behind her, and in a moment her sister was following alongside her with a smile. "Hey Sarah, could I borrow some money from you? I promise to pay you back," she cajoled with a grin.

Sarah chuckled as she carefully made her way up step by step. "You already owe me from past borrowings," she pointed out congenially. "Besides, you have tapped me dry. I am down to what I need to fund the fall season of pots and vials. I am afraid I have naught to lend." She paused a moment, doing a mental inventory of her short term list. "Well, how much do you need?"

"Only five pounds," replied Rachel impishly.

"Hah!" burst out Sarah, shaking her head at the sum. "Sorry, but I just cannot foot that kind of bill."

Rachel pouted prettily. "I will find it some other way," she replied, shrugging. She reached her room, slipped within, and gave a friendly wave before she shut the door.

Sarah shook her head in amusement, then slowly made her way along to her bed. It was only moments before she was sound asleep.

Chapter 3

When Sarah awoke the next morning, her mind felt far sharper than on the previous few days, and her hunger had definitely returned. It was barely dawn, but she was famished! She pushed herself out of bed, dressed quickly, and headed downstairs. She worked her way back towards the larder, figuring she would grab a hunk of cheese to keep her stomach from rumbling until lunch. She knew her mother would not mind, but Father Smythe was sometimes overzealous in his discussions on the wasteful sin of a breakfast meal.

As she passed a window near the back courtyard, a movement caught her eye. She stopped and looked out, curious. A man was there, working through a sword routine with quiet deliberation. She stood by the window, transfixed, watching him in action. She had grown up around soldiers, certainly, and had participated in practice to gain the basic skills necessary to defend herself while she was out on her own. She had seen plenty of men with swords, and understood the basic functions of attack and defense.

This was different, somehow. With the soldiers, the movements had been utilitarian, like a woodsman hacking down a tree. The man she watched now was elegant, seamless. It called to mind the times she had visited the master wood carver and watched him craft a fine piece of furniture. The tools were the same as other men used - and the material identical - but the control and finesse were on a different plane altogether.

Sarah stood, mesmerized, as Reynald flowed from one attack into another, deftly blocking with one motion while preparing a counter-attack with the next. He was so sure, so in control. He twisted to the side, then turned to swivel …

Suddenly Sarah was staring full into Reynald's gaze. He stopped abruptly, freezing mid-stride, then stood up straight. To her shock, Reynald strode slowly toward the keep, an intent look on his face.

Sarah blushed crimson, embarrassed to have been caught while so boldly watching his private meditations. She half ran down the hallway, quickly reaching the pantry door. She frantically worked the lock to the seclusion of the shelves and casks. In another moment the door was open and she was in the half-dark room, surrounded by the fragrances of a hundred different items. She took in a deep, steadying breath, moving automatically to the back area where the large, yellow wheels sat covered with cheesecloth. Putting her hand on one, she drew the cloth aside and pulled her dagger from her belt to cut off a hunk.

"There you are," murmured a low voice behind her. Her already keyed up emotions jumped to a higher state, and she let out a short shriek, spinning with her dagger out. Reynald put his hands out to the side, moving with lightning-fast speed to avoid the slicing weapon.

Sarah quickly lowered her blade, leaning back against the shelves. "You startled me," she offered in embarrassment, her face flushing with guilt at the near miss. "You are lucky I did not wound you." It occurred to her that it was his skill, and not luck, that had prevented injury; the speed with which he had pulled back from her swing was impressive.

Her heart hammered in her chest, but she forced herself to look up at him in the quiet dark of the large storage closet. Morning light filtered in gently through the half open door.

Reynald lowered his hands slowly and gave her a wry smile. "I did not mean to upset you," he apologized in a low voice. "I spotted you through the window. I came to offer my regrets in person for causing your illness. I am fully to blame."

Sarah cocked her head sideways, her breathing slowly returning to normal. "How do you figure that?" she asked with honest curiosity. "I was the one who traipsed through the rain. Lord only knows I have done that countless times in the past.

You just happened to be there when it chanced to be the time I fell ill."

"Still, I *was* there," countered Reynald. "I could have been gentler in the gazebo, so you felt more comfortable staying under shelter until the storm passed. I also could have offered you something to act as a cover from the rain, once you decided to leave."

Sarah chuckled. "I think you will find, Sir, that I am an adult and quite capable of choosing my own path. If I get into trouble, I will take responsibility for my action and look to blame no other." Her grin widened. "I have warned my patients enough times to stay out of drenching rain. If I do not practice what I preach, then woe be to me when I become annoyed with the consequences."

With that, she turned and carved off a hunk of cheese, then two. She turned back to the man before her. "So, now that is out of the way, would you like a morning snack? I imagine you might be hungry after that workout."

Reynald took the offering with a smile. He gave it a sniff before biting into the wedge. His eyes lit up with delight as he continued to eat. "This is quite good," he praised after a short while. "I will have to pack some of this in my day sack."

"Are you going out today?" asked Sarah, leaning against the shelf and nibbling on her own wedge. "Were the other midwives useful to you?"

"Yes, and thank you for your help. I did indeed spend Sunday afternoon visiting with each woman in turn, talking with her about her patients and experiences. It was quite illuminating; they had some fascinating stories to share. I did not get back here until long after dark." He paused for a moment, holding her eyes. "However, you know as well as I do that the discussions turned up nothing of value for me. None knew anything about the bandits."

Sarah suddenly felt the force of Reynald's stare. He had not changed position at all, and his voice was dead calm, but she became acutely aware that he stood between her and her only exit. He was, after all, a soldier, and he appeared quite determined to get the information he wanted. Her dagger would be little help.

Her mouth went dry as she considered her options. He would not be so rash as to threaten her, would he?

A jingle of keys sounded down the hallway, followed by a mild expletive as the footsteps neared the half-open door. A low muttering voice could be heard, saying, "Is she at it again? If her father finds out this time ..." A shape moved into the open doorway, and Reynald turned to see who it was.

Sally's young face fell open in shock as she met eyes with Sarah. "Oh! Miss ... it is ... I am so sorry ..." sputtered the woman in surprise. Her face burnished crimson, and she retreated quickly down the hall.

Reynald glanced quickly at Sarah, his face contrite. "I can go after her and explain -"

Sarah waved his concerns away absently, the spell broken. "Do not bother yourself about it. After all, we were just talking." She walked past him out to the hallway, looking around as she heard the sounds of the castle stirring to life. "I will see you at lunch, then," she added over her shoulder before heading out to the herb garden.

To her relief, he did not follow her there to interrupt her musings.

* * *

Sarah tried to take it easy during the misty day, keeping her efforts relegated to light weeding and pruning. She was indeed feeling better, but not quite full strength yet. True to his word, Reynald took his leave shortly after lunch, going out on a scouting expedition. Sarah knew that he was looking for the wanderers on his own.

She wondered nervously just why he was so interested in finding them. Had one of them stolen money from him on the road? Was she truly protecting lawbreakers? He had not volunteered the reason for his outing, and she had not wanted to ask and be drawn into a conversation on the topic.

The sun was heading down towards the horizon when a young, portly lad came running into the gardens, racing straight toward her side. "It is Cecily, M'Lady," he called without preamble, his breath coming in gasps. "She is in a lot of pain, and her husband is frantic."

Sarah was moving in an instant. "You go get some ale and take a rest," she instructed him as she strode back toward the keep. "You have delivered your message well. I will head out immediately." The boy collapsed onto a nearby bench in exhausted relief as she entered the main building and hurried up to her room. She sorted through her leather bag's contents, ensuring all necessary medicines were present, then stood quickly, turning to leave.

The room spun for a moment, and she put out a hand to steady herself on her dresser. She closed her eyes in frustration, willing herself to regain her balance. Now was not the time for her to be ill. A full term woman was depending on her to be alert and in full command of the situation.

She took a moment to savor several deep breaths, and then she was off. She took the stairs two at a time going down to the stables. Lou, well used to reading her moods, was at her side in a heartbeat as she entered. Together they had the steed saddled and bridled in record time. Sarah carefully secured her bag and was swinging up to mount when hoof beats came riding in the front gate.

Reynald raised his hand in a friendly greeting as he pulled into the stable proper, then his gaze focused on her face. He deftly wheeled his mount around to slide to a stop next to hers.

"A problem call?" he asked without preamble, his gaze piercing.

The need for haste pressed down on her, and her tone came out more sharply than she meant. "It is not the 'bandits'," she snapped in exasperation. "You can go on inside and get some ale." She finished settling into her saddle, doing one last check on her supplies.

Reynald did not blink at her comment; his eyes held hers with serious intent. "I have been a field medic for many years; I have probably seen far more medical emergencies than you could imagine. You could use my help."

Sarah looked up sharply, stunned into angry silence at his presumption. She needed *his* help? Of all the arrogance!

"I do not need any assistance," she insisted, turning to gather up her reins. "What I need is to go. Now."

"I *will* ride with you," insisted Reynald, his face set.

Time was wasting; there was little she could do to stop him. Sarah exhaled sharply in exasperation. "Fine, keep up with me then," she challenged. With a press of her legs she was flying out the main gates.

Sarah did not look back as she thundered across the meadows and into the forest. If Reynald thought he was going to use her to gather information, it was time she taught him a lesson. The fastest way to Cecily's home was through dense woods on an old animal trail. She knew it well, having ridden it weekly her entire life. If the roots and stumps slowed down the knight on her heels, she was not to blame. She leant low over her mount's neck and urged him to go at an even greater speed.

She leapt the first log with ease, and twisted left to avoid the muddy bog formed by a warthog family. There were a few low hanging branches to avoid, and then another log. She took the course with ease, pushing her horse to his limits. The tree branches flew by only inches from her face. There was the rocky outcropping … and the old oak stump …

As the track twisted and turned, a guilty ache gnawed at her. She should have warned Reynald more firmly off the chase. A fall here, at these speeds, could cause a serious injury. If he hurt himself because of her ...

She pushed the thought out of her mind. He was a grown man, capable of taking care of himself. He could slow or turn back at any time if he felt out of his depth.

Cecily needed her.

She pressed onward, focusing intently on the path ahead.

The miles flew by in a blur of trunk and rock. The strain carved deep in her shoulders by the time the forest began to open up before her. It had been a half hour since she had left the keep, but it felt like far longer. Peering through the remaining trees, she could see the low, one story cottage that Cecily and her husband Milo had built two years ago, just after their wedding. There - Milo, his rail-thin form a wisp in the dusk, was pacing up and down before the wooden door.

The worried husband looked up with visible relief as she came thundering into the dirt clearing. She pulled her mount to a hard stop, then turned in surprise as she heard another set of hoof beats closing behind her. Reynald reined in strongly, his face showing the marks of a few errant branches.

Sarah's temper flared with heat. Her admiration that he had managed to stay with her was quickly replaced with a fierce protectiveness over her ward. If he thought he was going to waltz in here and take charge of her patient …

Reynald slid off his mount with ease, motioning to her. "Go in, I have the horses," he offered quietly, catching his breath. Sarah paused a moment, startled at this apparent change of mood on his part, but she did not need a second push. She had her bag and was running through the open door in a heartbeat.

The cottage contained one large, well-kept room, and the simple wood-frame bed was against the far corner. Sarah dropped to her knees besides Cecily, taking in her strained face and sweat-drenched clothing in one encompassing look. Cecily's eyes were closed in pain, her face wan.

"I am here, Cecily. It will be all right," Sarah murmured reassuringly to the woman. She turned, sliding up the dress and chemise to take a look at Cecily's bulging belly. She arranged the blanket to cover Cecily's hips down to her feet. Sarah ran one hand, then two, across the rounded surface. Her face went white as she slid her hands carefully across the distended skin.

Milo strode into the room, with Reynald right behind him. After only a few steps Milo spun and shouted angrily at the stranger. "Who are you? This is my wife here!" His voice was near breaking with panic.

Sarah took in a deep breath, then spoke without turning her head from her patient, her voice low and commanding. "Milo, I know you are a jealous man. However, Sir Reynald is a knight, and I will need his help if your wife is to live. Make your decision quickly. Decide if you distrust his honor so much as to risk your wife's life - and that of your unborn child."

Milo's eyes rounded with shock, and he was speechless for a moment. Then, taking a shaky breath, he sat down hard on a wooden chair by the door.

"Is it as bad as that, then?" He gulped visibly, dragging a shaking hand through his hair. "Please, save her," he whispered, all fight draining out of him.

Reynald strode across the room to stand by Sarah's side, looking down at the exhausted pregnant woman before them. To her relief, he did not offer up questions or make any demands.

"How can I help?" he asked quietly, his eyes moving to meet Sarah's.

Sarah took in another a deep breath, then let it out with slow deliberation. She had only faced this problem once before in her years as a midwife; that had been ten years ago, with old Marigold as the lead caregiver. Marigold was gone now, and Sarah did not know if she was up to the challenge before her … but she had to try. She knew that none of the other midwives had ever successfully handled this issue. There was nobody else to call for help.

"The baby is breech; its feet are pointing downwards," she explained softly, moving her hands cautiously over the lower part of the protruding belly. "It cannot be born like this."

Reynald was nodding before she had finished. "My best friend, Charles, ran the stables for the Templars. Over the years of foaling we had this happen several times," he agreed in understanding. "With a horse, we can actually reach inside and use ropes to turn the foal." He looked down at the moaning woman before him. "I do not imagine -"

Sarah shook her head. "If only it were that easy," she commented wryly. "We must do this from the outside."

Reynald did not hesitate. "Tell me what to do."

Sarah glanced over at Milo. His thin frame was curled up; his face strained with tension. Her heart went out to him, and she gently called him over. "We will need your help," she commented with quiet calm. "Please bring us pots of hot water, any clean fabric you have, and a bottle or two of vegetable oil. That will help us turn the baby."

His face brightening with the task, Milo burst off to comply.

Once Milo had left the room, Sarah took Reynald's hands in her own, moving them across the protruding bulges where the baby's head, body, and legs were located. "There is not much room in there," she explained as they ran their hands over the taught skin. "It will take a while, but we have to help the baby rotate in that space without causing him any harm."

Milo stumbled back into the room, and Sarah took one of the oil bottles from him, pouring an ample amount on her hands and on Reynald's. Together they gently massaged Cecily's stomach, giving gentle motions to the young child within her, encouraging the baby to slide.

Sarah took the first shift, and Reynald organized the water and cloths within easy reach. Milo looked nervously between the two, twining his fingers together, stepping back out of the way.

Reynald motioned to the wooden chair by the door. "Milo, why not move that chair by Cecily's head and sing to her."

Milo's face crinkled in a frown. "I am not a very good singer …" he stuttered nervously.

Reynald waved a hand. "I am sure Cecily loves the sound of your voice. Sing her lullabies, as you would to your new child."

In a few moments Milo had settled himself by his wife, taking her small hand in his. He gazed down with loving devotion and began to sing. Sarah could feel Cecily's body immediately relax beneath her, and she sent a thankful glance in Reynald's direction before renewing her focus on the task at hand.

The hours moved by slowly as the two labored at their task. Sarah would work until her hands became numb, at which point Reynald would take over. Milo brought them food and drink. After a few hours Cecily drifted into a fitful sleep, and Reynald made an effort to distract Milo with tales of Jerusalem and other far off lands. Sarah only half heard the stories as she kneaded and massaged.

The night wore on. Slowly, ever so slowly, the baby began to move. Milo sang and resang soft songs to his wife, and Sarah kneaded ... kneaded ... she felt Reynald's hands over her own, and gratefully turned over the task to him for a while, collapsing into the nearby chair.

The morning sun sent glistening rays across the floor, and the baby was half turned. On they worked, trading places without a word, sharing a common goal.

The baby was three quarters around. Cecily's eyes were full of tears at the pain, but she bit down on a piece of leather and focused on her husband, on relaxing as much as she could so that the work could go more quickly. The hours dragged on …

The sun was long past down again before the baby gave a final wiggle and settled into a head-first position under Sarah's probing fingers. Sarah felt as if she had been working in this room, on this task, for weeks, and exhaustion seeped from every pore. She could not rest; there was still more to do. She settled back against the bed with a loud sigh, gathering her strength.

"There, we are ready," she announced, forcing her voice to echo enthusiasm. She looked up at Cecily, who had wearily opened her eyes. "Do you have enough energy to push?"

By way of an answer, Cecily struggled to bring herself into a sitting position. Sarah looked over to Milo, meeting his eyes. "Milo, you are going to have to hold your wife's dress up around her waist." She glanced briefly at Reynald, then back at Milo. "I can ask him to wait outside if -"

Milo looked past the point of exhaustion and shook his head. "Save my wife. I trust you both. She is too tired."

Reynald stepped forward and put his hand on Milo's shoulder. "I promise you, I will do everything in my power to help," he vowed, his eyes somber. "We will save her, and your child as well."

Together, the two men supported either side of Cecily, helping her to move over towards the clean cloths on the ground, then slowly squat down over them. A new look of strength came over Cecily as she settled down into position, feeling the baby move within her.

Sarah kneeled before Cecily, and after a few minutes she smiled in relief. "I see the head!" she called out to the three in joy. "It is all right! You can push! Push!"

Sarah cried out loudly as she bore down, relief and focus mingling with the pain of the contractions. The men firmly held her up on each side, and she leant against them as she might a pair of tree trunks. The baby slowly slid out and gave a hearty yell as it met the air. Another slip, and the tiny infant was in Sarah's arms. She gave a twist with her dagger to free the child, and the men eased the mother back onto the bed, smoothing out her dress.

Sarah gave the baby a quick wash in the now warm water, then bundled him up. She held him close for a moment, staring down at the bright blue eyes which gazed up at her with such trust. This little life had been held in her hands ... she gave the child a kiss on the forehead, then stepped forward to place him in his mother's arms. Milo moved down to hug his family gently, murmuring and laughing to his wife.

Sarah went through her evaluation of mother and child with careful deliberation, and to her delight she found no issues with either. Both were in fine health, with no bleeding or complications that she could see. She finally sat back on her heels, a pleased exhaustion overtaking her.

She looked up to Reynald, and found he was staring at her, his gaze lost in thought. Shaking himself, he glanced at the happy trio of the new family, then without a word took Sarah's arm and guided her out of the cottage. As she stumbled through the door, she found to her surprise that it was nearly dawn of the next day. It had seemed as if time stood still in that small room, trying to save the baby and his mother ...

Reynald brushed a few stray hairs from her face, looking down at her. She could feel his presence as a palpable force, sense every movement of his fingers along her brow.

"You were wonderful," he praised her softly, his voice husky. "I had no idea what midwifery involved. It was an honor to help you."

Sarah's conscience tugged at her. She had fought so strongly to keep him from coming – and he had been a valuable help in this emergency. "I do not know what would have happened if you were not here," she admitted slowly, forcing herself past her pride. "I was wrong to treat you as I did. Thank you for your help."

The door creaked open behind them, and Sarah instinctively took a step back, distancing herself from Reynald. Milo came out of his home with a light trot, a great smile on his face. "I cannot thank you both enough for what you have done," he gushed, beaming with pleasure. "Please, anything I have, it is yours. Would you like some mead? Some more food?"

Sarah shook her head wearily. "If I do not leave now, I will not make it home," she admitted. "I can stop by in a few days to check up on the mother and child, but right now I think sleep will do us all the most good."

Milo stepped forward and gave her a warm hug in thanks, then he turned and shook Reynald's hand with vigorous enthusiasm. He helped Reynald saddle up the two horses in only a few minutes. Soon Sarah found herself wearily climbing onto her mount. Reynald was alongside her in a moment, and the two walked back at a slow pace toward the keep.

Sarah's eyes lost focus, and she snapped herself back to wakefulness. "Please talk to me," she asked Reynald sleepily. "Otherwise I will fade and go right off my horse."

Reynald's horse moved easily alongside her own, and he turned to her, his eyes weary but alert. "What would you like me to tell you?"

Sarah's mind drifted. "You were spinning stories for Milo back there in the cottage, but I was only half listening. What was it that you did in the Holy Land?"

Reynald settled his gaze halfway between the trail ahead and Sarah, keeping both within his compass as he rode. "The order I belong to is the Knights Templar. We were founded to help ensure that pilgrims to the Holy Land can reach their destination unmolested."

Sarah nodded absently. "Yes, I know of them. It seems a noble enough cause. So you do not go out on the actual Crusades, taking over towns and villages?"

Reynald shook his head. "No, that is for others to do. My sole concern is with keeping the roads clear and the travelers on those roads safe. It is the bandits I take issue with, the ones who would plunder for their own gain."

Sarah winced at the mention of the word bandits. It brought to mind again the reason that Reynald was here, and the issue which lay between them. She was too weary to keep dodging the topic. "So, you seek to slay bandits wherever you encounter them, then? You have brought that fight home with you?"

Reynald's eyes sharpened, and he was silent for a while. He turned to watch forward as the path twisted and turned ahead of them. The dark forest scrolled past them as they moved, the early morning sounds of birds and insects growing in a gentle cacophony.

Sarah let the silence drift, her own thoughts going with them. On one hand, Reynald seemed a most admirable man. He had chosen a profession which let him keep others safe, and had volunteered to help her save a woman's life. He had provided a calm, level head in a situation that desperately needed one.

However, his arrogance in chasing down these bandits, his preemptory manner of wanting his own way in a situation … his flares of temper …

The world spun in lazy circles, then collapsed into darkness.

Reynald's arms were around her. "Sarah, we are almost there. Wake up," he called gently into her ear, giving her a soft shake. She struggled to open her eyes. Yes, the gates were up ahead, and the guards were pulling open the doors for the pair. She headed the horse over into the stables. Lou was dozing on a pile of hay in the corner, but at the sound of hoofbeats he came awake with a start and ran to hold the reins. Reynald was down beneath her before she could turn, and she gratefully lowered herself into his arms. Her eyes closed again, and she half fell against him.

A familiar, lilting voice rang out. “So *there* you are, sis!” Sarah’s eyes sparked open. She pulled back from Reynald’s body, turning to see Rachel standing at the stable doors. Her younger sister sported a wide grin as she looked between Sarah and Reynald, then she winked and ran off back toward the main castle.

Reynald took a few steps toward the door, his face resolute. “This time I will say something,” he growled in a low voice, his eyes following the running figure.

Sarah shook her head. “It will only make it worse,” she insisted sleepily. “Besides ...”

She attempted to take a step towards him, but her foot caught in the hay and she tripped. Reynald was beside her in an instant, steadying her.

“Let us first get you to bed,” he amended. “You are beyond exhaustion.”

Sarah did not argue, and allowed him to half lead, half carry her up to her room. He pulled aside the covers, and she crawled into bed fully clothed. She felt him gently pull off one boot, then the second, and in a moment the covers were carefully laid down over her. She pressed herself against the pillow, and the world faded away.

Chapter 4

Sarah found herself being gently shaken awake. She wearily opened her eyes. The late afternoon sun was bronzing the landscape, and a gentle breeze drifted through the open window, adding a flutter to the edge of her curtains.

Polly smiled down at her. "I am sorry to disturb you," she murmured. "I know you were out late. It is just that Simon is here, and he comes from so far away …"

Sarah sighed and pushed herself to a seated position. "Of course, yes, I understand," she nodded to her maid with a yawn. Would she never get a full night's sleep? "Please tell him I will be down as soon as I am able. I imagine you have him in the sitting room?"

"Of course, and he has some mead and cheese. I will go let him know right away," responded the maid, turning and leaving the room.

Sarah climbed out of bed, ignoring the aches and pains which seemed to have settled into every corner of her joints. Simon was a nice enough man, and she found him to be a friendly, intelligent companion. Unfortunately, she imagined that his long term aim was not just to have a friend to talk with, and her heart did not tend in that direction. He must have ridden for three hours to reach her, too.

She rolled her shoulders to loosen the knots, then stripped down to her thin white chemise. She dug out a muted sage green tunic to slide over it. She braided her hair back into a long plait, then gave herself a quick once-over before heading out of her room.

The keep was quiet as she made her way downstairs to the sitting room. She smiled with pleasure when she saw Sally approaching the room with a tray of breads, meats, and cheese for her, as well as a mug of mead.

"Thank you so much," she whispered with ardent appreciation as Sally preceded her into the room, setting the tray down on a low table by a leather chair. The young woman nodded and retreated from the room, closing the door behind her.

A row of large windows faced out over the back courtyards, their open lengths admitting golden streams of sunshine. Several comfortable chairs were spaced around the room, and a large, low wooden table occupied the central area. Hanging tapestries lined the other walls, displaying floral designs in blue and yellow.

Simon had turned from the leftmost window as she entered the room. He was tall, perhaps six foot three, with short, blond-white hair trimmed close to his skull. His skin was pale, and he verged on being too skinny for his frame. He wore an elegant, grey tunic with intricate indigo embroidery.

Simon's smile was genuine and friendly as he stepped forward to greet her.

"Sarah, how wonderful it is to see you," he glowed, taking her hand and lowering his head to kiss it. "It always makes the ride worthwhile, to find you waiting at the end."

"Please, sit down," offered Sarah graciously, taking her own seat with slow care. "I am sorry I made you wait for me. I see Sally has brought you some mead – would you rather have wine? Or ale perhaps?"

"Mead is quite fine; I am not particular," replied Simon easily. His eyes swept over her. "You look beautiful, as always," he added with warmth.

Sarah blushed. "You are teasing, surely. I am barely out of bed." She brushed a stray tendril of hair from her face. Leaning forward, she picked up a slice of cheese and layered it onto a piece of bread, taking a bite with relish. She was quite hungry, she realized as she gratefully swallowed the delicious morsel. "I had a long night behind me," she added.

Simon took a sip of his mead. "Oh, busy with the midwifery of yours? Yes, that is a lovely hobby for any single woman, to help out other families. I would suppose in a way it is great training for your own future, when you have a family of your own and can put that frippery aside."

She popped another piece of cheese into her mouth and nodded her head, half thankful for the inability to respond with words to that back-handed compliment.

Simon saw at once that she was ravenous, and he smiled. "Here, I am being rude. Please allow me to play you some music while you eat."

Sarah's face broadened with a thankful smile. "That would be wonderful," she encouraged him.

Simon moved to one of the walls, taking a lute from its hook and returning to sit down on a padded bench near the window. The tapestries on the walls waved gently in the breeze, and soon the gently strummed notes filled the room.

Sarah sat back against her chair, relaxing as the music echoed around her. Simon was talented with the lute, and she did relish this aspect of his visits. He was sweet, gentle, kind, and overly courteous to her. She ate another slice of cheese, glancing over his pale face, his watery blue eyes. He smiled at her attentions, then focused again on his fingering.

Sarah looked down at the tray, choosing a piece of roast beef. Why was it that she could not bring herself to be more fond of him? He obviously was courting her. She felt a tender friendship toward him, almost as if he was a younger brother. Still, she did not think they would be happy as a couple. He was too docile, too compliant.

She looked out the window past Simon, to the rear fields. The soldiers were practicing sword work today, and the muted clang of steel on steel came through faintly behind the gentle strums of Simon's song.

Sarah's gaze sharpened. She realized there was an unknown figure in leather armor moving amongst the men. After a moment, the style of his movement clicked. It was Reynald. She shook her head. Did that man not need to sleep?

She found herself watching him more carefully. Judging by the way he was interacting with the others, he was helping the men with their techniques. She could see how her guards attended to his actions, then mimicked them carefully, looking to him for approval.

With an effort, she brought her focus back into the tapestry-lined sitting room. She ate with relish, savoring the flavors, then finished off her midday meal with a long pull on her mead. Still, the image of Reynald nagged at her. She would not have thought a templar knight to be the type to spend time with common troops. Surely he had more exalted things to do, important people to speak with …

Her mind drifted back to the previous day's activities. Reynald had not complained once during the long hours of effort. He had been focused, attentive, and fully involved. He had seemed invested in helping and learning. Perhaps she had misjudged him …

She realized suddenly that the room was silent, and looked up to find Simon smiling at her. She clapped her hands, adding guiltily, "I am so sorry, I seem to have been swept away."

Simon executed an elegant, short bow, holding the lute against him. "It is the ultimate compliment to a musician, when the music transports the audience," he promised with a wink. His look became serious. "Perhaps it is a state you could enjoy more frequently, once we are together every day."

Sarah's attention was brought fully back to the room in a swift rush. So here it was. She had tried gentle hints and suggestions up until now, and she hated to hurt Simon's feelings. He was so kind. He deserved someone who would love him fully for his many talents.

She stood and walked toward him. He automatically stood when she did, and put his lute aside on the bench. She took a deep breath and took his hands in her own. She needed to do this gently.

"You are a wonderful man, Simon," she murmured, looking down at his slim fingers. "I enjoy talking with you, and your musicianship is superb. Somewhere out there is a woman who will adore you with all her heart, someone who will count her blessings every time you step through the door." She felt guilty even as she said it, but she knew it had to be done. She lifted her eyes to his, and saw the hurt reflected there already. "It is not me," she sighed. "I am sorry, but it is not me."

Simon gripped her hand even tighter. "I can change," he insisted softly, his eyes bright. "Tell me what is wrong, and I am sure I can fix it. Then you will grow to love me as I love you."

Sarah shook her head sadly. "You are wonderful just the way you are," she insisted. "We are simply different people." She searched through her mind for a way to explain it. "Imagine the most beautiful trout, enjoying its pond. Then imagine the finest horse, grazing in the field. You would not ask either creature to change one whit of what they are. Yet the creatures would simply not be happy if they tried to be partners in life. Some things were not meant to be."

She raised a hand to his cheek, touching him tenderly. "You are a dear friend, Simon. If I lose your friendship because of my honesty, I will be heartbroken. However, I do not want to lead you on when you might be courting another woman far more suitable for you. It would not be right. She is out there, and she loves you. You will love her dearly in return. You just have to find her."

Simon dropped his eyes. Several long moments passed, and Sarah could not think of anything further to say that would not make things worse. Finally Simon shook himself and looked up again.

"I think I should go now, I feel I have overstayed my welcome. Fare well, Sarah."

Sarah watched sadly as he made his way out of the room. She knew she had wounded him deeply, but could not think of any other alternative. To have let him keep spending his time on her would have been a greater harm.

She moved away from the window, feeling both guilty and strangely liberated. She had known for a while that she had to talk with Simon, and it had finally been done. She hoped that he would get over the hurt as soon as possible.

Sarah gave a long stretch, still sore and worn out from the previous day's tasks. Her mother had always liked Simon; Sarah wandered through the keep, wanting to tell her mother what had happened. She walked slowly through the rooms, but not finding Mathilde in the main building, her feet eventually led her towards the stables. She could see if her mother's horse was still here, and also check to see if Simon had in fact left already.

Simon's dappled horse was gone, but to her surprise, she heard Reynald's voice coming from the back of the wooden structure. Turning the corner in puzzlement, she found Reynald staring down at Lou, his face stern. The stable boy was shaking his head resolutely, and his voice was soft but firm in his response.

"Begging your pardon, sir, but I cannot say anything about that," he insisted. "You would have to direct any questions to the lady herself."

Sarah strode forward, anger suddenly rising within her. "Yes, please do," she confirmed with heat. Reynald's head spun at the interruption, and to his credit he flushed at being caught in this position.

Sarah moved forward to stand before him, staring up into his face with blazing eyes. "How dare you question our staff about my actions?" she bit out in fury. "You are a guest in our home, sir, and have no right. You will find that our people here both respect us and have the honor not to speak of our activities to strangers. It is an honor that you might deign to learn."

Reynald's face went white with tension, and his voice, when he spoke, was low and steely. "Are you daring to question my honor?" Lou took a step back involuntarily at the look in Reynald's eyes.

Sarah did not flinch. "If your activities involve pressuring young boys in back rooms to reveal the secrets of their employers, and you feel this is appropriate behavior for a knight, then by all means let us take this matter to my father and hear what he has to say." She swiveled in place and strode out of the dark stables. “I believe he is in the back fields, training with his troops,” she tossed over her shoulder as she marched resolutely toward the side of the keep.

She had reached the back gardens when she heard long strides moving to overtake her. “Sarah, wait,” called out Reynald, his voice half contrite, half exasperated.

A strong hand grabbed at her arm, and she turned suddenly, angrily shaking it off. Reynald released her instantly, putting his hands to the side in surrender. “Please,” he tried again, his breath coming in long draws from the run. “Let me just talk with you first.”

“I have seen the way you … talk,” growled Sarah, but she slowed her pace, moving to the gazebo rather than the gates which led toward the back field. As she stepped within, the cool shade and gentle breezes created an oasis from the bright summer’s sun.

For a few long moments she wondered if Reynald had changed his mind. There were no footsteps, no further calls. Slowly her pulse settled down to normal. A bird sang in a nearby tree, a lilting tune of tranquility. She stared out at the pond, wondering just what was going on in her world. First two births in as many weeks, and now this …

A voice sounded quietly from behind her. “Sarah?”

She turned her head quickly, shaken from her reverie. Reynald stood at the side of the structure, one foot on the stone step. His hand rested easily on the hilt of his blade, and his eyes held hers with a serious look.

“You have a right to know the truth, and I have been wrong to ask for your trust without providing you with any reason,” he admitted in a low tone. He paused for a few moments, looking into her eyes. “However, I know the timing may be poor for this discussion. Would you like to talk now, or do you wish to be alone, given what happened earlier between you and Simon?”

Sarah tilted her head to one side, her mind thrown completely off track. She had not thought anyone had overheard her conversation. “What do you know of this afternoon?” She flushed, contrite that Simon’s rejection had been overheard.

Reynald blushed slightly. "I had remained behind after the practice, and was cleaning my blade at the stone near your window when you had the talk with Simon," he admitted. "Then when Simon came out to saddle his horse, it happened that I was there in the stables, talking with Lou. Simon introduced himself to me and … well, he made a comment or two."

Sarah could not help herself. "Was he truly upset?" Her heart fell at the thought of Simon's emotional state. "I tried to be gentle …"

Reynald smiled, nodding his head. "I know you did. He seems to understand that as well, although I imagine it will take him a while to absorb it."

Sarah moved to sit sideways on the bench, drawing her knees up against herself. Her heart ached with weariness, her mind swirling with conflicting thoughts. She struggled to put them aside for now.

Reynald had been stirring up situations since he had arrived, and had never felt an explanation was necessary. If the headstrong knight was finally willing to explain what was going on, she needed to listen before he changed his mind and shut her out again.

She looked up and met his amber gaze. "Please, I would like for us to talk, to get a handle on the issues you seek to remedy. Help me to understand."

Despite the lingering pique she felt over Reynald's questioning of Lou, Sarah had to admit that she was curious about his motives. Something had been driving him hard since he had arrived at her home. Taking a deep breath, Sarah sat back against the low wall of the gazebo. Now that she had made the overture, she waited patiently for him to begin the topic.

Reynald took the few steps to enter the gazebo with her, then stopped. He seemed quite uncomfortable, and Sarah wondered what disturbed him so. He had been so sure of himself at other times. This was a new aspect of him.

He swept his eyes around the area, then lowered them to meet her gaze, holding it steadily. "What I am about to tell you, you must keep to yourself," he muttered in a low rush. "I have seen how well you care for others – both physically and emotionally. Indeed, you have been resolute in protecting even the wanderers from me." He paused, then continued more slowly. "I believe I have enough faith in your honor that you will guard my own privacy with the same care."

Sarah nodded encouragingly. "Of course I will abide by your wishes. If you wish me to keep this discussion secret, then I shall," she agreed readily.

Reynald paced along the width of the building. "I have a younger sister. I love her dearly. While she is sometimes foolish, she has a good heart. When I left to join the Knights Templar, I wrote regularly to hear news of her."

He paused for a moment, then continued, his face set. "About five months ago, my mother wrote to me. She reported that a local bandit had gotten my sister pregnant, and my sister had foolishly run off with him. My mother blamed my sister for taking up with the ruffian and refused to go after her or send a rescue party."

Reynald's eyes shadowed. "I could not believe my own mother would cast her daughter out - and her grandchild. Unfortunately, my mother can be old fashioned and stubborn about some issues."

Sarah considered this thoughtfully, watching Reynald. "So you came home to find her?"

Reynald looked down, not meeting her gaze. "I came to this area for several reasons. Right now, my sister is out there somewhere. I must find my sister and make sure she is safe." His voice turned steely. "If that rogue has hurt her in any way -"

His hand dropped automatically to the hilt of his sword, and he looked out over the pond, his face suddenly distant.

Sarah spoke quietly into the silence. "Well, then, what is her name?"

Reynald responded without turning. His voice was a mere whisper. "Abigail."

Sarah's heart stopped. "Is she about sixteen? Thin in build, with long, blonde hair?"

Reynald spun instantly, his eyes wide. “You *have* seen her then?”

Sarah’s eyes sharpened. “How many children did your mother have?”

Reynald answered without hesitation. “Three. I was the oldest, then David, who is with the Crusades in Antioch. Abigail came long after us two.”

Sarah held his gaze, keeping her voice neutral. “Did you know a young man named Lloyd?”

Reynald’s forehead creased with confusion. “There was a Lloyd who was a boy who worked at the stables. He was a lad when I left. He would probably be around twenty one ...” His voice drifted away, and his eyes held Sarah’s in challenge. “Are you saying my mother lied to me about the bandits?”

Sarah let the silence linger on for a moment, then she made her decision. “I am saying that Lloyd and Abigail are very much in love with each other, and that they are married. They are safely in hiding.” She waited a moment for the shock to pass on Reynald’s face before adding, “They are the proud parents of a beautiful baby girl.”

Reynald leant back against the support of the gazebo, his face relaxing into relief. “Thank God,” he breathed gratefully, all tension melting out of him. His eyes eagerly moved back up to meet Sarah’s. “So she is all right? The baby is all right? Are they healthy?”

Sarah smiled and nodded. “Yes, very much so. Abigail has been careful to take care of her health, and from what I see, Lloyd is an admirable husband.”

A frown swept back onto Reynald’s face. “Except that he has brought her in with the bandits.”

Sarah stood to face him, her face serious. “First, they are *not* bandits. They are wandering craftsmen. Second, Lloyd needed an environment that was secure and had food while his wife was in her final months. Kyle is there with them, to help keep her safe. Now that the baby is born, they intend to find a place to build a house, before fall gets too chill.”

Reynald's face shifted to a frown. "She should come home, where she belongs!"

Sarah's face became equally stern. "As you might remember, her mother does not welcome her there. Perhaps Abigail is better off somewhere she and her child are loved."

Reynald turned away at that. He was quiet for a while, looking off into the distance. "I will talk with my mother and get her to see reason," he decided finally. "In the meantime, I need to get my sister somewhere safe." He looked over to meet Sarah's eyes, his face resolute. "You must take me to her right away."

Sarah chuckled softly, her voice taking on a hint of steel. "That is for Abigail to decide."

Reynald's eyes flared with anger. "I am her older brother!"

Sarah's face shuttered instantly. "So you say," she pointed out shortly, crossing her arms. "However, I will wait to hear from Abigail, to see what she wishes to do about her own life and family."

Reynald's face twisted with emotion. At last he stepped back a pace, his voice apologetic and soft. "Of course, your obligation is with her trust. I appreciate that." He looked as if he would say something further, then he looked away in frustration. His voice came as a whisper. "It is just so hard, after all this time ..."

Sarah sighed, breathing in the anguish emanating from the man before her. It was, after all, very unlikely that he was lying to her. He clearly seemed concerned about Abigail's safety and well-being. She relented, and touched him gently on the shoulder to have him turn.

"You will not have to wait long," she consoled him. "I see her regularly, but on a certain schedule, for everybody's safety. Local thieves would love to know where their camp was, given the supplies the gypsies carry with them. Do not fear, I will be seeing her again in a short while. I will ask her, then, what she wishes to do."

Reynald looked as if he would argue, but, taking a deep breath, he bowed his head. "If there is a schedule you have arranged which keeps her safe, then I will not ask you to alter it," he agreed reluctantly. "I am sure, once you speak with her, that she will come home to me."

A lilting voice echoed across the gardens. "There you are!" Rachel strolled into view through the bright summertime sunlight. She was sporting a low cut green gown which clung to her curves as if the fabric was soaking wet. Sarah watched as Rachel moved right past her to stand before Reynald, her body moving sensually while she spoke.

"Sir knight, I hear that you ride very well! Would you be willing to escort me to the fair at Burbage? It would be quite gallant of you to provide this service, in exchange for our fair hospitality."

When he turned, Reynald's gaze gave no hint of the emotionally charged discussion which had just finished. His eyes were alert and he moved at once to agree. He gave a short bow, nodding his head. "I would be honored, Rachel. You should most certainly have a companion on your trip."

Sarah watched as he bowed in farewell to her, then headed back towards the keep in company with her younger sister. She sat in the gazebo alone for a long while, her thoughts torn between Abigail's difficult situation and how she had disappointed Simon's dreams.

* * *

Sarah found only her mother and father waiting for her at the head table that evening for dinner. They both looked at her expectantly as she sat down. Sarah waited until the mead was poured before she wearily nodded her head.

"I am sure nothing stays secret in this house for more than five minutes," she sighed with a half-smile. "Yes, it is true that I asked Simon to stop courting me."

Mathilde sipped her drink. "He was always such a nice young man," she murmured. "Still, you have to decide for yourself what path your life will follow. You are sure he is not the one?"

Sarah shook her head. "He is certainly sweet," she agreed, "and he creates lovely music. However, he holds a deep disdain for the things I treasure in life, and dismisses my opinions. I cannot imagine I would be happy in a household with him."

Her father leant forward, patting her hand. "You will know when the right man comes along," he promised with a smile. "Hold fast to your ideals. A man will come who shares them, and who respects you."

Sarah took a hunk of bread from the table's center, ripping off a small piece and chewing on it thoughtfully. "Still, I wish there could have been a way for it to … peter out naturally," she commented sadly. "He was so sure I was the one. He seemed so desolate when I told him there was no hope. If only …"

Mathilde chuckled softly. "Woe be to any baby bird or lost lamb who comes across your path," she smiled to her daughter. "You would keep every wayward creature completely safe from all harm and trouble. These are part of life, and they help to make us strong and mature," she pointed out. "Simon is a grown man. He will deal with this setback, move on, and find his match. For every pot there is a lid."

"I suppose so." Sarah's heart was not in her response. She still remembered vividly the sad look in Simon's eyes as she gave him the news, the fading of his shine …

She considered bringing up the subsequent events involving Reynald and Lou, but she took another drink of mead instead. Better to hold her tongue, to wait and see how things played out. One never got into trouble by being slow to share gossip. Instead, she talked generally about how her gardens were doing, discussing fall harvesting plans with her parents.

Dinner was almost finished when Reynald walked into the main hall, absently dusting the dirt off his tunic as he strode across the wooden floor. He came over to sit opposite Sarah and her parents, nodding his thanks as Sally brought him a trencher and a mug of mead.

Her father raised a glass in hearty welcome. "Greetings, Reynald, and well met," he called out. "I am so glad you were able to return from the fair in time to sup with us. The items they serve out at Burbage are sometimes … questionable." He chuckled at the thought, nudging his wife with a smile.

Sarah's heart roiled with concern. "Where is Rachel?" She knew her feelings were irrational; Rachel was certainly old enough to take care of herself. Still, she thought of Rachel as an innocent younger sister, and old habits seemed to die hard.

Reynald finished his mouthful of chicken before answering. "We ran into Simon," he explained between bites. "Simon said that he would see her home again when she was ready, and she seemed most interested in taking him up on his offer."

Sarah's temper flared. "You left Simon in her care?" she snapped with heat.

All eyes swiveled to her, and Sarah's mother chuckled softly. "I rather think Rachel is in Simon's care, my dear. Surely you trust Simon with her well-being? I rather thought you liked him, despite the way things ended between you two."

Confusion swept over her. "Yes, of course," she stammered quietly. "Simon is sweet; I trust him completely." She looked down at her plate, mixing the peas around absently with her knife.

She heard her mother ask Reynald for details of the fair, and the conversation swirled on around her. Her emotions rolled in a twisted maelstrom. The moment dinner was over, she walked over to the sitting room, moving to stare out the window.

Footsteps came in behind her, then stopped a few feet away. Reynald's voice was contrite. "I am sorry," he offered softly. "I did not think there was any harm in -"

Sarah waved her hand. "No, of course, you are right," she agreed wearily. "Simon is an upstanding man and would never hurt Rachel. I imagine she was most insistent that she wanted to be with him instead."

She turned to see Reynald nodding. "Indeed she was, and I did not feel it was my place to gainsay her wishes." His face creased. "However, if it has upset you so -"

Sarah sighed, sitting on the fabric-topped bench which had only a few hours ago held a gentle musician. "I am not sure exactly why I am upset," she admitted slowly. "Certainly, I have no claim on him. I have been hoping for him to find a wonderful woman for many months now. He deserves that joy and happiness."

Reynald's voice was quiet calm. "You want him to find love - but not with your sister?"

Sarah turned to look out at the darkening sky. "If she were serious, then perhaps I would not mind. It is hard to know. As it is, I imagine Rachel is not serious at all. The poor man's emotions are in turmoil, and she knows he cared for me. It just seems … wrong."

Reynald spoke from behind her. "Perhaps she seeks to distract him from his sadness."

Sarah chuckled wryly. "I do not know if it really helps, when one sister turns you down, to have the other dally with you for a day or two and then vanish as well. That would seem more likely to make things worse."

She shrugged. "Well, they are both adults, and I can only hope that Simon does eventually find the woman he is meant for. He is deserving of that contentment."

Exhaustion seeped through her bones, and her eyelids suddenly were enormously heavy. Simon's sad eyes seemed to stare out at her from the darkness beyond the windows. Taking a deep breath, she stood wearily. "I am sorry, but I am still exhausted from yesterday." She smiled tiredly at Reynald. "Thank you, for everything."

Reynald swept down into a bow. "Sleep well, Sarah," he offered with a quiet look.

She moved past him, making her way to her room. She glanced for a moment at the door one to the right of her own … her sister's room … before heading in to collapse into sleep.

* * *

Sarah's awareness slowly came into focus. Someone was knocking softly on her door. A voice came seeping through. "Sarah, wake up. Sarah!"

Sarah pushed off the covers and staggered her way over to the door, pulling aside the bolt she had thrown in a vain hope of, for once, getting some uninterrupted sleep. She slowly swung the door open.

Her sister tumbled into the room, her face glowing with excitement.

"Sarah, it was wonderful!" she whispered loudly, bursting into giggles. She hugged herself tightly, her blonde hair bouncing with her movements. "Simon is so sweet, so kind. His hands – they are so soft!"

Sarah rubbed at her eyes. What time was it? The night seemed pitch dark, with only soft moonlight filtering into the room.

Rachel plunked herself down on Sarah's bed with ease. "I must tell you *all* about it."

Something within Sarah snapped. She was tired to the bone, and hearing about Rachel's exploits with Simon was more than she could bear. The poor man …

She reached out a hand and took Rachel's, hauling her sister back up to her feet.

"Please, not tonight," she insisted sharply. "You can keep your Simon tales to yourself."

Rachel's face fell in disappointment. "I want to tell you!"

Sarah's eyes grew sharp. "Why is it that half of the time you deliberately hold things back from me and the family – or even lie about certain issues? Then when you feel that a bit of truth is advantageous to your own goals, you want to force us and others to hear it?"

Rachel pouted and her voice grew louder. "I am only trying to share my life with you," she grumpily huffed.

Sarah walked over to her bedroom door and stood by it. "The last ten men you dated, you did not say one word to me. You lied outright about two of them. Then suddenly, when you are seducing the man who was only recently courting me, you feel obligated to wake me up in the middle of the night to share every last detail?" She shook her head in frustration. "Do you even realize you do this? You lie frequently. You hide truths frequently. When you share truths, it is often in a situation which deliberately upsets others. Not tonight."

Sarah waited until Rachel had stalked out of the room before closing the door firmly behind her.

Sarah stood by the door for a few moments, taking in several deep breaths. She felt unhappy about snapping at her sister, but she was just so tired of everything … she slid the bolt home again with firm resolution, then made her way back to bed.

Chapter 5

Sarah skipped lunch the next day, instead grabbing some cheese and bread from the pantry and taking them to her room. As the day wore on, her tensions slowly lessened with the gentle breezes and a robin's melodic warbling which floated in through her window.

Finally, she climbed to her feet with resolution. Maybe she was just feeling worn down. It seemed that she had been on the go for weeks on end. Couple that with no sleep and the leftover guilt from having hurt Simon ... she needed a change. A quiet ride into town would do her some good.

She was cinching her horse's saddle tight when Reynald strode into the stables to join her. He scanned her activity with an interested look in his eye.

"So there you are," he commented lightly. "Your sister was looking for you earlier."

Sarah kept her eyes lowered. She strove to keep her tone even. "What did Rachel want?"

Reynald shrugged, leaning against the side stable wall. "She did not say. She left an hour or so ago, to visit a friend. Your father sent one of the guards as an escort for her."

"Hmmmm," answered Sarah with a noncommittal murmur, putting the issue out of her mind. She had to learn to let Rachel go, to stop treating her as a helpless little sister.

Reynald let the silence slide. His eyes moved to her horse's saddle with a steady glance. "No bag, and no haste. So this is not an emergency call?"

"No call at all," replied Sarah, looking up to meet his gaze. "I am heading into town for some supplies. The rosemary and sage should be ready to harvest soon, and I was going to acquire more pouches and glass containers in which to store them."

Reynald moved towards his own horse. “Please allow me to escort you, then.”

Sarah focused her gaze on her horse’s bridle, settling the leather gently against his face. “I hardly need an escort,” she pointed out with honest appraisal as she worked. “The supplier is only a half hour’s ride, and the roads are safe enough.”

Reynald gave a brief tug on his horse’s saddle. “A short ride, and yet you never can tell,” he commented quietly to himself. The sharp tone in his voice made Sarah dart a glance over at him, but his head was lowered to his work, and she could not judge his expression. Shaking her head, she mounted up.

“As you wish,” she replied easily. She was content enough that he would be riding with her, and had no real desire to drive him away.

The two headed out into the warm summer sunshine. A scattering of gilt-edged clouds drifted across the sky, the ivory shimmering against the cerulean blue. A flock of sparrows danced and soared overhead before spinning off towards a distant farm.

A golden glow seeped into her soul, nestling there, seeming to echo in Reynald’s amber eyes.

* * *

Reynald let the silence drift for some time, curiosity growing in him about the woman by his side. At first glance, she looked like many other noble ladies he had met over the years. Her locks were tawny, waist-length, and shone in the sun. Her dress was finely embroidered and well fitting. She handled herself with serenity and grace. In talking with her he had come to know that she was well educated and possessed a quick wit.

The more he spent time with her, however, the more intrigued he became. How many noble women would choose to ride out in the middle of the night to help a peasant give birth? How many would risk their own lives to deal with wandering gypsies and assist people they barely knew?

Finally he put voice to his musings. "Tell me, how did you become interested in midwifery?"

Sarah was silent for a long while, and Reynald rode alongside her, comfortable with the quiet. He had been on enough long rides that he understood the value of patience, of letting a story unfold in its own time. After five minutes had passed, Sarah looked up from the road.

"I grew up with two friends - Dorrie and Tanya - who were dear to me. We did everything together. Tanya was a little on the wild side, though. She would want to stay out late listening to the traveling minstrels, that sort of thing. Dorrie and I tried to look out for her as best we could, but as we grew older, it became more challenging."

She paused for a moment, lost in thought. Reynald let the silence extend, putting no pressure on her. A few minutes passed before she continued.

"Tanya had always been the scrawny one when she was younger. When she turned fourteen, she promptly filled out, in a womanly sort of way. She spent long evenings with the band members at local taverns. They plied her with food and drink. When her belly rounded out, we took it as a good sign, that she was finally getting enough food into her. We never thought to question it."

The pause now dragged on for quite a while. Reynald looked over at Sarah, watching her profile. She had a quiet strength in her, as well as a deep reservoir of emotions. He could see how difficult this was for her, to think back over the situation with her friend.

"She was pregnant," stated Reynald quietly.

"Yes," whispered Sarah softly, her voice more of a cry than an answer. She brushed away a tear. "She told no one. She was embarrassed, and afraid that her mother would get upset at her." She scoffed in despair. "Get upset? Her mother was the sweetest woman you could hope to meet. Still, you know how young girls can be sometimes."

"Everyone has their secrets they are loathe to reveal," commented Reynald softly. "It is part of being human."

Sarah looked out into the distance. "Perhaps you are right at that," she agreed. Her face became serious. "However, in this case, it meant that I found Tanya, bleeding, in the corner of her stables. Something had gone wrong with the baby. She pleaded with me not to tell anyone. She insisted that we could handle this on our own. She had already lost so much blood, though, that I knew it was beyond my help."

She sighed and looked down the path. "I ran for her mother, and a physician was fetched immediately. Despite his best efforts, it was too late." She shook her head, wiping away more tears. "If she had only trusted in someone - anyone - then she would be alive today. Instead, because she hid away, she died."

"So now you offer protection without judgment to women who are pregnant," finished Reynald in understanding. "That way, no woman is put in that position again."

"Yes," agreed Sarah, taking a deep breath. "No matter what, I will keep their confidence. My reputation spreads as I take on more patients. Then other women in trouble take that step to contact me. My reputation and honor are, in a way, far more important than any particular skill I have learned over the years."

"As well it should be," agreed Reynald softly, half to himself. He gave himself a shake, turning back to the woman by his side. "What did the mother do?"

Sarah looked down the road, lost in thought again. "She joined a nunnery," she commented with a quiet smile. "She works with young girls now, to help guide them and provide them with a friendly voice. I believe she has done a lot of good; at least that is what Dorrie tells me. She lives near the nunnery with her husband, and visits occasionally."

"That is some comfort, that she has found a way to spend her life helping others," mused Reynald.

The two rode on in quiet, each lost in their own thoughts.

* * *

When Sarah came down to lunch the next morning, she found that Reynald had left for the day already. Disappointment swam in at her, and she pushed the feeling aside. Her mother only had a vague notion of where he had gone – apparently he had eaten early and then ridden off. Rachel was still sound asleep, so Sarah enjoyed a quiet hour with her parents before preparing for her afternoon's tasks.

When Sarah returned to her room, she found Rachel coming out of her own room, bleary-eyed with sleep. Her younger sister smiled widely at Sarah as they passed in the hall.

"Morning, sis," called out Rachel, wiping at her eyes and yawning.

"Good morning indeed," teased Sarah gently. "Another late night?"

Rachel brushed the loose tendrils of blonde hair back from her face. "Maybe," she responded with a mischievous grin before heading down the stairs.

Sarah watched her go, considering. If she had been with Simon, maybe it was not such a bad thing. Rachel did like musicians, after all, and perhaps Simon's gentle ways would help to tame Rachel. Was the match really such a bad one?

She went through her supplies with practiced ease, choosing which ones she would need for her trip. Her schedule was a simple one – a half hour ride to visit with Melissa, who was only six months pregnant. The young seamstress had never given birth before, and was understandably nervous about the process.

Sure that she had everything she needed, Sarah allowed herself the time to catch up with her weeding and garden tending for an hour. Then, with the sun still high, she gathered her horse to head out.

She enjoyed the ride out to Melissa's home in the afternoon sunshine, covering the short, familiar route in no time at all. She spent a comfortable hour sitting with the woman, answering her questions and drinking mead. The time flew by, and Sarah was relaxed and content when it was time to head home again.

She was walking her horse quietly along the main road when she heard hoofbeats sounding behind her. Glancing back, she saw that it was Reynald approaching her, his horse streaming along at a hard canter. Once he realized who was sharing his road, he pulled in and slowed to a trot, then a walk.

"Greetings, Sarah," he called out with a concerned look. "You are out without a guard?"

The dust on Reynald and his steed indicated he had been out for quite a ride. Sarah wondered where he had gone to, but bit her tongue. If she began to pry information out of him as to his travels, he might feel equally inclined to pull details from her.

"Well met, Reynald," she answered in a light tone. "I was just over the hill with a friend, and am on my way home. I do not take escorts with me when visiting my patients. In any case, it certainly is a fine day for riding."

"Indeed it is," he answered shortly, his eyes scanning the forest. It seemed to Sarah as if he would say something more, but he took in a breath and turned his head. He rode at an easy pace, keeping his steed alongside hers.

After a few moments he spoke again, his voice calmer. "So everything went smoothly?"

"Yes," she acknowledged, "and I am very thankful that things are quieting down. I am looking forward to the pheasant stew that I heard was being made for dinner."

Reynald's eyes brightened. "Oh? That does sound like a good ending to this day. I am becoming quite spoiled, lodging in your home."

A furious gallop sounded behind them, and both turned quickly to see who was bearing down on them. Reynald's hand dropped to his sword, his eyes sharp. He relaxed visibly as the rider came into view. It was Rachel, leaning low over her roan stallion. She was on them in moments, pulling to a hard stop alongside Reynald, almost running her horse into his.

"There you are, you slowpokes!" she cried out in delight as her mount skittered sideways in agitation. "Plodding along on such a fine day! Come, Sarah, race me to the gates."

Sarah smiled gently at her sister, demurring. “I am sure you would win, Rach,” she pointed out. “Your horse is far faster on the short stretches. I concede victory to you.”

Rachel’s face wrinkled into a frown. “You spoilsport!” she cried out in frustration. “You could at least try!”

Sarah bit her tongue. Perhaps it did not matter if Rachel would win by default. Rachel simply wanted her chance to shine, and would it cost her that much to give her the opportunity? She smiled brightly. “You are right, of course,” she agreed. She turned to Reynald. “Would you give us the starting mark?”

Reynald nodded his head. “Three … two … one!” he called out.

Sarah pressed her legs into her mount’s side, giving the race the best attempt she could, but there was no contest. Rachel’s high strung horse was bursting off the ground in seconds, and it seemed that she was drawing ahead with every stride. Still, Sarah gamely struggled to keep up, pushing her steed to his limits. She heard Reynald following along behind and wondered with a smile just how much he was reining in his own horse in order to let the two women race unimpeded.

By the time Sarah reached the main gates, Rachel had dismounted and was handing her steed over to Lou with a casual flip of the reins. Rachel cavorted in delight as Sarah came into the courtyard. She lost no time in proclaiming her victory.

“I won! I won!” she cried out, pronouncing her triumph to all within hearing distance. “I am the best!”

Sarah pulled her weary horse in to a stop and slid off. “You certainly did,” she agreed with a smile, walking over to give her sister a gentle hug. “I am proud of you. You are an amazing horsewoman.”

Reynald pulled in behind the two sisters, dismounting. “Very nicely done,” he offered to Rachel. “That was a fairly won race.”

“My horse is one of the fastest in the stables,” boasted Rachel with pride. “He cost my father a pretty penny, but he was worth it!”

A page came running into the courtyard, stopping when he reached the group. "Rachel – your father wanted to see you as soon as you returned," he reported in quick staccato. Rachel flushed, then hurried after him into the main building.

Reynald handed care of his mount over to Lou, then turned to face Sarah, who was unsaddling her own. He helped her remove the tack as he spoke.

"You know, I am quite good with horses. I can help you select another mount if you wish," he offered with quiet solicitude. "One that is a bit more fleet of foot."

By way of an answer, Sarah glanced down at his sword. "That weapon you carry – it is not very well adorned," she commented with an appraising look. "I could find you several in our armory which are more decorative, with sapphires or rubies in their hilts."

Reynald automatically dropped his hand to his sword, a frown crossing his face. "My sword has proven itself in combat many times over," he stated firmly. "I would not trade its reliability for a more gaudy blade."

A moment passed, then a sparkle lit into his eye. "I think you were trying to make a point?" he asked with a smile, bringing the harness to hang on its peg.

Sarah nodded, patting her horse gently on his neck. "My steed is not the fastest here. That I fully accept. However, when he canters, he is as smooth as silk. I have carried women nine months pregnant to a surgeon without harm. I have brought newborn babies across great distances without waking them."

She chuckled softly to herself, leading her mount to his stall, pouring water into his trough with a fond smile. "He is not the fastest. That is fine. He is the very best for what I need, and it took me months to find him. I have had him for three years now, and every day I thank the stars that he is a part of my life. I would want no other."

Reynald's mouth quirked. "You do not mind that he is not as handsome as your sister's," he commented half to himself.

Sarah smiled despite herself. "To me, he is the most beautiful horse in the stables," she replied, her eyes shining as she looked into those of her steed. “He has never faltered. He has been there for me at every turn. He is perfect for me.”

She gave her horse a gentle kiss on the nose, then patted him and turned to leave. She was surprised to find Reynald standing in front of her, a distant look on his face.

Reynald’s gaze sharpened, and he looked down at her steadily. She found herself blushing under the intensity of his gaze, but she did not waver. Then, after a moment, he turned and strode from the stable, leaving her alone and flustered.

Chapter 6

Rachel and Reynald were both absent from the table the next morning when Sarah joined her parents for an early lunch. She gave her father a gentle kiss on the cheek as she sat down next to him and her mother, digging with relish into the warm oatmeal. Sally brought her over some cider, which she downed with pleasure.

Her mother leant over with a smile. "We will be riding into Mildenhall for the day, to do some shopping. Would you like to join us my dear?"

Sarah looked up at her parents, watching how they sat so comfortably together, how they still looked forward to spending time with each other after all these years. She sat back for a moment, then asked suddenly, "Did you know right away, when you met, that you would be so happy together?"

Her mother's peals of laughter filled the room, and her father chuckled ruefully. "Surely you have heard the tales, many times," he smiled at her. "How we met at a local faire, and promptly dismissed one another as being far too stuck up for our tastes."

Mathilde nodded her head, putting a fond hand on her husband's arm. "Your father was so stern looking, as if he could not be troubled with the frolicking and fun around him. I told my friends that he would be the last man there I would consider marrying."

Christopher turned to Sarah. "I thought she was the silliest creature I had ever met, only worried about who had the fanciest dress on. I thought she treated me poorly because I could only afford a simple outfit – not an embroidered one as the other young men wore."

Sarah looked between the two. "Then you met again, later, on the road home?"

Mathilde leant her head against Christopher's shoulder. "It began to pour, and I took refuge under a willow by the side of the road. A few of the young men from the faire passed me on their stallions, but they did not even see me – they were too concerned with riding quickly to save their outfits." She smiled up at her husband. "Then Christopher walked by. He spotted me right away, and came down to make sure I was all right. We spent hours and hours talking. I soon realized that he was not proud at all. He was shy, and embarrassed of his less than fine attire."

Christopher patted his wife's hand fondly. "I realized that she had been reacting to my attitude, not to my clothing. She was really quite a wonderful person, when I allowed myself to start afresh with her."

He sat back a bit, his eyes twinkling. "It is amazing how misconceptions can escalate. If you begin with the slightest mistake, you can build on it, bit by bit. Soon you are sure things are a certain way, and you feel you have 'proof' of your point of view. It is the way the human mind works. It likes to sort things logically. If you believe a person is a certain way, it is likely that you will pay attention to the items that support your belief, and overlook any to the contrary."

"How very true," came the reply from over her shoulder. Sarah looked up and blushed; she hadn't realized there was an audience to her discussion. Reynald stood a few feet away, looking down at her, considering her.

Sarah saw that he was dressed for riding. So he did not like misconceptions? "Where are you off to today, then?" she asked with casual lightness.

Reynald's eyes shuttered for a moment. His eyes shot to look at Christopher's.

Sarah's gaze followed his in an instant, and she turned to face her father. "You know what he is up to and are keeping it from me?" Her voice became more firm. "Does this involve the so-called bandits?"

Her father shook his head, patting her arm in a placating gesture. "No, no," he reassured her. "It is just that I did not want to worry you before we had fully worked out the situation. There is some danger involved."

Sarah's resolve sharpened. She had sensed something was afoot, and it bothered her that her own father was keeping information from her. "If there could be danger, then perhaps it is best I know of it now, since I am often out and about on my duties. Surely you do not think me so faint of heart that I would be unnerved by mere news of trouble?"

Her father shook his head. "It is not that, but rather that Reynald asked me to keep his information confidential. It is up to him whether we can discuss the matter further."

Reynald sat beside Sarah, his face solemn. "I thought to keep you and your sister sheltered from my true task here. However, I see now that I should have made you aware of this earlier, and it was wrong of me to try to … protect you." He looked again to Sarah's father. "I leave it to you, what to say."

Christopher sat back. He spoke in a straightforward manner to his eldest daughter. "Reynald has been sent by his order to find news of three renegade knights. They have been spotted around this neighborhood, and their appearance coincided with a rash of crimes."

Sarah looked between the two men, confused. She had assumed that Reynald's sister had been the main reason for his being in the family's keep, and that his other business lay in distant parts. It had not occurred to her that his remaining tasks had anything to do with her home town.

She focused on what her father had said. "Are you sure the crimes are related to them? Maybe the knights were simply tired of their duties, and are heading home through our region."

Reynald shook his head slowly. "If only it were that simple," he admitted with sadness. "One of them was a good friend of mine. His name is Charles. When his mother died a year or so ago, it affected him greatly. He fell into an association with two other men who were already being watched for suspicion of dishonorable behavior.

"I should have done more to help him. I was busy with other things and did not make the time. Before I knew it, the three had vanished. Funds were missing from the treasury. They are wreaking havoc wherever they go."

He gave a sigh. "I still cannot believe Charles is aware of what is going on with his companions. It is part of why I asked to come after them – alone – to discern the truth."

He paused for a long moment. "I even came without a squire or escort, and am growing my hair out. That way I can better blend in with those who live here. I am doing all I can to acquire the information I seek quietly."

Sarah glanced over at her father, disbelieving that their quiet landscape could harbor such a threat. "Have there really been reports of serious crimes in our area recently?"

Her father's eyes looked weary. "At first there was the odd tale coming in about robberies, but we discounted them as the work of common criminals. Now it seems that there is more of a pattern to the reports. Reynald has been out talking with the victims, to see if descriptions of the attackers match his quarry."

Sarah smiled slightly. "Well, I should be safe enough. I doubt highway robbers would be interested in stealing bandages and anti-nausea herbs."

Reynald's eyes shadowed. "It is your personal safety I would fear for," he reminded her gently. "They could do far more harm than simply steal a few baubles."

Sarah's cheeks grew pink, but she nodded in understanding. "That is fair enough," she agreed, "Or, if they took me hostage, they could pressure my father into who knows what concessions." She looked to her father. "If it is necessary, I will take a guard to ride with me when I go any great distance or must travel at night. I would not wish to cause any distress simply because I wanted to ride alone."

Her father pulled her close, kissing her gently on the forehead. "I knew you could be trusted to be sensible," he commented with a smile. "It is one thing to defend yourself against a common criminal – but if a Templar comes after you, one of our guards would be hard put to even delay him enough for you to flee to safety."

Sarah had not been considering fleeing as an option, but she bit her tongue and nodded to her father. These were all quite remote scenarios they were discussing, and there was no need to argue over something which would probably never happen.

She looked up at Reynald. "Well then, good luck on your interview visits. I hope they are productive in helping you find the men you seek."

Reynald stood, looking down at her for a long while. "As do I," he stated finally, his voice gentle. He nodded to her parents, then turned and left the room.

Sarah's father turned to look at her after Reynald had gone. "I would like to keep this from your sister," he advised her thoughtfully. "It would only upset her, and she is a handful as it is. I will ask the guards to keep an eye on her when she leaves our walls."

Sarah nodded. "As you wish," she agreed. Standing, she nodded to her parents before heading out towards the gardens, lost in thought. She found that her mind returned to Reynald often as she spent the day in quiet labor, tending to the sage, dill, and lavender.

* * *

Sunday morning dawned with gentle sunshine, and Sarah dressed herself in her traditional Sunday best, looking forward to the time in the chapel.

As the familiar sound of the litany washed over her, she found herself giving thought to the nature of what Reynald did every day for his chosen life's work. He protected pilgrims from all walks of life – high and low, rich and poor – who had decided to make the long, arduous journey to Jerusalem.

Sarah contemplated how difficult that trip must be, the miles to travel through all types of weather, along varying landscapes. Although many people she had met expressed an interest in going, only one person she knew had actually invested the time and effort to go there and return. His tales of the trip ranged from humorous to downright frightening.

Sarah imagined the hundreds of individual people, each making that life changing decision for whatever personal reason. Did they have a dying wife? A child in need of a proper spouse? Had they lost their way in the world and were seeking new direction? Maybe they had done a great wrong and were seeking redemption.

Each person, no matter how mean or base their background, was watched over along their journey by these knightly guardian angels. The Templars did not charge for their services. They looked out for the travelers without pride or notice. It was due to their ever-vigilant watch that the pilgrims could reach their destination unscathed, and return home again.

Sarah's eyes drifted ahead to rest on Reynald's strong shoulders. He sat in the pew two rows before her, alongside Rachel. His eyes were fixed on the priest, and he appeared engrossed in the sermon. His black hair was brushed back from his face, falling in soft curls to his shoulders. She imagined him standing alongside a quiet, dirt road in a foreign landscape, far from his homelands, ensuring that people he had never met made their journey safely …

Reynald turned suddenly, meeting her gaze with questioning eyes. Blushing fiercely, Sarah dropped her own eyes to stare down at her hands in her lap. She had heard that people could sense when they were being looked at – surely it could not be true! She forced her gaze to remain fixedly on her clasped hands for the rest of the sermon.

Sunday afternoon in her home was set aside for reciting passages from the Bible to each other, and if any visitors came, in quiet discussion with the guests. To her surprise, Reynald joined them in the sun-drenched sitting room. The family members passed a candle around from person to person, each recipient choosing a passage to share with the group. Reynald appeared to pay close attention to each reading, listening intently to what was being said.

When Sarah was done with her passage, she looked to her right, where Reynald sat, relaxing in a leather chair. Leaning forward, she handed the candle over to Reynald.

"You do not have to speak, if you do not wish it," she stated courteously as she offered him the candle. "Feel free to pass it along to Rachel."

Reynald smiled as he received the candle from her. "I would be quite proud to participate," he responded with grace. He only took a moment to settle himself, and began.

His voice was slow, rich, and almost melodious as he spoke.

"Psalm 15 - A psalm of David"

"Lord, who may dwell in your sanctuary? Who may live on your holy hill?"

"He whose walk is blameless and who does what is righteous, who speaks the truth from his heart and has no slander on his tongue, who does his neighbor no wrong and casts no slur on his fellow man, who despises a vile man but honors those who fear the Lord, who keeps his oath even when it hurts, who lends his money without usury and does not accept a bribe against the innocent. He who does these things will never be shaken."

Sarah was caught by the words. They resonated within her. She wondered for a moment if Reynald had meant them as a prod to her, to speak the truth about the location of the gypsies – but looking up into his eyes, she felt sure that this was not the case. This passage had special meaning to him. She could see it clearly in his gaze.

She wondered just what had driven him to take on such a rugged calling, living his days out so far from his home. She wondered how he sustained himself over the years, risking his life each day for the pilgrims who traveled his roads.

Reynald nodded his head in reverence, then passed the candle along to Rachel. She nibbled grapes idly for a while as she pondered. Sarah sat back peacefully in her chair, taking a sip of mead from the table beside her. She truly enjoyed these quiet Sunday afternoons, a chance to rest and reflect after a week of hard work.

Rachel cleared her throat, and all eyes turned towards her.

"John 8," began Rachel in a smooth, clear voice.

Sarah fought to keep her face serene, to prevent a smile from slipping into view. This was one of Rachel's favorite passages. Sarah appreciated that Rachel felt much put upon and unappreciated. Each time Rachel recited these words, Sarah tried her very best to find new meaning in them, to understand how Rachel felt. This was another chance for her to relate to her sister. She wanted to give this her best effort.

"Jesus went to the Mount of Olives. At dawn he appeared again in the temple courts, where all the people gathered around him, and he sat down to teach them. The teachers of the law and the Pharisees brought in a woman caught in adultery. They made her stand before the group and said to Jesus, 'Teacher, this woman was caught in the act of adultery. In the Law Moses commanded us to stone such women. Now what do you say?' They were using this question as a trap, in order to have a basis for accusing him."

"But Jesus bent down and started to write on the ground with his finger. When they kept on questioning him, he straightened up and said to them, 'If any one of you is without sin, let him be the first to throw a stone at her.' Again he stooped down and wrote on the ground."

"At this, those who heard began to go away one at a time, the older ones first, until only Jesus was left, with the woman still standing there. Jesus straightened up and asked her, 'Woman, where are they? Has no one condemned you?'"

"'No one, sir,' she said."

"'Then neither do I condemn you,' Jesus declared."

Rachel nodded her head with a satisfied sigh and looked around the room. Sarah ventured a glance toward Reynald, wondering if he had caught the omission. His face revealed nothing, and he nodded his thanks to Rachel for the reading, following the candle with his eyes as it was passed along to her mother.

The afternoon passed in quiet contentment, and when the readings were through, Sarah was drawn to take a quiet walk in the back gardens before dinner. She had made her way to the gazebo when she heard footsteps. She turned to find Reynald approaching. She smiled her greetings to him as he entered the structure to stand beside her.

"You have a devout and literate family," he praised her quietly, looking out over the pond.

"Thank you," responded Sarah with pleasure. "Both my mother and father felt it important that Rachel and I learn the scripture. I know families where only one person recites the Bible to the rest all Sunday long, and I really find it much more interesting when we each take turns to share a verse."

Reynald's face remained steady, but his voice had a light teasing quality in it as he answered, "Apparently your sister felt a subtle commentary was necessary in her reading?"

Sarah raised her eyebrows. Maybe he had noticed after all. "What do you mean?" she asked innocently.

Reynald did smile at that. "You know very well, it seems," he countered. "I believe the instructional passage your sister chose to read had a subsequent line she left off. Something about Jesus instructing the woman to 'go now and leave your life of sin'?"

Sarah chuckled in spite of herself. "Now that you mention it, I do believe Jesus tries to set the woman back on the straight and narrow path. However, the Bible does not tell us if his admonition was followed by said wayward lamb."

Reynald's tone remained light. "Your sister does seem to be a little on the impudent side."

Sarah shrugged. "Many men like that about her, that she is not uptight and formal. She certainly has her share of suitors."

"However, she is not yet married," pointed out Reynald.

"Nor am I," rebutted Sarah easily. "Not that Rachel needs to wait for me, of course. She is free to marry whenever she wishes. She chooses not to."

Sarah did not like where the conversation was heading. Her parents had been quite patient with her quiet avoidance of any talk of marriage, and she certainly was not going to get into the issue with a newcomer. Her mind switched gears with deliberation.

"Perhaps my sister's rebellious nature is simply a product of her birth order. I know several older sisters, and it seems in many cases that the older sister becomes the responsible one, while the younger sister has the freedom to rebel."

She gazed out at the pond, considering. "The older sister is trained from the moment another child is born to look out for the younger one. She is reprimanded when she fails at this. This responsibility is reinforced every day of her life."

Her eyes twinkled. "The younger sibling is equally trained, every day from birth, that she has someone watching over her – and telling her what to do. It is probably quite normal for her to both feel safe enough to be wild, and to resent the continual orders about her life by a person nearly her own age."

She looked over at Reynald, who appeared lost in thought. "Tell me about your siblings," she asked with curiosity.

"I have a brother two years younger, and then a half sister who is more than ten years my junior," he stated quietly. "I agree, what you say about younger siblings seems very true with my brother as well. He was always the wild one in our family. My father died just after he was born, and I tried my best to guide his growth – often to little avail."

Sarah turned to face him. "I am so sorry about your father," she offered gently.

Reynald shrugged. "I barely knew him. I grew up having to handle the responsibility of my younger brother, to make sure he was fed and kept safe. Our mother would often be away from the house visiting with friends, so it was up to me."

He looked out over the pond. "Then, when I was about ten, my mother remarried to a much older man. He was wealthy and stern. I imagine it was the first that attracted her to him. Together they had Abigail." A smile crossed his face. "From the moment I saw my new sister, I adored her. She was a delight. It was hardest to leave her behind, when I left for Jerusalem."

A high pitched squeal of laughter came from the main gardens, and Sarah turned in surprise. She saw Rachel dancing amongst the roses, with Simon moving alongside her, a smile on his face.

"See, sometimes things do turn out well," murmured Reynald beside her, his eyes following hers into the distance.

Rachel's voice rang out over the gardens. "Oh, and then my sister – my do-as-you-are-told, I-know-best sister, she is caught with him in the *pantry*! I heard it from the cook! Can you believe it?"

Sarah blushed crimson and leant heavily against the railing of the gazebo. Simon's muttered response was too low for her to hear, but Rachel's peals of delight rang out, echoing across the pond.

"You had better believe it!" she agreed whole-heartily. "Then the next thing I knew, they were going at it in the stables. The *stables* mind you! She calls *me* the wild sister?"

Reynald uttered a low growl next to her, and Sarah immediately put her hand out onto his arm, holding him still. She watched as the couple moved off in the direction of the keep.

"Let her go," she rasped, her throat tight. "She is entertaining Simon. She is … she is lessening my worth in his eyes. Maybe this will help him get over me more quickly. Her exaggerations will not cause serious harm."

Reynald's face was dark. "She is spreading gossip and affecting how others think of you. It is not right."

Sarah gave a weak smile. "The rest of the household knows of her tendency to dramatize events. They will not take her seriously." A thought struck her and she looked up with concern at Reynald. "If it is your reputation you are worried about …"

Reynald shook his head quickly. "No, I will stand by anything I have done, and will speak out if it is brought up." He looked into the distance. "If you will tolerate your sister's behavior, for her sake and for Simon's, then I certainly can as well."

Polly's voice rang out into the afternoon air. "Dinner's ready! Sarah! Rachel!"

Sarah shook herself, then stood up to go. Reynald moved easily at her right as the two walked in towards the keep for dinner, both lost in thought.

Chapter 7

The table was full when Sarah came down the following morning. Her mother and father sat facing Rachel and Reynald. Her sister wore an embroidered lilac outfit, complete with a lavender-dyed feather tucked into her hair. She was deliberately turning her head occasionally to tickle Reynald with it, which the knight was ignoring with calm patience.

"Good morning," Sarah greeted the group, sitting beside her father. The egg dish with sausage smelled delicious, and she eagerly began eating. "It looks like another fine day outside."

"Oh yes," replied her sister cheerfully, "I think it is a perfect day to get a new dress from the seamstress in Upavon." She turned her gaze to Reynald. "I would be very pleased if you would escort me there, my champion."

Reynald looked troubled, and he began slowly, "Perhaps it would be more appropriate if one of the regular guards …"

"Posh!" cried out Rachel, dismissing the idea immediately. "They are needed around home, for their 'regular' duties. You are the visitor here, and as hostess, it is my duty to show you around! This is the perfect way for you to get to know the neighborhood. You are best suited to keep me safe," she added with a sly smile.

Reynald's eyes flicked up to meet Christopher's, and Sarah's father shook his head slightly. Reynald's lips compressed, but he nodded slowly. "Of course, your safety is very important," he agreed soberly. "I would be quite happy to provide you an escort."

"Why, then we should leave immediately!" decided Rachel, springing to her feet. "No reason to sit around here all morning like fuddy-duddies." She grabbed Reynald's hand, barely giving him time to bow to her parents before half dragging him out the front door.

Sarah shook her head, looking back to her parents. Her mother shrugged.

"Do not look at me," she remonstrated. "Your sister has been willful since she became a woman. Now that she is an adult, there is little we could do that would change her behavior."

* * *

Sarah thought about her sister all day while working in the garden shed, drying and mincing herbs and organizing her supplies into small pottery containers. When she spotted her sister returning later in the afternoon, she hurried out into the garden, intercepting her where they could talk alone.

"Rach, I would like to speak with you for a minute," she began carefully.

"If it is about Simon, you can have him," responded Rachel with a smile. "He was all right in small doses, but I find him far too clingy. I shall not be going off to see him any more."

Sarah's heart fell. She wondered how Simon was taking this latest blow, and her voice came out gruffly. "Actually, I was not even thinking about Simon. I was thinking of how you have been behaving around Reynald."

"Oh, I see. Well, you cannot claim him," responded Rachel archly. "Reynald is single, and I have as much right to him as any other woman. I do not care if you are older. I am not going to wait around for years and years until you decide to finally marry someone."

Sarah's mouth hung open. The thought that Rachel would wait on her for anything was a complete shock. She recomposed herself and began again. "No, that was not it. I just wanted to suggest that you ... tone it down a little, how you behaved around him. He is a knight, after all, and -"

"And you want him for yourself," shot back Rachel with a pout. "Well, then, see if you can get him from me. I find that my wiles are working quite nicely, and I think you are just jealous that you do not possess my … assets." She wriggled her body demonstratively.

Sarah sighed. "Rachel, I am just trying to provide you some sisterly advice."

Rachel tossed her hair. "I hardly need suggestions from you," she replied sharply. "You are single. Therefore, you could not possibly have any quality advice to offer me."

Sarah felt a jab of ire at this irrational statement, then her eyes flashed with inspiration. "So the only person who could possibly offer you any words of wisdom is someone who is perfectly happy in marriage?"

Rachel opened her mouth to say yes, but quickly shut it again, shaking her head. "Oh no, not our parents," she stated. "On second thought, I do not want any advice at all. I am quite pleased with how I handle things."

Her brow wrinkled, and she added, "Whenever you or our parents try to tell me what to do, I feel like a cat that has been rubbed the wrong way."

Sarah's shoulders slumped. This was not going at all how she had hoped. "We are just trying to help you to be happy," she pleaded resolutely.

"Then support me in my choices!" cried Rachel in exasperation. "When I want to do something, give me praise for doing it my own way!"

Sarah shook her head. "What if it seems to be a poor choice, based on incomplete information?"

Rachel stamped her foot. "Have you not heard of unconditional love? I do not want your advice or your alternatives. I want you to agree with me on the way I want to live my life. I want you to tell me how proud you are of what I am doing."

Sarah took a step back at this, her eyes shadowed. "You are serious. You want us to lie in order to make you feel better about your choices?"

Rachel's lips curled down in a pout. "Why do you always have to put things like that? I just want to do what I want to do –

and I want my family to back me one hundred percent. Is that so much to ask?"

Sarah sighed. "Please, just … be careful," she pleaded.

Rachel tossed her head back. "I am always fine," she stated firmly. Turning, she stomped toward the main building. Sarah watched her go, her heart falling. How had the gulf between the two of them grown so large? She sat wearily on a stone bench, lost in thought.

"A family is never an easy thing," commented Reynald, stepping to stand beside her, looking in the direction of the keep.

Sarah looked down at her hands. "So you heard that, did you?"

Reynald chuckled wryly. "It was rather hard not to. I did not mean to eavesdrop, but -"

Sarah waved away his concern. "There are few secrets around here," she assuaged him. "My sister is the way she is. Undoubtedly she would say the same thing about me, that I am too stubborn, or unsupportive, or controlling, or rigid, or something. Who knows, perhaps I am."

Reynald's mouth quirked. "I did hear something of the sort, during our ride today."

Sarah lowered her head into her hands. "I do not even want to hear about it," she moaned softly. "It would only make me feel more helpless."

"My brother and I fought like cats and dogs," commented Reynald in a soothing tone. "From the moment we were both old enough to walk, we were beating on each other with sticks, throwing each other into the local pond, wrestling each other in whatever mud hole we could find." He smiled at the memory. "Despite all of that, we loved each other dearly, too. I remember the time that someone punched my brother. I was there in a heartbeat, defending him with my life. There was no question in my mind what I must do."

Sarah smiled, imagining a young Reynald scrapping with the neighborhood bully. "Girls do not fight physically like that," she mused. "With us, it was more of an emotional thing. Who would get more of our mother's affection, or our father's. Who would be in the spotlight more."

Reynald smiled. "That is why they call it sibling rivalry," he pointed out. "Children are not adults. By their nature, they act immaturely."

Sarah sighed. "I am sure that I did my share of grabbing for attention, of wanting to be first. Even so, most of what I remember of our childhood are the good times. I remember teaching her how to read and how to count. I remember holding her by the hand when we want walking, to keep her safe. I would make sure she remembered her cloak when it was cold. When we were given candies I would divide them up, one by one, to make sure she got her fair share."

She shook her head. "Somehow my sister remembers a different slant on things. She would figure that I divided up the candies to get as many of hers as I could."

Reynald sat down beside her on the bench. "It is the curse of being the eldest," he offered with a gentle smile. "We are always the ones expected to be responsible. Our parents look to us, every day, to watch out for our younger siblings. If we slip up even for a moment and act 'our age', our brothers and sisters will remember that moment forever, and forget the twenty three other hours we were there and caring."

Sarah looked up to Reynald, nodding. "In the meantime, they are never expected to be responsible. They are always being cared for, and expect that to be done perfectly. Any failure by the elder is cause for life-long repercussions."

She rolled her shoulders. "When my sister became a woman, she changed. I suppose all girls do. I had always defended her actions to my parents, putting myself between her and them as naturally as you did with the bully. Finally, shortly after my sister turned thirteen, my parents had had enough. They told me to stay out of the way – that my sister's problems should be faced by my sister on her own, and that I should let them discipline her directly, without involving myself at all."

Reynald's eyes focused on hers. "That must have been hard on you," he commented, intrigued.

Sarah nodded. “I wore mourning clothes for over a week in protest,” she responded. “It felt as if they had asked me to stop breathing. Defending my sister was what I did. Caring for her was my every day life. To tell me to abandon her – which is how it felt to me – hurt immensely.”

She reached down to pluck a stray violet, staring at its petals for a long moment. “When you think about it, parents should have the right to discipline each child individually for what they have done wrong. It never would have occurred to my sister to intercede when I was being punished, to protect me. Still, my whole life had been about keeping her safe, caring for her.”

Reynald looked back towards the keep again. “Now she is a grown woman.”

“Now she is a grown woman,” agreed Sarah. “Yet when she stands before me, I think of that young, wide-eyed doll who followed me around, who looked at me with those big, trusting eyes, and relied on me to keep her safe. It is hard for me not to be caught by that vision.”

She shook her head. “Maybe Rachel is right. Maybe I do tell her what to do, when I should stand back and let her try on her own – whether she succeeds or fails.”

Reynald’s eyes met her own. “That is a challenging thing to do,” he commented quietly.

Sarah dropped her eyes. “It eats me up inside, every day,” she responded. “If she fails … and fails again … and I can see her sinking, not learning from her mistakes …”

Reynald put his hand over hers, giving hers a gentle squeeze. “Part of being an adult is accepting the consequences of your actions, and learning that the things you do lead to results you must live with,” he pondered softly. “As a sibling, all you can do is offer to be there to give advice, and hope that someday they are of the mindset to seek – and understand – any wisdom you offer.”

Sarah looked up to him, her mind switching gears smoothly, caught by his tone of voice.

“So you would not try to drag your sister back, if she did not wish to go with you?” she asked softly.

Reynald held her gaze for a long moment, his look troubled. Then, finally, he nodded in agreement.

"As much as I long to do so – to bring her to safety, to protect her – I accept that she must make her own decision. I will make myself available to talk with her. I will offer all the advice I can. In the end, though, I understand that she has the free will to listen or to ignore me."

He took in a deep breath, then turned away. "I also accept, as hard as it is, that she may not even wish to hear my advice. Maybe she feels her own path is so well chosen that none could possibly help her any in mapping it out."

Reynald chuckled wryly. "Especially since I am not married, and do not have a child. By your sister's reckoning, that means I could not provide any suggestions at all on Abigail's situation that could be of value."

Sarah smiled reassuringly. "Abigail does not seem to have that mindset at all," she confided with a wry smile. "I will do my best to encourage her to speak with you, and to hear what you have to say."

Reynald's amber eyes were caught on hers, and she could see how much her words meant to him. Finally he spoke, his voice rough. "Thank you. It means more than I can say."

Chapter 8

Sarah gave her boot a final tug before turning and gathering up her leather bag of medical supplies. She hefted it over one shoulder, then made her way down the quiet hallway to the main dining area. Waves and smiles greeted her from the various tables as she made her way through to the head table. The foursome was just beginning a meal of stewed vegetables, and she eased down beside her father with a smile.

He patted her hand by way of welcome. "Off for a visit this morning, are we?" he asked gently. "Going far?"

"Not far," she responded with reassurance, taking in a bite of the steaming, fragrant stew. "Just over the hill to Devizes."

Reynald glanced up. "I was planning on riding to Devizes myself at some point over the next few days," he commented with interest. "One of the …" he glanced sideways at Rachel for a moment, then continued smoothly. "One of the individuals I want to talk with lives there. I can accompany you to the town, and we can meet up again when it is time to head back."

Rachel looked up with a frown. "I wanted to ride with you into Burbage," she huffed in frustration. "Why does Sarah's trip take precedence over mine?"

Christopher smiled placatingly at his younger daughter. "I will ask Cedric to take you," he offered. "You always were fond of his company."

Rachel tossed her hair. "I have long since grown tired of Cedric," she insisted. "He is stodgy and boring."

Her mother took a small bite of the vegetable medley. "Be that as it may, today Cedric will be your escort. I will ask him to be more cheerful in your presence."

Rachel looked down in stony silence, pouting. Sarah finished her food quickly, eager to be on her way. Reynald followed along as she walked to the stables and prepared her horse for the ride.

They fell into the preparation of their horses as easily as long time companions, and Sarah marveled at how comfortable it was to ride side by side along the sun-streamed path, how easily their conversation flowed from the best way to treat cuts to techniques for helping an ill patient relax and calm. At every turn Reynald was intelligent, curious, and open to discussing whatever topic she broached.

When the pair reached Devizes she found it hard to bring the fascinating conversation to an end. She had to remind herself that she was being waited for, and forced herself to smile brightly as she waved farewell to him.

"We will meet back here just before sunset?" she asked as she turned her horse's head.

Reynald nodded in agreement. "As you wish, my lady," he agreed, his eyes twinkling, offering a chivalric sweep of his hand.

A shiver of delight spun down her spine at the courtly reply. She nudged her horse into a trot down the road to hide her emotions, focusing on the task before her.

Her patient today was Melanie, a young woman who was pregnant with her first child. She was only three months along. Sarah spent much of her time answering basic questions, providing information on handling morning sickness, and soothing the young mother's concerns.

The time flew by, and soon the sky began to darken outside the window. Bidding farewell to her patient, she mounted and rode back to the meeting point at the edge of the village.

She had just about reached the spot when a woman's voice called out to her from a house at the side of the road. "Sarah, hold up a moment!"

Sarah pulled to a stop. "Cornelia! How are you?" She smiled down at the plump woman, admiring her simple but clean periwinkle-blue dress.

"I am fine, thank you," Cornelia responded, glancing in both directions down the long, quiet dirt road. "I do not suppose you have seen Ralph, my younger brother, on your travels?"

Sarah shook her head no. "I apologize; it has been weeks since I have run into him. Is he missing?"

Cornelia's eyes perked up at motion far down one end of the road, but her shoulders quickly slumped again. "Not him," she sighed. Her gaze returned to Sarah. "He has only been gone two days. I am sure he is off gallivanting with friends."

"I will let him know to come home, if I see him," promised Sarah dutifully. "How is your sister?"

"Dorrie is fine, thank you. She and Walter are quite happy together, and I hear from her often. She keeps telling me I should move closer to her, but my husband's family is here, as is my own."

Her voice edged with crispness. "I tell her that she and Walter should move back home again, but of course, they will not. It grieves me greatly."

Heat rose to Sarah's cheeks, but before she could respond, Cornelia added, "Speaking of which, how is *your* sister?"

There was the sound of quiet hoof beats, and Sarah looked up to see that Reynald had pulled alongside her. His gaze moved evenly between the two women. Sarah flustered, caught between defending her sister as always and being blanketed by the embarrassment of what had happened.

"My sister is well," she finally responded, striving to keep her tone neutral.

"Any hope of Rachel going off to the convent, to join Tanya's mother?" prodded Cornelia, her eyes sharp.

Sarah flushed. She should speak out for her sister - but what could she say? The idea that she could not do so in good conscience shamed her. "No," she responded shortly, dropping her eyes. She knew she should introduce Reynald, but she could not. Every bone in her body told her to ride away before she said something she regretted.

Cornelia pursed her lips, looking over at the newcomer with open curiosity. "I am sorry to hear that," she finally replied with a bitter edge. "Have a good ride home," she added, then turned to head back into her house.

Sarah nudged her horse into motion, sure that her cheeks must now be a deep crimson color. She turned her eyes to the side of the road, keeping her face turned away from Reynald's sharp gaze.

To her relief, Reynald did not say anything at all – he simply rode at her side, matching her pace. As the miles rolled on, Sarah's composure returned. She took in several deep breaths, rolling her shoulders.

"It is not as bad as you may think," she began, her eyes flickering sideways to meet Reynald's. "You might even say it was a sort of a misunderstanding."

"Things often can blow out of proportion," agreed Reynald with an even look, "when people do not take the time to learn the whole truth."

"I was only sixteen," continued Sarah, thinking back in time. "Rachel was fourteen."

"That can be a rough age," mused Reynald. "One can become caught between wanting to be independent and not having the experience to make wise choices."

Sarah nodded, the words beginning to flow more easily, her comfort with him drawing her to speak where normally she would have stayed silent. "Rachel was always bright, but she would sometimes act before she thought things through. She was just at the age where she wanted to come and spend time with my friends at our more 'adult' get-togethers. She had always followed me in the past, so I suppose this was no exception. I swore to my mother that I would keep an eye on her, and keep her out of trouble."

"As always," commented Reynald quietly.

Sarah nodded. "One of the men in our group was older – twenty one – and charming, in a rakish sort of way. He was the special beau of my good friend Dorrie. His name was Walter."

She looked down for a moment. "I have to admit that I had a crush on Walter at the time, but I never acted on it in the slightest way. To me, the fact that Dorrie and Walter were a couple meant that he was completely off limits. It would have been the ultimate betrayal for me to have gone after him."

She sighed. "I explained all of this to my sister before she began joining our group. I told her who the various members of our circle were, and how each was related to the other. She knew how I felt about Walter, and she knew that he was a taken man."

She rode along in silence for a few moments, and Reynald did not seek to break the quiet. It took her a while to gather the strength to continue.

"One evening, I came home late, after dark, from visiting with a patient. I had been assisting old Marigold with a case she had, to learn more about midwifery. When I got home, Rachel was not there. She had not returned from her visit to Roundway to see a friend. My mother was supposed to meet up with her there and escort her home."

Her eyes shadowed. "I was furious with my mother, more than I had ever been before. I thought my mother had forgotten to pick up Rachel. I had images of my poor sister waiting, abandoned, at a dismal, dark crossroads, hoping plaintively for someone to come to her aid."

Sarah ran a hand through her hair, her lips pressed tight together, then took a breath. "I yelled at my mother in a way I had never imagined I would. How could she forget my sister like that? I was all set to race out to rescue her myself."

She shook her head. "To my surprise, my mother did not even flinch at my tone. She seemed to take it in stride. She explained that she *had* gone to retrieve my sister – and that my sister had not been there. That it appeared that my sister had instead gone off with Walter."

Sarah looked down at her hands. "She was just fourteen years old. What was she thinking?"

Reynald's voice came in a low, tense rumble. "What was *he* thinking?"

Sarah glanced at Reynald in surprise. In all her years of going over the story in her mind, she had never looked at it in that way.

She moved on with the tale. “My mother and father went to fetch Rachel home. I kept myself apart, and could not bring myself to defend her as I usually had. She had betrayed my trust. For the first time, my complete devotion to her had a chink in it. This had been a man important to me for several reasons, and she had thrown it all aside for … for I do not know why.”

Reynald met her eyes. “So Walter and Dorrie moved away?”

Sarah nodded. “They were married soon afterwards, and they live quite happily in Bisley. I try to see Dorrie when I can, but there is still a bit of… well, uncomfortable feelings between the families because of the situation.”

“I imagine it also caused a rift between you and your sister,” commented Reynald.

Sarah sighed at the memory. “It was as if a line had been crossed. I still do not think my sister understands at all why it mattered to me. To her, she was better at ‘getting a guy’ than I was, and she felt sure I was upset to have lost. However, to me, he never should have been approached. He was sacrosanct. That she could have done that …”

She shrugged. “I suppose I still have that wide eyed doll image in my mind, of how my sister was when we were young. Perhaps I would have her stay that way forever. It is an unfair thing to ask of anyone.”

“You were not asking her to stay young and immature,” pointed out Reynald quietly. “You simply were asking her to match your own levels of honesty and respect for others.”

Sarah looked up to him. “Is that even a fair thing for me to ask?” She sighed in confusion. “Every one of us has different measuring sticks, different values we feel are important. My sister thinks nothing of lying blatantly to our parents. She routinely leaves out important parts of her life when talking with them, lies of omission. She says she is justified in doing this because they will not support her unconditionally in her choices. She does not want to have to listen to their criticism or suggestions, so she does not tell them anything they might disagree with.”

She ran a hand down her horse's mane. "I, on the other hand, simply tell the truth. If my parents disagree with my choice, I accept that and move on. I would never want my parents to lie to me, to claim they felt one way when they really felt another. Nor would I want to hide things from them. They are my family after all, and they would undoubtedly find out what was going on later for one reason or another. Lies rarely survive for long."

She sighed. "However, if I am honest with myself, even I keep some things from them. I do not tell them the names of my patients, for example."

Reynald watched her face with consideration. "That is a reasonable exclusion. You are protecting the privacy of the women you work with. I understand that."

Sarah met his gaze. "Still, what if something happened to me? What if I fell and was hurt on the way to someone's home? My parents would have to track down where I was going in order to find me. They would know the truth eventually. Also, after all, once a woman births a child it becomes known soon enough. It is not an eternal secret. Would it really be that wrong to tell my parents – and perhaps the guards – as a balance for my safety?"

"Then where do you draw the line of who you trust to tell?" pondered Reynald.

Sarah nodded. "Everybody draws a line somewhere. We all draw those lines in different places. So perhaps it is unfair of me to say that others around me must choose to maintain the exact same lines I have chosen for myself."

Reynald thought about it for a while. "Still, there are some general guidelines that society as a whole has adopted. I can kill someone who is trying to attack me – but I cannot ride down the road and kill a random stranger because I want his possessions."

"Most situations are not quite that cut and dried," responded Sarah with a chuckle. "Nobody dies when Rachel creates a false impression."

Reynald's eyes held hers. "Her honor is diminished – and your ability to trust her is lost. That is not something to be dismissed lightly." He paused for a moment, then added,

"Especially if she has allowed her own desires to override any concerns about your emotions."

There was a long stretch of silence, and suddenly Reynald spoke up with a lighter tone. "Here we are, safe and sound."

Sarah looked up and saw that the walls of her home were coming into sight. She was astonished again at how quickly time seemed to fly by when she was with Reynald, and how much she enjoyed talking with him.

Reynald's eyes stayed on her, and when he spoke, his voice was rich with respect. "I have to tell you, Sarah, I have not had conversations like this with any other woman before." He paused for a few moments before adding, "You are quite a companion."

Sarah was caught off guard by the praise and by the echo of her own sentiments towards him. She turned to steer her mount into the stables, dismounting and handing the reins over to Lou, who was patiently waiting within.

She turned to find Reynald standing close to her, his dark curls almost tinged with gold in the glow of the sunset. She could smell the musk of his aroma, the leather of his armor, the tantalizing hint of cedar that clung to him. Her chest, suddenly, felt as if it were caught in iron bands.

"Thank you for the escort," she offered throatily, her eyes caught by his.

His hand moved up to her cheek, cupping it for a moment, and Sarah thrilled in every movement of his finger along her cheekbone. His voice was soft and rich when he spoke.

"Someone, after all, should look out for you."

He held the gaze for a heartbeat, then turned quickly and walked toward the keep. Sarah forced herself to stand still, to wait until he had entered the building, before moving slowly after him.

Chapter 9

Sarah stepped into the main hall with a dancing step, breathing in the fresh morning air, her eyes sweeping towards the head table – and her heart fell in disappointment. His chair was empty. Her step seemed to drag as she moved to take her place.

Her mother's eyes twinkled as she greeted her daughter. "Your sister is off visiting friends, but I am sure she will be back soon," she reassured Sarah. The grin on her lips indicated that she knew well who it was Sarah was really missing.

Sarah nodded, picked at the roast hen, barely hearing what her parents said to her.

Finally, as the meal drew to a close, her father spoke up. "My dear, my duties are light today. Would you like to take a walk for a while?"

Sarah's heart lightened. She rarely had time to talk alone with her father, and looked forward to moments such as these. "Yes, gladly," she replied with a smile.

In a short while the two were heading out the main gates, their feet moving along a quiet path. They walked for a spell in silence, enjoying the bird song and quiet forest shelter.

Sarah glanced sideways at her father. He had always been a steady rock in her life, a man of serene wisdom and firm action. "Do you think there is just one person for each of us?" she asked suddenly. "Like you and mom?"

Her father smiled. "I think what you will find in life is that having the right partner for you is not so much about finding just the right person, but in *being* just the right person."

"What do you mean?" asked Sarah, confused.

"Some people are miserable with their lives. They do not like the way they are living, and feel unhappy with their world.

They seek out a person to come strolling into their life to make everything better. They want a soul mate who will appear, make them perfectly happy, and sustain that feeling forever."

"That does seem like a nice idea," commented Sarah with a smile.

Christopher shook his head. "Unfortunately it rarely works, for many reasons. First, if you cannot be happy on your own, it simply does not work for another person to 'make' you happy every day. Few relationships can survive under that strain. Next, who would want to be with you in the first place, if you were always unhappy?"

"So the key is to be happy?" asked Sarah.

"The meanest of peasants can be completely content with their lot in life – and the richest kings can be miserable," mused Christopher. "We each have within us the ability to be happy with what we have. I am not saying we should be stationary. There is always cause to strive for something better, to improve ourselves each day. Still, these should be healthy, goal oriented pursuits which we relish. Activities should not be forced, knee-jerk reactions to an existence we thrive on despising."

Sarah thought to one of her patients who she suspected was in an abusive marriage. "What if you are trapped in a situation beyond your control?"

Her father nodded. "In a way, all of us have aspects of our lives that are beyond our control. I cannot change that I am male. You cannot change that you are my daughter. Yet so much of our world *is* within our control, if we only take the time and energy to confront the situation. There is always something in our life we can appreciate. There is always some small task we can do to make things better."

Sarah warmed in relaxation, strolling alongside her father through the bright July afternoon. "I have been blessed in many ways," she commented after a while. "I have a loving family, a secure home, and I am very content with my life's calling. The problems I face are tiny compared with what many deal with every day. I do count myself as being happy." Her mouth quirked as she looked up at her father. "Why, then, am I not surrounded by soul mates?"

Her father glanced at her with a mischievous look on his face. "Maybe you are," he commented wryly.

Sarah looked away, blushing. "Just because I might be interested in a man – and I am not admitting here that I am – it does not mean at all that he is interested in me."

"Then he is not right for you," stated her father with firm conviction. "A partnership can never be about one person luring in the other, or tricking them into a match. If you feel a man is perfect for you – and he does not feel the same way – then he is in fact *not* perfect for you. You are simply blinding yourself to the problems, and focusing only on the advantages to yourself."

"Surely there must be something to the alluring that women do," Sarah felt obliged to point out.

Christopher nodded his head. "By all means, promote your assets – you are the only person who can make sure they are known properly to others," he acquiesced, "but to try to go beyond that simply will not work out over the long term. I have several friends who were captivated by a woman who claimed to share their interests – fishing, riding, whatever it happened to be. Each man married with the expectation that he had a life long partner he could trust and depend on."

He sighed, looking down the path. "In each case, the woman was able to keep up the charade for a few months, but as time went on, her true feelings became known. Now the men feel taken advantage of and the trust – the cornerstone of any relationship – has been damaged. If the women had simply been honest and presented themselves truthfully, the relationship most likely would have been drawn together anyway and the men would have been far more content. As it is, the deception at the beginning seriously damaged their chances of a truly happy marriage."

Sarah looked over at her father. "So you and mother went into your relationship with open eyes?"

Christopher chuckled. "Completely open. She was very forthright about the things she loved to do. For example she gently let me know that she would not have any interest in falconing with me. It was, in fact, a refreshing change from the other women who simply parroted an interest in each hobby of mine." He smiled fondly.

"I have other friends I can falcon with. Only your mother is my confidant in life, the woman who I can trust with anything. I treasure her honesty more than anything else in the world."

Sarah spoke half to herself. "So I simply have to wait, to see if what I am is what he wants?"

Her father wrapped an arm gently around her shoulders, giving her a hug. "You are one of the three most special women I know," he reminded her gently, "and you are quite unique. Many men would be incredibly proud and fortunate indeed to have you as their partner in life. Give it time. When it is the right match for you, you will know it – and so will he. Do not settle for someone who does not love you as whole heartedly as you love him."

Sarah's stomach twisted in doubt, but she put her own arm around her father, and the pair walked in silence for a long while.

Sarah's steps grew slower, her heart heavier, as she thought ahead to her afternoon task.

When they approached the back end of the keep, Sarah saw the men drilling in the fields. Reynald was in amongst them, working with two of the younger guards, sparring against both of them in turn. Sarah watched the Templar in admiration. His skill with the sword was graceful and controlled. Equally impressive was his patience with the lads as he corrected their swings with calm encouragement.

She was half tempted to change and join in the practice, as she sometimes did, to keep her sword skills from getting too rusty. She knew she could not. She had other things on her mind today, and she put aside her desire.

"I will be heading out to Devizes in a short while," she informed her father as they stood watching the men. "It is a well traveled road, but if you wish I will take along one of the guards, as a precaution."

Christopher nodded without hesitation. He raised his voice and called out to the men. "Cedric, I need an escort for my daughter," The burly guard looked up from his sparring instruction, running a hand through his short-cropped black hair. Reynald laid a hand on his arm, then trotted over to stand before the two.

"Cedric is busy here, but if I am not being presumptuous, I will gladly go in his place," he offered, looking between the two. "My rounds are complete for the day, and I am at your leisure."

"By all means," agreed Christopher contentedly. "I will leave you to it. I could use some practice time myself." He gave each a nod, then headed into the keep to change.

Reynald looked down at his own outfit, which was covered in dust. "Perhaps I should change as well?" he asked with curiosity. "Where will we be going today?"

"To a cemetery in Devizes," explained Sarah, her face somber. "You are fine; my friend will not mind at all how you are dressed. She was always a simple soul, possessing a most beautiful heart." She paused for a long moment, lost in thought. Seeing a waving mass of daisies nearby, she walked to them and gathered up a bouquet of the white flowers. When she had them settled in her arm, she turned.

"I am ready to go now, if you are."

By way of answer Reynald wiped down his sword, sheathing it with one easy motion. Together they walked over to the stables, and in short order they were heading down the sunny road side by side.

Reynald did not speak as they traveled, and Sarah was glad to let the silence grow around them. Her heart shadowed, melancholy and lost, despite the streaming sunshine and medley of wildflowers which lined the lane. It was just one year ago now … one long year since that tragic day. She felt rather than saw Reynald's looks of concern, and was glad that he did not break the silence.

The cemetery at Devizes was behind their stone church, surrounded by a low grey wall of fieldstone. It was quiet as they approached and tied up their horses, the lines of grey markers standing resolutely in the summer sun. There was the drone of a bumblebee as it moved amongst flowers in the far corner of the yard, but other than that sound the area was silent.

Sarah moved through the grass to the stone she sought, the grave standing alone in a back corner. The marker was small and simple.

Ysabel Brown
Aged 16
Loving daughter and sister

Sarah knelt before the stone, laying the flowers before it in a blanket. Reynald had come to a respectful stop at the entrance to the cemetery, and she was alone in this holy place. She let her head drop, thinking back to that long night, to the look in her friend's eyes, the long gaze of sadness and understanding. The quietly whispered words, "You did your best." The tears came, and she let them flow unhindered.

There was a noise behind her, and Sarah turned, then rose to her feet in one smooth motion. A young man in his early twenties was stumbling along the side wall of the church, heading in their direction. His clothes were dirty and torn, his dark hair an unruly shock. He glanced up, seeing the cemetery was not empty, then his eyes narrowed in fury. He drew his sword in one angry movement. Reynald's own blade was out in an instant, and he stepped to fully block the opening in the stone wall.

The man's voice was a low growl when he spoke, shot through with seething hatred. "This is not your battle, sir," he directed at Reynald dismissively. "That woman desecrates the ground she stands on. She has no right to be here!"

Sarah took a few steps forward, staying behind Reynald but moving so she could be seen. "Ethan; I am sorry to intrude on your day of remembrance. We will leave you in peace." She wanted to say more, but held her tongue, not wanting to inflame an already tense situation.

The surly man shook his head. "Leave me in peace? How can I ever find peace? My sister is dead. You took her from me!" He took a menacing step forward, his sword held high. Reynald held his position, dropping slightly into a more defensive stance. He did not say a word, his eyes never leaving Ethan's.

Sarah kept her voice low, soothing. "I did everything I could to save your sister," she promised gently. "It was too late – she had already lost too much blood …"

Ethan's eyes went wide with fury. "So it is my fault?!" he cried out in anguish, and in a second he charged. Reynald blocked, Ethan spun to attack again, and the clang of metal on metal rang out into the stillness. Sarah was frozen in shock, unable to move. Her skills were clearly no match for either man who parried and thrust in furious rhythm. She was rooted, unable to turn and run for help. If Reynald was hurt, or killed …

As she watched, she realized that Reynald was holding back, blocking more than attacking. He was redirecting the blows, carefully timing his own movements to push Ethan to retreat, to build distance between the aggressor and his prey.

A shout came from the other side of the church, and in a moment a larger man rounded the corner, a taller, sturdier version of the wild-eyed swordsman before them.

"Ethan, God's blood! You are on holy ground! Put up your weapon!" called out the newcomer, racing forward. When Ethan hesitated a moment, the man reached around, ripping the sword from his grasp. Reynald stepped back warily, looking between the two men with caution.

"Elijah, thank God," breathed Sarah in relief. "I am so sorry …"

Elijah shook his head, taking in deep breaths. "It is I who should apologize for my brother's behavior," he growled out, looking down in anger at the younger man. "He has been in a state all day, but I never thought … I should have kept him at home." He looked over at Reynald, scanning him appraisingly. "You are not hurt, sir?"

Reynald lowered his sword, shaking his head. "I am unharmed," he responded shortly.

Elijah's brows rose in respect. "Then you have a good arm, sir, for my brother is well known for his skill. I am glad he has met his match." His gaze returned to meet Sarah's. "You know that none in our family hold you responsible for what happened to Ysabel," he added, his voice more gentle. "Ethan's impetuous behavior aside, we know you did all there was to be done. It was already too late for hope."

Sarah dropped her eyes, guilt filling her. "I will leave you to mourn in peace," she responded quietly.

Elijah prodded his sullen younger brother to slide a few paces to the side, and Reynald moved to stand between them and the dirt path, his posture at high alert. Ethan's face remained mottled with fury, his eyes glancing quickly between Sarah and Reynald's ready blade.

Sarah kept her eyes lowered, walking quickly along the narrow path. As she moved past the pair, she could feel Ethan's eyes boring into her. She was nearly by when his sharp voice stung at her back.

"Your sister, I hear, has spread her legs for coin," Ethan shot out in a snide tone.

Sarah froze mid-step, fury flaring through her at the wild charge. It was all she could do to keep her hands stationary, to not lower them to the weapon at her waist and make him pay for the slander. She took in a deep breath. Anything she began, Reynald would be forced to finish for her. Ethan was simply insane with grief. He was lashing out.

Even so, it took all of her force of will not to defend her sister. She let out a long exhale. Then she put one foot down in front of her, then a second. She focused on the motion.

Ethan was not done. "Speaking of your sister … how is your fiancé Dirk doing? Oh, wait, he is your ex-fiancé now, is he not?"

Sarah felt the blow as a physical attack, and she nearly doubled over in pain. Her face went white; her breath gasped out of her in shock. How could he know? How could anyone know? She could not turn … she could not move …

A hand gently took her right arm, and she set back into motion, leaning against Reynald, moving alongside him around the corner and across the front of the church. Finally she could breathe again, could focus on the horses before them, could go through the motions of checking the saddle, pulling herself up on her steed, turning his head toward home.

* * *

Sarah let five minutes pass in silence, then ten. Reynald did not ask anything, did not so much as look at her inquisitively. He had laid his life on the line for her without question or hesitation. She knew she should say something, but could not bring herself to begin. Finally she forced herself to speak.

"Thank you for defending me," she commented softly. "I had no idea that Ethan would be in such a state. Indeed, I had hoped to slip in and out unnoticed."

"It was my honor," responded Reynald, his voice low. He did not ask anything further, keeping his eyes on the forest and trail ahead.

Sarah appreciated his silence, and almost gave in to the temptation not to speak one more word. However, her honor could not allow it. He had put himself in harm's way to keep her safe. He deserved an explanation.

"Ethan's sister was unmarried, and her lover was a visiting musician, only in town for a week or two," she began quietly. "Ysabel was a sweet girl, but rather naïve. When she realized she was with child, she hoped she could bear it without anyone noticing, and leave it on the church steps. She had heard one too many fairy tales, I am afraid."

Reynald nodded in understanding. He did not interrupt, but stayed at her side, a ready listener.

"Ethan found her in labor, and was furious. He spent time berating her for getting into this situation, rather than fetching help. He was a squire for a local knight and his first thought was how this would damage his prospects. By the time I was called for, there was little hope for the girl. I tried my best, but she was gone."

"I am sorry for the family's loss," mused Reynald. "As to the brother, I can see why he is so upset," he added, his face somber. "However, if he wishes to be a knight, he should learn to own up to his mistakes, rather than blame another."

Sarah shook her head. "He has abandoned that path now. He stays home all day, submerged in a gloom. I am afraid he has lost his way."

"I hope, for his sake, that he finds a new one," commented Reynald quietly.

Sarah knew there was more to be said, but her will faded, and she turned her gaze to the ground passing beneath the horse. The riders lapsed into silence, moving easily as the sun slowly tinted the sky from turquoise to deepest crimson.

Chapter 10

When Sarah awoke the next day, butterflies instantly began fluttering in her stomach. She always became nervous when heading out to the wanderers' location, and with the added complication of Reynald, she was overcome with an additional dose of trepidation.

He seemed almost too good to be true, with his care for her family and his concern for others. His protective duties as a Knight Templar, watching over innocents, drew her in to trust him with her own thoughts. Still, with all he had said about his sister, she knew that his main reason for being here was a serious mission, given to him by his superiors, to find the three renegades.

With that in mind, she had to consider the very real option that she was being played. Was the friendly behavior a carefully laid plan, meant to lower her defenses? Was he still planning on using her in order to get to the gypsies and track down his quarry?

There was no way to know for sure. She could only try her best to discern the truth.

She dressed carefully, putting on an outfit that was loose fitting and dark in color. It would allow her freedom of action if it came to a fight, and the ability to become lost in the shadows. She braided her hair along her brow line, coming down to a thick braid down her back. A sword and dagger completed the outfit. She sighed when she looked at her reflection in the small mirror on her dresser. She was hardly the ideal, alluring female now - but in the end it did not matter. The safety of her patient was foremost in her mind.

She heard laughter as she came down the stairs, and steeled herself to keep moving. She knew before entering the hall what awaited her. Her sister had escalated her outfit. The crucifix was nestled even lower in her bosom, and unless Sarah's eyes deceived her, the rouge which had brightened Rachel's cheeks had now highlighted other aspects of her anatomy as well.

Sarah averted her eyes and moved to her seat by her father, nodding generally to the others at the table. She focused on consuming her oatmeal as quickly as possible so that she could get about her work. Her parents, sensing her mood, talked between themselves, and her sister was exclusively focused on flirting with Reynald.

Sarah finished her meal in record time, pushing herself up to stand. "I will be out for the day," she offered to her parents. "Reynald will be coming with me today."

Rachel stood up immediately, her face flushed. "He went with you last," she insisted hotly. "Today should be my turn."

Reynald's face remained passive. Sarah wondered if she imagined a flicker of impatience in his eyes that was quickly tamed. Was it her own wistful thinking? Was she coloring his responses with what she hoped to see?

"Today's ride is something I need to do," Reynald commented quietly to Rachel. "However, I can spend the day with you tomorrow, if you are available," he added with the hint of a smile.

Rachel brightened. "Promise? All day?"

Reynald nodded, his face serene. "Yes, Rachel. I will be available on Friday for escort duty with you."

Sarah did not wish to hear any more. She turned and headed out of the main hall, heading towards the stable. Before she knew it, Reynald had joined her to move easily at her side.

Their saddling and preparing of the horses seemed a natural ritual now, and they moved past each other in a dance as they fetched tack and gear. Together they rode side by side out of the castle gates.

To Sarah's surprise, Reynald did not ask any questions at all as she led him down the road. He seemed patient, content to follow where she led. She found that she enjoyed the peace of the quiet ride as much as she had liked the conversations of previous days. The two walked their horses across the miles, the morning sun streaming down across the quiet wooded path.

Sarah's mind drifted to Abigail, the reason he had given for accompanying her on this ride. Something struck her as odd about his story.

"Reynald, if your mother remarried and had Abigail with a new husband, why can Abigail not go to her father for support? Surely her father would wish to see his granddaughter?"

Reynald shook his head. "Mitchell was the name of the man my mother married when I was ten. He was elderly at the time, and he aged quickly once he became her husband. He passed away almost two years ago."

Sarah looked down. "Oh, I am sorry. That must have been very hard on Abigail."

Reynald kept his gaze on the forest around them; the branches and thickets grew more dense the further they traveled into the woods. "It did not seem as if it was a great loss to her," he admitted quietly. "Her father had never been attentive. I am afraid she looked more to me than to either of her parents for caring and support. She took it hard when I left."

He let the silence drift on for a while. "I did send them money regularly, and wrote letters to her. She liked that, and wrote me frequently."

Sarah thought about that for a while. How would it be when she was forced to live apart from her sister, to abandon Rachel to the fates? How would her sister fare when she was not there to keep an eye on her? She knew that siblings could not live together forever – and yet it was a hard step to contemplate taking.

Time rolled on, and they moved along smaller and less well-defined paths. Finally they reached a quiet glade with a small stream running alongside it.

Sarah pulled to a stop. Reynald reined in alongside her, his eyes curious but calm.

"This is where we part company," explained Sarah with a quiet smile. "Sit tight, and I will return to you after a while." Her eyes became more focused on his. There was still the possibility that this was all subterfuge. "I promise you, however - if you attempt to follow me ..."

Reynald held his hands up, his face serious. "I value my sister's safety as much as you do," he vowed with meaning. "I will not do anything to compromise that. I am sure after you talk with her that she will agree to see me, and I am willing to wait."

He paused for a long moment, holding her eyes. At last he spoke again, his voice tight with emotion.

"I do not deny that this is hard on me. Please tell her ... tell her I love her. No matter what else she may feel, she should know that much."

Sarah sat for a long while, looking him over. He was the consummate soldier - broad shoulders, well-muscled, his eyes sharp and clear. She knew that he could overpower her in a fight without batting an eye. Even so, he was willing to wait, to abide by her wishes. She could see in his eyes that he meant what he said.

She nodded at him, then pulled her horse to turn down the path. Over the next half hour she doubled back repeatedly, stopping to listen at random intervals. She had no sense that she was being followed. Finally she pressed forward toward the camp.

Lloyd ran forward with a smile as she rode into the clearing. "Sarah, it is so good to see you!" he called out before she had even drawn to a stop. "Abby is eagerly awaiting your visit!"

He escorted her with a quick step through the camp to the tent. Abigail sat out in front of the structure, her young baby held in her arms. Sarah was pleased to see how happy and healthy she looked, and knelt down immediately before the pair.

"Oh Sarah, she is just perfect," gushed the new mother. "Sure, she wakes us at all hours of the night, but she is such a darling. She cannot help it if she gets hungry! She is growing every day, and is just an angel."

Sarah gave mother and daughter a full evaluation, and was quite satisfied that both were progressing well. She sat alongside the pair, taking the baby's tiny hand in her own. She looked up at Abigail, and her face became more serious. "Abby, a man came to see me recently about you."

Abigail suddenly became quite still, and drew her baby in against her breast. "Who was it?" she asked in a soft whisper, her face tense.

"His name is Reynald, and he says that he is your brother. He is a Knight Templar ..."

Abigail looked behind Sarah, scanning the clearing, her voice tight with panic. "Is he here? Did he come with you?"

Sarah patted her gently on the arm. "It is fine, he is not here," she quieted Abigail. "He said to tell you ..." she blushed, but continued. "He said to tell you that he loved you, no matter what."

Abigail's eyes welled with tears, and she held her child close for a long while. Sarah waited with patience for the woman to speak at her own pace. When Abigail finally looked up again, Sarah saw that her face was now streaked.

The girl's voice was tremulous. "Reynald is not angry with me?"

Sarah's heart swelled with sympathy. "He is sincere; I believe in him," she reassured the girl. "He agreed to wait a distance away. He wants to see you and the baby, but he understands the situation you are in. He is willing to do this in a way that keeps you completely safe."

Abigail's face melted with relief. "He ... he wants to see me? The baby too?"

Sarah held the girl's hands in her own. "He loves you," she repeated. "He wants to see both of you. If you are willing …"

Abigail nodded enthusiastically, and Sarah was touched by her love for her brother.

"Well, then, here is the plan. When I return in two weeks, I will bring a horse for you both. The baby will be a full month by then, and it will be safe for you to ride a short distance. I will escort you from camp, so your companions are not in any danger. Reynald will be able to talk with you, to see for himself that you are safe."

Abigail looked down. "What if he tries to take me away from Lloyd?"

Sarah shook her head. "He knows that you love each other, and are married. He respects that. He just wants to hear, from your own lips, that you are safe and happy. He wants to do what he can to help you."

Abigail brought her eyes up again. "How about my mother?"

Sarah gently gave a squeeze to Abigail's hand. "It does not seem that she has changed any," she related sadly. "Parents can be like that. Do not worry about that for now. Your brother loves you, and he will stand by you. You have him, and you have your husband and the baby. That is a lot."

Sarah's eyes shone. "Aye, that is," she agreed with a smile. "I had not thought to have even that much."

Sarah talked with her for a while about the baby, and about her health. She desperately wanted to know more about Reynald, about what type of a brother he had been, about the type of child he had been growing up. She held her tongue, knowing her hours with Abigail were limited. There was enough time for such frivolous discussions later. For now, the safety of the mother and child were paramount.

It seemed all too soon when it was time to go. She gave Abigail's hand a squeeze, promising her she would be back in two weeks with the horse. Then she was off at a gallop, returning to the clearing.

Reynald was waiting alertly when she came in to meet him, and his face relaxed into a smile when he saw the look on her face. "Abby is doing well? The baby also?" he asked before she had even drawn fully to a stop.

Sarah dismounted easily, going over to stand before him. "She is a beautiful mother," she praised in reassurance. "The baby is a delight, and growing at a healthy rate. Do not worry, you will see soon enough for yourself."

Reynald's face lit with joy. "She has agreed to see me?"

Sarah had not seen him so honestly happy since she had met him, and the thought warmed her immensely. "Yes," she confirmed immediately. "Your sister was very pleased with the news that you wanted to meet with her. She will come to see you in two weeks, with her child."

Reynald sighed in relief. "I cannot tell you how much I appreciate this," he murmured to Sarah, taking her by the hand. "Abigail was always the sweetest of children. She was a treasure in our household, and it was very hard for me to leave her. Out of all of my family, it is she that I miss the most."

Sarah held his hand in her own. "I understand, really I do," she replied softly.

The afternoon sunlight streamed in to the small clearing, and warblers were calling from the trees. Sarah saw the love in Reynald's eyes as he thought about his younger sister. Suddenly she wished that he felt that same affection for her - that he would gaze at her with that same look.

She flushed, drawing her hand away, turning from him. She mounted her horse, heading back towards home. In a moment, she heard Reynald following along behind her.

Sarah became lost in thoughts of loving one's sister without hesitation, without any limits. She thought of Rachel's recent request for money, and wondered what she had driven her sister to do by refusing to help.

When they had arrived at home, Sarah headed off in search of her mother. She tracked down Mathilde in the sitting room; the woman was embroidering a shawl by the long windows. Sarah sat down across from her mother, admiring the fine, elegant stitches being laid down on the cloth.

"So, what can I do for you on this fine afternoon?" asked Mathilde with a generous smile. "It appears your ride went well?"

"Yes, very well," agreed Sarah with a nod. "I actually have a favor to ask of you."

"Yes, what is it?" prompted her mother, laying aside the needlework.

Sarah hesitated, her face turning crimson. She reminded herself that this was for her sister's sake. She pushed herself to speak. "I … I need to borrow five pounds."

"Oh? What for?" asked Mathilde with amused interest. "You rarely ever …" She shook her head quickly. "No, never mind. You do not need to tell me the cause. Yes, certainly I will do that." She called out for Polly, who came into the room in a few minutes.

"Fetch me my lock box," Mathilde asked the maid with a nod. It was only a short while before Polly returned with the engraved wooden box cradled in her arms.

Mathilde drew a slim iron key from the collection at her waist, and carefully turned it in the lock. Propping the lid open against the window, she carefully counted out the coins for her daughter.

"Use them wisely," she cautioned her daughter with a smile. "Money does not grow on trees, you know."

Sarah gathered the money up in her hands, standing and nodding. "Thank you, I appreciate this," she said to her mother, dropping a small curtsey. She turned and headed up the stairs to her room. Once there she dug an old scabbard out from a lower drawer and slid the coins down into its base for safe keeping. She lay the scabbard on her dresser top, then sat at the foot of her bed, staring at it for a long while.

* * *

True to his word, Reynald left early the next morning for a ride with Rachel. Sarah watched the two of them head out the gates, willing herself not to be jealous of her sister. Reynald was not hers, after all, and he was free to spend time with all members of the family equally. Besides, it was comforting that Reynald was keeping an eye over her sister, if there really were rogue Templars out there seeking to cause harm.

She spent the day busying herself in the garden, tending to the plants, and making up new poultices. She focused on her father's words, that she needed to be happy and content in her own world.

It was not that she was *un*happy, she thought as she weeded through the sage, enjoying its fresh aroma. She had pretty much everything she needed here. She had good food, a soft bed, and parents who cared for her. She was living her daily life in a way which suited her.

She sighed deeply. She remembered back to the night with Cecily, when she was handling the breech baby. Having Reynald by her side, being able to count on him to help her and support her, had been such an incredible feeling. It was one thing to have her mother provide praise for her when she returned from a call. It was quite another to have a man by her side actively supporting her in her life's work. Once she had realized just how powerful a feeling that was, it was hard to go back to being on her own.

The day slipped by in a long train of thoughts, and she forced herself to focus on her planting, to immerse herself in her work. She had managed to finally lose herself so thoroughly that she jolted in surprise when her sister grabbed her around the waist, bubbling out in a burst of laughter.

"There you are, you stick-in-the-mud!" cried out Rachel in delight. "I should have known to look for you out here. I had so much fun with Reynald! Did you know he is an excellent rider? Few men can keep up with me and my steed, but Reynald managed it! He did not even complain when I took the fences by the old pond, like our stodgy guards do! He is an amazing man."

Sarah smiled, standing and brushing the dirt off of her dress. "I am delighted you enjoyed yourself," she offered with a warm laugh. "It is true, few can keep up with you and your energy!"

"He even bought me some fresh tarts when we visited town," remembered Rachel, licking her lips. "They were delicious! What a sweetie he is."

The mention of money swept Sarah's mind back to the slur at the graveyard, to Ethan's innuendo about Rachel's activities. Sarah dropped her eyes for a moment. "Rach, you know how you said you needed five pounds? I was able to get it for you after all. I have it, up in my room."

Rachel shook her head, doing a spin around the garden. "Hah, you silly, that was days ago. I got the money for myself. You are so behind the times!"

She did another twirl then ran off towards the house. Sarah watched her go with misgivings. Part of her wanted to ask how Rachel had acquired the cash, but another part of her felt it was better not knowing. She sighed, then moved slowly back down to her knees, pulling gently at the weeds sprouting amidst the sage.

* * *

Sarah fought the urge to look again at Reynald's empty chair, to wonder what corner of the realm he was delving into today on his quest for the wolves' heads.

She needed a distraction.

She took up the last spoonful of venison stew, then turned to Rachel. "How would you like to go for a ride to Melksham, to listen to some music?" she asked, drawing a smile on her face. "I hear a new band has come into town."

Rachel's face lit with pleasure. "That sounds wonderful!" she gushed. In no time at all the pair were riding out together in the open sunshine. Cedric trailed along a short distance behind, wearing his typical leather armor with long sword.

Sarah enjoyed the afternoon's ride immensely. Her sister was witty, offering insightful, if often cynical, commentary on the people and places they rode past. They finally reached the village and stabled their horses before strolling around town. Cedric took the opportunity to visit with his sister and young nephews at the edge of town, leaving them in the safety of the crowd. Sarah had great fun shopping and enjoying the open air with her sister.

At last they came to the main building on the green, the two-story tavern with its wide windows and peaked roof. The interior of the tavern was comfortably laid out. There were several circular wood tables, a large fireplace in one corner which sat dormant, and large, open windows which sent a nice cross breeze through the room.

Sarah and Rachel settled themselves at a corner table, and an attentive waitress made sure they were supplied with ales and meat pies.

Sarah found that the musical talents on display for the afternoon were quite good, and looked forward to the featured act for the evening. It seemed no time at all before the men were introduced to the audience.

The lead musician was a tall, sturdy man with blonde hair and a quick smile. His voice was rich and resonant as he called out a greetings to the boisterous crowd.

"Hello, Melksham! My name is Michael, and I want to welcome you all this evening. My friends and I have travelled extensively throughout France and Venice, and we have an eclectic selection of songs to offer. Sit back and enjoy!"

The band immediately burst into a merry dance tune, and the floor was soon full of spinning and whirling couples. As the songs flowed one into another, Sarah marveled at the wide variety of tunes the band had to offer. She enjoyed herself immensely, tapping her toes to the music.

Rachel appeared equally entranced, her eyes fixed on Michael as he moved to and fro across the stage. Soon it became harder to see the group as the crowd swelled in size with each passing tune.

Night was falling in earnest when the group finished its first set and called for a short break. Waitresses moved amongst the guests, lighting candles and stoking up the main fire. To Sarah's surprise, she saw a blond haired figure moving towards them. Michael made his way easily through the throngs over to their table.

"Greetings, young ladies," he called out jovially, sweeping into a bow. "As you know, I am Michael, and I am at your pleasure. How are you enjoying my music?"

"You are wonderful!" called out Rachel, her eyes shining. "That tune you played from Castile, it was so lively and full of spirit! Have you really been there?"

He nodded, his wide mouth crinkling into a warm smile. "Yes, indeed. The landscapes are stunning, and the wine is rich and delicious." His eyes turned to meet with Sarah's. "And you, miss, how do you find our offerings?"

Sarah smiled, leaning forward slightly to be heard above the room's escalating volume. "I am very impressed with your musicianship," she offered. "Many of those songs have difficult arrangements, and your group moves through them as if they are no trouble at all."

His blue eyes lit up with the praise. "We have been together for many years, and we are each accomplished in our own area," he boasted with pride. "It is why we can play songs from so many different cultures, providing the feel of each one accurately." He glanced back up at the stage. "Maybe you would like to come meet the other members, where we can talk at greater length?"

Rachel stood immediately. "I would love that!" she eagerly enthused.

"You two go ahead, I will stay and guard the table," agreed Sarah with a smile. "Otherwise we will have nowhere to sit when we return."

Rachel looped an arm through Michael's and turned him to head back toward the stage area. Sarah looked after them, watching as her sister was introduced to the other members of the band.

Her mind drifted. It would appear Michael was in his mid-twenties, and that he was single. Few would think twice to ask him why *he* was not yet married. He was doing what he wanted, traveling to fascinating locations, and enjoying what life had to offer.

She took another pull on her drink. It seemed unfair that women were expected to marry as soon as they were legally able, as if that was the only thing they were good for. Their purpose in life was to start making babies as soon as they possibly could.

Her brows creased. What of the women who, for whatever reason, were unable to have a child? Were they therefore failures in life? That seemed extremely harsh, given that the situation was completely out of their control. It made as little sense to count someone as a failure because they were born with freckles, or with red hair.

Long minutes passed, and she became lost in thought. It startled her when Rachel plunked down into the seat next to her, a wry grin on her face. The musicians launched into an energetic folk song, filling the room with its rich sound.

Sarah leant over. "So, how was it, meeting the band?" she asked congenially.

Rachel wrinkled her nose. "Michael kept asking me about you," she admitted with a chuckle.

Sarah smiled in return. "I am sure you were able to distract him from that line of thought before too long," she teased her sister.

Rachel's eyes twinkled. "He asked me to come back and hear them next week, when they are playing for a summer festival here. So I certainly hope so!"

Sarah gave her a toast, her heart warming with the joy in her sibling's face. Rachel had a zest for life that she envied. She wished with all her heart that Rachel would find a safe path to a long term happiness.

Chapter 11

Sunday brought dark, roiling clouds and a furious storm. Sarah and her family raced, laughing, through the pelting rain to reach the sanctity of the chapel. The sermon was barely audible over the crashes of thunder and the steady thrumming of rain on the roof overhead.

Sarah did not mind the noise. She found that she spent much of the morning's sermon musing over what Christianity laid out as the path for women. She had been raised devoutly by her parents, and her father had taken part in the Crusades. She felt strongly that faith and duty were important parts of a well-lived life.

And yet … just what had Jesus said about the role of women? He had not treated them as mindless children. He had forgiven the adulteress, knowing she could reach greater heights. He had kept Mary Magdalene by his side during his travels, relying on her wisdom and experience. When he arose from the dead, it was Mary he first went to.

When all others had abandoned him at the cross, it was his mother and Mary who stood beside him, willing to risk antagonizing the Romans to be true to him.

The Bible repeatedly stated that women were caring, were wise, and were morally judged for their actions. When Lot's wife had looked back, she had not been treated as a child. She had been held responsible for her decision, as a mature adult, and the consequences were significant.

The image stayed with her, and Sarah recited that passage that afternoon, passing the candle along when she was done. She barely heard the words the others chose, instead remaining lost in thought.

A voice sounded in her ear. “Anyone in there?” came the low, teasing query.

Sarah looked up from her spot on the window bench in surprise. The room had emptied, and only Reynald remained, smiling down at her.

Sarah ran a hand through her hair, shaking the cobwebs from her thoughts. “Sorry about that, I was just … ruminating,” she admitted quietly.

“Oh?” asked Reynald with a noncommittal look, his amber eyes curious but gentle.

Sarah turned to look out the window. The storm had broken and the afternoon sun was baking down, sending waves of heat into the room. “Apparently I must be a failure,” she mused, half to herself.

Reynald’s reaction was immediate. “Who said such a thing?” he asked in shock. “Who could believe such a thing?”

Sarah shook her head. “Nobody has said it. Still, it seems clear. A woman is supposed to marry as soon as she is able to safely bear children. I am, what, six years overdue? My sole task in life is to create as many children as I can in wedlock for my husband.”

Reynald sat down at her side, looking into her eyes in confusion. “First, that is not true. Women choose many other paths; they are nuns, they are healers. They are midwives, like you are. And second …” he paused for a moment, then continued quietly. “Do you truly *not* want to marry, not want to raise a family?”

Sarah sighed, dropping her eyes. “I do want that,” she admitted softly. “It is what I dream of, someday, to have a husband who loves me, to have a safe home where my children play and grow.”

Reynald’s voice came in an unguarded hush. “I am surprised you have not already been swept away by some lucky man.”

Sarah blushed crimson. The words tumbled out before she thought. “There was someone, once, who I was interested in. His name was Dirk, but -”

She forced herself to turn away, to gaze out the window. “Things happen,” she finished half-heartedly. “That was many years ago.”

Sarah’s heart swirled in confusion. She wanted to tell Reynald everything that had happened, to finally unburden her soul of this pain it had held for so many years. Glancing back at him, her will to stay silent almost failed her. His eyes seemed full of tender understanding, his face reflecting patience. He would never press her for more than she was willing to give. She knew he had seen far worse, survived far worse, in the years he had spent on the roads to Jerusalem. It would be such a relief to have someone to confide in.

Still, could she really trust him? Could she even be sure she understood him, after such a short period of time? She barely knew anything about the man at her side. Why had he gone off and become a Templar, living so far from home? Why had he left his sister?

Another thought flashed through her mind, and she stiffened, turning her gaze once more to the fields beyond the window. What of her own sister, flirtatiously moving against him at every opportunity? Was he really so immune to her charms?

Many long minutes passed in silence which neither sought to break. Finally Sarah shook herself and rose to her feet. If she remained here for too long, she might say something she would later regret.

Reynald instantly stood at her movement.

Sarah glanced at him with a shaded look, muting her feelings under his sharp gaze. She nodded her thanks to him, then turned to go. To her surprise, Reynald took her gently by the hand, and she paused, keeping her eyes lowered to hide the sudden beating of her heart.

“I am here,” offered Reynald softly, his voice hoarse. “Please find me at any time if you wish to talk. I promise I will listen without judging.”

For some reason, Sarah’s mind skipped back a few days. “Is that not all my sister was hoping for?” she mused to herself, lost in thought. "She wanted someone to listen to her without judging, simply supporting. I was hesitant to offer that to her."

Before Reynald could respond, she moved past him, back up toward her room. She knew she had many chores, many tasks waiting to be done. She could not bring herself to face any of them. She stood at her window for a long time, but even the bright sunlight seemed too much for her. She pulled the curtains closed fully, immersing the room in darkness. She tucked herself onto the chair in the corner, bringing her feet up, losing herself in thought.

The door flung open suddenly, and Sarah blinked in the light that streamed in from the hallway. Her sister danced into the room, blonde hair bouncing with Rachel's movements.

Rachel called out in laughter, "are you in here?" Her eyes roamed the room until, adjusting to the dimness, she spotted Sarah curled up in the corner. "Oh, there you are! What is this, your cave?" Her mouth curved into a teasing grin. "I have always wanted a cave of my own."

Sarah's mind was far distant, lost in her musings. "I just want to be alone for a while."

"Sure thing, we will enjoy dinner without you!" chuckled Rachel with merriment. She turned and headed out again without another word, closing the door solidly behind her.

Sarah turned her eyes back to the heavy curtains, her mind far away.

* * *

Sarah's mother seemed in exceptionally good spirits the next morning, engaging in lively conversation with her husband and Rachel in turn. Sarah found her mood lifting as breakfast was served, and smiled when the talk came around to her.

Her mother's brow raised in friendly curiosity. "So, where are you off to today, or can you tell? I am not sure that much can hold up to the musician's evening, if Rachel is to be believed!"

Sarah chuckled, being drawn easily into the insouciant, carefree atmosphere. "The players were quite good. However, I have something more sedate planned for today. It is the two week check-up for a patient of mine."

Reynald's eyes brightened. "The one I assisted with? I would like to come along, if that would be all right."

Sarah looked over in pleased surprise. "Certainly, if you wish it. I am sure they would be delighted to talk with you."

Sarah took the ride at a slower pace this time around, moving at a gentle canter through the woods. She loved this path, with its mossy leaps and dappled turns. As before, Reynald stayed with her for every twist, and she admired his horsemanship as he took a leap over a small stream with ease. His personality, his skills fit as snugly against her needs as two spoons nestled together in the drawer.

Longing filled her soul, and she gave a deep sigh, focusing on the next log in her path. She turned her mind away from Reynald with firm resolve. He was a temporary visitor in her home, and nothing more. Once he had met with his sister in person, and tracked down the rogue Templars, he would be gone back to Jerusalem. As far as she knew, Templars made their vows for life.

It was a short period of time before they had pulled up outside the quiet cottage. Cecily and Milo were waiting for them outside, sitting on a low bench by the front door. Cecily held the infant wrapped in a blanket in her arms, gazing fondly at the small face.

Milo stood with a smile as the two reined in and dismounted. "Sarah! Reynald! It is wonderful to see you! Come, see how much young Chilton has grown!"

Sarah sat beside Cecily with a smile, accepting the offer when Cecily handed her the small infant. She looked over the child from head to toe, and Cecily blushed in pleasure when Sarah pronounced him healthy and growing well.

Sarah nuzzled the young child with a smile, looking at his tiny fingers and toes with joy. It was amazing to think that new life was sparked so easily, although the ensuing nine months were certainly less of an enjoyable task. Still, this tender fragility could be nursed, with care, to create a full sized adult. It truly seemed a miracle.

She looked up at Reynald, and was caught by the emotion on his face. He was gazing down at her, warmth brightening his cheeks. She wondered if he was thinking of his sister, who he would be seeing in a short period of time.

Reynald blinked at her gaze, and turned quickly to Milo. “How have things been going for you?” he asked, looking around at the cottage. “It seems that you are doing quite well.”

Milo smiled with pleasure. “The weather has been perfect, and our crops are growing nicely,” he agreed. “Cecily has been able to rest and relax, and spend time with our son. It has been very easy for me to keep things running along smoothly these past two weeks, and give her time to heal.”

He glanced to the north. “I count my blessings, given what happened to the Johnsons.”

Reynald’s brow creased. “Who are they?”

Milo smiled. “I forget you are not from around here. The Johnsons live about two miles northwards. Sarah here helped them with both of their children. It was because of Bethany’s recommendations that Cecily asked Sarah to help her with her own pregnancy. Sarah was an angel for both women.”

Reynald looked over again at Sarah, where she sat cradling the young child. For a moment Sarah thought she saw longing in his eyes, but in a heartbeat it was gone, replaced with firm discipline.

When Reynald spoke again, his voice was rough. “What has happened to the Johnsons?”

Milo sighed. “We had that lightning storm yesterday, you might remember. Their house is on a hill, and the trees around them took several strikes. The blasts brought down sections of fence. Now the deer have gotten into their crops, and the Johnsons are having quite the time sorting their life back to normal.”

“That is a shame,” mused Reynald, considering.

Milo nodded. “I would go over to help, but with Cecily in the state she is in, I feel I should be here, just in case. She is not quite ready to travel yet.”

Reynald patted him on the back. “You take care of your family,” he agreed. “There are plenty of others who have the ability to help. I am sure everything will be settled out for the Johnsons soon enough.”

The afternoon flew by in quiet discussion and admiration of the new life. Sarah found that she felt almost reborn as she took the path home, sailing through the woods, Reynald keeping close alongside her.

The two horses rode side by side into the stables easily, comfortable with each other’s presence, and with Lou’s help they were quickly stabled and brushed. Sarah and Reynald were just walking to the main doors when Rachel rode in, her stallion glistening with sweat.

Sarah gave a warm laugh. “Rach, where have you been?” She took in the state of horse and rider with one long glance. “Did you ride to London and back?”

“Cedric would never have allowed that,” shot back Rachel with a grin, looking around as the soldier galloped up the path, reining in heavily as he drew close. “Not that he can keep up with me when I want to run!”

Cedric shook his head as he dismounted. “You really should stay near me, Rachel,” he admonished as he led his horse over to Lou.

“Posh!” cried out Rachel with glee, leaping down from her horse. Her eyes lit on Reynald, and she grinned. “Come help me with my steed,” she entreated. “I know you love horses!”

Reynald glanced at Sarah, and she smiled in return. “I will go tend to my gardens. You two have fun,” she offered, the enjoyment of the sunny day drawing her on. She headed out through the stable doors, turning left to move toward the back gardens.

A sparkle caught her eye – a broach was discarded by the outer stable wall. She moved toward it, recognizing it as a ram design that her father had given her sister as a present several years ago. Chuckling, she picked it up, preparing to head back in to give it to Rachel.

Rachel's resonant voice came to her as she neared the stable doors. "So then, I went to talk with her, and you would not believe what she had done! She turned her room into a cave! It was pitch dark in there! A sunny day, people all around, and she is hiding out in a cave! What is she, a troll?"

The energy drained out of her; the world dimmed. She put a hand out against the door for a moment, hearing only a murmur of response from Reynald. Turning, she kept her gaze downcast at the ground as she moved her way back toward the keep. She idly rotated the broach in her hand as she went, her thoughts muddled.

Chapter 12

Sarah woke with a resolute focus. She knew where her energies should be directed. She would find something to do out of the house for the day, and to help others. It was the best way to draw herself out of her funk.

She kept that thought in mind as she headed down to breakfast. Rachel maintained a flirtation with Reynald throughout the meal, but Sarah studiously ignored the pair, her mind deliberate on her plans.

She finished her meal quickly, then headed out to her garden, already bright with the summer sun. She took her time gathering her seeds, trowels, and fertilizers. When the bags were full, she lugged them over to the stables, packing them all securely onto her horse until there was barely room for her to sit.

Finally ready, she mounted up and made her way slowly to the Johnson's home.

The trip was pleasant, the warm summer sun bringing a fresh glow to the wildflowers which lined the lanes. It seemed in no time at all that she was reining in at the small two-room cottage nestled into a clearing in the woods. A line of clothes hung drying to one side, drifting in the breeze.

She had barely dismounted when a pair of young children came running up to greet her, squealing with delight. Behind them walked their mother, her round face beaming with pleasure.

"Sarah, what a surprise!" called out Bethany, dusting the dirt off of her simple home-spun tunic before welcoming her friend with a gentle hug. She smiled down at her two youngsters. "John, Susan, go fetch some mead for our friend. She must be thirsty."

The two ran off with glee. Sarah turned and unstrapped the packs and leather bags from her steed. Once those were in a pile by the cottage wall, she removed the saddle and bridle, carrying them to stow them to one side of the cottage.

To her surprise, a similar set of items was already tucked into a corner. Looking up, she could see a steed grazing on the far side of the clearing.

"Did you get a horse?" she asked with a smile, gratefully accepting a proffered cup from Susan, the cherubic blonde who had just turned five.

Bethany shook her head, turning to point out into the field. "No, that horse belongs to the man who came to help Jack with the fence work today. We have been doubly blessed; I am sure we will get everything repaired and replanted in no time now that you are here."

Sarah followed her gaze. There was Jack, his portly build easy to spot, pulling a log clear from the fenceline. And alongside him … her face blushed. Surely, that was Reynald, down in the dirt alongside him, wrenching the log free of some impediment.

Bethany's keen gaze met that of her friend. "So you know him, then? We thought him a godsend when he arrived this morning, offering to help. He dove right in, no questions asked."

"Reynald and I were with Cecily and Milo yesterday," explained Sarah, "checking in on their new child. Milo told us of your plight. I had no idea that Reynald would come out here, though." She watched him for a moment; his movements were sure and steady. She shook herself and turned her attention back to her friend. "Reynald is a Templar, visiting the area. My parents have put him up in our keep while he is here."

Bethany gathered up a few of the bags. "What do you think of him?" she asked with a friendly smile.

Sarah took the other half of the items, and walked with her friend alongside the fence. Together they knelt in the rich dirt at the beginning of the garden area.

"It is complicated," Sarah admitted slowly. "He is only here for a short while, on a mission. Certainly he seems very honorable."

A chorus of young voices sounded near them. Susan's young voice piped up. "I want to plant!" she insisted, pulling her younger brother in tow. "What can I do?"

John's eyes were bright with desire. "I can help too!"

Bethany smiled indulgently and provided digging tools to each child in turn. With great seriousness, the pair dug out shallow holes, spacing them evenly down the row. Behind them, the two women carefully planted the seeds, surrounding each pocket with loose dirt and nutrients.

The sun moved slowly across the sky, and Sarah's energy seemed to renew with each row. The children laughed merrily as they did their part, and Sarah and Bethany made quick progress, replacing the eaten plants with fresh seeds for fall-growing crops. They talked and joked as they went, enjoying the beautiful weather.

After a few hours, Bethany stood and brushed the dirt from her tunic. "How would you like to stop for some food?" she asked Sarah with a smile. "We could have a picnic on the grass."

"I brought some supplies for just such an event," responded Sarah, standing and heading toward the side of the cottage. The children ran to call in the men, and shortly the group was converging on a blanket laid out in the shade beneath a large apple tree, to one side of the home.

Reynald strolled up to Sarah as the others worked in the house gathering serving plates and cups. "Well met, Sarah," he offered with a warm smile. "I did not think you would have come out here today, or I would have ridden in escort with you."

Sarah dropped her eyes, suddenly flustered in Reynald's presence. Every day revealed a new aspect of him, another feature of his honor which drew her in. She turned to rummage in the bag at her feet, drawing out wrapped bundles. "I brought along bread and cheese," she commented quietly, "for my midday meal. There should be enough here for us both."

Reynald's smile grew wider. "As did I," he responded, "with the help of Sally. I think between us that we shall have enough to feed the whole family."

Together they laid the provender out on the blanket. Soon the group was settled in the shade, laughing and talking. Sarah cut off pieces of cheese for the children with her dagger, amusing them by carving the shapes into simple animal designs.

The meal time flew by, and in short order the men were back at the far end of the fence, continuing to mend the broken lengths. The children went in for a nap, and Sarah and Bethany worked their way further down the rows, now planting near where the men were performing their repair work.

Another hour drifted by in peaceful talk, with both teams shouting encouragement to the other as they moved through their tasks. The children, bleary eyed, stumbled out into the bright sunshine. Sarah looked up at Bethany, but she waved the two off.

"Let them play," she mused with a chuckle. "They have done enough for one day, and we are nearly finished." She licked her lips. "I am thirsty, though." She pitched her voice to carry to the young ones. "Susan, fetch us a fresh bucket of water from the pond for mint tea, would you?"

John threw his small head back with pride. "I can do it!" In a moment he had gathered up the bucket from beneath the eaves and was trotting across the clearing. Sarah watched his progress with amused eyes.

The small pond was at the far end of the homestead, tucked in against the woods. John carefully pulled the wooden bucket through the water to fill it, then wrestled it to sit upright on the shore. Despite planting his feet and pulling with all his strength, he could barely budge it from that spot.

Sarah laughed in amusement, her eyes twinkling. "You hold tight," she offered to the equally merry mother. "I will go and help the young water carrier." She stood and strode across the distance to come up alongside the boy.

John's face was crimson with exertion. "I can do it," he insisted stubbornly. He pulled hard against the handle. The bucket slid an inch, then stopped.

"I know you can," agreed Sarah with a smile. "However, I was sick a short while ago, and still need to rebuild my strength. Please let me carry this, so that I can get better."

John looked up and studied her with a serious frown. "All right," he agreed after a moment. He took a step back, his eyes looking out at the woods.

All of a sudden, he froze still, his eyes growing round and white. Sarah followed his gaze. In a flash she stepped before him, drawing her dagger in one smooth movement.

A pair of yellow eyes stared in unblinking focus from the woods. A step, then two, and a large she-wolf emerged from the shadows, facing them, not twenty feet away. At her feet tumbled two young cubs, their faces still wet with water. The youngsters scrambled to stay close behind their mother.

A low growl emerged from the wolf's throat, and Sarah's hair stood on edge. The noise made every muscle in her body scream for her to run away, to escape those sharp teeth and rending claws. She swept a hand behind her to take a firm grasp on John's arm, drawing him in behind her body.

"Stay perfectly still," she ordered him beneath her breath, her voice firm. His body instantly went rigid against hers.

The world seemed to slow down. She could hear every chirp of a grasshopper, sense the lazy drift of a butterfly over a daisy. Behind her, there was a long, drawn out shout, but Sarah did not look away from the eyes. She knew if they ran that the wolf would be drawn to chase. She dropped into a lower crouch, settling herself in. If the wolf sprang, she would need to absorb the full impact so John could escape unharmed. If she was lucky, she might drive the dagger into the wolf's chest or throat. If she were unlucky … well, John would get away.

She turned the blade in her grasp and made a flicking motion at the wolf. "Go," she growled, her voice hoarse.

To her surprise, the wolf blinked once, twice … then turned on its heels and headed in a fast trot into the depths of the forest.

The two cubs stayed close at her side. A second passed, then two, and they were gone from sight.

The world spun back up to speed again, and Sarah took in a long, deep breath. Life exploded into motion. John was ripped from behind her, and she heard Bethany and Jack cry out in panicked relief. A shadow fell across her as Reynald landed heavily before her in a crouch, dagger out, shielding her with his body. Reynald scanned the forest with sharp eyes, every muscle tense and alert for trouble. Finally reassuring himself that the threat was gone, he stood upright, then turned to look down at Sarah, his eyes moving up and down her body with rapid evaluation.

"Did the wolf harm you? Are you all right?" he asked in staccato, his breath still coming quickly from his sprint to her side. "How many were there?"

Sarah shakily reseated her dagger back into her belt, her gaze moving past his to reassure herself that the animals had indeed left. "It was a mother with two cubs," she explained, her voice tight. "I imagine they had come down for a drink."

"God's teeth," swore Reynald under his breath, looking back out into the shadows again. "A mother defending her young; anything could have happened." His gaze returned to the woman before him. "What you did was incredibly brave," he added, his eyes going to the weapon at her side.

Sarah chuckled wryly, working to slow her breathing. "It is what any mother would do, to defend her cubs," she pointed out, her gaze lost in the depths of the forest.

Warm arms wrapped her in a bear hug as Bethany enveloped her from behind. "Oh, thank you, thank you," her friend gasped, holding her for several long moments before releasing her. "You saved my baby."

Sarah looked around. John was high up on his father's shoulders, and Jack held him there securely with both hands. "I will gather up the villagers tomorrow," he promised, his voice somber. "We will drive the pack far from here, deep into the woods, and kill them if they return. This is no place for a wolf to be raising its young." He glanced around the clearing. "The fence is done, but it was meant to keep out deer. Wolves would be another problem altogether."

The group moved as one back toward the safety of the cottage. In the bright sunlight, with the fence stretching securely around them, and the long line of crops planted and laid out, the danger began to fade, to seem a bad dream.

Bethany gave her daughter a pat on the behind. "You go play in the house with your brother for now," she instructed the blonde girl. After she had ensured both youngsters were safely indoors, she turned and looked over the fields, allowing herself to relax and admire the result of the day's efforts.

Sarah's eyes ran along the edges of the clearing, her heart still pounding, but she forced herself to smile with encouragement at Jack. She pitched her voice in what she hoped was a casual tone. "So your work is complete? The fence is whole?"

Jack looked over at Reynald, nodding, returning to more immediate matters. "Yes, we had just finished the last of the spans," he reported with a gleam of pride. "Everything is more sturdy than before, thanks to Reynald here. I could not have asked for better help."

Reynald smiled in acknowledgement, but his eyes went to Sarah's, bright with admiration. His voice was light when he spoke, but Sarah could see how his tone differed from his inner emotions. He had other comments for her which he was putting aside due to the presence of their hosts. She wondered what he would have said if they had been alone.

"Did you accomplish all you dreamt of?" he asked quietly, his voice hoarse.

Sarah was caught in his gaze, sensing the emotion behind his seemingly casual comment about their planting. All she dreamt of .... Her throat went dry as she remembered how he had leapt before her, risking his life to protect her …

To her relief, Bethany answered for her, covering her lapse. "We might have fewer summer turnips. However, we will have plenty of spinach, which perhaps is just as well." She glanced up at the sky. The sun was dropping lower, and evening shadows were stretching across the clearing. Bethany looked between Sarah and Reynald, her look full of friendly welcome.

"We do not have much, but please, come in and have some dinner with us. It is the least we can do."

Sarah looked down, then glanced up at Reynald with nervous concern. The family would be short on food for a while, regardless of Bethany's statements. She did not want to be rude, but Sarah did not want to add to their already burdened life.

Reynald understood immediately and shook his head.

"I am afraid I have business back at the keep," he informed the couple with a wry smile, "and given today's events, it would be best if Sarah rode back with me." He offered his hand to Jack. "I will certainly take you up on the offer another time, though," he added with a smile.

Sarah accepted warm hugs from Jack and Bethany, promising to return soon for a visit. The four gathered up the horses, saddling them and packing the bags on in preparation for the trip.

Soon she and Reynald were walking their horses quietly along the path home, the evening sun streaming across their path.

After long minutes of silence, Reynald looked over at her, his eyes somber. "Your actions by the pond were beyond courageous," he commented quietly. "If that wolf had leapt …"

Sarah kept her eyes on the road, drawing in a deep breath. "If the wolf had leapt, my dagger was out, and I would have done the best I could. I have been trained with a dagger, and perhaps I could have found my mark. If nothing else, I hopefully would have delayed her long enough to allow John to get to safety."

Reynald's voice dropped into a growl. "I should have been there."

Sarah shook her head. "You cannot be in all places, to protect all people," she pointed out. "It is why I practice with knife and sword. I may not be very skilled with either, but I can at least try. It allows me to help others who are less strong than even I am."

Her mind drifted back over the day's events. "Speaking of which, what made you come out here today? I never would have dreamt to find you there." She thought of the long hours Reynald had spent in manual labor, setting spans and digging fence post holes. "I know the family well, but you had never heard of them before."

"I knew they were in need of assistance," murmured Reynald as they moved through a dusky section of the forest. His eyes scanned the shadows alertly, his hand resting lightly on the hilt of his sword. "That seemed enough reason to help them out."

Sarah pondered Reynald's response, and wondered how many other people would consider that enough of a call to action. The couple drifted into silence again, and although Sarah had ridden this road countless times in the past, she felt reassured having Reynald alongside her, his eyes ever alert for danger.

Chapter 13

By the time Sarah had come down to eat the next morning, Rachel and Reynald were fully involved in plans to ride out to a local lake for the day. Sarah left them to their discussions, preparing herself for an afternoon in town.

She made her way out alone. It was a ride she had done for countless years, but for some reason it felt odd to be traveling without a partner. She pushed the thought from her mind.

Sarah valiantly engrossed herself in buying supplies, visiting vendors to place new orders, and catching up on the news of the world. She sought out every familiar face to greet and spend time with.

Yet, every moment seemed to remind her of Reynald. Every new bit of information seemed one she wanted to get Reynald's opinion on.

Sarah knew it was petty of her to want to keep his attentions all to herself. She had no claim on him, and he was certainly free to do as he chose with his time. Even so, every hour she was away from him she wondered what he was doing and thought about when she could see him next.

The ride home was long and lonely. When the pair was not home for dinner, Sarah retreated to her room, embroidering for hours by the window to distract herself.

She found her luck had not changed the next morning when she descended the stairs. Reynald was gone, apparently tracking down more news of his Templar quarry. Rachel tripped off merrily to visit with friends, and the house settled into a restive quiet.

Sarah normally relished these peaceful times, but today she felt restless. She fought to engage her interest with caring for her garden, practicing her swordwork, working on mixtures and poultices.

No matter what activity she attempted to focus on, she found herself wondering what Reynald would think. Would he praise how she blocked to the lower left, or would he suggest a better angle?

Rachel returned shortly before dinner, and Sarah strove to immerse herself in the daily family discussion around the table. The meal was delicious and Sally kept the glasses topped off, but Sarah felt the hole. Despite her best efforts, she found herself glancing occasionally at the empty seat.

By the time the meal was over, Sarah knew she had to do something to get her mind off of him. She grabbed Rachel's hand and brought her over to the thick rug in front of the fireplace, currently cold and dormant. The two sprawled in front of an onyx-and-white-marble chessboard, placing their pieces with care, sipping at mugs of mead while they plotted their moves.

* * *

Reynald handed his horse off to Lou with a smile, shaking the dust off his outfit before turning to head into the keep. It had been another long day, but he felt that he was making progress. Soon he would narrow down the exact location of the three Templars he was seeking. Once he had been able to meet with his sister, he would move after them in earnest, to convince them to return to Jerusalem with him. If they would not go, the local authorities could certainly gather the force necessary to insist that they join him.

He found his stomach rumbling as he moved into the main hall. It was easy enough to ignore the demands of the body when he was out engaged in a task, but now that he was home again, it was easy enough to be again reminded of that hunger.

He chuckled quietly. 'Home' indeed. He had only been here three weeks, and already he had found himself settling into the routine. After so many years in a foreign land, it was decidedly easy to be comfortable.

His eyes scanned the room. Most of the household had already finished eating, and Sally was clearing away the plates and trenchers. Christopher and Mathilde were not to be seen; perhaps they were in another room talking. But there, on the floor …

His gaze became caught as he looked down at the two sisters. They were so alike, and yet so different. Rachel was eagerly contemplating her next move, knight in hand, threatening to move it to first one location, then to another, watching to see her sister's reaction. She laughed gleefully at some comment, leaning forward to add a retort. Her blonde hair glistened in the candlelight.

Reynald's eyes moved across to the older sister. Sarah's face was more quiet than her sister's, her tawny hair a more muted version of the blonde brilliance. She lay quietly by the board, watching her sister's moves without reacting. Her hand rested gently by her queen, almost in a protective manner.

Reynald stepped back into the shadows, taking a seat in the corner of the room. Sally quietly brought him over a mug of ale and a serving of food. He sat there quietly, watching the pair, lost in thought.

* * *

Sarah could feel Reynald's eyes on her, and she blushed, willing herself not to look up. She had been listening intently for his footsteps, and her heart sang when he had walked into the room. Now that he was here, it was all she could do to keep her focus on the board before her.

Rachel seemed to have no such qualms. She looked up at Reynald with a mischievous smile, putting down her piece for a moment. "So, Sir Knight, do you play chess?" she asked with a playful air.

Reynald nodded. "Yes, certainly," he agreed with a smile. "It is a great game of tactics."

"This set was given to me when I was nine," continued Rachel, indicating the elegant board before her. "A family friend gave it to me for my birthday. Then Sarah stole it from me."

Sarah ran her eyes over her remaining pawns. "I traded it to you for a trio of French dolls," she corrected Sarah with a gentle nod. "I agree, though, it was wrong of me to push you into giving up your present." She gave a wry smile. "My only defense is that I thought you were too young for chess on your own. I thought that I could figure out the rules and then help teach you. We have certainly played many games together since then." She finally decided on a pawn to the left, carefully sliding it forward one row, leaving her finger on the piece for a long moment before releasing it.

"Yes, but you could have taught me with my own set!" argued Rachel, grabbing her castle and attacking the pawn immediately, laughing with glee as she swept the piece off the board.

"You are quite right," agreed Sarah tapping her finger against her lip in thought. "Once again, I am sorry for trading for your game when I was eleven. I have offered the set back to you several times; the offer still stands." She eyed her rook for a long moment before carefully sliding it two spaces.

"Hah, you would like that, to just pretend it never happened," shot back Rachel with amusement. She grabbed up one of her knights, sending it into the fray. "Look, Reynald, that is you, racing in to protect me!" she called out with a laugh.

Sarah's mouth quirked into a smile. She surveyed the board for a moment, then moved her queen forward, taking the knight. "I am afraid his chivalrous gesture was short lived," she chuckled. "Queen takes knight."

Rachel shrugged, sitting back and taking a long drink of her mead. "That is fine, I have another knight," she pointed out cheerfully.

Christopher walked into the room, glancing over his daughters' game for a moment and chuckling to himself as he saw the layout on the board. Then he shook his head, turning to

Reynald. "If you have a moment, I would like to speak with you," he asked in a low tone.

Reynald was on his feet in moments. "I am at your pleasure," he responded simply, and turned to follow the older man from the room.

Sarah watched them go for a long moment, then turned back to finish off the game.

Chapter 14

Sarah was riding back from Melissa's house the next afternoon when a steady thrum of hoof beats jogged her from her thoughts. In a moment, Reynald had ridden up to pull alongside her, his eyes scanning the woods in a sweep before bringing his gaze to hold hers.

"You really should have a guard with you," he advised with concern. "I realize this is a well-traveled road, but it cannot hurt to be cautious."

Sarah was too content to argue. "You are here with me now, so I am all set," she pointed out, her mood serene.

Reynald settled back into his saddle, drawing closer to her side. "I am beginning to sense a pattern in your rides," he commented as they moved along through the sunlight. "So you check in on your patients every two weeks?"

Sarah smiled back at him, nodding in agreement. "It is not so much that they need that frequency of health checkups, although with infants it can often be helpful," she explained. "I think it is more that the women like having someone to talk with about their concerns, to know they are being thought of. They often have issues they feel uncomfortable bringing up with family or friends."

"It is good of you to provide that service to them," replied Reynald. "I am sure they appreciate it greatly."

"I enjoy it, myself," responded Sarah. "It is a chance to help others out, and often the issues one person resolves can be shared with other women who face the same problem."

Reynald thought about this for a while, and the silence stretched in pleasant relaxation for Sarah. The gentle clop of hooves and cheerful bird song filled her world.

Reynald's low voice slid into the medley, quiet and unobtrusive. "You are spending your life helping women become good mothers and wives," he commented, his eyes focused far down the lane. His voice remained neutral, without pressure. "Yet you and your sister choose to remain single."

Despite the quiet tone, Sarah's independence flared, a frisson of annoyance interrupting the peace of the day. Looking away, she took in a long, deep breath. She had certainly fielded this very question from enough well-meaning people over the years. If Reynald wanted to go down this road for some reason, so be it.

In a moment she had regained her balance. "I suppose we choose our own path, at our own pace," she replied evenly. "Not every life fits into a neat schedule." She had a feeling that Reynald was looking for a more personal answer, but she was not in the mood to pursue that thread.

She flicked her eyes to meet Reynald's for a moment. It tweaked at her that he was delving into this wound of hers, and she sought to redirect the conversation. "For example, do people ask you regularly why you have not married, why you are spending your life riding around the wilds of Jerusalem?"

Reynald nodded in understanding. "I realize it is different for men and women. Still, do not think that makes it better for one or the other of us. Women are expected to bear children as soon as they are able because soon they become *un*able to do so. Age makes it more difficult to bear a healthy child. Educating and tending to a child becomes more difficult."

Reynald's gaze drifted out to the path. "Also, men cannot bear a child. That ability is reserved for a woman. It is a great responsibility – a great mystery – that she can cause a simple act to result in a perfectly formed child. To see that baby, with its little fingers and toes … it was truly a miracle. To think that a woman could not want to experience that – when men are fully shut out from ever hoping to – can be difficult."

Sarah chuckled wryly. "So that is the great burden that men bear, the burden of not being able to give birth?"

Reynald shook his head. "No, it is different. I know you may find it a bit unfair, but a woman, to be accepted, only has to dress prettily and become pregnant. She instantly has her place in the world then, and the more children she has, the more valuable she becomes."

His gaze moved down the road. "For men, it is more challenging. We must prove our worth as a life-long supporter of a family. It is not enough to be loving. We must spend years proving we are of value, to amass the skill and savings to provide for our family." His voice dropped to a quiet murmur. "By the time we do that, the woman we grew up with has already chosen another beau."

Sarah looked up with curiosity. This was something new. "Chosen another?"

Reynald glanced up, his eyes momentarily shadowed with pain. He appeared surprised that he had spoken of the incident. His response was short and curt. "While you may have waited to wed, many women do not."

He looked back down the grassy lane. His gaze became unfocused, and they rode for a long while in silence. When he finally spoke, his voice had taken on a cynical bite. "In my younger days, I was quite fond of a girl in my village. Michelle was her name. She was smart, friendly, and she loved horses as much as I did. We courted for years. Finally we pledged ourselves to one another, and gave each other silver bracelets."

He held up his left arm, and Sarah saw a thin, silver loop gleam against his forearm. She remembered it now from Cecily's labor, when his strong hands had slid over hers, taking their turn at the endless efforts.

His voice went on. "Our love was not enough. Michelle's father made it clear to me that I would need to make something of myself before we would be allowed to wed. He wanted to see proof that I was a man of responsibility. So, as much as it pained me to leave my family, I joined the Knights Templar, agreeing to a term of five years. It seemed a field that would suit my nature and prove myself to Michelle's family."

He paused for a long while, his mind lost in past recollections. "When I joined the Knights Templar, Michelle's family was indeed pleased. More importantly to me, Michelle was quite proud. She liked the idea of my protecting innocents."

Reynald's face became set as he remembered those years. "We wrote each other regularly at first, letters full of passion and fire. Then, as the months passed, her letters came less and less frequently."

Reynald's gaze clouded. "Finally I received a message from her parents. She had become engaged to another man – someone ten years her elder. He had already proven his valor, apparently, and was worthy of her right then. She decided there was no need to wait for me when a suitable man was immediately available."

Reynald shrugged, his eyes on the path ahead. "So you see, it is not easy on either end. You come of age, and the world is presented to you. You are pressured to choose someone – but if you choose to wait a few years, you are no worse off for that. On the other hand, when men come of age, they see the women they love go off into older men's arms – and they are instructed to wait, to prove themselves, to save up and prepare. Eventually, if they are lucky, they might deserve a family."

Sarah chuckled. "It is hard to feel too sorry for you," she commented wryly. "Women get stuck with older men who are tired out. Men are required to satisfy themselves with young, active, healthy girls on the cusp of maturity."

Reynald's eyes caught at hers, and she saw the serious look in them.

"Not all men are solely interested in a firm body and an immature soul," he commented quietly. "For my part, I am in this for the long haul. I would much rather have a partner in life with whom I could talk at length, who shares my values. I would much rather have a mature mate to understand my troubles, rather than a giggling girl who has just escaped from her parents' clutches. Bodies fade over time, regardless of how they begin. A great soul remains steady."

Sarah looked away. "Is she so hard to find, then, this woman you seek?"

Reynald was silent for a long time before answering. The miles drifted by in a haze of summertime sun. When he did speak, Sarah got the sense that he had chosen his words with great care.

"It seems that most women are married young, unformed. By the time they reach a healthy stage of maturity, they are a long time spouse of someone who does not appreciate them. It is too late."

The thought whirled in Sarah's mind; she had not thought to view the situation in this light. She looked ahead down the path, to where it wended its way, eventually, to her quiet home. The image of her father and mother came to mind, of the adoration in their eyes when they held hands, of the way they treasured each other, even after all these years.

Her shoulders eased. "Yet sometimes fate does bring together two who can appreciate each other with all their being."

His voice was hoarse. "Yes, it does."

She flushed; was he thinking of Michelle, the woman he had loved, and had tragically lost? She glanced again at the silver bracelet he wore around his wrist. It must have been ten years ago that he had pledged his heart to the woman, and he still wore her token. She knew that Templars swore to chastity. Had he remained true to her all of these years? Perhaps his service in the Holy Land had become a form of refuge for him, hiding from a past wound which had not healed. Sarah felt the pain of that revelation all too clearly.

Her eyes moved up from the bracelet to his eyes – and stopped. He was gazing at her with a steadiness which seemed to ease into her very soul. Her instinct was to turn, to look away, to maintain the distance between them. At the same time, she basked in the strength he gave her. They rode like that, their horses' hooves making a soft clop on the dirt road, and at last a soft smile came to her lips.

He gave a knowing nod, and she was lost.

Chapter 15

Rachel was nearly aglow with delight when Sarah came down to eat the next morning. The blonde smiled warmly as Sarah sat down next to her father.

Rachel took another bite of her butter-soaked turnip, then leaned forward. "So, where are you and Reynald off to for the day? Maybe getting some new pots for the fall herb storage perhaps?"

Sarah glanced across at Reynald in surprise, but judging by his baffled expression, he knew as little of this as she did. "I do need some new pots," she admitted slowly. "I had not thought to bother -"

Reynald spoke up with a smile. "I would be glad to be of service. Tomorrow is Sunday after all, and the person I now need to follow up with is not available until Monday. I have the day open."

Sarah smiled suddenly, illumination hitting her. "Oh! Today is the day of that summer music festival, featuring Michael the musician," she chuckled.

Rachel's mood lost a little of its zing. "I would have thought you would be tired of going out, after last week," she offered hopefully.

Sarah patted her hand. "Not to worry, dear sister of mine. I have more than enough to keep me busy for today. You go enjoy the music all you wish."

Her father leant forward. "Speaking of interesting men," added Christopher with a grin, "We had a message arrive for you today, Rachel. It is from Seth." He called over to one of the servants, who handed a slim, cream-colored scroll to Rachel.

Rachel took the message with a sigh and unrolled it, scanning the words quickly. She tossed it back onto the table, going back to her meal. “He wants to see me again. I guess he cannot take a hint.”

Her mother smiled at her father, then leant forward with a teasing glance. “Oh, but Rachel, one hears that he is *very* rich …”

Rachel rolled her eyes. “He must be, what, fifteen years older than me! I would wear him out in a week!”

Mathilde patted her husband’s arm tenderly. “Not all mature men are so easily worn down,” she chuckled. “However, Seth lives in London, right? That *is* rather far away – and then there are the various exigencies of city life …”

Rachel lit up. “I would love to live in London! The excitement, the taverns … but to live with Seth?” She turned to grin at her sister. “Remember the last time he came to visit us a month ago? His hands were so weak, it was like being touched by a cold fish. Could you imagine being caressed by those hands?” She shivered.

Sarah winked at her mother. “I am sure you could get used to anything, given the right motivation …”

Rachel shook her head. “Not me!” She took a last bite of her roll, then stood. “Well, I am off; be sure not to wait up for me tonight!” She gave Sarah a quick hug, then practically skipped out the front door.

Christopher shook his head to his wife, chuckling. “I wonder if this musician knows what he is in for,” he commented wryly. “I suppose we shall hear all about it tomorrow. Then again, depending on how well it goes, perhaps we will not hear a word …” He motioned to Cedric, and the man slipped out the door, following after Rachel.

Sarah watched her sister go, then sat back to take a long drink. “Why does she keep encouraging Seth to come and visit, if she is so sure she does not like him? Is that not unfair to Seth?”

Mathilde chuckled, looking fondly at her older daughter. “You never quite understood this about women in general, and your sister in particular,” she commented wryly. “It is not all about what the woman does! Rachel is not the only person involved in her flirtations. The men are not helpless thralls in her presence. If they choose to flirt with her, and to dally with her, it is because they enjoy it. Men do, in fact, have free will."

Sarah stared into her cup, morose. "It certainly does not seem that way sometimes," she murmured half to herself.

She saw Reynald and her father exchange an amused glance. Piqued, she finished off her drink, then stood. She nodded to her mother and headed out the main door.

Sarah found it almost second nature to walk with Reynald out to the stables and saddle up their mounts. Even their horses seemed comfortable strolling side by side as they headed out toward the village of Market Lavington.

Reynald looked over with gentle calm. "So, where are we going again?" He drew his eyes again to the quiet road. "Not that it really matters, on a day as lovely as this one."

"We are going to see my good friend Lily," responded Sarah with a chuckle. "She makes the most beautiful pottery, and she specifically makes items to suit my needs for storing herbs and ointments."

"Did you meet her during one of your midwife tasks? Was she a young maid in need of a friend?" Reynald relaxed back into his saddle for the ride.

Sarah burst out into peals of laughter, the thought amusing her greatly. A great joy bubbled up out of her, and she felt lighter than she had in many weeks. She knew Reynald was watching her, an odd, distant look in his eyes, but it took her a while to settle back down.

After a few minutes, she was able to talk through her chuckles. "I am sorry, you will understand when you meet Lily," she explained with a smile. "I believe she is in her late sixties, and she lives alone. She was married once, long ago, but her husband died in an accident just a few years after they were wed."

"She never remarried?" asked Reynald with curiosity, his gaze focused on the road ahead.

Sarah shook her head. "She says she never found anybody else to tempt her," she replied easily. "She and her husband had both loved pottery, and their home was filled with their implements and wares. When he passed away, she became a sole proprietor and perfected her art. The things she creates are awe inspiring."

Sarah chuckled softly. "Lily says if she tried to bring a new man into her world now, there would literally be no room for him! Unless he showed up with naught but the clothes on his back, and a soul-deep desire to work with clay every day, it simply would not work out."

"Is she lonely, then?" wondered Reynald, "to be all alone for so many years?"

Sarah shrugged. "She says she is not. She gets lost for hours in a project, and she has enough adoring fans to fill her evenings with conversation if she wishes. Other than that, you shall have to ask her yourself."

They rode on for a while in silence, and soon pulled up to a small but cozy cottage. The windows were lined with beautiful clay vases in a variety of styles, each holding a different type of bouquet. A large kiln behind the home sent a steady stream of smoke into the air.

A white-haired woman with a strong frame came instantly to the door, gazing out at the pair. "Sarah, my dear, how lovely it is to see you!" she called out, moving forward to take a hold of her horse's bridle. "Come for your pots, I imagine. Who is this with you?"

Sarah dismounted and gestured to Reynald. "Lily, this is my good friend, Reynald. He is a Knight Templar, and is staying with us while he works on something for his order."

"My, how dashing," offered Lily with a smile, presenting her hand to be kissed. Reynald took it with a sweeping bow, gallantly pressing his lips to it.

Lily's eyes twinkled at the flirtation, and gave a courtly curtsy. "Well met, sir knight. Please do enter my abode." She gestured with a large movement, ushering the pair into her home.

Sarah glanced around at the crowded room. She felt as if she was in a museum each time she visited. Every corner and nook was being used to showcase some sort of an elegant bowl, delicately crafted urn, flower-filled vase, or decorative dish.

Reynald gazed appreciatively at the items around him. "These are truly works of art," he murmured. The objects were created with a variety of glazes, raised pieces, and patterns, so that no two were alike. Some were indigo and swirled like the ocean at night. Others were translucently thin, with white patterns interlaced with the natural creases of the clay.

Lily blushed at the praise. "Sit, have some cheese and wine," she offered, settling herself on a wide couch. She took a trio of elegant, sage-green cups down from a shelf behind her and laid them out, grabbing a bottle from beneath the couch to pour.

Sarah sat beside her, cutting the hunk of cheese into smaller slices with deft movements of her knife. She nodded her thanks as Reynald passed her a trio of small plates on which to lay the pieces.

Lily distributed the cups. "Here we go, one for each of you," she instructed with a smile. "And now, a toast – to long life with health and happiness. For one is not of much value without the other two." The trio clinked their mugs, and drank down the wine.

Sarah smiled in appreciation. "Delicious as always," she congratulated. "Let me guess – blackberry wine?"

Lily shook her head. "No, this was blueberry. It keeps me young!"

Reynald took another sip of his wine before putting it down. "It is quite rich, and very flavorful," he commented. "I might buy a bottle or two from you, if you could spare them."

Lily smiled with pleasure. "Of course, I am always glad to share my bounty," she offered cheerily. "And now, sir knight, if you could reach behind you, you will find the box with my young friend's current items."

Reynald dutifully looked for and located a medium sized wooden box, which he carefully lifted with both hands and placed on the table before them. Sarah removed the lid with the expectant glow of a child on Christmas morning.

"Oh, Lily, they are gorgeous," gushed Sarah, reaching in to withdraw the small containers. They had been created with a forest green glaze, and the top handle of each pot's lid was in a different shape. Of the first two she removed, one was an acorn, another a caterpillar with a hunched back. The items were made with exquisite detail.

Reynald examined one lid which portrayed a small, speckled mushroom on its top. "You truly have an artist's touch."

Lily smiled. "It can take me hours to get a single pot done properly," she explained, "but the result is worth it, to see that look on Sarah's face. Of course, she pays me, too," she added, her face lighting up with mirth.

Sarah turned one of the pots around in her hands. "I still think you should raise your prices again," she insisted. "I have seen no finer work anywhere."

Lily looked around her. "What would I do with more money? My house holds what I make. I make as many items as I wish right now; I would not want to make them any more quickly. They sell out almost immediately. I enjoy what I eat, I enjoy what I drink."

Reynald took another sip of his wine. "You could always hire a helper, someone to keep you company," he suggested quietly.

Lily glanced between the two, then laughed again merrily. "A helper would only drop my things and break them. Besides, I am rarely alone. You two are here now; others will be by in a few hours. I have friends coming and going all day long. My nights are blissfully quiet. If I had someone else here, undoubtedly they would snore!"

Sarah looked up at her friend. "So you never thought about marrying again?"

Lily shook her head. "Maybe for a moment or two, but never seriously. To tell the truth, the only thing I missed sometimes was being held. Just the contact of skin on skin, that someone cared for me. But soon I realized that many of my friends in the area had children, and then grandchildren. The tykes would be thrilled to sit in my lap for hours while I told them stories and listened to their tales. I think we both benefitted from the attention."

Sarah raised a toast to her. "I am sure you did." She drank down the rest of her wine, and Reynald topped her glass off with a smile.

Lily chuckled, waggling a finger at her friend. "Do not let that priest in Devizes see you overindulging in my wine, young Sarah. He was over picking up a new dish for his church last week, and when he spotted my horde of bottles, do you know what he said to me?"

Sarah leant forward in anticipation. The priest was known to be quite conservative when it came to heavy drinking. "No, do tell," she encouraged.

Lily drew herself up and added a high nasal whine to her voice. "He said, '*Vitio format perit, vino corrumpitur aetas.*'

Sarah could not help herself. Lily's impersonation was dead on, and the phrase – 'By wine beauty perishes, by wine youth is corrupted,' was normally recited to tender girls, not to aging adult women! She burst out in peals of laughter, the glee of the moment filling her. She could just imagine the priest reciting this in stern admonition, and Lily's amused response.

Lily joined her in an enthusiastic, long chortle, and Reynald sat back, watching the two women with a smile on his face. Lily had tears streaming out of her eyes in a moment, and wiped them off with the back of her hand. Her breath came in gasps.

"Can you even imagine?" she managed to say to Reynald, "Him saying that to me? Youth is corrupted? Beauty perishes?" She was off again, her face crimson with merriment.

After a moment she drew in a deep breath, looking over at Sarah. "If he was going to worry about beauty, Sarah there is the one he should talk to, do you not agree?"

Sarah was still chuckling about the outrageousness of it all, and flashed a brilliant smile to Reynald, playing along with the story. To her surprise, Reynald did not respond to the gibe in a playful manner, as she expected him to. He seemed caught off guard as he gazed at her. He held her eyes for a long moment before turning to look again at Lily, his tone quiet.

"Yes, I do," he offered gently, raising a toast to the elderly woman. She clinked her glass against his with an understanding smile, taking a long drink.

Lily turned the conversation deftly to discussions of local politics and intrigues, drawing them both in with her playful banter. Over an hour passed in friendly conversation, and soon hoof beats sounded from outside, indicating another group was coming in.

Lily gave a warm laugh. "See, never a dull moment around here," she teased as Sarah and Reynald stood to go. "I barely have time to work on my pottery any more! Still, that is fine. Soon there will be enough snowy days to indulge my muse. Nature is like that, keeping your world in balance."

Reynald helped Sarah tie her new wares down on the back of her steed, then the pair nodded in greeting to the new visitors before heading out on their way.

Reynald patted the leather pouch holding the pair of bottles he had acquired from Lily. "She really is quite a lovely woman," he noted with a smile. "I will have to savor these wines during a special occasion."

"Do not keep them for too long," warned Sarah with a grin. "I find sometimes it is better to declare an occasion special, and to enjoy it, rather than wait years and years for a suitable one to present itself bowed and tied."

Reynald nodded in understanding. "Well then, let us open the first one together after I visit with my sister next Thursday. That will be a day to celebrate, after all."

Sarah looked away. Was it coming up that quickly? It seemed like only yesterday Reynald had arrived in her life, and his stay was already coming to an end. She found that her throat had grown tight, and she took a deep breath before responding.

"After that, you will be leaving?" she asked, her voice level.

Reynald was quiet for a long while, then replied in an equally even tone. "Yes, I imagine so. It will be time for me to chase down the trio of Templars in earnest, and to escort them back to Jerusalem if I can."

Sarah's heart dropped, but she said nothing. She had known the truth of it from the start, and she needed to accept it.

* * *

Sarah was not surprised when dinner came and went without Rachel arriving. With the music festival going on, her younger sister would likely meander in at dawn, if then.

Sarah found a window at the front of the keep and settled herself into it with a pillowcase, embroidering a rose pattern onto it as her mother's birthday present. She figured it would keep her occupied until she was ready to turn in, and keep her safe from Reynald's company. She knew she was becoming far too fond of the Templar, and that her heart would be sorely pressed when it came time for him to leave.

The light was just starting to fade when she heard hoof beats coming into the main courtyard. To her surprise, it was her sister who rode in. Her state of mind showed clearly in the rough way she handled her mount.

Sarah leapt to her feet, allowing her embroidery to spill to the floor unheeded as she hurried out towards the main door. She met up with her sister in the entry way. Rachel's face was a mixture of frustration and cynical acceptance.

Rachel looked up at her sibling as she came into the room, drawing to a sudden halt. "Things were going very well until his wife showed up," she blurted out, a wry smile on her face. "Once she was there, it became a bit uncomfortable for me. I decided after a while that I was just as well off heading home again."

Sarah shook her head in shock. "You mean Michael? He was married? He did not tell you?"

Rachel shrugged, moving past Sarah to head inside. "He might have mentioned it to me," she responded casually. "I did not think the wife would actually come this evening though. Silly me."

Sarah stood still, her mind spinning. Her sister moved on into the hall, calling out for some mead. Sarah bit her lip, unsure of what she could say. Should she commiserate with Rachel for her bad luck in having the wife show up? Comment that perhaps it was to be expected? No matter what she said, the conversation was bound to go awry.

She turned to head upstairs, and flushed crimson when she saw Reynald standing off to one side. He was staring after Rachel, a thoughtful look on his face. He was holding Sarah's embroidery in one hand, and she realized that he had meant to bring it out to her.

Sarah spun and took the steps two at a time to reach her room before he saw her. The vision of Reynald staring after Rachel was burnt into her brain. Maybe Reynald saw this as his chance to get Rachel on the rebound.

Sarah ran her father's words through her mind like a mantra as she reached her room and closed the door behind her in one quick move. If Reynald was the man for her, then he would love her on his own. If he chose another path, he was not the man meant to be by her side.

She undressed quickly and climbed into bed, but found herself lying awake, unable to fall asleep.

* * *

Reynald watched as Rachel sat at one of the tables, drinking her mead and joking with the man who brought her some leftover dinner. He wondered again how the family that could have produced one sister had also molded the second. What different influences had caused them to be so varying in their outlooks on life?

He glanced back down the hall, but to his surprise Sarah had vanished. He pursed his lips, looking down at the embroidery in his hand. He had thought he might have an opportunity to talk with her alone, but apparently it was not meant to be. He laid the pillowcase down on a side table, then moved up the stairs to his own room.

The keep was settling down for the night, and he stood for a moment, looking down the long hall. The main bedrooms lined the front end of the keep, looking out over the courtyard. His room was at the far left end of the hall, a small storage room separating his from Sarah's. Then came Rachel's room, another small storage room, and that of her parents.

Reynald found his footsteps slowing as he approached Sarah's door, and gave half a thought to knocking on her door, if only to tell her where he had put her embroidery. He scolded himself and moved past. It would be highly inappropriate for him to wake her; he could certainly let her know tomorrow.

Reaching his room, he entered and let out a deep breath. Only a few days remained before he saw his sister, and after that? There would be no more excuse to intrude on the hospitality of his hosts, and every reason to move on in pursuit of his missing comrades. Time was slipping away from him.

He unbuckled his sword belt with practiced ease, laying it against the bed from long years of habit. He placed his dagger alongside it. He sat at the end of the bed, pulling off one leather boot with a tug, then the second. Then it was time for the leather tunic, which he slowly pulled over his head.

A quiet knock sounded on his door, and Reynald's heart quickened. Maybe it was Sarah, coming to ask after her sewing. He had thought she had seen him standing there. He glanced down his clothing quickly. He still wore his pants and socks, and his white linen shirt, while not neatly pressed, was still clean and proper. He moved quickly to the door, pulling it open with a smile.

It was not Sarah who returned the smile with an even wider grin. Instead, Rachel stood before him, her eyes shining, a glass of mead still in her hand. She took a quick step toward him, tripping as she came, and he automatically put out a hand to steady her. She wrapped herself around it, pressing herself up against him.

Her voice was a soft purr. "Finally, I have you alone, all to myself." She put the glass down on a nearby table. Her hands moved along his wrists, drawing them down toward her.

Reynald strained his ears for any sound of motion in the hallway. If he was seen in this position … he gently tried to extricate himself from her embrace.

Rachel frowned at the motion, then wriggled herself even more closely against him, her actions insistent.

Reynald's patience with Rachel's behavior snapped. Done with niceties, he pushed her away, and she fell hard against the door jam. He felt something snap on his wrist, but his concern was quickly directed to Rachel, who looked as if her surprised shock might move to full outcry.

He quickly stepped forward, speaking in a low voice.

"Are you all right?" he asked in a hush. "I did not mean to hurt you."

Rachel looked down in her hand. Reynald followed her gaze, and saw that she held his silver bracelet there. Her eyes gleamed through their muddled haze, then looked up into his, hopeful. "Maybe I can keep this?" she asked with delight.

Reynald sighed in relief. Perhaps this situation would end peacefully after all. "Yes, of course," he responded more gently. She was probably just drunk and would be more reasonable when she had slept it off.

He pitched his voice to be reassuring. "You look exhausted. Go get some rest; we can talk all you wish in the morning."

He exhaled in relief as she turned out into the hall and staggered in the direction of her bedroom. He closed his door and bolted it shut.

He sat down wearily on the bed, dropping his head into his hands. Thank all that was Holy that she had not woken anybody up with her shenanigans.

* * *

Sarah heard a bumping noise outside her room and was half tempted to get up to see what her sister was up to now. She had no doubt that Rachel was out there. Instead, she rolled over, pulling the blankets closer around her. If only she could fall asleep …

There was a faint knocking on her door, and she sat bolt upright. It was Reynald. She knew it must be him. He had come to return her embroidery, perhaps. If it had been an emergency with one of her patients, Polly would not be so gentle.

She hurriedly climbed out of bed, wrapping her robe around her. She gave herself a final look-over before pulling open the door.

It was not Reynald. Rachel stood there, a wide grin on her face. She pushed past Sarah into the room, waving one hand in the air.

"I just came from Reynald's room," she boasted. "The man has such strong hands. It makes me shiver just to think of them. Look what he has given me!" She held her arm out for Sarah to see.

Sarah knew in a glance what it was. She had seen that bracelet on his wrist when he was helping her with Cecily's birth. It had been there when he rode with her, talked with her. And now it adorned her sister.

"It is … very nice," she was able to croak out, her throat closing up.

"Yes, it is beautiful, is it not?" agreed her sister, raising it up to admire it. "I had best get to bed now; he wants to spend more time with me tomorrow." She winked at her sister, then sashayed out of the room and toward her own.

Sarah closed the door slowly, leaning against the back side of it once it latched. It was one thing for her sister to chase after men in their own home – but to come by and boast about it afterwards?

She knew she was being uncharitable. Her sister had been happy, and had wanted to share her happiness. That did not make the news any easier to bear …

Sarah flung herself onto her bed, the tears streaming from her eyes. It was no use denying her feelings any further. She cried as her heart broke in two.

Chapter 16

Sarah went through the motions of dressing for church the following morning. She spent a long while sitting on her bed, holding the cross in her hands, running her fingers along its smooth, wooden edges. She had so much already in life to be grateful for. It seemed petty to complain that her emotions had been sorely abused. Others had borne so much more without complaint.

Still, she waited until the hour of mass was nearly upon her before heading downstairs. She nodded in greeting to her family, avoiding Reynald and Rachel as she moved forward to the chapel.

As the sermon sounded around her, she struggled to focus her attentions on the ceremony. She kept her gaze fixedly away from the sight of Reynald's dark curls, his strong shoulders alongside Rachel's long, blonde waves. Soon he would be gone … soon he would be gone. This would all be a distant memory.

She gave a heartfelt "amen" when the sermon was over, and waited patiently as her parents moved their way out of the chapel. Rachel trailed after them, chatting animatedly with her father, answering some question about the afternoon. To her chagrin, Reynald waited at the end of her pew. She set her face firmly and slid down the pew without looking up. When she reached the end, she stood and turned to walk past him.

He reached out and gently took a hold of her arm. "Sarah, please wait a moment," he asked softly, his voice almost hesitant.

Sarah whirled in anger, yanking her arm away from him as if his grasp was red hot. "Do not touch me," she hissed at him, her anger leaping to the fore. His face flashed between guilt and shame, and her fury grew.

Her voice was cutting when she spoke again, fighting to keep her tone low. “Should you not be with my sister, rather than me?”

Reynald’s face went pale, and he murmured quietly, “she told you, of course.”

Sarah flared. “Of course she did,” she snapped. “Were you hoping for her silence to protect you, or perhaps her lies?”

Reynald went even more pale, shaking his head. “I take full responsibility for my actions,” he insisted. “I only wanted to explain -”

Sarah took a step toward him, her eyes blazing. “I am sick and tired of having revelations pushed on me,” she growled. “Whatever is between you and my sister should stay that way. I wish to hear no more of it.”

She turned on her heel and stalked out, moving past her surprised family and heading into the keep. She stopped in the main hall for a moment, taking in a series of deep breaths. She had to get control of herself.

She heard footsteps coming up behind her, and whirled in anger. If Reynald thought to press the issue …

It was her mother, whose mouth opened in surprise at the look on Sarah’s face. “My dear, what is it? What is wrong?” she asked with consternation.

“It is nothing,” insisted Sarah, her voice hoarse. “Nothing at all.” She turned and strode up the stairs to her room.

She stalked around her bedroom, part of her tinged with guilt for snapping at her mother. Surely her mother did not believe her evasions for an instant, but Sarah did not have any desire to explain the situation. Long minutes passed as she breathed in deeply, fighting to slow the wild beating of her heart.

She finally calmed down enough to sit by the window, looking out into the courtyard, her emotions slowly coming under control. An hour passed, then two.

Hoofbeats sounded from far off, and she looked out, drawn from her thoughts. Her interest turned to concern when she saw it was Milo riding in on a strange brown steed. She immediately ran from the window, tripping down the stairs, heading toward the main door at a half run. Out of the corner of her eye she saw the family gathered in the sitting room, looking up at her hurried flight.

"Milo, what is it?" she called out in alarm as she ran across the cobblestones towards her friend. "Is Cecily all right? Is it Chilton?"

Milo's face was a wreath of smiles as he dismounted. "I did not mean to frighten you!" he called out warmly. "A friend of mine lent this horse so I could come out and bring you a present of proper thanks."

Sarah's heart slowly calmed, and she put her hand to her chest. "Thank God," she vowed fervently. "You did not need to do that," she added with relief. "Why not just wait until I next visited?"

Milo shook his head. "You have done so much for us, I could not wait," he insisted. "After all, Sunday is for visiting those you care for."

Reynald and Rachel came up behind Sarah, and she turned automatically, feeling the weight of social convention bear down on her. It would not do for her to act churlish in front of a guest.

"Rachel, this is Milo," she introduced with a sweep of her hand. "Milo, this is my sister, Rachel."

Rachel gave Milo a dismissive once over with her eyes. "Why bother to learn your boyfriend's name?" She turned to shrug to Reynald. "She goes through them so quickly, she will be on to the next in no time."

Sarah's mouth opened in shock, and she closed it again with a resolute snap. She would not allow her sister to drawn Milo into trouble. She immediately strode forward and took Milo's arm, steering him into the stables. Once safely inside, she took in a deep breath, then let it out again.

"Never you mind her," she instructed Milo with a wry grin. "It is simply my sister's way."

Milo shook his head, then chuckled. "If you say so," he agreed with a smile. He opened the leather belt pouch hanging at his hip, and withdrew a small ivory figurine. With a bashful smile he handed it to Sarah. "Here, I carved it for you from bone," he offered.

Sarah took the carving and ran her fingers over its smooth form. It was an image of a mother wolf, standing protectively over her young pup. The little ears, the twist of the tail, every detail was just perfect. Even the steady focus of the wolf's eyes, the strength in her form, was tangible.

Sarah's eyes misted. "Why, Milo, this is beautiful," she whispered, turning the image over in her hands.

Milo beamed. "I am so glad you like it," he enthused. "I put a lot of work into that. I thought it was perfect for you. The way you cared so determinedly for my wife and child, how you watched over them, was awe inspiring."

Sarah wrapped her fingers around the small figure, pressing it to her heart. "I will treasure it forever," she vowed, stepping forward to give her friend a tender hug.

Milo's face burnished crimson. "I have one for Reynald too," he added. "I know he was not nearly as much help as you were over the months, but he did do his part in the final hours, and we want him to know we appreciate it."

Sarah flushed. Her mind skipped back to those hours of work, of Reynald's sure hands beside hers, of his steady, calm demeanor. A sharp pang twisted in her heart, and she resolutely pushed it aside.

A deep voice came from the doorway. "Thank you; it was my honor to assist." Sarah turned, her heart pounding. Reynald was framed in the wide doors, the sun shining past his shoulders. He stepped forward as Milo retrieved another figure and passed it into his hands.

Reynald turned the male wolf figurine in his fingers. "Your carving skills are exceptional," he praised with a smile. "The detail on this is quite impressive, Milo."

"I figured it was well suited to you," explained Milo, blushing even further. "Loyal, protective, and intelligent. It seems to fit you perfectly."

Sarah looked away, her heart racing. The stables seemed to close in on her. She had to get out of there … "Would you care to come in for a drink, Milo?" she asked hopefully. "Maybe something to eat?"

Milo shook his head, moving back out toward the horse. "I only borrowed the steed for a short while, and I need to get back to Cecily." He mounted up, then gave a friendly wave. "Thank you both so much!" he called out. He turned the steed, and in a moment he was riding back out through the main gates.

In the same moment, Rachel came running into the courtyard from the main keep, leather bag at her hip. "He is gone? Oh good. Now we can go for that ride, Reynald. Come on, time is wasting!" She grabbed him by the hand, dragging him eagerly back into the stables.

Sarah took in a deep breath, then turned and walked slowly up the stairs into the keep, returning to her room. She placed her wolf figurine at the center of her dresser, then sat at the end of the bed, staring at it, lost in thought.

When Sally hesitantly poked her head into the room to ask if she would like a meal brought up to her, Sarah gratefully agreed. She spent the rest of the day holed up in her bedroom, the weight of her emotions nearly smothering her.

* * *

Sarah awoke Monday morning with a new firmness in her heart. She only needed to last until Thursday, until his meeting with Abigail, and then he would be gone. Surely she could last three more days in her own home. She would consider it a test of her patience and strive to be civil.

Still, she was overcome with relief when she came down for food and found that Reynald had left already for his meeting. Rachel was off on some adventure. Her parents were atypically quiet and she felt rather than saw the worried glances they sent in her direction.

She ate quickly, retreating to her gardens as soon as she was able. She spent the day tending to her plants, focusing on the daily routine she had followed for so many years. Once Reynald was gone, everything would return to normal.

Tears welled as she thought the words, and she pushed them harshly away with her fingertips. He was not worth the sorrow. She would get over him, and move on.

* * *

Tuesday morning dawned with Sarah more secure in her strength. She would be out talking with Melissa during the day, enjoying the sunshine. She only needed to get through morning and dinner with Reynald.

She dressed in a rich, burgundy colored tunic, laying the cross over the top as usual. She willed herself to feel no emotion, but even so her foot paused for a moment as she stepped into the hall. Rachel was not there, but Reynald turned to look at her as she entered the room. She steeled herself and pressed on, keeping her gaze on her parents who sat across from him.

The table was silent while Sally moved amongst them, setting down bowls of steaming oatmeal. Sarah dug into hers eagerly, losing herself in the rich, fragrant steam which wafted from her bowl.

Her mother leant across her father, her voice casual and light. "So, my dear, what do you have planned for today?"

Sarah heard the underlying concern in her mother's voice, and made an effort to respond pleasantly. "I am heading west for a visit," Sarah replied in between spoonfuls. "I imagine I will be gone for the full day."

Reynald looked up, his eyes shadowed and distant. "Please allow me to escort you," he insisted in a low voice.

Sarah's voice shot out of her in tight directness. "No."

Her parents both glanced up to stare at her in surprise, then turned their gaze questioningly toward Reynald.

A sharp bite of remorse hit Sarah. There was no call for her to bring censure from her parents. Reynald had done nothing wrong. He and Rachel were consenting adults, and whatever they chose to do together … her throat closed up and she took a long drink of mead. She coughed once or twice, as if to clear her throat, and then strove to speak in a more normal tone.

"What I mean is, I am not going far. I will be back before nightfall. There is no need to take you from your duties to chaperone me."

Reynald held her gaze with his own. "My research is done; I know where the men are holed up." He glanced at Christopher before continuing. "They are not far, and it is becoming less safe for you and your sister. Apparently someone has been asking after you both, learning your schedules. My guess is that you are considered high value hostages. You really should not go out alone."

Sarah blanched. She had always considered Reynald's task as a distant one, something he would move on to once he had talked with Abigail. She had not seriously thought that it might pose an immediate threat to her region, or to her personally.

She looked down to her meal, re-steeling her resolve. "I will go with Cedric, then," she insisted quietly.

Her father's brow creased in confusion. "But why -"

Her mother put her hand gently but firmly on her father's arm. Her father turned to glance at her mother, then nodded quietly.

"As you wish," he conceded. "I will have him ready shortly."

Sarah focused on finishing her food, ignoring the man across from her. When she was done, she nodded to her parents, then headed straight for the stables.

Cedric met her there in a few minutes. He smiled with gentle familiarity at Sarah as he came up alongside her. He was perhaps ten years her senior, and had grown up at the keep. She had known him her entire life, and trusted him intimately.

Still, riding along the road with Cedric was nothing like her travels with Reynald. Cedric was courteous when spoken to, but quiet, without thought or insight otherwise. His stolid attention remained focused on the path ahead, on the shadows in the woods. Nothing else held any importance.

Cedric waited outside while Sarah spent several hours with Melissa, relaxing with her, answering her questions and sharing advice. Melissa appreciated the extra time, but Sarah knew that she was delaying her return home as long as she could.

Eventually the sunlight tinged with dusky shadows, and Sarah realized it was long past the hour to head back. It was one thing to stay away from home to give herself time alone. It was quite another to risk Cedric's life for her own personal pleasure.

Cedric waited patiently as she mounted and gave her farewells to Melanie. Then the two were riding back toward the keep. Sarah found she did not mind Cedric's vigilance this time. Reynald's caution had transmitted to her how serious he had been, and she kept her own hand on the hilt of her sword as they rode. She watched every tree, every shadow for movement.

She sighed in relief when they reached the main gate, riding over to the stables. Cedric dismounted first and held her reins while she climbed down. He walked the two horses over to Lou to be unsaddled.

She stood against the stable wall, lost in thought. She felt the contrast again with how Reynald had been. Where Cedric was brisk and efficient, Reynald had been considerate … caring …

She looked up in surprise as Reynald rode quietly into the stables. His movements with the reins seemed weary, and he looked up in surprise when he saw her step away from the stable wall.

He drew to an uncertain halt. "I … I thought you had gone in already," he stated slowly. He paused for a moment, then dismounted and turned to loosen the saddle straps.

Sarah took a step toward him. "You followed me …?" Fury flared up within her. He had no right!

Reynald shook his head quickly. "No," he stated. "Well, yes," he amended after a moment. "But only to the village. I stopped where we had met on our previous trip. I figured that since I already knew that part of the trip, it would not cause you any harm to have me ride that length." He took a deep breath, removing the saddle and placing it down on a nearby support. "I had to hope that Cedric would do a good enough job while you were out of my sight."

Sarah watched the tightness of Reynald's shoulders as he moved through his task. Slowly the heat of anger eased from her. When she gave it objective thought, he had respected her wishes, and done his best to abide by her request for privacy.

"Was it really necessary?" she asked in a quieter tone. "Surely the danger is not that imminent?"

Reynald tugged at his horse's bridle and tack, moving to hang it on a hook behind him. When he turned back to face Sarah, his face was haggard.

"A young woman was raped and murdered two nights ago, about five miles from here."

Sarah's world went still. "Who was she?"

"Her name was Carrie Brown; she was only sixteen. Her family farmed land around Pewsey." He looked down for a moment. "The funeral is being held tomorrow."

Sarah was touched by the pain in his eyes. She took a step forward to stand before him. "It is not your fault," she promised softly. "These men are responsible for their own actions. With your help, they will soon be brought to justice."

Reynald looked up to meet her gaze, and his eyes held infinite sadness. Her heart went out to him. When he spoke, his voice was distant, lost. "I let myself get distracted by my sister," he insisted. "If I had spent those extra days searching for the trio of men, just one or two more days, Carrie might be alive now."

Sarah reached out to take his hand, and then stopped. She gazed at his bare wrist. That silver bracelet now adorned the arm of her sister.

She turned suddenly, forcing herself to walk into the keep. If Reynald needed support, she was certain that her sister would be there to provide it.

She brought a bowl of venison stew upstairs with her, spending the evening working on her mother's pillowcase. As night fell, she changed into a fresh chemise and climbed resolutely into bed. She knew what her plans would be in the morning.

Chapter 17

Sarah dressed somberly, laying her cross down on the front of her dark brown tunic. She strapped on her sword and dagger, then stood for a while, looking out the window. A woman had been slain, and the men responsible were still out there. She had to do her part to support the bereaved family, but she was also aware that she could not afford to make the situation worse. She could not provide them with another target.

Resolute, she opened her bedroom door and moved down toward the main hall. She steeled herself for an argument. Whatever terms her father and Reynald might insist on, she would comply. That being said, she *would* go to the funeral.

The table was full as she entered the hall. Reynald and Rachel sat opposite her parents, and a meal of fried eggs and spiced sausage was laid out. Her parents were quiet as she approached, and Reynald did not turn.

Rachel, however, was bubbling with bright energy. "Make sure you tell Helga to serve that beef stew this afternoon," she instructed Sally merrily as Sarah took her seat. "Seamus will be coming by to spend some time with me, and he says he loves that dish." She flashed a wide grin at her sister.

Sarah glanced between Reynald and her sister, sure she was missing something. "Seamus? As in Seamus, the Irish friend I met two years ago who played the bodhran?"

Rachel chuckled with delight. "I knew you would remember him! Yes, the very one. I ran into him yesterday at the market; he was passing through on the way to some festival or another in London. I flirted with him for a while and invited him over for dinner. When he heard we had a real, true-to-life Templar staying with us, he was fascinated and wanted to meet him."

Sarah cut into her sausage, confusion sweeping over her. She had not seen Seamus in a year; not since her friendship with him had been tainted. She had been fond of him – and had thought he appreciated her as well. Then during one visit she had brought her sister along. The next thing she knew, her sister was curling up close to him. That was upsetting enough, but to her disappointment Seamus did not resist; he spent his time with Rachel, leaving Sarah alone on the couch for the evening. It had been part of what had stretched the distance between her and her sister.

Rachel had not been serious about the relationship, of course – she discarded Seamus without a second thought once Sarah had separated herself from him. So what was going on now? Why would Rachel wish to bring Seamus in to the mix, when she already had Reynald? Why would she want the two men meeting each other?

Sarah's mind spun through the possibilities. Was Rachel trying to make Reynald jealous, and more interested in her? Was she tiring of Reynald and happened across Seamus as a new man-of-the-moment? Was she not really interested in either, and simply curious how each man would compete for her attention in the presence of a rival?

A surge of anger poured through her. It was bad enough that Rachel was playing these games, but to do it on the day of Carrie's funeral? She took a few deep breaths, seeking a way to divert Rachel's aims without sounding hostile.

To her relief, Reynald spoke up with a somber voice, handling the situation for her. "I am sorry, Rachel, but I will not be here to meet your friend. I will be going to Pewsey for a funeral."

Sarah looked up quickly at that. She had thought it would be a challenge to request a guard to go with her to the funeral. She had not dreamt that Reynald had meant to go himself. Her gaze met his.

"As am I," she stated quietly. She waited for a rebuttal or argument from him, but he merely held her gaze for a few moments, then nodded. "I will see you there safely," he vowed, turning to speak to her father. "You have my word on that, sir."

Rachel stopped with a link of sausage halfway to her mouth, looking between the men. "What is this about a funeral? Has someone we know died?"

Sarah's mother glanced at her father, then leant forward to put her hand on Rachel's wrist. "It was Carrie Brown, from the village of Pewsey," she advised her daughter quietly. "She was murdered by outlaws two days ago."

"Oh, yes, I heard about that," agreed Rachel, finishing her bite. "Seamus told me all about that."

Sarah looked in confusion between Reynald's tormented face and Rachel's look of blithe contentment. "You do not intend on going … with Reynald?" she finally asked.

Rachel glanced up at her as if she had lost her mind. "I just told you, Seamus is coming over. Did you forget already? I have plans, and it is a shame that Reynald cannot make time for them." Her voice held a light, teasing tone.

Sarah's world swirled around her. It was too much. Was Rachel truly that uncaring? She pushed herself to a standing position, staring at her sister. "But …" she was at a loss for words. At last she motioned toward her sister's wrist. "But the bracelet!" she called out in confusion.

Rachel sniffed haughtily, her face aglow with self-assurance. "What, do you think one small present means I am at this man's beck and call for the rest of his life?" she shot back, her head held high. "I do not think so!" She spun the bracelet on her wrist absently. "Plus, the clasp was broken. I had to repair that myself."

Sarah's voice was tight with pain. "But the bracelet is -"

Reynald quickly interrupted her, standing as well. "It was a mere trinket," he interjected quietly, his gaze locked on hers. "A keepsake I should have stopped wearing long ago."

Rachel shot hotly to her feet, staring at her sister with open jealousy. "It is mine, I tell you," she insisted, her voice sharp. "You *always* try to take the things I have. You will not get this. It is *my* present."

Sarah's throat grew hoarse, and her anger surged. "I am not fond of your method of acquiring … presents," she bit out.

Rachel's face colored crimson, and her voice rose in pitch "I shall have you know that Reynald gave this to me in apology after he hit me."

Sarah rounded immediately on Reynald, her fury transferring in a lightning flash. Her parents stood alongside her as one. "You *hit her*?" she screamed, anger turning her shoulders into steel. The thinnest thread of self-control held her from drawing her dagger and launching herself at him, Templar training be damned.

Reynald threw his hands out to his sides, clearing them of his weapons in one smooth motion. "I swear to you, I did not," he called out to Sarah and her parents, his face pale and serious. His voice came out in a quick staccato. "Rachel came to my room, drunk, and I pushed her away from me. She hit against the door jam, and she pulled loose my bracelet as she did so. I swear to you, this is the truth of the matter."

Rachel smiled brightly, all cheerfulness. "See, he admits to it! He threw me into the side of the door. All I got in return was this one measly bracelet. Now you expect me to do penance by going with him to the funeral of someone I have never met?"

Sarah's world spun around her. She pushed away from the table, walking blindly out the main door, out to the stables. She had reached her horse's stall when she heard the footsteps, heard the stride as Reynald caught up, then stopped behind her.

She turned and looked up into his eyes, so full of pain and guilt. When he spoke, his voice rasped.

"Sarah, I am so sorry," he apologized, his voice haunted. "I did not mean to encourage your sister in any way. When she appeared at my door, my only thought was to get her away safely. I never meant to hurt her."

Sarah could only stare at him as if she was seeing him afresh for the first time.

"You did not give her the bracelet as some sort of … token?"

Reynald's features twisted in confusion. "A token?" he repeated, looking at Sarah in bewilderment. "Do you mean … of affection?"

Lou hurried in from a side door, and Sarah turned away from Reynald, her heart pounding. She moved to her horse's stall, focusing her attention on preparing him for the ride. She had no desire to learn more about Rachel's dalliances with Reynald. A girl lay dead, and today she was to respect the loss. With well worn skill she put all thoughts of her sister and the past away.

She led her horse into the central area. In a moment she had settled the saddle onto his back, snugging the girth. Alongside her, Reynald moved with practiced ease to get his own mount ready for the road.

In short order, the pair was moving quietly along the main road, heading towards the village of Pewsey.

Reynald's demeanor had changed greatly since the last time Sarah had ridden with him. He seemed to be watching in every direction, and his body radiated a primed alertness which made it seem that he would be at her defense in an instant. She felt both reassured and unnerved by his behavior. If things had gotten this bad … she kept her own hand by the hilt of her sword. She knew she was no match for his skills, but she could provide what help she was able if it came to that.

They did not speak until they reached the small village. Mourning ribbons were hung on many of the doors, and a crowd was gathered by the stone church on the common. Sarah and Reynald tied up their horses, then moved in to join the group. Sarah spotted Bethany and Jack standing to one side, and moved over to join them.

Sarah drew Bethany into a tender embrace. "How are the children?"

"They are with my mother," responded Bethany, her eyes somber. "It is a tragic thing," she added in a moment. "Carrie was a sweet child. It is hard to believe something like this would happen in our area."

Reynald flushed, and his eyes became hard. "I swear to you, it will be stopped," he vowed.

Lily moved over to join the group, her normally cheerful face a mask of sadness. “Oh, my friends, to meet on such an occasion,” she offered in sorrow, exchanging hugs with Bethany and Sarah in turn. “Such a bright spirit, taken from us far too soon.”

They heard a clearing of a throat, and all turned to face the priest. He stood in a somber, black robe, motioning that he was ready to begin. The group followed him into the church, settling into the pews. Reynald slid down the wooden bench to sit at her side, his thigh pressed lightly against hers. She could feel every contact point with searing heat, and soaked in the strength of the man at her side. She held off the longings with effort, focusing on the words of the priest.

The sermon was lovely, and Sarah was touched by the words offered by several of Carrie’s family and friends. When the eulogy was finished the group moved out into the summer sunshine.

Looking at the bright sky and white clouds, it seemed to Sarah an unsuitable day for a burial. She sighed, recognizing that nature knew no change in its cycle. People would be born and die on every day, at every hour. Life rolled on in its continual circle.

Sarah stood beside Reynald as the family members lowered Carrie’s body into the ground. After several intercessory prayers, Sarah was blanketed by an immense sense of sadness as the young woman was covered with earth. Carrie had been so young, barely starting out in life. All of her hopes and dreams had been snuffed out in one violent act.

Sarah looked over at Reynald, and saw a new sense of resolution settle into his face, into the set of his shoulders. She knew that he still felt responsible for this death, and imagined that he would do everything he could to prevent its repetition.

Together they walked over to the grieving family. Sarah waited patiently for her turn, and then approached the couple and their children.

"Dear friends, I am so sorry for your troubles," she offered quietly. "I cannot even imagine how you are feeling right now. If I can help in any way, please let me know."

"We appreciate your coming," responded the mother, her face streaked with tears. "It means a lot to us that others will take note of her passing." Her eyes traveled to the man at Sarah's shoulder.

"My name is Sir Reynald, and I am visiting with Sarah's family," he introduced himself somberly. "I also want to offer my assistance, in any way that I can."

Carrie's father took the offered hand and shook it firmly. "Your presence here is enough," he commented quietly. "That Carrie's departure from life is so well marked, we can hope that she is somewhere far better off now."

"I am sure of it," replied Reynald with great seriousness. "I will pray for her daily."

Sarah and Reynald moved aside, allowing others to step forward and offer their condolences. Lily gave her goodbyes, and then Bethany and Jack left as well, and still the couple stood by the grave, lost in thought. Sarah felt it was the least she could do for the young woman who had been so ruthlessly slain.

Footsteps sounded, and Reynald tensed beside her. Looking up, she saw Ethan and Elijah closing in on them, their demeanor serious. They were dressed far more neatly than when they had met in the cemetery. Reynald's hand dropped to the hilt of his sword, his gaze even on both men.

Ethan spoke up promptly as the pair stopped before them. His voice was low but clear. "I want to apologize to you, Sarah, for my behavior the other day. It was unfair of me to take out my grief on you, when I know you did all within your power." He turned to look up at Reynald. "You, sir. You were drawn into a fight which you had no part in. I am glad you were not hurt because of my rashness." He stood before them, humble and ready for any response.

Reynald turned to Sarah, allowing her to speak for them.

Sarah gave a somber smile. "I cannot imagine what it must be like to lose a sister. I know if my sister died I would be overwhelmed with grief for years. I am only sorry that I could not do more to help."

Ethan turned crimson. "Speaking of … I mean … I am also sorry for my jibes about Rachel, and about Dirk. They have rung in my ears ever since that day. It was cruel for me to bring those up. I am sorry – very sorry – for causing you any pain."

Sarah blushed deeply, but she nodded reassuringly. "You were upset, and that is in the past. All is forgiven."

Elijah stepped forward to stand by his brother's side. "We will be going to Bisley, to join up with Walter's forces there. They are training men to take action against these bandits. Word is we should be ready in about a week to ride out."

Reynald glanced at Sarah before responding. "I will be with that force," he informed them. "I will be honored to ride at your side, to clear this land of the scourge."

The men shook hands, and the two brothers headed off to offer what comfort they could to the grieving couple.

Sarah was torn by the talk of the upcoming fight, and of Reynald leaving the keep. Why had he not mentioned this? She pushed down her questions, giving one last look at the fresh grave. Whatever needed to be done to end this threat, she would accept. There would be time enough for discussion afterwards.

Reynald's gaze dropped down to meet hers, and she turned away, walking toward their horses in silence. They mounted as one, turning their reins to head the steeds onto the quiet road back to their keep. They took the ride in somber silence, the miles drifting by in a sun filled river.

About halfway home, Reynald broke the silence, his voice slow and careful as if he had been crafting his question for many miles. "Dirk was the man you once loved … a man in your past?"

Sarah's cheeks flamed with heat. Of all the questions Reynald could ask her, this was the one she was the least willing to talk about. She could not lie … and she felt churlish about telling him to mind his own business. After all he had done for her, if he truly wanted to know, she could at least give him some portion of the story.

"I was seventeen," she sighed wearily, tension settling into her shoulders at the mere thought of the situation. "Dirk seemed everything I could have wanted in a man. He talked frequently of honor. He had a military background. We were betrothed after only a month or two of meeting. I thought my life was heading down a wonderful path."

She ran a hand along her horse's mane. "Time passed, and Dirk became uncomfortable with my interest in being a midwife. He turned to another woman, one who solely wanted to stay home and tend to his needs. They were married a short time later."

She took in a deep breath, then let it out again. She let her gaze drift along the side of the road, watching the wildflowers wave in the summer breeze. "I do not blame him, of course. I was not what he wanted in a woman. Maybe there is no man who would accept a woman with her own sense of purpose."

Reynald's voice was a mere murmur. "I am sure there are men out there who treasure you exactly the way you are," he commented softly. His head turned so that he caught her eyes. "Ethan mentioned your sister …"

Sarah, if possible, flushed even more brightly at this. She could not maintain his gaze; she turned her head to the side, facing out into the woods. A long while passed as they rode side by side down the quiet lane. Several times Sarah began speaking, and could not make any sound. Finally she shook her head in anger. This was silly. The event was in the past, done with. She should be able to mention it without this trauma.

"It was only perhaps a year ago that my sister brought up Dirk's name. After all that time, I had thought he was an old story. But my sister decided to tell me -"

Her throat closed up on her. Tell her, indeed. Her sister could lie with little provocation, and hide secrets for decades if they served her purpose. Here, her sister had felt it necessary to share.

She swallowed her pride and pressed forward. "She told me, one night while we sat chatting, that she had slept with Dirk, early in our betrothal. During one of his visits to our home. She claimed she had been drinking at the time. She did not apologize, or say anything further."

Sarah's body went rigid at the memory. "My sister had just admitted to having an affair with my future husband. *My future husband!* She never told me back when it would have mattered! She could have told me right then. She could have warned me that my future husband had no honor after all. Instead, she waited for years before she revealed this truth. She waited until we were already apart. By that point she knew the knowledge could only cause me pain, and serve little other purpose."

Reynald's voice was tight with anger. "What she did was wrong. Still, why do you always forgive the men in these situations? Dirk is equally responsible; perhaps more responsible, if she was drinking and he was older."

Sarah lashed out; the pain and shame and fury of the event poured out through her after years of denial. She had never spoken of this with any other person, and the floodgates had been opened.

"What he had done was sleep with a willing partner. You should have seen the way she flirted and laughed any time he was around. Yes, I was upset to find out he was a man without honor, but it was a lesson I took to heart. Men cannot be trusted to resist temptation."

Reynald opened his mouth to speak in rebuttal, but Sarah ignored him, her fury driving her to speak. "But *her?!* Rachel bedded the man I had chosen – in *my home!* I could not even imagine kissing a man she had chosen to wed. It would turn my stomach, like kissing a brother. Yet she let him touch her – even in a drunken state – without crying out? Without screaming for help? Without fighting tooth and claw?"

Tears streamed down her face. "When you are drunk you lose your inhibitions for things you *want* to do. You sing too loudly, you dance too wildly. You kiss that beau you have always lusted after in your heart."

She plowed on, unable to hold back the flood. "What did she do afterwards? When she was sober? If I had been in congress with a partner of hers, I would have gone to her immediately and warned her of the danger she was in. I would have explained that he could not be trusted, that she should get away from him immediately. I would have dragged her away myself, to keep her safe from him and his deceptive charms."

She hunched over, pain worming its way into every muscle in her body. "What did she do? She let him keep wooing me, keep touching me. She let me move forward with plans … plans to *be* with him for the rest of my life! While she knew what he really was!"

The agony staggered her. "Is that the act of a sister? Is that the act of *anyone* who cares for me?"

Reynald was silent at her side, and Sarah took in a long, shuddering breath. Her voice was hoarse, her emotions spent. "When she finally deigned to tell me, after so many years, after he was gone from my life, what was I supposed to say? Thank you for sharing that you cheated on my fiancé with me and never told me? Thank you for allowing me to make plans with a known adulterer? I appreciate your honesty, now that it is long past too late?"

Her throat closed up. "I could not say anything."

She was exhausted now, and ahead she saw the keep slowly coming in to sight. Her voice dropped down to a mere whisper. "I took it on as my burden, as the older sister, to let it go. I did not call her out for her actions. I did not rail at her for giving in without crying out for help. I did not berate her for staying silent afterwards, for condemning me to a life with a man who could not be trusted. I did not even scold her for being … the way she is. I let it go. I could not say I forgave her; perhaps that is what she sought. Still, I let it go, and put that part of my life in the past."

They came in through the main gates, and the horses moved without prodding into the stables. Reynald dismounted in a smooth motion and came over to help Sarah down from her horse.

When she had gained her feet, Reynald stood before her for a long moment, looking down at her. His voice was raw when he finally spoke.

"Sarah …"

Sarah turned her head to the side, unwilling to look at him, unwilling to talk further. Her heart had already been ripped raw; she could say no more. She moved away from him, walking deliberately out of the stables. She strode straight into the keep and up to her room.

She sat there for many long hours as her chambers descended into darkness. Her mind swirled in circles, thinking of Carrie's death, her mistakes of the past, and the prospects of a bleak future.

Chapter 18

Thursday morning dawned with sultry waves of heat. As she lay in bed, a gnawing tension rooted deep in her neck and shoulders. The trauma of yesterday's talk mingled with the seriousness of today's visit with the wanderers. She pushed her twisted emotions aside with an effort and wearily climbed out of bed.

She dressed slowly, reviewing her preparations item by item to ensure she was ready. The sword, the dagger, the loose clothes, and braided hair. More than ever, she was pressed down by the obligation that she had to keep Abigail safe. Seeing the dead girl being lowered into the fresh grave had made the risks all too real.

It was one thing to worry about bringing danger into the wanderer's camp. There were many armed men there to help defend the weak. Once she brought Abigail out of that security, she was responsible for her well-being - and the safety of the baby.

Sarah truly did not care what Rachel was doing when she came down the stairs. Her thoughts were completely on Abigail and the day ahead of her. That one focus needed to be her every waking thought.

She took in a deep breath as she walked into the main hall. It was as she had figured. Her sister was dressed in full attack regalia, with the crucifix, the exposed bosom, the bright smile. Reynald's eyes turned to meet with hers when she walked into the room.

Sarah saw in one glance that the display was wasted on Reynald.

His eyes looked her up and down, from the tight weave of her braid, down to the sword at her hip, well oiled and ready.

His eyes came back up to meet hers, and she saw the admiration, the appreciation, in his eyes. She flushed slightly, but held his gaze as she moved down the hall to sit by her father.

The standard morning activities flashed by in a whirl she almost did not see. She gave farewells to her parents, heard the complaint of her sister. Her father made a comment to Reynald about agreeing to meet with him later in the evening. Each was but a tiny interruption. Sarah ignored it all and pushed on with the task at hand.

She moved through the keep to the stables, then saddled up her horse. Reynald was at her side at each step, quietly matching her. They prepared a third horse for Abigail, a steady mare with a quiet temper. Then, as one, they rode out through the main gates, their gaze focused on the road ahead.

They moved together on the long path towards the clearing, side by side, not speaking. The miles and hours passed as a steady stream of time. When they arrived, Reynald pulled to a stop without a word. His face held a quiet seriousness.

He fished in a side pouch and brought out a small carved wooden whistle. It was looped on a long leather strap.

"Take this with you," he offered, his voice low and gruff. "She may not be able to ride far. Wherever she feels is best, blow this whistle. I will come to find you there. That way she can rest assured that her friends are safe - but she and the baby can go only as far as they wish."

Sarah pulled her horse alongside of his, nudging it close. She moved her head forward, and Reynald leant to drape the whistle over her head. A tingle ran through her as the warmth of his hands lay against her neck. She looked up to meet his eyes and was instantly lost in their steady depths. She almost broke; almost asked him to ride in with her, the wanderers' concerns be damned. They could be ordered to trust in him, to rely on her judgment.

Shaking herself, she nudged her horse back, breaking his contact. She could not risk all because of her momentary weakness. The camp members would react poorly to the sudden appearance of a stranger, and their behavior would be unpredictable. She could not jeopardize Abby's safe haven. The plan must be followed.

She turned without a word, gathering the reins of her horse along with the mare's lead rope, and headed at a steady pace toward the camp.

Sarah kept to her protective habits. They were more necessary than ever now. She backtracked and turned, paused at random locations, and listened with every ounce of attention she had. It was nearly a half hour before she was positive that she was not followed, and moved forward. The miles drifted by. At last she was drawing up to the outskirts ...

Something was wrong. She knew it before the camp drew into sight, before she saw the smoky tendrils curling up from charred ruins which once were tents. Her sword was in her hand without conscious thought, and she leapt off the horse, her eyes alert for any sign of movement.

A sharp noise came from behind her, and she suddenly remembered the whistle, that Reynald was waiting on her call. She realized with hammering immediacy the dangerous situation she was in. Even while she was turning around, she was grabbing the whistle with her free hand, and blowing ... blowing ... blowing ... the high piercing notes rang out loudly across the silence, across the clearing and the woods.

No attacker stood behind her - but a young man lay sprawled across the dirt, his eyes fluttering open at the noise. He hazily gazed in her direction, his face wracked with pain. A ragged wound laced down his right side and his arm lay twisted at an unnatural angle.

Sarah's breath sucked in with a sudden movement. It was Lloyd, Abigail's husband. She dropped down beside him, her hands moving to probe the injury.

"Lloyd, God's teeth, what happened here?" she rasped out in shock. She ripped free a strip from the bottom of her dress, binding his wound as best she could. "Where are Abigail and the baby? Where is Kyle?"

Lloyd looked away, his eyes filling with tears. "They took her, Sarah. They took all of the women and the young children." He struggled to a sitting position. "We tried to stop them. Kyle was struck down; he was one of the first to fight when he realized what was happening. I was on the other side of the camp, so I do not know what began it."

He shook his head, his eyes losing focus as he thought back. "All I saw was Kyle and the other leaders talking with some men - and then suddenly there was chaos."

"Is Kyle injured?" asked Sarah, scanning the area for signs of danger. The camp was blanketed in silence; not even a bird's song interrupted the deep hush. By the dried blood on Lloyd's wounds she guessed he had been unconscious for several hours. Yet there were no guarantees the attackers were gone. She kept alert for any sound, any sign of movement.

Lloyd winced against the pain, his face white with strain, his voice shaky and weak. "The last I saw, he was over near the main campfire ..." His voice faded as he shuddered against another spasm.

Sarah finished winding the bandage tightly about him. "Hold still; I will be back in a moment," she promised him, helping him to lay back down against a grassy mound. Then, sword in hand, she eased cautiously across the camp.

Her stomach turned as she picked her way through the wreckage of the wanderers' homes. Burnt out shells of tents and dead bodies were strewn in disarray like the abandoned toys of a child. Several blood trails led out into the forest. Apparently a few survivors had dragged themselves off into the relative safety of the dense foliage.

Suddenly she spotted movement to the right. A man was laying on his side, struggling to sit up. She bolted towards him at a dead run.

It was Kyle, blood streaming from a head wound. He shakily climbed to his feet as she reached him. "Was that you whistling?" he asked tremulously, his eyes glazed. "I thought I was having another hallucination, but then I saw you, thank the

Lord." He stumbled, and Sarah was there in an instant, helping to support him.

Going slowly and carefully, she walked with Kyle back toward the horses. She helped him to sit beside Lloyd, and ripped another strip from her dress, using it to bind the cut in his forehead. The area was dead silent; not even an insect's chirp interrupted the baking heat of summer. Sarah's heart pounded, and she wished they were not quite as exposed. They would be easy targets, should the wolves' heads return.

Finished with her ministrations, she looked between her two patients, then glanced around the clearing again. "We must get you out of here," she urged in a quiet voice. "This area is not safe. I have two horses with me, and I am light. One of you can ride with me." Her eyes looked between the two of them, making her decision. "Kyle, I know this is tough on you, but do you think you can hold your seat in a saddle? Lloyd has lost a lot of blood."

Kyle did not hesitate. "I can do it," he promised, forcing himself to focus. "If you keep a hand on the rein, I will keep myself awake."

A thundering of hooves sounded, and Sarah leapt to her feet, sword instantly held at the ready to one side. If the attackers were back, and they had taken out an entire camp of armed men, she knew she stood little chance. Still, she would not abandon her friends without a fight. She steeled her courage and faced in a defensive stance toward the sound. Her heart thudded in her chest as the noise of crashing brush grew louder.

A large, black horse thundered into the clearing, and a surge of adrenaline rushed through her body. She drew her arm back …

A cascading wave of relief washed over her, making her giddy. She was saved. It was Reynald.

His sword was raised high, and he pulled his horse up hard as he reached the clearing. He dismounted in one smooth motion, taking in the destruction of the area and Sarah's guarded stance in one swift glance. He ran over to her immediately, encompassing the two injured men and the chaos around him in a sweeping scan.

"Abigail?" he asked quickly, his eyes continually moving to take in details of the rest of the camp as he spoke.

"She has been taken," related Sarah bluntly. "We have to get these men back to the keep, and gather up a force to go after them."

Reynald turned back to his horse, his face set. "Your way home is clear and safe. Head back with those two. I will go after Abigail," he vowed fiercely, his eyes already far away.

Sarah did not hesitate - she ran to stand between Reynald and his steed, her sword brought up. "Reynald, think!" she challenged him. "This was an armed camp! The attacking group slew almost everyone here. They have undoubtedly returned to a lair which is both fortified and well-defended. You are Abigail's only hope of rescue. Do not throw that away."

Reynald's face twisted in agony, but he drew to a stop. "Those bastards have her ... I cannot leave her to them!"

Sarah lowered her sword, slowly taking a step forward. His right hand was clenched where it held his sword to one side; she put her hand on top of his, holding it tenderly. She looked up into his gaze, her eyes full of compassion.

"Reynald, your sister needs your help. She needs you to rescue her, not to lose your life in futility. We need a larger force. If we are to save her - and her baby - we need to mount an attack." Her voice dropped, and she moved even closer to him. "Trust me ... please. This is how we save them."

Reynald's face reflected his indecision; she could see the tension in his jaw, through his neck. Then, all of a sudden, he let out a deep breath and nodded. He looked back up at her, his eyes shining with new focus. "Then we must hurry," he insisted.

Sarah needed no prodding. "Let me just make sure there are no more injured," she requested in a rush, "while you get those two onto the horses." Reynald nodded, and Sarah sprinted off to move amongst the fallen bodies.

Sarah raced through the camp as quickly as she could. One after another, Sarah knelt by each prone shape, feeling for a pulse. Surely others must have been left alive besides Lloyd and Kyle? Each time she pressed a finger with fervent hope, and each time there was no answering throb. She stood and scanned the clearing – had she checked each one? There was another body by the far side of the campfire; she raced to reach him, quickly kneeling at his side.

Suddenly there was a snarl, and the flash of cold steel as a sharp dagger was pressed hard against her throat. She let out an involuntary cry which cut off short as the blade cut into her neck. She was dragged up to her feet by a strong arm.

The low growl in her ear was rich with fury. "You whore - how dare you!" She flinched, and the knife slid tightly across her neck in warning. A thin stream of warm blood trickled down her throat, sliding along her skin.

She fought down a rising panic. Her captor was much stronger than she was, and the dagger he held had already proven its sharp edge. Her hands hung uselessly at her side as he slowly dragged her backwards. She was completely at his mercy. She had no say at all in her own life or death. The helplessness of her situation threatened to overwhelm her, and she fought to think, to think ...

The man behind her gave her a shake, breaking up her efforts. His voice rang with hatred. "They are still warm, and yet you -"

A low, calm voice echoed across the clearing.

"You have made a mistake."

Sarah's heart stopped. She lifted her eyes in desperate hope.

Reynald stood across the campfire in a casual stance. His hand rested loosely on his sword hilt, the sword point down in the ground. His eyes slid to meet hers for a moment, and she breathed in the strength of their reassurance before he returned to gaze steadily at her captor.

"This woman is not responsible for the attack," he added with certainty.

"She was apparently willing to profit from it!" shot back Sarah's assailant with venom. His hands shook with fury. "I have never seen such a vulture in action!"

Reynald's eyes remained quiet, soothing. "She is a healer," he countered evenly. "You can ask Kyle and Lloyd, the two men she has already bandaged up. She was only hoping for more survivors to help."

The hand at her throat wavered for a moment. "I myself came back for Kyle and Lloyd," the man admitted slowly. "The other men who survived are all in safety; they were the last two left behind."

"We will bring these two with us," reassured Reynald, "and return shortly with a force to rescue the hostages. However, before anything can be done, you must let the healer go." His voice was calm, but Sarah could see the coiled power in his stance. He would be at her side in a moment if things went badly. Her eyes moved from his strong hand, resting with deceptive ease on the hilt of his sword … the tense muscles in his sword arm … the set of his shoulders … he was everything she could hope for, and it might not be enough. The man behind her could still slay her with one draw of the knife, and there would be nothing she could do about it, nothing Reynald could do. The panic rose again.

Reynald's eyes flicked again to meet hers, and she could viscerally feel the silent promise in them, the reassurance that he was there, that everything would be all right. She lost herself in his eyes, allowing herself to believe completely in him. Then, in a heartbeat, he was staring again at her captor, all attention focused on the man's slightest movements.

A long moment passed. Reynald's voice dropped into a lower, more steely bass. "Let her go," he ordered the man, the command clear, the threat palpable.

For a passage of time the world stood still. Sarah could hear every breath her attacker took as he considered his options. Reynald's eyes narrowed infinitesimally, and she could see his hand tighten on the sword at his side.

Then, with a smooth movement, the knife at her throat was lifted away. She was free.

Reynald put out his left hand, and Sarah did not hesitate. She ran pell mell into his arms, felt his left arm close tightly around her as she pressed herself hard against his chest. She began to tremble and closed her eyes tightly, willing herself to remain calm. She knew she should get behind him; leave him free to fight, but she could not bring herself to leave the safety of his embrace.

The harsh voice came again from behind her, slightly penitent. "You talk of soldiers; I assume you must come from the keep. If you can truly bring back a rescue party, we will join with your force to go after them," the man promised resolutely. "We will wait here until dawn. If you are not here by then, we will delay no further, however. We will go without you."

There was the sound of footsteps heading off into the woods, then silence.

Sarah sighed in relief as Reynald's arms pulled her in more tightly. She relished the encompassing feeling of the embrace. She was safe, secure … she did not want the moment to end. Her breath came out of her in long, low shuddering moans.

After several minutes a pair of lips tenderly rested against her forehead, and then she was gently pressed back a step. "Are you all right?" asked Reynald with concern. His eyes moved to the wound at her neck, and his eyes narrowed in anger.

Sarah absently wiped the back of her hand against the thin cut. "It is nothing," she promised resolutely. She drew in several long, cleansing breaths, her center returning. The burnt out camp around her seeped back into her awareness. She tried to shake off the spell of Reynald's presence, to focus on the problems around them. "Really, I am fine. We have other things to worry about right now. Let us get the two men mounted, and get home."

Reynald laid his hand gently against her cheek for a moment, then nodded and turned with her. They moved quickly back to Lloyd and Kyle. Between the two of them, they managed to get the two injured men up onto the horses. Sarah put herself before Lloyd, instructing him to hold tightly onto her waist. Then, as soon as everyone was set, they headed back towards the keep.

The ride seemed interminable. The injured men tried their best not to complain, but with their injuries the travel was sheer torture. Sarah and Reynald had to stop several times to allow the men to rest rather than faint from the pain.

It was nearly nightfall by the time the keep gates came into view. Sarah called out for help as soon as they neared the gates and soon the entire household was roused. Rachel, Christopher, and Mathilde were drawn out with the rest, streaming in waves over to the stables to help with the injured men. Rachel's eyes lit up with interest when she saw Lloyd holding onto Sarah tightly on the back of the horse. She ran over to their side at once.

"Here, let me help you down," she called up with enthusiastic concern, offering her arm to Lloyd. He stumbled down wearily, and as soon as he had gained his feet Sarah climbed down after him. Rachel ducked under one of Lloyd's arms to support him, moving with him in the direction of the main keep.

Sarah left Lloyd to her care and ran over to Kyle, who had been helped from his horse by Reynald. The two were talking quietly, and were joined by two of the castle's guards. As Sarah drew close, the guards each took up one of Kyle's arms and helped him struggle toward the building. Reynald turned to face Sarah and her father, now side by side in the stable's main hall.

"Kyle confirms that there was a Templar with the attackers, as I feared," stated Reynald, his face cold and shuttered. "The men were attempting to forcefully merge the wanderers into their own group. When the leaders refused, death was the only other option. The Templar apparently took the women and children to bolster their power, to hold them as hostages in return for money and food."

Christopher nodded in understanding, his gaze serious. His voice was sharp with decision. "It is long past time for us to do something about these wolves' heads," he agreed. He turned his head. "Cedric, call in all of the forces," he ordered shortly. "We leave as soon as possible."

The burly man saluted and sped off toward a nearby group of soldiers.

Christopher then turned back to Reynald. "It will undoubtedly take several hours for the men to be brought in from the villages. Come in and fortify yourself with some food and drink. I imagine it will be a very long night."

Together they moved into the main hall, where the kitchen staff scurried into action. Soon mead and chicken were brought out, as well as bread and cheese. Sarah wolfed it down hungrily; she had forgotten how long it had been since she ate last. Small groups of men began to arrive in twos and threes from neighboring villages. They seemed eager to join the action, chomping at the bit to head out for the rescue.

Time sped by in a blur, with guards coming and going, the story being told and retold to each new arrival. Reynald finished his meal quickly, and then turned to Sarah, his eyes serious.

"Once I rescue Abigail and the baby, I want to be prepared. If Abigail is unconscious, what should I check the baby for, and what should I do to help her survive until we get them back here to you?"

Sarah's mouth hung open in shock. "You, tend to an infant? Back here to me? I am going with you!"

Reynald's eyes widened in surprise. "No," he responded flatly. "You are not."

Sarah shot to her feet. "You are in no position to tell *me* what to do," she insisted hotly. "I know these lands intimately, as you do not. I have been to that camp more times than I can count – could you even find it? To think that I could tell you in a few minutes how to care for an injured baby!"

Reynald rose to his feet, his eyes steadily on hers. "My sister is already in grave danger," he replied, his voice tight. "There is no way that I would possibly subject you -"

"Subject, my foot," huffed Sarah in anger. "I will go where I wish to go, and I will not be stopped by the likes of -"

Sarah's father rose to put his hands placatingly between the couple. "Please, now, we must head out soon, and we need to be as cohesive as we can. There is a serious battle ahead of us; this is no simple bandit group we face."

He looked fondly at his daughter. “Sarah, I know that if we try to forbid you to come with us that you will simply trail behind our group. You know I have great respect for your skills. However, you must also acknowledge that compared to the serious training of a Templar, you are as lacking as many of our guards in defense.”

“Yet your guards are going with you,” snapped Sarah, her eyes sparking.

“They are,” agreed her father. “If one of them gets into trouble, we handle it as part of the plan. However, if *you* get into trouble, the entire line will fold, because the men will abandon all else to rescue you. You are that dear to them.”

Sarah sulkily dropped her eyes. “That’s hardly *my* fault,” she growled.

Her father gently patted her shoulder. “I might beg to differ, but be that as it may, the men adore you.” He smiled at her fondly. “So this is my compromise. You may come with us.”

“What?” cried Reynald, clearly outraged at the idea. “Surely it would be -”

Sarah’s father cut him off with a stern glance. “Believe me, Reynald, she will come whether we say yea or nay.” He turned to face his daughter. “However, you will swear this vow on the Bible. The moment we come into a situation of conflict, you will retreat to a safe distance and remain there until all fighting is over.”

Sarah’s heart ached as if he had wrenched it from her chest. “I can help!” she insisted plaintively. “I know I am no match for a Templar’s sword. I accept that. What if it is just a regular bandit guard? What if it is a scout, about to warn -”

“No,” instructed her father, cutting short all discussion. “Any situation can escalate, and any other guard here can take care of the dangers you mentioned. Either you agree to these terms, or I swear I will lock you in the cellars until we return.”

Sarah’s blood ran cold, and her face went white with shock. “You would not dare ...”

Her father did not say a word, and she knew in the depths of her heart that yes, he would do that, if she forced him to. Her emotions swirled in a maelstrom. If she made such a vow, she would be obliged to follow it. What if it came down to a life or death choice, and her father's life hung in the balance? What if it was Reynald's life at risk?

She turned to look up at Reynald. His eyes were rich with concern. She realized in an instant that she would rather be by his side - no matter under what restrictions - than trapped in the keep praying for his safe return. She did not hesitate a moment further.

"I swear, on the Holy Bible, that I will stay out of any conflict," she vowed solemnly, her eyes fixed on his.

Reynald's gaze took on a haunted look, and he reached out a hand to take hers. Her father discreetly drew away, allowing them a measure of privacy. Sarah moved to stand near Reynald, and a warmth flowed through her at his nearness.

Reynald's voice was hoarse. "Sarah, this is going to be very dangerous." His eyes moved to her throat, lingering on the cut which still gave a faint throb of pain. "I cannot begin to express how courageous it is that you wish to help my sister. But I would not put you both in peril."

Sarah's eyes flashed. "I have already sworn to stay out of any fight," she reminded him fiercely. "You will not get any more from me."

His hand moved tenderly to her cheek, shushing her. She half-closed her eyes, leaning against his touch. "I know that ... I know that," he murmured softly. "Please, just stay safe. For me."

"For you," she echoed gently, and for a moment it almost seemed that he was going to draw her in against him. Then there was a loud cheer as another force arrived, and Reynald was called over for introductions.

Sarah glanced around for her mother and sister, and could not find either in the crowded room. She made her way through the throng to her father's side.

"They are in the infirmary," replied her father shortly to the query. "Where you should be, I might add." He turned to give final instructions to Cedric, who stood at attention by his side.

Sarah took a step back, stung by his remark. It was true, of course. She had years of medical experience; she could be a help to the injured men currently under their care.

She shook her head, moving to the stairs to gather supplies from her room. There might be a few wounded men currently in the keep, but the upcoming fight promised to provide many more patients needing her attention. If she were at the actual battle site, she could save men who might otherwise be lost.

By the time she came downstairs again, the men were massing in the courtyard, many of them mounted. Lou had already prepared her steed for her, and she smiled at him in thanks as she pulled herself up and got settled for the long ride ahead. In a few moments the group was heading out through the main gates.

Sarah led them through the darkness straight towards the camp, all thought of secrecy long gone. They were thirty men strong, with many seasoned fighters in the mix. A few were concerned to hear that a woman would accompany them, but when it was explained that only Sarah knew where the camp was, and had been to the area many times, they reluctantly accepted her as a guide.

The time passed quickly as they thundered through the night, riding past village and forest in a blur of motion. It seemed that no time at all had passed before they were back at the location of the burnt tents and smoking ruins. A group of twenty armed men awaited them in the clearing, their eyes glowing with fierce anger. The motley crew gave brief greetings to the incoming keep's forces before forming up to move out.

Christopher turned to his daughter as the milling men settled into order. "It is time for you to take the rear position," he ordered in a low voice. "We will be following their trail from here." Sarah bit her tongue and complied without response. She knew she was lucky to be there, and did not want to question him in front of the troops. Reynald and her father took positions at the front of the team, and waved them to start into motion.

It was not difficult to pick up the path of the attackers. The bandit group had moved north, leaving behind a clear trail, even in the moonlight. The pursuers followed the route over a stream, down a long ravine, and up through a clearing.

As the night wore on, the group eased to a slower pace. Each member watched the forest with sharp eyes, careful to ensure they did not miss any turnings of one or more in the party off of the main path.

Sarah had ridden these trails many times over the years and did her best to watch at open junctures for stray footprints, faint marks in the moonlight. Maybe a child had gotten away … maybe a mother had left a token for them to follow. The group headed past a burbling brook, then turned down into the base of a narrow valley.

Something struck Sarah as odd, and she rolled it around in her mind. She knew this ravine well. There was always a large partridge flock nestled in here for the night. Why were they not scattering at the troop's movements, as they always did when she rode through in the dark? She drew her horse to a stop for a moment, looking around to reassure herself that she was not mistaken about their location.

It certainly was the ravine; she remembered that stony outcropping quite clearly. There, behind it, a glint of metal in the moonlight …

"Reynald!" she cried out in alarm, starting forward instinctively. There was a flash of motion and instantly a wave of men flooded in from the left and right, drawing a loop closed around the soldiers. Her companions reacted in a heartbeat. Swords flew out of their scabbards, and the area became locked in combat, the noise of steel on steel ringing out all around her.

Reynald swung his mount in a circle, clearing away the two attackers who had descended on him for a moment. His eyes sought out Sarah's and held them for a long heartbeat. Sarah nodded to him in resolution, understanding his plea. Every ounce of muscle in her body insisted that she fly down to help, join in the defense, but she held herself still. She determinedly backed her horse up to a higher location, making sure she could be seen by her father and Reynald, staying well away from the attack.

She watched, heart in throat, as Reynald leapt from his horse and cleared a path through the bandits. His sword moved with sure precision, his muscular body cycling through positions in an easy flow as he overtook each enemy in turn. He seemed aware of every man around him, and several times stepped in to help shield a companion from attack before turning to take on a new opponent.

Dragging her eyes away from his progress, Sarah turned to scan the combatants for her father. She finally spotted him at the far end of the field, locked in combat with a muscular man several inches taller than he was.

Sarah blanched in fear, her fingers tightening on the reins. She had always idolized her father as an invincible fighter, a man who could not be bested. However, his opponent seemed far more capable than the rabble of bandits around him. The burly attacker swung his sword with precision, laying down a series of thrusts that her father only barely fended off.

Sarah was nearly overwhelmed by the urge to race into action. She harshly reminded herself again to stay out of the fray. If she went down into the raging battle, she would only serve to distract the men who desperately needed to stay focused. Her own skills and additional blade could hardly make up for the disruption her presence would cause. Still, to see her father in trouble ...

Her eyes sharpened, and she gazed down at the battlefield in confusion. Suddenly it seemed as if her father's opponent had two weapons. Was it a mere shadow? There was the sword in his right hand ... and what was that ...

The man turned sideways, and the moonlight hit him more clearly. She now saw that he held a thick wooden branch hidden behind his back, clutched tightly in his left hand. He sprang into motion, spinning it with great force at her father's knee. She thought she could hear the loud crack as his leg broke, even over the cries and clangs of combat filling the night.

"Father!" she screamed out in anguish, stretched to the breaking point.

Reynald looked up instantly at her call, then followed the direction of her gaze to where her father now collapsed to the ground. In a heartbeat he was running full tilt, interjecting himself between the attacker and her father. She cried out in relief, her knuckles turning white with the strain of watching.

The battle slowly eased into quiet; most of the bandits had either been slain or had run off. Only Reynald and his opponent remained, slowly circling each other.

"Bruce. I should have known it would be you," growled Reynald, his voice carrying easily in the night air.

Bruce shrugged dramatically, spinning his blade in his grip. His blonde-white hair shone in the moonlight. "Reynald the dutiful," he taunted. "So it has been you hounding us this whole way." He seemed an equal match to Reynald's height and build. Sarah glanced between the two men in nervous apprehension.

Reynald eyed his fellow Templar with smoldering anger. "You were tainted even in the Holy Land. There were always reports of missing items when you escorted pilgrims down your stretch of road."

"As well there should have been," Bruce chuckled in return. "Those pilgrims were wealthy beyond measure, and we were putting our lives on the line for them! They could easily afford to pay us ten times what I took."

"You made a vow," snapped Reynald. "You swore to protect the innocent."

Bruce lunged without warning. The two men crossed blades in clanging reverberation several times before they separated and circled each other again.

"You were always far too loyal to those vows," sneered Bruce defiantly. "Live a little. Life is too short to take too seriously."

Reynald swung his blade into a high position. "Life is too short to be without honor," he responded crisply, his eyes focused.

Bruce laughed out loud. "Then let me help make yours even shorter," he agreed. Without another word, he launched into a fully involved attack.

Sarah was transfixed by the flurry of swords. Both men were consummate soldiers, blocking and striking with the speed of a cobra. They turned and twisted, rolling beneath a slicing blow, spinning from a lunging attack.

The fight caught her absolute attention, and the world fell away. Reynald ducked under a vicious strike, turning to spin his blade at Bruce's calf. Bruce leapt back with only inches to spare, and was swinging a fresh assault in the same movement. Sarah gasped, sure the sword would connect with Reynald's arm, but somehow he twisted aside, only a thin red line tracing along the arc of the blade. He threw a shoulder hard into Bruce's side, and the men blurred into motion anew.

Sarah held her breath. She could not tell if either man was gaining ground as they spun in a whirlwind of moving blades. She watched, fixated on each movement, praying that Reynald would make it through.

The men slammed together with a loud crash, and she could not tell where the blades landed. Then suddenly the pair was staggering apart, both men weaving unsteadily.

Sarah's world came to a screeching halt, and her heart thundered from her chest. Was Reynald hurt? Was it a serious injury? She strained forward, desperate to see …

Bruce took a menacing step towards Reynald, and a cry escaped from her lips. It could not be …

As she watched, frozen, Bruce's forward foot failed under his weight. He timbered forward, falling in slow motion, landing hard on his face with a thud. There was an echo of the sound, and then he lay still, unmoving.

Reynald stood alone at the center of the clearing, standing over his fallen fellow knight, his face weary with sadness.

Sarah hesitated one moment, then two, then her knees were driving into her steed's flanks, driving him into a hard gallop. Reynald moved with fatigued slowness to talk with the nearby group of solders. He seemed all right … suddenly her father's more serious injury hammered at her attention.

She raced her horse down the slope, driving directly toward Christopher's side. As she reached the edge of the group surrounding him, she was off her mount in an instant, grabbing her bag and sprinting at top speed. She slid to a stop alongside her father and pulled aside his leggings.

Her father gasped out in pain. "It seems to be broken." He slumped back against the ground.

Sarah could see that clearly. She called out to whoever was nearby, "I will need some sturdy branches for a splint -"

A calm voice answered by her side. "Already have them." She glanced up to meet Reynald's eyes, and she let out a deep sigh. She owed him so much already ...

"Thank you," she offered him, putting all of her emotion and feeling into those two words. She saw that his smile of acknowledgement understood her meaning, and as he handed her the pieces of wood, he held her hands for a moment.

"No, thank you for staying out of the fight," he responded softly. "I can only imagine how hard that was for you. I know if it were me, it would have eaten me up alive."

Sarah blushed crimson and turned her face down to the task at hand. She quickly cleaned up her father's wound as best she could, then wrapped and splinted it. Soon Reynald and another soldier were helping him onto his horse.

Sarah looked around. A number of the other guards were injured as well, although none as seriously as her father. She moved from man to man, tending them as best she could, preparing them for travel home.

Finally done with the last injury, she stood wearily and surveyed the scene. The soldiers had gathered up the bandit bodies and draped them over the horses to bring them back to town and have them identified. Everybody appeared ready to move out.

Reynald and her father, both already mounted, were deep in conversation at the head of the group. She walked briskly over to Reynald's side, scanning the two men as she went. Reynald's arm had the red scratch running down its length, but the blood had already begun drying. He appeared otherwise unhurt. Her father's leg was well bandaged and he was seated on his horse with the help of a wedged blanket.

The two broke off their discussion at her approach. She looked between the two men in concern.

"I know I am here only as a medic, but I hope you are deciding to retreat and gather more men, rather than to press on with what we have left …?"

Reynald sighed, but nodded. "Yes, I have accepted that," he admitted. "It can be discussed when we return to the keep, how best to mount this attack." His look slid over to Bruce's body, draped over a nearby horse. "We did take out one of the captains, however. That, at least, should make it easier to finish off the assault the next time."

Cedric came over leading Sarah's horse, and she mounted quickly. In a moment the group started into motion.

The troop headed back toward the keep, making their way slowly but steadily through the night. Sarah stayed alongside her father, checking to make sure he was alert and upright in the saddle. It was nearly dawn before they came to the gates, but despite the early hour the entire keep's inhabitants waited tensely in the courtyard, eager for news.

Mathilde flew forward at the sight of her husband in bandages, drawing him into her arms as he carefully dismounted.

His face creased in pain. "It is all right; it is only my leg," he reassured her hoarsely. He did not argue as she insistently helped him move toward the main keep doors, calling for the doctor to assist her with her husband.

Sarah watched them hobble away, her brow furrowed with concern. She had always thought of her father as able to take on any challenge. To see him so ruthlessly injured ... she shook her head, wearily lowering herself from her own mount, gathering up the strength to tend to the injured.

A squealing form ran past her, and she turned to see her sister, barely dressed in a bright red wrap, running to embrace Reynald. "You saved my father! How can I ever thank you?" the blonde apparition cried out in adoration. "You are so strong, so brave. Please, let me get you some ale. Would you rather have wine, or mead? Just tell me what you want, and it is yours." She snuggled against him in delight.

Sarah's cheeks flared pink with shame, and she strode quickly to the far side of the courtyard, burying herself in the work of bandages and poultices. The scene replayed over and over in her mind as she tended to the injured. She flushed with embarrassment over her sister's blatant behavior.

Yet, as she turned over the situation in her mind, she had to admit that another part of her echoed the feelings Rachel had so boldly displayed. She was giddy with relief that Reynald had saved her father. She shone with overwhelming admiration for how Reynald fought during the battle, helping all those around him.

She knew that a large part of her was jealous of Rachel. Her sister was able to unabashedly shout out emotions that Sarah held trapped, hidden, in her own heart.

Finally each man was tended to and under the care of the doctors. Sarah pushed the hair back from her brow and stumbled through the main doors, heading to the stairs which led up to the bedchambers.

She paused as she reached the steps up to her room, then shook her head. She was not ready for sleep yet. Despite her body's exhaustion, she was emotionally keyed up even as dawn stretched its first fingers of light across the horizon. She would not be able to fall asleep, not for a while yet.

Resigned, she moved through the keep and out the back doors, making her way to a stone bench by her garden. Perhaps if she sat for a while her mind would settle and let her body rest.

She watched as light slowly filtering across the landscape, listened as the first birds added their song to the world. There were so many thoughts jumbling in her mind. Thoughts of her father fighting for his life, the bandit looming over him. Thoughts of her inability to move, trapped on the outcropping, watching events play out. The image of Reynald, swift and sure, riding in to the rescue …

The images took on a dream-like quality. In her dream, Reynald turned to look at her, surrounded by the fray. His eyes met hers, and he saluted her. He was her protector … he was her partner …

It was as if a warm light was suddenly shining down on her, illuminating her in its glow. She knew what she had to do. She had to tell him how she felt. She had to tell him before it was too late. Her whole life was about truth, and honesty, and this was her test.

A rough voice sounded at her ear. "Good God, Sarah."

Sarah blinked her eyes, the gritty surface of the stone bench pressing against her cheek. Reynald was kneeling down beside her, his eyes bright with concern. "Sarah, have you been out here since we came back?"

It was still early morning, and a gentle mist swirled around the gazebo. Reynald had changed into the outfit he wore for his morning practice. Apparently even a night-long combat was not enough to dissuade him from his dawn routines.

Sarah sleepily rubbed at her eyes, pushing herself wearily up to a sitting position. "I wanted to talk with you," she explained fuzzily, her thoughts not quite connecting together.

Reynald's brow furrowed in confusion. "Talk with me about what? Could it not wait until after you had a decent sleep? You must be exhausted!"

Sarah shook her head. "It could not wait." Her eyes drew into focus, and she found herself eye to eye with Reynald, her hands held in his. His eyes were tender with concern. He did not press. With infinite patience, he knelt by her side, waiting for her to begin.

Sarah's mouth went dry. The man before her emanated strength. It was not just his broad shoulders and well-muscled form. It was the knowledge that he would stand by his vows, that he would speak the truth. She had wanted to praise him for his efforts of the night before, to thank him whole heartedly for rescuing her father from certain death. Yet, at his steady gaze, all such thoughts fled her mind, and only one remained.

I love you.

Reynald blinked in surprise, and Sarah blushed as crimson as a rose in full bloom. She looked down immediately, lost in confusion. She had not spoken the words aloud, but she wondered how clearly the message had projected in her eyes. She had not meant to let him know the depth of her feelings. Her dream aside, she did not have the strength to broach that subject. Not with his stay here numbering in hours. Not with Rachel …

She struggled to find her voice, keeping her eyes lowered.

"I wanted to tell you ... how grateful I am for what you did last night," she stated, her voice weary. "It was an honor to see your strength in action, and I know I speak for everyone here when I thank you for saving my father's life."

Reynald put a hand beneath her chin and slowly raised her face to meet his own gaze. "I know how much strength it took you to remain still, to wait for the area to clear before coming down," he replied tenderly. His eyes remained focused on her own, searching for something ...

Sarah turned her head again, unwilling to have him see more than she wished to share. She was exhausted. "I should probably get to sleep now," she yawned, her body completely drained of energy. "I will leave you to your morning routine."

She allowed Reynald to help her stand, but then waved him off, making her way to the door. "I am fine from here," she insisted. "Please, go on with your practice."

It took all her strength to turn her back on him, to make her way alone up the stairs and into her room.

Chapter 19

Sarah slept straight through the day, and into the night. By the time she had come down for food the next morning, Reynald and her father were deep in conversation with several of the guard captains. Her father looked older than she had remembered, bundled into a large chair by the main table, his leg well wrapped in bandages. Her mother sat to his side, a look of quiet concern on her face.

Her father looked up. "The group is going to Dorrie's. A messenger has already been sent," he announced without preamble as Sarah entered the room. "Yes, you can go with them, to set up a medical base at the keep there. Your skills will undoubtedly be quite useful. That keep is the most central location for a larger force to gather. They can be ready to leave from there in two day's time."

Rachel's voice rung out with delight. "This is wonderful - I will go too, then!" she cried. "I have not seen Walter in many years!"

"No," called out her father harshly, and Rachel blinked in surprise. "You know that would not be appropriate," he added in a quieter tone of voice.

Rachel plunked back down in her chair, her face sullen. "I do not see why *she* can go and I have to stay behind," she grumped. "That is not fair at all."

Reynald turned to Rachel, his voice gentle. "We will only be gone a few days. I am sure we all will greatly appreciate the homecoming preparations you have made for us at that time."

Rachel brightened at this, and Sarah bit her tongue. It was Rachel's own doing that the tense situation existed between her, Walter, and Dorrie, but she imagined that Rachel did not see it that way at all. She gave quiet thanks that her father had set down the rule, rather than leaving it to her to tackle.

Sarah ate and dressed quickly, gathering up the supplies she would need. Her practiced haste served her well; when she went down into the main hall with her gear she found the forces still in disarray. It was clear it would be another hour or two before the group was ready to move out.

Sarah went by the infirmary, checking in on Kyle and Lloyd. Both were sound asleep, and she verified their wounds were well tended to before leaving them in peace. She stopped by the sitting room, but even that normally quiet refuge was a temporary headquarters for several wanderers discussing their plans. They looked askance at the woman who seemed an intrusion.

Sarah carefully lifted the dulcimer off its shelf and tucked it under her arm, heading out to the gazebo. Her body almost hummed with a tense, unsettled feeling. Playing alone always helped to soothe her nerves. She tucked herself onto the stone bench, lowered her eyes, and picked out a low, drifting tune.

The steady rhythm of the notes, the gentle cascade of tones, slowly eased an order to her thoughts. The knots in her shoulders gradually lessened, her breathing settled into a relaxed calm. She moved on from song to song, focusing on the note progression, allowing all other thoughts to drift from her mind. The echoes of the final verse faded away into the afternoon.

A soft voice over her shoulder. “That was … stunning.”

She jolted upright, nearly tumbling the instrument from her lap. Reynald was staring at her from the entryway of the gazebo, a lost look on his face.

There was a pattering of feet, and Rachel came running toward them. “There you are!” she shouted in glee. “Oh, and look, you are playing the dulcimer. I always wanted to learn the dulcimer, but any time I touched it, Sarah would take it and start playing!”

Sarah shook her head and stood wearily, the spell of the moment broken. “I know, and I am sorry.” She looked down at the instrument. “When we first got it, I was a young teen and became enamored with it. It was wrong of me to not let you play. It was just -"

She bit her lip, looking away.

"Just that you could not stand me enjoying anything!" shot out Rachel triumphantly.

"No," retorted Sarah quickly, "No, that was not it at all." She took in a deep breath, remembering back. "I just felt things so … passionately, back then. I was in love with the dulcimer, I loved the songs. They transported me to another world. The times I heard you play, it filled me with an incredible longing to play it myself. I was thirteen … fourteen … but I should have been less selfish. I should have resisted, I should have let you have your turn playing and enjoying."

Sarah shook her head. "I imagine it was only a handful of times that I possessively took over the dulcimer while you were playing – but I also understand that it discouraged you from trying again."

"Now it is too late," muttered Rachel.

Sarah looked up. "That is hardly true! Many people learn new instruments long into adulthood. I thought you told me Michael had learned the recorder only a few years ago, and look how well he plays!"

"It is not the same," grumbled Rachel. "I should have been playing the dulcimer when I was eleven."

"I was out of the house frequently, with Marigold, learning the basics of being a midwife," pointed out Sarah. "You could have played for hours without interruption while I was gone."

"I did not want to play then," retorted Rachel. "You should have let me play when I wanted to play."

"Yes, you are right," conceded Sarah, "and I am very sorry about that. I cannot undo my mistakes from when I was a child. I can only offer you the dulcimer now, and I will teach you anything you wish to learn."

"I do not want it now," refused Rachel, shaking her head.

Sarah sighed in exasperation. "Well then …"

A shout came from the keep. “Rachel, what are you doing?” called out Mathilde with a hint of edge to her voice. “You were supposed to be finding Lou to saddle the horses!”

Rachel turned guiltily at the call, and headed off at a trot toward the stables. Sarah watched her go, her heart heavy, before reseating the dulcimer beneath her arm and walking back toward the keep.

Reynald’s voice was low. “I know it is not my place,” he murmured, “but why do you let her do that?”

“Do what?” asked Sarah distractedly.

“Berate you for incidents in your childhood, sometimes more than ten years past,” he pressed.

Sarah sighed, looking down. “She is right, I was selfish. I was at fault. I traded away her chess set because I felt I was better suited to have it, to teach her the rules. I took over the dulcimer the times she tried to play it, because it called so strongly to my soul.”

“You were only a child,” pointed out Reynald. “She has complaints about what you did when you were nine, that you should have known better. However, when she was nine, she complains that she was too young to make the right choice. At fourteen you should have controlled your love of the dulcimer – but she made no move to check her far more damaging passion and actions involving Walter when she was the same age.”

Sarah pulled to a stop, turning to face him. “What am I supposed to say?” she asked wearily. “Shall I tell her that her feelings are invalid? That she should simply stop feeling the way she does? Should I berate her for the mistakes she made as a child? That hardly seems like it would help.”

She ran a hand through her hair. “I am an adult now, and hopefully past those childhood mistakes. She is my sister, and for whatever reason, she is dissatisfied with her life. Rather than seeking to be happy, and to make improvements on her life each day, she is choosing to focus on all the wrongs done to her previously which she surely believes caused her to be the way she is now.”

She sighed. "I can support her. I can apologize for the past. I can work hard not to make those mistakes in the future. I can hope that someday she finds peace, that she accepts who she is and works to bring positive new skills into her life. However, I cannot walk that path for her – and she bristles if I try to make any suggestions to her on how to live her life. So I can only do what I can do."

"Still, you do not need to be trodden on by her," he insisted softly.

Sarah looked down. "She is my sister, and if this is what she needs to heal, to move forward, then I am happy to oblige," she insisted. She reached the door to the keep, pulling it open with a tug. She nodded to Reynald, then turned to head toward the sitting room, to replace the dulcimer and make her final preparations.

It was only a short while later that the party was heading out the main gates. Sarah glanced with calculation at the sun as they embarked on their journey. It was a full day's ride to reach where Dorrie and Walter lived, and even at a quick pace they would be hard pressed to reach there by nightfall.

They moved steadily along the road, crossing the miles in silence. The men were wary, keeping a constant eye on the surrounding fields and woods.

The way became more forested as they went, and Sarah did not argue when Reynald put her at the center of the group. As the sun eased lower in the sky, the forest slunk into ebony darkness, the branches and tree limbs twisting in the shadows along the sides of the road.

The sun dipped below the horizon. Sarah's fertile imagination picked out a wealth of threatening shapes in the shadows, and she rested her hand on the hilt of her sword. Dorrie's home was only a few miles ahead, and she was grateful they would soon be safe. It seemed as if around every corner was a new obscure form, a new sliding scurry.

The group came out of the woods' closeness into an open clearing, and Sarah peered into the surrounding shadows. The soldiers around her pulled in closer together, sharing her sense of foreboding.

Suddenly a shout filled the air. "Revenge for Bruce!" A chorus of voices took up the call. In an instant there were armed men all around, closing in quickly. Reynald wheeled to ride up beside Sarah, grabbing her reins and pulling her horse forward with his, lunging towards an opening. He slapped her horse hard on the rump to send him through it, then whirled to engage the men on either side of him.

"Run!" he cried out to her, and then he was a flurry of motion, battling to maintain two fronts at once.

Sarah's heart ripped ragged with pain. She had vowed to stay out of battle - but even her meager sword skills might at least help to distract an enemy from Reynald's embattled form. She teetered on the edge of action, watching the men below her. Then she caught Reynald's agonized glance at her in between swings, and she realized how true her father's words had been. The men would worry about her safety - and that could easily lead to their deaths. She could not allow that to happen.

She spun her horse to the east and dug in her heels. In a moment she was flying at top speed, her path leading her far away from the conflict.

Sarah thundered through the night, small branches whipping her face and arms as she rode. She ignored them, focusing on the stars above her, maintaining her route by their guide. The river came up suddenly, and she drove her steed in, fording it without hesitation. Both were soaking wet as he clambered up the steep bank on the other side.

Now she simply had to meet up with the road ...

There, the road came up on her suddenly, glistening in the glimmers of dawn. She immediately turned right on it, straining for glimpses of civilization ahead. The miles passed beneath her feet, and she could feel her horse begin to flag. It could not be that much longer ... perhaps a mile or two ... there! She saw the shape of a town ahead, and a keep up above the town. She pushed her horse to greater speed and soon was pulling to a hard stop at the gates.

It took her a moment to catch her breath as the guards hurried forward to see what the commotion was about. She struggled to gasp out, "I am Sarah. I am a friend of -"

"Of course!" cried out the guards in unison, recognizing her. They rushed to pull open the gates, and one ran forward to alert the house guards. Sarah had barely dismounted from her horse when Dorrie and Walter had hurried down the steps to join her. Dorrie, tall, lithe, with long blonde hair streaming behind her, was at her side in a moment, drawing her into a strong hug.

Walter's voice was rich with bewilderment. "Sarah, what is it?" His dark, sturdy body came up behind Dorrie as a bull approaching a swan. "Where is the rest of your party?"

Sarah waved him away for a moment. She cupped her hands and drew water from the horse trough, her throat blazing in pain. Once she felt could speak, she turned back to face the couple. Her eyes moved between Dorrie's pale face and Walter's ruddy one.

"You have got to help. The Templar bandits have the group surrounded, in fields to the west of here."

Walter did not hesitate for a moment. He swung his dark head up, calling to a nearby guard. "Get the troops mounted; we leave immediately." Activity buzzed around the courtyard at once, with men running to gather arms and horses.

Heedless of the activity, Walter turned back to Sarah, his eyes serious. "Do you remember any landmarks of the battle site?"

Sarah took a deep breath and looked around the stables. "If you have a spare mount I will lead you there," she insisted. "I can recognize it by sight, but I would not know how to explain its location to you."

When Walter hesitated, Sarah snapped in anger, her frustration lashing out. "It is Reynald out there! I have already sworn not to get involved in any combat. The least I can do is help guide you to save them!"

Walter paused a long moment, considering. Finally he nodded in acceptance. A man ran up to his shoulder, drawing to a stop. "All are ready, sir," he reported in clipped tones.

Walter turned to scan the gathered troops, mentally checking that all men were present. Finally, he turned back to the woman standing before him.

"Lead on, then," he instructed Sarah gruffly. "However, be sure to hold by your vow."

Sarah clambered onto the fresh horse brought to her. Fighting down her weariness, she spun her mount and headed back out the gates.

The ride back seemed to go more quickly, now that she knew where she was going. Walter rode at her side, his muscular bulk a reassuring presence, and the thundering of the force behind their back filled her ears.

Sarah strained to press forward as speedily as the night would allow. Every hoofbeat seemed to echo loudly in her heart as she wondered how Reynald and his men were doing. Were they hurt? Had they been captured? They had seemed outnumbered when she had left, and her mind imagined torment after torment as she rode.

Suddenly the area before her became familiar. She pulled her horse in to a trot, and at her side Walter motioned to the men to follow suit. Sarah exchanged a glance with Walter, and then despite the desperate desire in her heart, she pulled up short, waving him on. She was half crazed with worry to know how the fight had gone, but she pressed her urge down with desperate effort. She had made a vow.

As her companions plowed ahead into the darkness, she retreated to the shadows, letting them pass her by.

There was a cry up ahead, and then the group thundered down the hill with a bellow of attack. Sarah's heart raced, and she allowed herself to cautiously ride to the crest to look down into the clearing. A group of twenty men were clustered at the center of the area, surrounded by a group of bandits. Her heart pounded as she saw bodies littering the area, both dead and alive, both bandits and soldiers. Her eyes scanned … seeking …

Her heart leapt. Reynald was standing in the center of the group, his sword held out in defiance. The bandits had been circling their quarry, but they started in surprise with the cries of the new attackers. Yelling with rage, the cutthroats spun to face the fresh threat. In this instant her father's guards saw their chance. The tides of war reversed, and suddenly the ring of bandits were surrounded on both sides.

Sarah dug her nails into her palms, her body tense in anxious worry as the battle flowed back and forth. She could not spot any leader in the bandit ranks; certainly no man of the talent of the Templar Bruce from the previous fight. She wondered if Reynald had already slain the leader of this ambush, or if this group had not been headed by one of the remaining Templars.

The fight pressed on; slowly the bandits were worn down. There were five men fighting, then four. Reynald moved through them with a sure arm, joining the fight at every turn. The bandits put up a fierce battle, and two of Walter's men dropped back, wounded. Walter and Reynald circled the remaining attackers. Walter delivered a sudden thrust, and then there were three. The two men moved in with a flurry of swordwork, dodging and attacking in resolute deliberation. Another bandit fell. The men paired up …

Reynald and Walter circled and fought, their styles different, their aims aligned. Walter was short and bullish, his dark hair flying as he launched himself into each thrust. Reynald was taller, his muscular arms spinning his sword with a sure grip, blocking high and then driving for a low attack. He twisted left, and then with a quick movement drove his sword into his opponent's chest, drawing it out again in a turn, seeking Walter's location to see if he needed help. In the same moment, Walter slammed himself into his enemy's chest, bowling him over onto the ground. A slash of his blade, and the bandit lay motionless.

Sarah's heart beat into life again. The clearing seemed almost silent without the clanging of swords, even as the men moved through the area, calling out to each other as they turned over the bodies and checked for survivors.

Taking one last look over the clearing to ensure the fight was truly over, Sarah kneed her mount into motion. She pulled her steed to ride back away from the ridge, meeting up with a dark path which led down into the clearing. Once in sight of the group, she rode directly to Reynald's side, leaping down lightly as she reined up. Her feet barely touched the ground as she ran over toward him.

He glanced up as she approached, his face weary and streaming with sweat. She scanned his body as she moved. There was a cut on his upper arm, and a river of red was streaming down his right thigh from a deep gash.

"You are hurt," she called out, the swirling emotions of her mind cloaked within a professional calm. She dropped to kneel at his side, then instinctively reached to her dress to rip a long swath from its bottom. She did not stop for a moment, but worked to contain the wound.

"It is just a scratch," he insisted distractedly, but he did not seek to hinder her motions. His eyes scanned the area, alert for new threats to the men.

An ordered flurry of motion surrounded them as the soldiers helped each other onto horses and prepared to move out. The moment Sarah was done with the bandage, Reynald moved amongst the men, checking on injuries and preparing the group to head to safety. Sarah, aware of the danger, stayed out of the way of their efforts, helping with injuries where she could.

In a few moments the men had gathered themselves back into a mounted troop. Seeing that all injured men had been loaded up, Sarah mounted her own horse, dutifully falling into the center of the group without being asked. She stayed quietly in her place as they quickly made their way back to the keep.

The ride sped by in a blur; it seemed only a short while later that the company moved through the main gates and into the courtyard of the keep. There was a whirlwind of activity as the soldiers climbed down from their horses, medics came to tend to the injured men, and grooms led the exhausted steeds away.

Sarah dismounted wearily, the activity of the evening catching up with her. Even so, adrenaline still surged through her body, warming her blood. She gave her mount a pat on the rump as a stable boy led him away, then turned ...

Reynald was standing before her, his hand resting lightly on the hilt of his sword. His body was drenched with sweat and gave off a deep, musky aroma. A thin line of red traced down one cheek, and his leather armor was torn on one bicep.

It was his eyes that caught her. Even as they were worn with exhaustion, she could see the admiration as he gazed at her, patiently waiting for her to come to him.

She walked over to stand before him, hesitantly reaching out to touch the scar on his face. All pretense drained out of her, and laid herself bare. "It was an agony to ride away from you, Reynald," she admitted with quiet honesty. "If you had been seriously hurt ..." she sighed, her fingers tracing down his face.

He brought his hand up to rest it on top of hers. "If you had not returned with help, we would all have been lost," he stated plainly, holding her gaze with his own. "I know how hard it was for you to leave us, to abandon the fight. Because you did, and fetched assistance, alone, we survived. Your courage is beyond all measure."

Sarah took another step forward, and suddenly they were entwined in an embrace, pressed hard against each other. She nestled her face against his chest, overwhelmed with emotions. It had nearly killed her to leave him behind, to ride those long minutes away from him, certain that he needed her help. That he appreciated what she had gone through ...

She turned her head up to his, seeking his lips with her own. He groaned under his breath, lowering his head to kiss her - first tenderly, then with a fiercer passion. Everything else faded around her, as she lost herself in the kiss. Every part of her glowed with heat ...

A loud whinny from a passing horse reminded Sarah of their public location, but she did not hesitate for more than a moment. She took Reynald's hand and led him forward across the courtyard, into the keep, up the stairs towards the room she always took while staying here. He followed light-footed behind her, his face caught up in the same smoldering emotions.

She pressed open the heavy wooden door, and as he came through it behind her, he turned to press it shut, then to drop the bar across it. That done, he turned around to face her.

Sarah saw the passion in his eyes, the hot need of his body. Even so, he held back, not moving towards her. "God, you are beautiful," he groaned huskily. "Are you sure ..."

Sarah was never more sure of anything in her life. She crossed the two steps between them in one fluid motion, entwining herself around him with fierce passion, pressing her mouth against his in an open kiss. "Yes," she murmured against him, her voice hoarse with desire. "Yes, yes ..."

Reynald let out a low groan. He lifted her with one easy motion and carried her over to the bed, kissing her as he began stripping off layers of his clothing. Sarah wriggled out of her own, and soon they were stretched nakedly together, their bare bodies blending. Sarah's desire mounted in her until she was near bursting. She pulled Reynald down against her, feeling him slide against her. She wanted him ...

Reynald was over her, pressing in – and then suddenly he stopped. His eyes flew wide with shock, and he looked down at Sarah's face.

She pulled at him again, craving him, insistent that he continue.

"Sarah," he whispered huskily, his eyes searching hers. "You are untouched. Are you sure this is what you want?"

Sarah's eyes opened fully at that, and she nodded, her eyes holding his. "I am very sure," she breathed huskily. "Please ..."

Reynald gave out a long, ragged sigh, lowering himself to kiss her tenderly on the mouth. Then, holding her eyes with his, he moved slowly against her, easing the way. She felt the pain, but it was distant, a long way from the pleasure of the man within her arms. He held still for a few moments, then began moving against her, more and more quickly. Soon they were both reaching the heights of pleasure. The ride seemed to go on forever …

It was a long while before their breathing slowed. Laying in a tangle, Sarah was content beyond all measure. She smiled as Reynald kissed her tenderly on the cheek.

"That was far more beautiful than I had ever imagined," sighed Sarah, holding Reynald's body down against her own. "Stay just like that ... stay ..."

Her eyes closed, and sleep swept her into its gentle embrace.

Chapter 20

Sarah awoke the next morning to streaming sunshine. It was obviously long after dawn, based on the way the golden light danced through the windows. She stretched slowly, deliciously relaxed.

Suddenly she snapped awake, memories of the previous night flooding her head. A jumble of thoughts came over her at once. She was stark naked. The sheets were tangled from the lovemaking she and Reynald had shared. And most importantly … she was alone.

She climbed out of bed and moved to the dresser, finding a light robe in one of the drawers. She donned it, then moved to the window to stare out and get her bearings.

There was a fair amount of activity down in the courtyard. Men were strapping on armor and grooms were preparing horses. There were clanking noises from the armory as last minute repairs were being made to swords and greaves. Sarah looked through the hubbub for a sign of Reynald or Walter. She saw Ethan and Elijah sharpening their blades, and she recognized a few of the men from her own keep. However, the men she sought were not part of the tumult below.

She ran a hand wearily through her long hair. It was perhaps too much to ask that Reynald lounge in bed for a morning talk, with the next fight so close at hand. She should count herself lucky to have stolen even a few hours of his time. She wrapped her arms around herself tightly, thinking of the dangers he faced in the coming hours.

It was time she got dressed and joined the group. She pulled out her sword, dagger, and other gear and laid them across the end of the bed, preparing to put on her clothes.

The door swung open slowly, and she hurriedly pulled the robe closed around her. Reynald eased into the room, his eyes focused on the bed, his brow creasing in confusion when he found it empty. He swung his gaze across the room, smiling fondly as he locked eyes with her – and promptly frowning again when he spotted the gear she had laid out to wear.

"Oh, no," he warned her in a low voice, stepping forward and closing the door behind him with one smooth action. "You will not be coming with us today, Sarah."

Sarah's hackles rose. This was not how she had planned on beginning her day's conversation with Reynald! "I will most certainly be part of the group," she insisted with heat. "We have had this discussion before. I have sworn – on the Holy Bible – to stay out of any fight."

Reynald's face was firm. "That was when we thought there was a hope of there being no conflict," he stated resolutely. "We have already been viciously attacked twice in two days. Each time we barely survived. If we move on their main camp, this is going to be a serious battle. Nowhere will be safe. There will be no spot for you to sit and watch from that will not be dangerous."

"What about Abigail? What about the baby?" pressed Sarah, desperation mounting in her.

Reynald shook his head. "I love my sister very much, and once the battle is over, we will get her to safety. However, first we must win it – and that is no sure thing." He paused for a moment, his gaze serious. "It could very well be that we are all wiped out – and that it takes a fresh attack from new forces to clear this menace. We can only try our best."

Sarah blanched at the thought, and it made her even more determined to be there. Her voice became steely. "You have no right to prevent me from going," she pointed out.

Reynald took a step forward, and Sarah forced herself not to retreat in response. His eyes blazed with strong emotion. The words shot out of him full of fury and frustration.

"No right? It is my duty to keep you safe – as any man of honor would do for his future wife."

Sarah was shocked speechless by this proclamation. It was a few moments before she could pull herself up straight and stare him in the eyes to respond. Was this how he would take complete control of her actions?

"Your duty? Your wife? I believe you forgot an important part of this sequence – the proposal, and my answer."

Reynald flushed, and he opened his mouth to speak, but just at that moment a hammering came at the door.

"We are preparing to head out," called the page in a clear voice, thudding on the door a few more times before moving down the hall.

Reynald's face became caught between emotions, and he glanced quickly between the stout wooden door and the fury on Sarah's face. Sarah's anger mounted as he turned to walk toward the door. So he was going to leave this way? Well if that was how things were going to be …

To her great surprise, he stopped before the door and slid home the bolt which barred it. He turned around in place, putting his back against the door. He took a long, deep breath, and began again, his voice much quieter, his tone one of gentle reason.

"I started this all wrong, Sarah. I am sorry. It is just that we are pressed for time and everything is happening at once."

He strode the few steps toward her and dropped to one knee. He tenderly took her hand in his own, giving it a gentle kiss before looking up at her. His voice came slow and deliberate, as if he had been reciting these lines in his head for a long while.

"Sarah, from the very first days that I knew you, I realized you were a special woman. Your wisdom, your patience, your intelligence, and your honor are all traits I have sought in a partner for years. The trust others can place in you, your respect for duty, your ability to tell the truth in all situations, these have great meaning to me."

He paused, his eyes gazing deep into hers. "I would be immensely proud to have you by my side."

Sarah's heart melted with the words, words she had dreamt of hearing for so long. He respected her … he was proud of her.

She looked down at where his hand held hers, at the strength and capability represented by that grasp.

And still … a seed of doubt lodged in her heart. He had not said he loved her … and this proposal conveniently came when he wanted her to follow his orders. Was he expecting her to turn into his obedient slave once she said yes? Would her answer of a single word remove all independence of thought and action? Would he, like Simon and Dirk, expect her to give up her midwife activities, her chosen way of life? The thought stung her.

Just how real was this proposal, after all? She had not seen any signs of courtship from him in the past. All in all it seemed rather convenient; a guaranteed method to force her to remain behind.

Her anger flared that she was being so heartlessly manipulated.

She tossed her head at the tumbled sheets. "You speak of duty?" she asked him harshly. "Perhaps this sudden proposal is naught but an act of duty, then. It is your required, 'honorable' response to what we did last night, and your aim to have absolute say over my actions in the coming days." Her shoulders tightened at the thought of being a helpless minion with no say over her life. It would not come to that, not if she could help it!

The thought insistently pressed at her again that he had not mentioned love in his proposal. It drilled into her heart that this was an action of logic, not emotion. She found herself adding in a low growl, "Surely if you really *cared* for me all these weeks as you say, you would have courted me properly."

Reynald flushed and looked down. "You are right. I should have resisted the temptation of last night," he admitted with a mixture of frustration and shame. "Despite your insistence that we go through with it, I should have refused."

Sarah's fury piqued at this, her brain jumping to a new thread for no logical reason. "Are you saying I am incapable of deciding for myself what I want and when I want it? That you need to decide for me what is right for me?" She knew she was overreacting, but she could not help herself. It seemed to prove again that Reynald's aim was to control her life, to tell her what to do and think.

Reynald looked up at this, shaking his head quickly even as she finished. He seemed to be choosing his words with care now, his face serious, pleading. "It is not that at all. If you are saying you would rather have had a proper courting first, I should have known that and respected it."

Sarah sighed in exasperation. Everything was coming out wrong. "That is not what I meant at all. I did not mean you had to court me in order to lie with me."

Somehow that sounded even worse.

She took a deep breath and began again. "Reynald, I am quite content with my decision to be with you last night. You are heading out into a fierce battle – a battle which could take your life." The realization ran through her again just how serious the day's events were going to be, and she blushed, looking down at the man who knelt at her feet. Her voice became quieter and gentler as she continued, "Truly, Reynald, I am very much at ease with what we did. I would not take that back for anything. Still, it does not mean I expected anything in return."

She looked away for a moment, letting the anger settle out of her, struggling against the confusion that remained. Just what was it that she really feared here? After a moment she attempted to put it into words.

"I have seen too many couples marry because of one indiscretion – and endure years of agony as a result. I would not have that be the situation here. What I was pointing out is that you had not shown any inkling of courting me in the past. It is hard for me to believe you suddenly have these strong feelings for me. It is quite a step to jump from a casual friendship to a life-long marriage." She paused for a moment, then pressed on. "To do it because of one night's actions seems … impulsive."

Reynald glanced out the window at the rising noise of the milling troops, his face caught up in torment for a moment. Then he stood again to move in front of her gaze, ensuring she saw his face. His face eased from tenderness to a more deliberate, serious look.

"We do not have the time to go into the past right now. Let us deal with what is before us."

He took in a deep breath, then let it out. "Sarah, this is not simply some abstract sense of duty," he pressed. "There is the very real chance that you are with child now, as the result of our actions. If I die today, I would not want that child to be treated as a bastard – to be ridiculed his entire life as a son or daughter who was unwanted. I want to ensure that the world knows how much I care for you. I want the world to know – if you will let me – that I have every intention of recognizing and raising that child as my own."

Sarah flushed at this. She of all people should have thought of the consequences of her action. Reynald was right – and his aims were quite worthy of praise. She looked down in confusion.

Reynald put a hand beneath her chin, raising her eyes to meet his. "I want to have some arrangement known just in case … but I will only ask for an engagement," he suggested quietly. "If I return safely, let me prove to you – over time - that I can be a good husband, that I have the financial ability to care for you and our family. Let me speak with your father, and elicit his approval. Whatever questions you have, I will answer them with complete honesty. Whatever concerns you have, I will do my best to address them."

A look of worry shaded his face. "If it turns out that you truly do not want to be with me, and a month has passed so that we know no child has been created, then we can end the engagement with little fanfare."

He took a deep breath. "Even if you are with child – if you would raise the child alone, or with another man rather than with me …" His voice caught for a moment, but with visible effort he forced himself to continue. "I will respect your decision, and not contest it."

He took both of her hands in his own, and his eyes became full of tender pleading. "Just know this, Sarah. *I love you.* I have loved every new aspect of you that I have discovered over the past weeks. You would make me the happiest man on earth if you gave me the opportunity to grow and learn with you for the rest of our lives."

Sarah's breath caught at his words.

He loved her.

This was not just about duty and honor. This was not simply about a child. He loved *her.*

A flood of emotions overtook her, and she found the strength, finally, to give voice to the doubt which had been lodged in her heart since the first moment she had seen Reynald.

"What about Rachel?"

Reynald froze. "Rachel?" he asked in confusion.

A louder hammering came on the door. "We are leaving *now!*" called the sharp voice.

Reynald turned, his face a mirror of anguish. He took the few steps toward the door and slid the bar free. "I am coming," he growled through the door, putting his hand on the latch. He turned back to look towards Sarah, his face tight.

"Please, at least, think about it …"

Time stopped. She could see every movement in his face, in his body, as he began to turn away from her. Her feelings descended on her in a sudden rush, and she was running … running …

"Yes! Yes!" she cried out, wrapping her arms around him, clinging to him with all of her might. "If you truly want me as I am, then I will be honored to have you as my husband."

Reynald's arms folded around her to draw her in close, and he lifted her up to spin her in a circle. When he placed her gently back on the ground again, he stepped back a pace to smile down at her. He slowly pulled free his signet ring from his hand. He took Sarah's left hand in his own, placing the ring on her finger with tender care. When he had finished, he looked up and held her gaze.

"You will not be sorry," vowed Reynald. "I will wait as long as you wish before we announce the engagement, and for the ceremony. I would just like to tell Father Xavier who manages the chapel here. I spoke with him briefly this morning, while you were asleep. That way we have a witness, in case I am slain and you are pregnant."

He pressed a tender kiss against her hair. "I will do everything I can to prove to you that I am worthy. Over time I pray that you will grow to love me as much as I love you."

Sarah's voice caught. A rock of doubt still nagged her. It was time to bring it out into the open. Now was not the time for half measures. If Reynald appreciated the truth, here it was.

She took a step back from him, to stand in the center of the room. "Now that we are engaged," she instructed him with a calm she did not feel, "I need you to tell me your true feelings about Rachel. Be fully honest – I promise I can accept anything, as long as it is the truth."

Reynald took a step toward her, his face layered with joy and caution. "You are sure you wish to hear this now?"

Sarah nodded mutely. She steeled her heart to be strong.

Reynald seemed uncertain, but he visibly braced himself. "Then let this be our first test, the first proof that I will do as you ask, and not mince words."

He took a deep breath, then let it out. "I find her to be self-absorbed and immature. She has little regard for how her actions affect others around her. When she presses on me so that she touches me, I feel as if I have accidentally stepped into used dishwater." His lips clamped shut, and he stood silent, waiting.

Sarah reeled as if she had been struck. Her eyes flew wide with shock, and she saw Reynald retreat slightly within himself, almost preparing for a blow. She could only manage to gasp out, "Is this truly how you feel?"

Reynald nodded. "You have asked for the truth, and that is what I have given you."

Sarah could not take it in. "Rachel is buxom," she protested in confusion. "She is bubbly, flirtatious, friendly! She is beautiful, blonde … everything I am not."

Reynald looked at her in growing wonder. "How can you see your world so differently than I do?" he mused. "Do you forget the suitor you just had to turn away? Do you not see the admiration in the eyes of the guards who have ridden with you these last days?"

He took a step forward. "There is no doubt in my mind. It is you that I love, you that I respect." He searched for a way to explain his feelings in a way Sarah would understand. His eyes lit on the carved wooden cross at her throat. "That necklace you wear, it is not golden and jeweled, as the one your sister has. Why do you treasure it?"

Sarah's hand automatically went to her neck. "It was hand made personally for me, from a man I helped," she reminisced. "The care put into it is far more valuable than gems or jewels to me."

Reynald nodded. "When I look at Rachel, I see all the men she has waved her body at, men she had no interest in, men she used and discarded. It makes her attractions … cheap." His eyes tenderly held hers. "When I look at you, I remember the way you were ready to defend your friends at the burnt-out camp. I remember the dedication you poured into helping Cecily. Your honor and perseverance are far more appealing to me than any short-lived flirtatious charm could ever be."

A wave of relief swept over her. She finally had a glimmer of understanding about Reynald's feelings. Had she really been mistaken all this time?

"I thought you lusted after Rachel!" she blurted out, tears springing from her eyes. She let them fall, overwhelmed with joy.

Reynald shook his head in wonder. "You know me, Sarah. You know my drive for honor and truth. There was never any question about how I felt." His eyes held hers. "I tried to tolerate her, for your sake, but it was you I cared for, from the first. You were so distant; I thought if I showed you how well I could fit in with your family -"

"Distant?" cried out Sarah, her heart overwhelmed with how wrong she had been. "I love you! I have loved you since … I do not know since when. It seems now as if I have always loved you, from that first day when you carried me in your arms …"

Reynald's face went pale, and he took a step toward her, holding her arms. "You love me?" he asked in a shaky voice. "I have only dared to hope that maybe … someday …"

"Yes," murmured Sarah, her eyes captivated in his gaze. "Oh, how I love you …" Tears cascaded down her face, and she paid them no mind. Nothing else mattered.

There was a loud crash behind them, and the door flung open. Walter stormed into the room, his eyes blazing with frustration.

His gaze swept across the room, taking in the bloody sheets, Sarah's tear-stained face and Reynald's grasp of her arms, and his look went from frustration to fury in a heartbeat. He drew his sword and moved on Reynald with a stormy glare.

Reynald threw his arms wide, keeping them clear of his weapons. "Wait, I can explain!"

Walter's sword was at his throat in a moment, and the burly man held it there with a firm grasp.

Sarah flew to Walter's side, gently pulling him backwards. "Let him be," she reassured Walter, wiping the tears from her face. "These are tears of joy, I swear it!"

Walter's voice came out in an angry growl. "The cur took advantage of you, and battle skills or no, we will have him punished!"

Sarah shook her head, still pulling back on Walter. "It was I who wanted to spend the night with Reynald," she insisted. "He offered to stop, several times. I pressed him to continue. It was my choice."

Walter did remove his sword from Reynald's neck at this, and turned to stare at Sarah, a shocked look on his face. "Sarah – this is behavior more worthy of your sister!"

Sarah's face blazed in anger at the comment. Was Walter so innocent, himself, that infamous night he had run off with her sister? Out of the corner of her eye she saw Reynald's hand drop instinctively to the hilt of his sword.

"I am an adult," she snapped at Walter, her voice full of steel. She tossed her head at the bloodied sheets. "Also, as you can see, I do not give my favors out lightly."

She took a step backwards to stand at Reynald's side. "I love Reynald. He has earned my respect a thousand times over. The last two days have shown me how little time we may have together. This is hardly the time for a wedding or any other such ceremony. If this was to be our last night together, then by God I will spend it with him in the way that I wish!"

Walter slowly lowered his sword, and a wry grin spread across his face. "Now there is the Sarah that I remember," he chuckled. His eyes raised to meet Reynald's. "Sir, what are your intentions?"

Reynald held his gaze firmly. "I have proposed to Sarah, and she has accepted my offer. She is to be my wife." He put an arm gently around her shoulder.

A thrill coursed through her at his words, and she leant in against him. She was going to be with Reynald, raise a family with him … wake up every morning next to him …

Footsteps came racing down the hall, and in a moment Dorrie burst into the room. "There you are," she cried out, spotting her husband. In a rush she drew in the state of the bed, Sarah's disarray, and the fact that both men had drawn weapons. "What in the world?"

Sarah stepped forward, interceding immediately. "We are engaged to be married!"

"Oh, Sarah!" cried out Dorrie with joy, and she ran forward to give her friend an enthusiastic embrace. Sarah's joy glowed through her as if she were filled with all the stars of the night sky.

Chapter 21

Once the other three had left the room to head downstairs, Sarah hurriedly donned her clothes, leaving behind the sword. She did understand Reynald's concerns about the fight, and as much as it would cause her anguish, she would remain here rather than put him in further jeopardy. If it would keep him even a small bit safer, it was a sacrifice she was willing to make.

She ran down the stairs to join up with the group. Reynald spotted her the moment she came into the main room, and put out an arm for her to join him at his side. There were cheers and congratulations shouted all around, and Sarah blushed. It had all happened so quickly …

She looked up at Reynald, aware again that this might be the last time she saw him. Worry lanced her soul, and she pressed herself against him. He wrapped his arm more closely about her, holding her near.

Sarah's voice was hoarse. "If only there was a way to have a parlay with them," she sighed, her mind running through any possibility which might be helpful. "You said that Charles, at least, was once a friend of yours. If only there was someone he could talk to as an intermediary - a priest, his father, anyone."

Reynald put a gentle kiss on her forehead. "I am afraid we have chased down every possibility we could," he informed her resolutely. "It comes down to a fight."

He tilted his head down to hers, and Sarah gave him a slow, tender kiss, pouring all of her love and affection into the action. It was several moments before he drew away. Around them, the men were heading out into the courtyard, and Reynald reluctantly moved with them.

Dorrie came up alongside Sarah as their two partners found their horses and prepared to mount. Sarah found herself near tears again. "How do women do this?" she asked Dorrie, her voice shaky. "How can you watch them leave, knowing you might never see them again – that they will die without you there to help, to give them a final farewell?"

Dorrie gave her friend a tender hug. "In our own way, women are as strong as men are," she commented softly. "We must have the willpower to stay behind, when it is our being safe that gives our husbands the ability to fight with the greatest focus."

Sarah shook her head. "If only there was some other way. If only Charles' priest was still alive … if only his mother was still alive …"

Dorrie turned her eyes to stare at Sarah. "Charles of Swindon? He is the Templar you are after? But his mother *is* still alive," she offered with confusion.

Sarah turned to face her friend fully. "What do you mean? I thought Charles' mother died years ago."

Dorrie shook her head. "When her son left for the crusades, Charles' mother was furious. She therefore left her life – she sold off her belongings and joined a nunnery. She had it put out that she was now dead to the world."

Her brow wrinkled in surprise at her friend's confusion. "Surely I have told you about her? I see her occasionally when I go to visit Sister Cora - Tanya's mother. They are at the Holy Mary of Grace nunnery, perhaps a twenty minute ride."

Sarah did not hesitate. She lit out at a run straight to Reynald's side. He looked down as she came, his brow creased with worry. "I know this is hard, Sarah, but -"

Sarah skidded to a stop. "Charles' mother is alive!" she shouted, her heart pounding. "There is another way!"

Walter's head came around to stare at the couple. "Are you sure?" he asked, his voice echoing his disbelief.

Sarah nodded with her head towards Dorrie, who was watching the scene with confusion. "She has seen her at the nunnery several times. Charles' mother didn't die – she simply chose a new life."

Walter looked at Reynald with a glimmer of hope in his eyes. "That is a short ride from here. We could be there and back in no time, and if it is true …"

Reynald called over to the grooms. "Saddle up two horses for Sarah and Dorrie." He looked over to Walter. "I hope you agree – I believe they should come with us. This might be a situation that needs a women's touch to sort out."

Walter nodded in understanding. "My wife has been to visit the nunnery many times. They know her there. This is a task that is best handled with the softest of kid gloves."

The men waited as the horses were brought and the two women mounted. In only a few moments the four were headed out the gates, toward the nunnery.

Sarah relished the simple pleasure of cantering alongside Reynald through the beautiful morning sunshine. She glanced over to the man at her side every few minutes, caught up in just how proud she was to be engaged to him. He was all that she could ask for in a man – strong, trustworthy, and honorable.

Her looks did not go unnoticed; Reynald nudged his horse closer to hers as they rode down the lane, giving her a smile of contentment that melted her heart. She treasured every moment with him, and prayed that the nunnery would provide a solution that saved the men from a brutal battle.

All too soon they pulled up to the main gates of the nunnery. The guards recognized Dorrie at once. "Greetings there, M'Lady! Is this your husband you have with you? Who are your other two friends?"

Dorrie smiled down at the men. "The lady is my life long companion, Sarah. With Sarah is her new fiancé; they were just engaged this morning!"

Sarah blushed as the guards shouted out their congratulations and encouragements while pulling open the large iron grate gates. There was a large open area, and she saw that one low stone building to the right held the stables. Other stone buildings were laid around the grassy courtyard, and the main church and halls were straight ahead.

The four moved towards the stables, relinquishing their mounts to the sister who waited within. Then they turned to head to the main hall.

Sarah saw movement in one of the upper windows, but before she could discern who it might be, a short, plump woman came hurrying towards them from the herb gardens to the left.

"Dorrie, is that you?" called the woman with delight. "It is always wonderful when you visit. Who have you brought …" Her eyes opened wide with surprise. "Why Sarah, it has been years!" she cried out. "Do you even remember me?"

Sarah stepped forward with a tender smile. "Of course I do, Cora," she protested gently. "You were like a second mother to me. How are you?" She gave the woman a warm embrace, then stepped back to allow Dorrie to take her turn.

"This is my husband, Walter," introduced Dorrie with a smile. "And the other gentleman is Reynald, newly engaged to Sarah."

"My congratulations!" cried out Cora with a wide smile. "I am so happy that you have found someone to be with." Her discerning eyes moved from Reynald to Walter, then back to Dorrie again. "I see that this is not a social visit …?"

Dorrie nodded. "You are astute as usual, my friend. I am afraid that we need to talk with sister Gertrude about her son."

Cora's eyes became shadowed. "I thought it might come to this at some point," she admitted with regret. "I will bring you to Mother Superior. She will insist that we have the conversation in her presence. Wait here, and I will find someone to fetch Gertrude as well."

She hurried off toward the stables. After she had left, Sarah turned to Reynald, her mind sifting through the situation. "I imagine Charles would not believe us if we simply told him his mother was alive. We will have to ask to bring her with us to him – so that he sees her in person and agrees to speak with her."

Reynald's eyes sharpened as he looked at Sarah. "We? I thought we had agreed that you would remain behind."

Sarah kept her tone even and straightforward. "That was when the only solution involved an all out war. I understand that I would have little to offer in that situation. Now you are bringing an elderly woman on a journey of several days, in order to have a truce discussion. She will need someone to help her, someone to assist her in ways which would be inappropriate for a man. If you are to keep her safe, it is no harder to keep both of us safe."

Reynald took in a deep breath, but Cora was joining them again, motioning them forward. They headed up the stone steps, passing into the large, decorative main hallway. In a few moments time they were moving up a long set of wooden stairs to a landing. Before them stood a pair of ornate oak doors, with a sign beside them indicating that this was the Mother Superior's receiving room.

Cora had barely knocked on the doors when an austere voice called out, "Do come in."

Cora slowly opened the door. The room within was richly furnished with fine mahogany chairs, shelves, and a desk to one corner. A trio of large windows overlooked the main courtyard, and a fireplace lay dormant on the back wall. The summer sun streamed in warmly, and two windows let in a gentle breeze.

Cora made the introductions while the group bowed and curtsied. Sarah and Dorrie took a pair of seats side by side, and their men stood behind them, putting themselves quietly in a subordinate position.

Footsteps sounded outside the door, and Sarah turned to see a woman in her sixties, looking leathered rather than wrinkled, enter the room. She was tall, perhaps five foot nine, and straight as a pole. Her arms and legs were well muscled, and her eyes carried a no-nonsense look in them. The sole decoration on her simple habit was a wooden pin above her breast, in the shape of a dove.

She made her obeisance to Mother Superior, then turned to scan the occupants of the room. "I knew it would come to this," she snapped out in a rough, deep voice. "Well, out with it. What has my son done now that you need my help with."

Mother Superior's eyebrow twitched, but her face was serene as she motioned towards a chair. "Perhaps you might sit, Gertrude," she offered with solicitude. "This could take a little while to explain."

Gertrude shrugged and took the seat indicated, planting her feet down solidly once she had settled in. "Fine, talk away," she agreed, looking to Dorrie and Sarah with a tolerant air.

Dorrie glanced at Sarah before beginning. "You know who I am; we have spoken several times on my previous visits. The man behind me is my husband, Walter. With us are Sarah, who is known to Cora, and her fiancé, Reynald. Reynald served with your son in the Knights Templar."

Gertrude's glance flickered to Reynald's, her eyes stoic. "You poor man," she offered with a short laugh. "I imagine that was not much fun." She immediately looked back to Sarah and Dorrie, dismissing him. "So?"

Dorrie turned to Sarah, who took up the thread. "Charles was a well respected knight, and performed his duties fairly," she explained to the mother. "That was, up until he heard news of your passing. The grief that he was not with you at your deathbed overwhelmed him."

Gertrude scoffed at this, but Sarah could see a softening of her eyes. Encouraged, Sarah pressed forward with the story. "In his despair, Charles took to drink, and he fell in with a rough crowd. The two men who he spent the most time with were far from ideal companions. They turned him from his proper path, slowly, and finally convinced him to leave the Holy Land to return home. They now seem to use their skills and strength to harm those they should be protecting."

Gertrude nodded. "I had heard of the goings on in the area. I knew it sounded like the typical bullying of Templars." She snorted a laugh. "How that group ever got the power they have now, I am sure I do not know."

Sarah could sense Reynald stiffen behind her, and she spoke quickly to diffuse the situation. "These cutthroats are renegade rogues. They have violated every Templar pledge with their actions. We have already killed one of the trio in a fight. Your son and the other Templar have a large group of men at their command, however. If we cannot find a peaceful way out of this, dozens of men will die in the next day or two before peace returns to this area."

Gertrude sat back, considering. "It does put a damper on my weekly riding plans, to have cutthroats loose in the woods," she murmured with a distracted air. "Also, I suppose I do have some responsibility for the whelp that I raised."

She stretched languorously, then cracked her knuckles and looked at Sarah. "Fine. When do we leave?"

The mother superior, who had been watching the interchange with a tolerant gaze, put up a hand. "Not so quickly," she reminded the group. "There are still some issues I would like to have settled before I agree to this."

All eyes turned to her, and she waited a moment before continuing. "First, Gertrude, talk with Cora before you go. You may be gone for quite a while; the rehabilitation of your son may take longer than you think. Be sure Cora understands your current assignments."

"Done," responded Gertrude without a pause. "Cora and I swap off tasks every few days, to keep our minds agile. She is fully aware of everything I do and can take over immediately."

"Next," ticked off Mother Superior, moving smoothly on, "I do not want for you to be the sole woman in a group of soldiers. That seems inappropriate for a woman in your position." Her gaze swept to Dorrie and Sarah. "Perhaps one of you would be capable of attending to her?"

"Of course," offered Sarah instantly, detecting a gleam in the old woman's eye. She smiled her thanks while keeping her voice even. "I would be quite proud to escort your nun safely to and from this task."

Mother Superior stood, and the assembled people moved to rise with her. "Then it is settled. I see no cause to delay further, then," she prompted with a steady smile. "Be on your way, and God's grace light your every step."

True to her word, Gertrude was only ten minutes in gathering items from her room before she rejoined the others down at the stables. Sarah was not surprised when the athletic woman climbed easily onto a sturdy mount, wheeling him about with a practiced hand. Gertrude hardly seemed a woman who needed a chaperone.

Sarah looked up at the main hall, and saw a woman's figure standing in the windows there. She lifted a hand in farewell and thanks, and saw the figure mirror her action.

At first the men set a slow pace, wanting to be gentle on the nun in their midst, but after five minutes she gave an exasperated snort and spurred her horse into action, stretching him out into an easy canter along the road. Walter gave Reynald an amused grin before moving to match her speed.

In no time at all they were pulling into the courtyard. The men were stirring in an anxious mob, and all heads turned as one when the horses came in amongst them. Reynald pulled up alongside the nun, looking towards her with solicitous concern. "Would you like to rest a while before we head out?"

Gertrude scoffed and spun her horse around. "Get this show on the road," she called out, her face lighting up in anticipation.

Reynald exchanged a look with Walter, and Walter moved his horse alongside Dorrie's. He took her hand in his, giving her a tender kiss which he held for a long moment. Then with a nod of his head, the force moved out through the bright summer sunshine.

Sarah found herself enjoying the ride immensely. Gertrude had a rough demeanor, but her mind was quick as a whip and she offered lively discussion. It was soon clear that she was thrilled at being a part of this adventure. Ethan and Elijah, assigned to their protection, rode close alongside the two women. The men kept them within reach at all times, their eyes sharp on the surrounding woods.

Reynald and Water took turns riding ahead of and behind the group, talking with the troops and watching the landscape they rode through. Every member of the entourage was on edge and alert, well aware of the dangers which surrounded them.

As the sun dipped toward the horizon, Reynald called a halt to the group, and they set up camp in a clearing to one side of the road.

Sarah took care to ensure that Gertrude was comfortable, and brought over bread and cheese for them to eat as a simple dinner.

"Are you sure this will be enough for you?" Sarah asked the older woman with concern as the pair sat back against a large oak tree.

Gertrude smiled with pleasure, looking around the woods, at the quiet hubbub moving around the campfire. "Are you kidding?" she asked jovially. "This is great! After all of this time of being cooped up in the nunnery, it is wonderful to be out."

Sarah took a bite of her bread. "Why did you join the order, then, if you do not enjoy it?"

Gertrude patted her on the arm. "Ah, lass, I do enjoy it. I have the company of great friends, and we accomplish wondrous things when we work together. It is simply nice to get out into the world every once in a while, to explore beyond those grey walls."

Sarah smiled, looking around her. "It is very lovely here," she agreed. Her eyes came back to Gertrude, then to the wooden dove at her breast. "That pin is beautiful as well," she added thoughtfully. The delicate artistry of the work brought to mind the cross she wore around her own neck. "Where did you get that?"

Gertrude's face softened for a moment, and she lowered her hand to hold the piece for a moment. "My son carved it for me, before he left me on his fool's errand," she whispered, half to herself.

Her gaze moved to rest on Sarah, and her eyes took on a look of gentle pity. "You know, my dear, that once a man goes off with the Templars, he changes. His world is the open sea and far off horizons. He can no longer be bounded by the close confines of an English town."

Iron bands crept close around Sarah's chest. "What do you mean?"

Gertrude pressed her lips together for a moment. "When Reynald catches these two Templars, what will he do next?"

"He said he had to …" Sarah moved a hand to her chest, words failing her. He would have to escort them back to the Holy Land, for justice. And, as his wife, he would expect her to go with him. She could be away for years, away from the women who depended on her, away from her family who relied on her.

Gertrude nodded quietly in understanding. "Life is rarely as easy as one might hope."

Sarah wrapped her arms around herself, coming to terms with the knowledge. She had known it was too good to be true, after all. They could share their love until this current quest was completed. And then she would have to let him go.

There were footsteps, and she drew a smile on her face. She would treasure every moment she had with him, and count each one as valuable as the most precious of jewels.

Reynald stopped before them bearing a pair of sturdy metal cups. He handed them down with a smile to the two women. "How are you bearing up?" he asked the nun congenially.

"Could not be better," responded Gertrude heartily. She grabbed the cup and downed half of the mead in one long pull. "We should do this more often."

Reynald shook his head, his eyes holding hers. "We are on a serious mission," he reminded the nun, looking carefully at her.

Gertrude took another drink of her honeyed beverage. "Life is serious," she snapped evenly. "The longer you live, the more you learn to appreciate the good moments amongst it all." She looked up to meet Reynald's eyes. "Do not worry. We will get your sister out of this in one piece, and her child as well. Charles will see reason once he talks with me." Her eyes looked off into the distance for a moment. "Abigail was one of the good ones; we will get her out of this."

Reynald's eyes snapped to attention. "You know my sister?"

Gertrude shrugged and nodded. “Yes, certainly. Cora and I exchanged jobs frequently, and Cora’s special interest was in helping local teenage girls. I imagine it is how Abigail knew about Sarah, that she was a trustworthy midwife.” Her eyes moved to Sarah speculatively, then returned to meet Reynald’s.

“Yes, Abigail came in a few times. She was a bright enough lass, and helped me with my gardening more than once.” Her eyes twinkled with amusement. “She told me about you, Reynald. Said you were a bit big for your britches.”

Reynald sputtered in surprise. “She said what?”

Gertrude chuckled. “Relax, there, son. Abigail loves you very much. She just felt that your big brothering was sometimes a little … overzealous.”

Reynald’s face grew serious. “I only wanted to keep her safe.”

Gertrude shook her head. “There is no safety in this life. You have to live it to the best of your ability, and take responsibility and pride in your actions each day.”

Reynald nodded quietly in agreement.

There was a call from the other side of the camp, and he glanced up. “Good evening, ladies,” he offered, then moved along to check on the rest of his men. Sarah finished her meal in silence, lost in thought, and then helped Gertrude settle in for sleep.

Once the nun was asleep, Sarah rose, restless. So many things had happened today … she looked around and caught Reynald’s eyes. Without a word he came over to her, took her hand, and led her out of the main clearing into a secluded corner of the forest.

The moment they were alone, Sarah pressed herself hard against him, feeling his arms come up around her, holding her, pressing her in close. She raised her face to his, and he tenderly kissed her, his embrace firm and strong.

It was a long while before he pulled back from her, gazing down at her with glowing eyes. “It feels like a dream,” he whispered softly.

Sarah's heart tinged with sadness. "I wish it were a dream, that it could go on forever like this," she admitted quietly.

A shade of worry crossed Reynald's brow. "What do you mean?"

Sarah pulled away slightly, looking away from his insightful eyes. "I am the trout, and you are the horse," she muttered softly to herself.

Reynald's face went white, and he gently turned her head to face his again. "Tell me what you feel, and together we will find a solution. Surely there is nothing we cannot overcome as a couple."

Sarah was caught in his gaze. He was at once so strong and so vulnerable. She was pulled by the urge to turn away, but fought against it.

"This small region of England, as tiny as it might seem to you, is my world, my pond," she explained wearily. "It is only a portion of one island, and that island is but a tiny part of the larger world. I know that, and yet I love it here. I love being with my family, visiting my friends, helping those around me. It is where I want to be."

She took in a deep breath. "You live in a vast world, and you cross it at will. Your duties lie in the dust-filled world at the far eastern edge of the Mediterranean Sea." Her eyes filled with tears. "God, I love you, Reynald, I truly do. Yet I do not know how this can work."

Reynald gave a deep, cleansing sigh, and his eyes lit with hope. "Is this the only impediment that concerns you, that you would be ripped from your home?"

Sarah nodded cautiously. "Is that not serious enough?"

Reynald leant forward to tenderly kiss her on the forehead. "I have already talked with your father about this. The sheriff in your region is old and considering retirement. My name has been offered up as his replacement. There is a fine house to go with the position, a few miles away from your parents' keep. Surely you know the one I speak of."

Sarah could barely allow herself to hope. "But your Templar duties?"

Reynald ran a hand down her hair, reassuring her. "I have given the Templars over a decade of my life. That is enough. My obligation with them is long past paid. Once I have returned the prisoner or prisoners for justice, I will be done with their order."

His face became shadowed. "I do have a duty to finish out that specific task, though. This could take several months, between the travel time and other associated tasks involving the courts. I understand your duties are important as well, and I will leave you in your father's care until I return."

His face stilled, and he looked down at her. His voice dropped to a mere whisper. "If you did not wish to wait for me, I of course understand."

"Oh, Reynald," sighed Sarah, tenderly laying a hand against his cheek. "I have waited for you for twenty-two years. A few more months will be as the flight of a swallow's wings. Of course I will wait for you."

She thought of how quickly the months would spin by while she tended to the women in her care. During that time, Reynald would be traveling across interesting landscapes … back in the exciting world of the Templars. He would be surrounded by exotic sights … exotic women …

Her voice became hushed. "Even so, I would understand if, once you are back at your life's work, that you decided not to return to England after all."

Reynald pulled her into a hard embrace, pressing his face down against hers. "What a pair we are," he sighed softly. "We will have to learn to trust each other, to have faith."

They stood together for a long while, not speaking, before heading back into the main camp to sleep.

Dawn came with gentle tendrils of light, and Sarah was struck with the quiet beauty of the woods. A soft mist lingered in the valleys, and she stood, stretching. She spotted Reynald standing by the main path, looking down the road ahead. She moved to stand alongside him.

"Today will be the day," he stated softly, not turning. "It will tell whether we fight or negotiate a peace."

Sarah lay her hand on his arm, gently reassuring him with her presence. "Charles will see reason," she whispered encouragingly. "We will save your sister and your niece."

Behind them, the myriad of clanks and groans grew as the camp stirred into life. As one they turned to help with preparations for the day.

It was a much more somber group that took the trail after breakfast, all eyes and ears on full alert. They had a general idea where the bandits had set up their base, but undoubtedly scouts and other outliers were scattered about the area. The hours moved by slowly, and although the sun climbed up into the highest reaches of the sky, the forest remained musty and dark.

Reynald moved to the front of the column, and at his orders the group slowed its pace. The forest seemed to widen into a clearing ahead. An owl gave a call to his left, and although many of the soldiers turned their heads, seeking to pick out the source of the sound, Reynald's eyes focused straight ahead. A motion of his hand, and Ethan and Elijah pulled in even more closely alongside Gertrude and Sarah, drawing their weapons. Sarah's hand strayed to her own sword, but she stayed silent. She glanced sideways at Gertrude. The nun was stoically quiet, her eyes calm and prepared.

The clearing was somber and empty as they entered. Ahead of them a large wall of rock stretched, and a small pool lay to the left. Dense woods ringed the other sides of the opening. Sarah felt as if she could hear every twig snap, every horse's soft whinny as the group moved out into the open area.

Suddenly a tall, broad shouldered man walked out onto the top of the cliff, twenty feet above them. A line of archers moved into view on either side of him, bows drawn. Reynald instantly put up a hand, and the group of soldiers as one pulled to a stop. Reynald then rode ten feet ahead of his troop, looking up at the figure.

"Charles, it has been a while," he called up to the man. "It is good to see you."

"I have left your world behind, Reynald," warned Charles in a deep voice. "You do not belong here. Because you were once my friend, I will give you one chance. Leave now, and I will let you go in peace."

Reynald shook his head. "You know I cannot do that, Charles." He paused, and when he spoke again, his voice held a quiet poignancy. "What happened, Charles. We made a vow."

Charles took a step forward, coming to the very edge of the cliff. "You have no right to talk to me of vows, of fairness," he ground out, his voice hoarse. "I gave the best years of my life to the Templars. I spent months in the rain, in the mud, risking my life. What does life provide in return? My mother dies, alone, uncared for!"

He scowled and swept his hand. "I have formed a new clan with like-minded men. We will live in the woods, beholden to none, responsible solely for our own mouths."

Reynald's voice tinged with a harsh edge. "How about the men you killed at the wanderer's camp? The innocent women you took captive?"

Charles shook his head in disagreement. "That was Bruce. He and I parted ways. Denis, too, is on his own. I have harmed no person – and I will not be ordered by the likes of you. I tell you again. Return to where you have come from. I am alone now."

There was a movement to Sarah's side, and Charles' mouth fell open in shock. He staggered forward, his face going white.

Finally, he was able to make a sound. "Mother?"

In a second he was half scrambling, half falling down the slope, tumbling and running and crying out in joy as he sped towards Gertrude. She had dismounted, and her hard face had melted into softness as she opened her arms to her son. They embraced in a tender sweep.

Several long minutes went by before Charles took a step back from his mother, his face wet with tears. "But … I thought you were dead …" he croaked out in confusion.

Gertrude put a hand to her son's face. "Not my body, dear child. Simply my soul. My faith had been reborn, and I entered a new life."

Reynald walked softly toward the pair. "Your mother lives not far from here, Charles," he explained in a quiet voice.

Charles' face lit up with a contented smile. "You live …"

Without turning, he motioned his hand in the air. Behind him, twenty sets of bows slowly lowered to point toward the ground.

Gertrude's face took on a more serious look. "Now, Charles, I hear you have some guests here."

Charles reddened, and he glanced at Reynald for a moment before looking down again. "Those visitors were brought in by Bruce, and I did not question him on his aims. I know that I should have spoken up. I lost direction when I thought I had lost you," he admitted to his mother in a low voice. "I have done things that I am ashamed of."

Her gaze did not waver. "The Lord is merciful. Now it is time to begin to undo that damage," she agreed quietly. "The guests?"

Charles nodded and turned. "Release Bruce's hostages," he called out toward the base of the cliff. A few moments passed, and then individuals straggled out of an opening at the base of the cliff. Reynald scanned the women and children moving into the open, the captives blinking as they emerged into the bright light. Suddenly he cried out with joy. He broke into a run, and in a moment he had swept up Abigail and her child into his arms, tenderly cradling them against his body.

"Oh Abby, are you all right?" He pulled back to look her over carefully, checking her from head to toe until meeting her eyes again.

Abigail's eyes shone with relief. "Reynald, I knew you would come for me. We are fine, we are both fine," she promised. "They fed us well, and never threatened us at all, not once we reached this base." She glanced past Reynald to look at Charles. "Bruce was rough and loud, but Charles, that man over there, took good care of us. He checked in on us and made sure we were provided with food and water."

She shuddered for a moment, then looked back up at her brother. "The third man, I think he was truly crazy." She looked around her, scanning the crowd. "Is he here?"

Reynald snapped back to an alert status. "I do not know," he responded shortly. "We need to get you all back to safety." He escorted his sister and the other women toward the larger group of soldiers.

Gertrude nodded complacently to her son, looking with satisfaction at the released prisoners. "What else is in that cave?"

Charles did not hesitate. "Ralph, bring out the chest," he ordered one of his men. Sarah turned, realizing in surprise that the young man he called to was Dorrie's younger brother. A few moments passed before Ralph and another man moved into the main clearing, carrying a trunk between them. Opening the lid, Charles revealed a pair of canvas bags.

With a heft, he pulled out one of the bags, then reclosed the lid and motioned to the soldiers. "This trunk now holds what was taken from the wanderer's camp," he informed them. "Find a way to carry this along with you."

Turning, he called out to his men, who by this point had gathered at the base of the cliff. "I know that you joined with me because of my promise to live with you freely in the woods," he informed them. "I will no longer make this trip with you, but I wish you peace, whether you do choose to form your own village or whether you find other paths in life."

He pulled open the bag, revealing a collection of coins. "This is what remains of what Bruce took from the Holy Land. Each of you come forward and take a share, if you can tell me truthfully that you will use it to seek a life of peace."

One by one the men stepped forward and talked quietly with Charles. The Templar clasped each man's hand in farewell. When Ralph had taken his share, he moved over to stand with Walter, the two engaging in a long conversation.

Reynald watched over the process with careful attention, motioning to his men to gather up the women and children onto their horses.

A sense of relief swept over Sarah. It was done. The situation had been defused without any bloodshed. Abigail had been rescued, and the baby was safe. She would take the time to look over each hostage once they had retreated from the camp, but she understood Reynald's desire to get the innocents to safety first.

She helped one of the younger boys up to sit before Cedric, then turned to see if anybody else needed assistance. Most of the women and children were now mounted with a soldier. Walter and Ralph sat side by side on their steeds, their eyes scanning the forest. Reynald was standing to one side, watching the motley crew of bowmen gather up belongings, preparing to make their ways back to their homes. Charles was walking slowly with his mother, holding her hand, escorting her back to her steed.

As Sarah watched them go, she saw a small object shake loose and fall to the forest floor. It was the wooden dove Gertrude wore at her chest. Sarah skipped over to pick up the small item, then reached forward to catch up with Gertrude and Charles.

"You have dropped something," she called out with a smile.

Someone punched her, hard, in the back, the force spinning her half around. She took a deep inhale in shock, the wind knocked out of her.

Who? What?

Her front felt … funny. She looked down. A barbed arrowhead was protruding from her lower left belly, just above her hip. She stared at it in confusion, the world seeming to slow around her. There was no pain from the wound. It just glistened in the sunshine, a red ooze beginning to leak out around it.

This was going to hurt. It was going to hurt a lot, and the pain would be starting any moment now. Maybe it would be a good idea to faint first.

When the world began to spin, Sarah did not resist. She let herself spiral deep into the blackness.

* * *

Reynald was assisting his sister onto a horse when Ethan came up to him, motioning his head up into the hills beyond the camp. Reynald turned at once, carefully scanning the area. It did seem like there was a movement … beyond a stand of birches …

Suddenly, Denis stepped out from the woods, bow in hand. In one smooth movement he had nocked an arrow and raised the feathers to his cheek. Reynald spun his head to follow the direction of the aim. Denis had drawn a bead on Gertrude's back.

Reynald raced forward, calling out the alarm. To his horror, he saw that Sarah was also moving in Gertrude's direction.

"Sarah!"

His feet flew in a flat-out sprint.

Something flashed across the clearing, and Sarah was spun around by the force of the impact, the arrow impaling her through her left side. It seemed that she was suspended upright for a moment, then she crumpled to the ground in a limp heap.

The clearing erupted in chaos, with soldiers diving for cover and the newly released men taking up arms. Reynald flung himself over Sarah's body, covering her with his own, and he saw Charles move to shield his mother.

Reynald turned to look up into the hills – but the area was quiet. Denis had vanished into the treeline.

Walter's voice called out in an echoing challenge. "A reward of fifty pounds for whoever brings me in Denis – dead or alive!"

There was a cry of approval from Charles' men, and immediately a swarm of pursuers headed high into the hills, scrambling through the briars and bushes. In a few moments, only the soldiers and rescued hostages remained in the camp area.

Reynald looked down at Sarah. Her face was pale, and her eyes were closed. Gertrude appeared without a word at his side with a wad of cloth, and he pressed it down around the front of the wound, making a dam to hold in the blood.

"Sarah, hang on," he pleaded to her hoarsely while he worked.

Her eyes fluttered open at his voice. They slowly regained focus. "Abigail?" she croaked out.

"They are all fine," reassured Reynald as he made the bandage firm. "Nobody was hit but you."

Sarah looked up with serious attention into Reynald's eyes. "Bad?" she asked weakly.

Reynald pursed his lips, then nodded. She deserved honesty. "Yes, it is bad. We need to get you back to the keep immediately." He stroked her face gently, gazing into her eyes. "You need to focus on me, on my voice. Save your strength."

Sarah took in a deep, shuddering breath, then marshaled her energy. "Rachel. I must … forgive Rachel ..."

Reynald ran a hand across her forehead, resting his fingers against her face for a moment. "Yes, you will be able to forgive Rachel. I will bring you to her. You just hang on."

Sarah nodded weakly, then lay back, her eyes falling closed again.

Reynald gathered her up in his arms, calling for Sarah's horse. Walter quickly brought it over, his eyes creased with concern.

"Are you sure you do not want my mount, or your own?" he asked in confusion. "Surely either one is faster."

Reynald shook his head. "As a wise woman once told me, a steady horse is better than a fast horse when injuries are involved. The key is to go at the perfect combination of speed and smoothness – and this horse is a master."

He raised Sarah up into the saddle, then quickly mounted behind her, holding her in place. He glanced around the clearing, taking in the situation.

Walter patted the horse on the neck. "We have this under control," he promised resolutely. "We will be out of here in under five minutes, and with the chase underway after Denis, I do not see any problems at all. We will be right behind you. Now fly!"

Reynald needed no further prodding. He dug his heels into the steed's sides, and they were racing through the forest, driving towards the keep.

Chapter 22

Sarah lay muffled in a blinding white silence. Had she been trampled by an angry bull? Her entire body ached; some places presented stabbing pains, while others were slow, steady thunders. Her head was throbbing. Even the light against her eyelids burned. She struggled to raise a hand to her face to block out the glare.

A flurry of noise and movement surrounded her, and the room went dark. She struggled to open her eyes, finding they were stuck shut. With some effort she was finally able to force them apart.

A number of faces peered down at her, presenting a mixture of concern and happiness. Between the darkness and lack of focus it was hard to make out shapes. She managed finally to identify her mother, Abigail, Gertrude, and Polly. Her mother took up a wet cloth, sliding it gently over her face to wipe away the sweat and dried tears.

"Oh Sarah, you are awake at last. Thank God," she moaned softly. She spoke over her shoulder to Polly. "Run and wake her father; let him know the good news." Polly was gone from the room in a flash.

Once her mother had wiped her eyes, Sarah was able to focus more clearly, and saw she was in her own room. The curtains had been pulled shut, blocking out the midday sunshine which still poked through the corners. Sarah looked again at the faces, at the level of concern shown on them. Had she been injured that badly?

She tried to speak; the barest whisper of a croak emerged. Her mother immediately brought over a mug of mead, bringing it to her lips. She took down one swallow with an effort, then two. Her throat slowly eased into motion.

"How … long?" she was finally able to gasp out.

Her mother nodded, brushing the hair back from her face with a tender hand. "You have been delirious for nearly two weeks," she told her daughter quietly. "The doctors were quite worried about you. I knew you would pull through, though. You are quite a fighter."

Two weeks! Sarah lay back against the pillow, her body aching in every extremity. Her mind went back to the attack, to laying on the ground, looking up at Reynald. He had carried her … she remembered moments of awareness, with the forest thundering by. He must have brought her first to Dorrie's keep, and then to her own home.

Her eyes sought out her mother. She took a deep breath, wincing against the pain, and tried to formulate a new word.

"Reynald?"

Her mother shook her head, a frown forming. Behind her, Sarah saw the other women exchange worried glances.

"He is not here," soothed her mother quietly. "He is out." She brought over the mug of mead again. "Here, drink some of this. Your father should be here soon."

Sarah focused on the cup being brought to her lip, willing her muscles to contract, fighting against the pain.

She pushed the worry from her mind. Of course Reynald was not here. Denis was still out there, apparently, and undoubtedly he was causing trouble. They had stirred up a hornet's nest, and Reynald was fighting to keep a fragile peace.

She pulled back from the mug, her thoughts muddled. If Reynald was out finding Denis, why was her father asleep? Was his leg still bothering him that much, that he was not organizing the strategy? Was there great danger in what Reynald was doing? Was that part of why everybody looked so concerned? Was it something about her injury?

She thought back again to when she had been wounded. The arrow had gone in near her hip. Hopefully nothing critical had been struck there. She was alive, after two weeks, and while she hurt a great deal, she could still wiggle her toes and fingers.

She remembered lying on the ground, looking up at Reynald. Her concern had been … Rachel. She had wanted to talk with Rachel, to apologize.

She looked back up at her mother again, her voice coming more easily this time. It still took an effort to put the breath behind the word.

"Rachel?"

This time, Sarah knew she was not imagining it. Her mother looked away from her, dropping her eyes. Her voice was low and strained. "She is not here," she admitted, reaching for a different mug this time.

A bolt of fear shot through Sarah. For Reynald not to be by her side was one thing. There was a murderer on the loose who needed to be brought in. But for Rachel to be missing as well – and for her mother to be holding back from her …

Sarah pushed herself into a sitting position, causing the women in the room to draw forward, calling out in alarm. Her mother was there in an instant, raising the mug to her mouth.

"Where? Where?" insisted Sarah, her voice croaking in a harsh rasp. She could not help but drink the liquid being put to her lips, and the moment the thick liquid hit her throat, a strange lethargy overtook her.

No, she did not want to sleep. She wanted to know what was going on … but her body would not comply. Against her will, her eyelids eased shut, and she was drawn down into darkness.

* * *

Sarah's eyes fluttered open. It was early morning, judging by how the light was gently filtering in through the window. The room was quiet, and her body drifted in a subdued sea, the pains and aches substantially lessened. Abigail sat to one side contentedly nursing her young child.

Abigail's eyes brightened as she saw Sarah was awake, and she laid the child in a nearby basket before coming over with a mug. "Here, drink some mead," she offered gently.

Sarah was thirsty, and she drunk gratefully from the mug before nodding her thanks.

"It is Monday the seventeenth of August," offered Abigail without prompting, settling Sarah back down against the pillows. "You have been fading in and out of consciousness, but the doctors feel you are doing much better. We are all taking shifts now, so that someone is here any time you wake up."

Sarah nodded, her mind still fuzzy. Images of Reynald and Rachel floated through her mind, and after a few minutes they connected together. She remembered what had been said and implied during her last awakening, and her brow creased.

Surely she had misunderstood. Her sister was here; she had just been out on some chore the last time she had asked for her.

"Rachel?" she rasped out hoarsely, her heart hopeful.

Abigail flushed bright pink and looked away, out the window. "Your sister is not here," she admitted slowly. She looked back at Sarah, her face twisted in concern and hesitation. "Maybe I should fetch your mother. She is asleep, but I am sure – "

Sarah held out her hand. "No," she pleaded, her throat tight. She would not wake her mother in order to be told bad news. Not now … but still, she had to know at least some small part.

She motioned toward the mead, and Abigail promptly brought over the mug, helping her with a long swallow. Sarah felt sturdier with the warm liquid in her, and gathered her resources.

What did she really want to know? Her mind seemed to latch onto only one solution for this dilemma. It was the only explanation which made sense to her scattered mind. Her throat was still in agony, but she fought to form her query with the few words she could manage.

"Reynald … chased after *her*?" she asked finally, her voice harsh and low. It was too late to mourn what was lost, but perhaps for once she could not lay the entire blame at her sister's feet. She had to know if Reynald had proactively been involved. Reynald had always chided her for laying all responsibility on her sister. It was time for her to look equally at the men involved in such trysts.

Abigail almost looked away again, but she bit her lip and met Sarah's stare. After a few minutes, she nodded quietly. "Yes," she admitted. "You deserve to know. Your parents said to keep all news about Rachel and Reynald's situation from you, but you are her sister. You should be told about their relationship."

She let out a long sigh. "Reynald made sure we all knew that he took full responsibility for what went on between the two."

Sarah's heart dropped into a deep ocean. She turned on her side, facing away from the window, and closed her eyes. It was a long while before she was asleep again.

* * *

Sarah floated into awareness. The room was immersed in gloom, with only a low fire painting the furnishings in a soft glow. Her father sat at her side, his face creased with worry and pain. A sharp stab of guilt coursed through her in seeing him so upset. It made her heart sick that she could be even part of the cause.

"Father?" she called out softly to him, her voice coming more easily.

"Sarah, my child, you are awake," he replied with a half smile, shaking himself out of his musings. "Here, have some broth. How are you feeling?"

Sarah gave a gentle stretch, and found that many of her aches had faded. "Much better, thank you," she admitted hoarsely, her throat far less tight than before. She let him help her to a sitting position, and soon he was feeding her from the bowl, tilting it toward her to allow her to sip the warm liquid.

"I am so glad you are doing better," he sighed absently, carefully handling the bowl. His face showed a weary distraction "With everything else that is going on, your mother is simply a wreck. It will make her happy to have one small part going well. With Rachel and Reynald …"

He glanced down at his daughter guiltily. “Oh, but you should not worry about any of that,” he soothed her quickly. “You need to focus on getting better, on resting and gaining your strength. Everything else will work out … somehow. Do not think about that now.”

“I am sure everything will be fine,” agreed Sarah, her concern for her father growing. His gaze was unfocussed, and his shoulders slumped with exhaustion. Whatever else was going on, she would not add to his burdens.

When she finished the soup, she lay back against the pillows, allowing herself to drift back to sleep.

* * *

It was evening; the warm, rich colors of sunset were glowing throughout the room, and she breathed in the rich crispness that came sometimes with the oncoming darkness. She stretched with delicious ease. Her body was finally healing. Perhaps soon she could be out of this bed and rebuilding her life.

She heard a movement at her side, and she turned her gaze. Her breath came in with one long, swift draw.

Reynald was there, kneeling at her side. His face was a tormented mixture of guilt and sorrow, of apology and fixed determination. He reached a hand toward her cheek, and she drew back instinctively. His eyes shadowed, and he brought his hand back to his side in a slow, reluctant motion.

Sarah flushed with overwhelming desire to be held by him – to be cradled by him, to be told that everything was going to be all right. A dark desperation blossomed within her, that he could be so close and yet out of reach.

The smallest glimmer of hope tantalized her. She still had not heard any admission from his own mouth. Maybe she had misunderstood.

When she found the breath to speak, her voice came out more sharply than she had intended. “Where is my sister?”

Reynald flinched as if he had been struck, but he held his gaze steadily on hers. “It is my fault,” he admitted quietly, his voice rich with regret. “I am sure you have been told by now what happened between us. I know you tend to blame her in these situations, and I want to make it clear. I take responsibility here.”

He paused for a moment, then added more quietly, “I am afraid you will have to believe me in this matter, as Rachel is of course no longer in the keep.” His face flushed with guilt, but he held her gaze with steady will, ready to accept any punishment she chose to lay on him.

Sarah’s body layered with ice. Reynald had already installed Rachel as mistress of his new home? Slowly, carefully, she brought her hands together and drew Reynald’s ring off her finger. She raised it to him.

“This is yours,” she offered, her voice steely.

Reynald hesitated for a moment, then nodded and took the ring back from her. He did not put it on his own finger, but carefully placed it into the small bag at his belt.

Sarah’s face hardened. Was he so quickly planning on giving it to her sister, then? Her voice became harsh.

“Get out,” she ordered him. When he did not move, she pushed herself into a sitting position, her voice growing louder. “Get out!”

Reynald stood quickly. “Please, you are still ill,” he pleaded with her. “I will leave and will fetch you some help.” True to his word, he turned and quietly left her room, and in moments Polly had entered. The maid did not speak, but moved around the bed quickly, offering her a mug of mead.

Sarah rubbed at the spot on her finger which had held the ring, tears coming slowly to her eyes as she sipped the liquid. Seeing the rivulets, Polly murmured soothing comments to her as she drank.

“Do not cry, miss. Everything will work out somehow. I know it is hard, right now, but it is always darkest before the dawn. I am sure that somehow things will work out …”

Sarah fell asleep to the quiet litany of her promises.

* * *

Sarah was being shaken awake. "Come on, sleepyhead, it is time to get moving," came the strict instruction. Surprised, Sarah opened her eyes to find Gertrude standing over her, hands on her hips.

"You have been coddled for long enough," instructed the woman, her feet planted solidly. "It has been almost three weeks – plenty of time for you to get more than mead and broth into you! We are going to start with strained turnips today. But first, we are going to sit up."

Gently but firmly, Gertrude helped Sarah to settle into a sitting position. After a few mouthfuls, Sarah had to admit that she felt much better, and eating the semi-solid food was quite refreshing. Her sorrow eased as her stomach filled with the vegetables.

"That is a start at least," agreed Gertrude once the bowl was empty. "Next, we have to get your muscles working again."

She pulled the blankets away from the bed and sat by one leg, making it bend and then unbend. Sharp pains shot through Sarah at the motions, but they felt good, as if a long unused piece of machinery was finally getting its gears moving again. She braced herself against the back of the bed, giving in to Gertrude's ministrations.

By the time Gertrude was done with the full body's worth of workout, Sarah was exhausted. She drank down another bowl of soup, relishing the warmth that filled her from within.

When Polly came to remove the bowl, Sarah looked up at her. "Could you send Cedric to me in the morning? I have something I need to talk with him about."

"Of course, dear," responded the woman with tenderness. "You get some sleep now."

Sarah nodded, drawing the blankets over her head, falling into a tired sleep.

* * *

The next morning, a semblance of Sarah's old strength eased into her muscles. Gertrude was there with strained carrots, and Sarah found that she could feed herself. With Gertrude's help, she swung her legs around to the side of the bed and hobbled around the room, leaning heavily on the nun for support.

The courtyard was quiet outside her window, and after she had spent every last ounce of energy on walking and moving, Gertrude sat her down by the window for a well earned rest.

There was a knock on her door, and Cedric stuck his head into the room. When he saw she was up, he came over to stand before her. "Sarah, I am so sorry," he stated hoarsely, looking over her from head to toe. "If only -"

Sarah cut him off with a wave. "We are lucky to have gotten through so much fighting with so few injuries as we have seen," she offered him tenderly. "I was told by many to stay behind, to stay safe. It was my own choice to be there, to be at risk." She paused for a long moment. "That was the second time in five days where I had been caught unawares. I blame no one for that but myself."

She looked up at the soldier before her. "I know you have trained me for many years on the basics of combat, with both sword and dagger. Now I want you to try to teach me something different. At the wanderer's camp, I was held captive by one of the men. I was completely helpless." Her lips pressed together tightly. "I never want to feel that way again."

Cedric nodded in understanding. "It will be my honor," he responded simply. "We can start tomorrow, if you are ready."

"I will be," promised Sarah with feeling.

Cedric bowed, then turned and left, closing the door gently behind him.

Sarah sat there for a long while, the summer sun soaking into her body. Strength was returning to her, step by step. Her heart still echoed with hollow despair. She sensed it would be much longer before that wound healed.

Evening shadows stretched across the courtyard, and suddenly the sound of hoofbeats carried across the clearing. A group of soldiers came riding in through the gates. She spotted

Reynald at their center, and recognized Ethan, Elijah, Walter, and several other men.

Sarah sat forward, her brow furrowed with thought. Where had they gone to? Were they still out hunting down Denis?

To her surprise, Reynald looked up at her room as he dismounted. He stopped suddenly as he saw her sitting there. Sarah turned her head sharply, putting him out of her vision. When she looked back several minutes later, the men had gone inside, and the courtyard was quiet again.

She sat by the window, lost in thought, until darkness descended. She climbed her way back to the bed, and fell asleep.

* * *

The next few days passed in rapid succession. Sarah's strength returned as she progressed to venison stew and mashed turnips. With each hour she could walk more easily around her room. She worked with Cedric for an hour each afternoon, going through the moves slowly at first, then more quickly as she learned the skills. Gertrude helped her with her flexibility and strength training

Sitting at her window, Sarah watched the group of soldiers leave each morning and return each evening. They did not appear to be engaging in any fighting – they returned without any injuries, and only the weary dust-ridden look of a long ride. Each evening Reynald looked up at her room as he returned, and each evening she turned her gaze, unwilling to meet his.

Sarah tucked her feet beneath her, watching the full moon rise up over the distant forest, lost in thought. Was Reynald riding to see Rachel every day, and returning here to report news of his search for Denis to her father? Had her mother refused to allow Rachel to visit the house? What had been going on while she was unconscious all of those weeks?

It had been weeks … a thought suddenly occurred to her. Her monthly bleeding had always begun a day or two before the full moon – but it had not appeared yet. It was now almost a month from when she had slept with Reynald.

A deep shuddering sigh was torn from her chest. With everything else that was going on, surely she could not be pregnant as well! She knew how injuries and stress could affect a woman's cycle. Surely it was just the chaos of her life, her injuries, her situation with her sister -

Her mind filled with fury. She'd had quite enough of this hiding in her room, pussy footing around the situation. Tomorrow she would confront Reynald, in front of witnesses, and discover exactly what was going on.

Chapter 23

Sarah was ready and alert when Gertrude walked into her room the next morning. She spoke up before the nun had a chance to sit. “I believe I will surprise my family by coming down to eat with them,” she offered in a low voice. “Could you bring up a bath, but not let them know my plan? I would like it to be a surprise.”

“Yes, of course,” chuckled Gertrude with a grin. “You are definitely ready to get out of this room and on with your life!” She was gone in a moment, and in short order a trio of servants had brought in a large wooden tub, ferrying in several large buckets of warm water to fill it up.

Gertrude came over to the side of the bed, but Sarah waved her away. “I would like to do this alone,” she asked quietly.

Gertrude nodded, her leathery face creasing in understanding. “I will see you downstairs,” she promised, then turned and left, closing the door firmly behind her.

Sarah undressed carefully, then spent an hour luxuriating in the suds, wiping away the grime and sweat of weeks. The heat felt glorious on her aching muscles, and she was refreshed and renewed when she toweled herself off.

Her legs were weak but able to support her, and she dressed with resolve in a long, tan dress over a white chemise. She braided her hair down her back and fastened the belt. She steeled her heart to hear whatever was going to be said. She wanted to know the truth – and she was going to face it, no matter what it led her to.

She pushed open her door and moved slowly down the hall, taking care on the stairs. While she knew her will was strong, she also respected her body’s recovery and did not want to push herself beyond her limits. It was a few minutes before she reached the bottom, turning the corner to walk into the main hall.

The murmur of conversation came to an abrupt halt as she entered the room, and all eyes turned towards her. She held her head steady as she walked slowly across the room, her gaze fixed on the main table. Her father and mother sat at the large oaken span, with Reynald by her father's side. Her sister was nowhere to be seen.

Fury boiled within her. That was *her* seat that Reynald was in! Had he moved in so quickly?

Both men stood immediately as they saw her approach, watching her movements with cautious surprise.

Sarah stopped before the table, putting her hands on the wooden surface for support. Her eyes swept past her mother and father before connecting with Reynald's. He looked so strong … so sturdy … she pushed those thoughts out of her mind and focused on the task before her.

"Where is my sister?" she growled, leaning forward on her hands.

Her mother spoke up gently. "Now, Sarah, I think -"

Sarah motioned her to stop speaking with a wave of her hand. "I want to hear this from *his* lips," she grated, her eyes not moving from his.

"I … I do not know," he admitted quietly.

Sarah's anger snapped. "What do you *mean* you do not know?" she called out, her voice rising.

Reynald took in a deep breath, then let it out again. "We send numerous search parties out every day. We have asked every village, every small outpost for help. Wherever Denis has made his camp, it is well hidden."

Sarah's mind spun with fury. Reynald was being deliberately obtuse! How dare he try to distract her from her sister with mention of this other task!

Reynald's face was dead serious. Beside him, her parents were pale and resigned.

Sarah took in a quick breath, realization sweeping over her. With sudden insight she saw that he was being absolutely honest. He was answering her question.

Rachel had been taken by Denis.

Her fury burst from her in a tidal wave of emotion. "You let her be stolen away by *Denis*?" she screamed, aghast. She was torn between wanting to fly at Reynald, to pummel him for his inability to protect her sister, and to race after her sister herself. Her family instincts won out, and she turned to run toward the main doors and the stables.

Strong arms grabbed her from behind, and she struggled futilely against them. "How long has she been in his clutches?" she railed, pulling with all her strength. "We have to save her! You abandoned her!" She twisted, but could not get free from the embrace.

"Shhhh," murmured Reynald in her ear, soothing her. "I am sorry … I am so sorry … but you know you are too weak to go. We are doing all that can be done. You need to focus on healing."

Sarah's energy gave way, and she collapsed back against Reynald, spent. Tears flowed freely down her face. With everything else that had gone on, now her sister was under the control of that madman.

Reynald held her against his body, supporting her, giving her his strength and comfort.

Finally, Sarah wearily brushed away her tears. She shook Reynald's arms off of her, and stumbled toward the main doors. She heard the footsteps following behind her, but she did not stop. Rather than turning toward the stable, she moved into the small stone chapel beside the main building.

A measure of serenity settled over her shoulders as soon as she entered its cool, damp walls. A row of candles lay flickering to one side, and she moved to the row, taking a small stick to light a fresh candle. Then she sat heavily on the front pew for a moment before dropping to kneel before the statue of Mary.

An image of Rachel, scared, alone, came to mind, and she put all of her strength and energy into sending waves of support to her sister. Any fortitude, any endurance she had, she wholeheartedly turned over to help her sister get through this trial.

Whatever else Rachel had done, she was her younger sister. Sarah thought back to all the times she had watched over her sibling – supporting her sister against their parents, teaching her new skills, looking out for her, caring for her. It was part of her being, part of what she was. Rachel was in trouble now, and Sarah would do everything she possibly could to rescue her from it.

She vowed to spend every moment building up her own strength, healing as quickly as possible, so that she would be ready at a moment's notice to go do what must be done to save her sister. She might not be able to fight, but she could gather information, talk to every person she could. The bandits must be somewhere. It was only a matter of time and energy to ferret them out.

Sarah bowed her head, kissing her cross. She had a plan, and she would see this through.

Reynald's face came to mind, and pain coursed through her heart. As much as she had learned to accept her sister's behavior, it was still a blow to her that Reynald had been so quick to fall into temptation. Yes, he had refused Rachel's drunken advances of a few weeks ago, if his story was to be believed. Apparently he had not been as strong after Sarah's injury – and he fully accepted the responsibility for that.

She looked at her hands. Perhaps it was unfair of her to have expected him to resist. Despite his claims to the contrary, she still found his marriage proposal to be a bit hasty, more of a knee-jerk reaction to their night together than anything else. Would he have proposed if they had slept apart that night? She did not think so. With her then near death, perhaps it was not so surprising after all that he had accepted Rachel's generous offers of comfort. She was younger, more curvaceous, more lively. He might have counted himself lucky to escape a poor match.

Tears rolled down her face, and she did not move to wipe them away. Today was the day for forgiveness. She had forgiven her sister for her deceptions and affairs. These were a part of Rachel's nature and she had accepted that. It was time for her to forgive Reynald for …

For what? For being fickle? For preferring her sister over her? For doing the right thing and proposing marriage to a woman he had slept with? Sarah shook her head, the stream of tears moving in a slow, steady flow.

She had to forgive him for breaking her heart.

Sarah took a deep breath, and thought about the situation for a long while. He could not be expected to stay in a relationship that he simply did not want. It would never work. She could not desire that of him. If he did not want to be with her, then he had done what was right. He had, as far as she could tell, been as discreet as could be expected. She could ask no more of him.

She held her cross in her fingers for a long time, and finally she brought it gently to her lips. Yes, she forgave him. Her life would go on. Finding her sister was now the priority, and the only thing she would allow to occupy her mind.

She stood slowly and turned to head out of the chapel. Reynald stood within the shadows by the entryway, his face somber and quiet. He took a step to move into the light, and he held her gaze with quiet strength. His eyes took in her tears and weary expression in one long sweep.

"Whatever can be done, I will do it to retrieve your sister safely," he vowed to her, his voice hoarse. "You have my word."

"Thank you," she responded simply, and was satisfied that her voice was even when she spoke.

He stepped forward to move by her side, and put out an arm for her to lean on. Sarah hesitated for a moment, but relented and took a hold of it, allowing him to escort her back to her room.

Chapter 24

Sarah dressed herself with determination the next morning, putting on her riding clothing despite the aches and pains that tweaked at her joints. If she was going to heal up and be a help to her sister, she needed to make every day count. She strapped on her sword and dagger, acknowledging to herself that they were more for show than use at the moment.

A momentary gladness lifted her heart when she walked into the main hall and saw that her usual seat was open; Reynald had chosen to sit across from her parents for the meal. The three looked up solicitously as she approached the table, and in short order Sally had brought over the ham and eggs which comprised the current menu.

Sarah saw Reynald and her father glance at each other with a worried frown, but it was her mother who spoke gently to her. "Sarah, my dear, are you sure it is a good idea to be riding? You are barely healed from your injury. The doctors said it might be several more weeks before you were ready for strenuous activity."

Sarah smiled reassuringly at her mother. "My horse is not any work at all to ride; he is as smooth as silk. If I am to get back into shape, I need to exercise regularly. I will not go far – just enough to allow my body to regain what it has lost."

Reynald's voice was low. "I will accompany you then, to keep you safe."

Sarah was prepared for this, and focused on keeping her voice in a gentle, reasonable tone. "I appreciate that, Reynald, but you are far more important in the long range searches which I cannot yet assist with."

Her father's eyes were sharp. "You are *not* going out alone," he declared in a tone of voice she had rarely heard him use. "I forbid it."

Sarah put her hand tenderly on her father's arm. "I would not dream of it, father. There has been enough angst for one family to bear." She looked over to both of her parents. "I will take Cedric with me; he is quite capable, and I imagine not nearly as indispensable with the main task. Also, I promise that I will stay near the castle grounds."

Her father nodded morosely, mollified by her quiet acquiescence. "See that you do," he murmured before returning to his breakfast.

Sarah's heart sank. Her parents had always been rocks of stability; to see them so worried and upset concerned her greatly.

When she stood and walked out to the stables, Reynald moved quietly at her side. She waited until they were in the shelter of the stables before turning calmly to meet his gaze.

"You do not intend to follow me again, do you?" she asked with a deliberately light tone. "Finding my sister should take precedence."

Reynald nodded, his look serious. "I realize that. Still, I wanted to emphasize to you how volatile this situation is. Please, I know I have no right to ask this – but be as safe as you can be. Do not take any unnecessary risks."

Sarah was touched by his concern. "I will be careful," she promised. "I know I am not up to full strength yet. I want to make sure I heal as quickly as possible, though, so I can be a help to the effort sooner rather than later."

Reynald looked down at that, and took in a deep breath. When he looked up again, Sarah's heart stopped. His gaze was so full of angst … of sorrow …

Reynald's voice was almost a whisper when he spoke again. "I am so sorry for allowing harm to come to you … for allowing this new pain to enter your life," he offered softly. "I cannot undo past mistakes. If there is anything I can do for you now – anything at all …"

Sarah forced herself to smile, and she stepped forward to hold his arm. "Find my sister," she instructed. Then she turned and walked to her horse's stall, to saddle him for the ride.

She did not mind at all that Cedric was silent during their hour ride around the keep walls. She was acutely aware of the dangers they faced, and it took every ounce of her strength to stay on the horse's back, balanced and alert. Still, she was pleased by the end of the ride. She felt tired, but in a good way. She had confidence that she would regain herself in only a short while.

She returned back to her room, and after a short nap, she spent the afternoon on exercises that she could do around her bed. She worked on practice moves with her sword and dagger, and was reassured when she found she could wield both with at least some degree of strength. She pushed herself right until dinner, and then after the meal was over, turned in for an early rest.

* * *

Sarah was pleased when there were no comments by her family or Reynald when she arrived for lunch the next morning prepared to ride again. Her father and Reynald spent the meal discussing the area the men would cover in the daily sweep, and her mother sat quietly, apparently lost in thought. Sarah wished there was something more productive she could offer to the effort, but knew that her best chance lay in bringing herself back to full strength.

Reynald followed her out to the stables again, but this time did not utter a word. He simply watched over her as she went through the activity of preparing her mount. She found his presence reassuring, and nodded to him when she and Cedric rode out for the morning.

Sarah breathed in the fresh afternoon air as they headed out. Her muscles had quickly gotten used to this activity again, and the day was bright and warm. She turned her horse's head in the direction of Lily's home.

"What did you have in mind for today?" asked Cedric quietly. His tone was not curious; he simply was asking for the plan.

"Of all the people I know, Lily reaches the widest range of individuals and locations," explained Sarah as they moved. "She is only a short ride away, so we should only be gone for an hour or so. That is well within my current limits. Once we enlist her support, she can spread the word throughout her network and find out more for us in one week than we could discover in a month."

"It seems a good idea," agreed Cedric. "This road is well traveled. I do not see any issues at all."

They alternated between short canters and periods of walking, with Sarah paying careful attention to how her body reacted to the activity. She wanted to balance the exercise she needed with the knowledge that she was still healing. She was grateful when Lily's home came into view.

Lily came bustling out immediately when she saw who her guest was. "Sarah, my lamb! Are you sure you should be out? I heard you were injured …" She quickly helped Sarah down and into her room, pouring out wine for the pair.

Sarah took a gulp of her wine, grateful to be relaxing on the couch if only for a short while. She turned to Lily, her gaze serious.

"I am here about my sister. She has been abducted by Denis, a Knight Templar who is a known bandit in this area."

Lily's face went pale at the news. "I have heard rumors about that, but I had hoped they were not true! Have you heard from the kidnappers?"

Sarah shook her head. "None. There has been as yet no demand for ransom. The men at the keep are performing searches every day, and a reward has been posted, but so far there has been no news. I thought, perhaps, with your wide network of friends -"

Lily put her hand on her friend's shoulder. "Say no more," she instructed. "I have a market day coming up tomorrow. I will make sure that every person I speak with knows what to watch for. I will make sure they know it would be a personal favor to me if they could tell every person they meet or know in the coming days. We will get the word out."

Sarah sighed in relief. "Thank you so much. I am sure that, with your help, we can track her down. She must be somewhere …"

Lily glanced at the door. Through it, Cedric could be seen tending to the horses and maintaining an eye on the forest beyond. She turned back to Sarah. "That man I know; he has been a guard with your family for many years. Where is the courtly gentleman who was with you on your last visit? Reynald was his name, I believe?"

Sarah looked away. "Reynald is out looking for Rachel." She was tempted to say more, to spill her torment and emotions. She had nobody to confide in, nobody to draw reassurance from. However, if Lily was going to be out discussing the situation with many people over the coming days, Sarah did not want any chance of the wrong comment slipping out accidentally. She trusted her friend, but it was better this way.

Lily watched Sarah's face for a long moment, then nodded quietly. "I am here, if you want to talk any time," she offered.

Sarah forced herself to smile. "I know, and I appreciate it. Maybe once we find Rachel, I will take you up on that."

She finished her wine in a long swallow. "I think I should be heading back now," she admitted to her friend. "I do not want my family worrying about me as well, with all that is going on."

"Of course, I understand completely," agreed Lily. In a moment the two had risen and moved back out into the yard.

Cedric helped Sarah climb back up onto her mount, then was ready at her side in an instant. Sarah smiled and waved goodbye to her friend, then followed Cedric as they headed back toward home.

Her soul eased as they followed the quiet road through the woods. Her wound was healing more with each passing day, and she had done something productive to help in the hunt for her sister. If she focused on small, meaningful steps, she was sure that their efforts would result in success.

She did not even feel frustrated that they took the peaceful road back at a slow walk. She had made good progress today. Tomorrow she would accomplish even more.

There was the sound of hoofbeats behind her, and she gave a wry smile. So Reynald felt it necessary to check up on her, after all. She found that she looked forward to finishing up the ride with him by her side. It was time she began looking on him as a good friend, to put aside her romantic feelings. Today was a good day to begin the change.

She reached forward to pull to a stop, but was caught by the look in Cedric's eyes. He had turned half sideways to see who was approaching them, and his gaze was sharp, his hand moving towards the hilt of his sword. His voice held a low, warning tone.

"Sarah …"

Sarah spun her head. Four cloaked men were riding toward them at high speed, their swords glinting at their sides. Their look was rough and rugged.

Cedric spun his mount to press alongside hers.

"Run!"

Sarah needed no further exhortation. She dug her legs into her steed's side, and in a flash she and Cedric were racing full tilt down the road.

Sarah's heart pounded in her throat, but a glance behind her showed that the men were steadily gaining on them. She pushed her mount as fast as he could go, but she knew it was hopeless.

She looked sideways at Cedric, who maintained a constant presence at her side. "Go ahead!" she urged him. "You can outrun them! Get help!"

"Never!" ground out Cedric, his face reflecting his determination. "I will not leave you."

It seemed only moments before they were overtaken, the bandits grabbing at their reins and pulling them to a hard stop. There was a clatter of hooves as the horses spun into a dusty group, Sarah and Cedric drawing swords in unison to ward off the attackers.

Sarah found herself facing two of the bandits, and she spun her mount to keep them from pinning her in on either side. She desperately used wide, sweeping motions to keep them away, but their reach was longer than hers, and their strength much greater. It only took two or three hits before her weapon was thrown from her hand. In a moment they had moved their horses in on either side, holding tightly on her reins and pressing their swords in at her side to keep her quiet.

She looked with concern to Cedric. He had injured one of his attackers, but the men he faced were good with the sword. Cedric fought valiantly, but she could see that he was flagging under the onslaught. He blocked a blow from the bandit to his right – and suddenly from behind the other bandit slammed hard into his horse, causing him to lose his balance. Sarah cried out in horror as he went down into the sea of churning hooves.

One of the bandits cried out in rough urgency. "They said not to kill anyone from the keep!"

Immediately, the other bandits pulled back from Cedric's location. She saw that he had curled up into a fetal position, both shielding his head and nursing his left side.

One of the bandits leapt down, his sword held at the ready. He glanced over Cedric's wounds with an offhand look. "Bah, he will live," he called back. "Someone will find him eventually, if we leave him here."

Sarah's captor gave a barking laugh. "That is good enough for me. Plus, we have two fine mounts in the bargain. Time to head back!"

Without further comment, the four men launched into a fast gallop down the road, keeping Sarah at the center of their group. Sarah's only consolation was that the relatively slow pace of her own horse would check their speed. If only someone would come across Cedric before it was too late …

Her hopes dwindled as, in a few minutes, the bandits moved off of the main road and delved into the thick forest. They wended their way through the woods with ease. Sarah was completely lost in a short period of time as they backtracked and circled their way through the ancient oaks.

It was past nightfall when they came into a small clearing against a hill. The soldiers pulled up, then dismounted, forcing Sarah to do the same. They escorted her with gentle prods towards an opening in the hill. Torches lined the entryway. One of the men stayed behind with the horses, while the other three brought her inside.

The cave split off into three tunnels, and they led her down the leftmost one for several minutes. A rough wooden doorframe was wedged into the tunnel, and when she stepped through, they closed the heavy door behind her. She heard the sound of a lock turning.

The carved out room she stood in was lit by flickering torchlight. A draft swept the smoke upwards into a small hole cut high in the ceiling, far overhead. The room was lined with boxes and bags. A pile of blankets to one side appeared to form a rough bed. A small fire was banked against one wall, and Sarah could see a figure leant over, working at a pot. The person turned at the sound, then rose …

Sarah raced forward, her heart bursting. She wrapped her arms around her sister, calling out her name over and over again.

"Rachel … Rachel … you are alive ... you are all right …" she breathed in helpless relief, squeezing her sister. "We were all so worried …"

Rachel gave her sister a gentle hug in return, then pressed her back away. "It certainly took you long enough to get better, to get out of the house," she commented dryly. "You were starting to make me look bad. I am sure by now Denis thinks you are some sort of a weakling."

Sarah shook her head in confusion, then moved toward the door. She examined the frame in detail, pressing for weak points. The hinges were on the outside of the door, and the lock seemed sturdily built. She threw her shoulder against it experimentally, and the frame did not budge.

"Please, do not do that," sighed her sister wearily. "I do not want to have them tie you up. It is so much nicer when we can sit and talk together."

Something in her tone got through to Sarah, and she turned in shock. She took another look at the room, and at her sister. Her sister's face was layered with grime, but she did not seem afraid at all, or eager to seek an escape. In fact, her sister seemed … almost proud.

"But, surely you wish to get free?" asked Sarah, her voice echoing her confusion.

Rachel sighed, and squatted back down by the fire again, tending to her food. "There you go again, assuming that other people feel the way that you feel. You never think about how I feel, about the things I want. You never ask me what I think. You just tell me what to do."

Sarah moved to kneel in front of her sister, weakness and confusion threatening to overwhelm her. "We have all been worried sick about you. The men are out every day desperately searching to find you. Please … explain to me what is going on here."

Rachel smiled and looked up. "That is better." She sat back and arranged her dress around her. "I was on my way to buy a new dress, enjoying the afternoon, when Denis rode up. He seemed so similar to Reynald – the Templar crest on his armor, a strong build, a sword at his side. I decided if you could have a Templar, then so could I. I found a man exactly like yours, only stronger. He had the power to go out on his own."

Sarah eyed her sister in confusion. "Rachel, the two men are nothing at all alike. Denis has been killing people, taking hostages, and stealing!"

Rachel shrugged. "Are you claiming that Reynald has not killed anyone?"

Sarah shook her head. "I am sure he *has* killed people. It is his job to protect innocent travelers from bandits. However, he has only killed *criminals*."

Rachel rolled her eyes with elaborate drama. "Oh, so now the people Reynald chooses to kill *are* worthy of death, but the people Denis chooses to kill are *not* worthy of death? That seems fairly arbitrary."

Sarah bit down her frustration. She had to figure out what was going on. "It does not matter right now," she demurred. "Please explain this to me. You felt Denis was just like Reynald, so you spoke with him."

Rachel nodded with a grin. "He was so commanding, so sure of himself. He had this presence that I could not resist. When he told me I should come back with him to see where he was living – that he trusted me with his secret lair – how could I say no?"

Sarah forced herself to remain calm. "So you went with him voluntarily?"

Rachel chuckled. "I knew what a stir it would cause for the family. Everyone would be paying attention to me! They would all be out looking for me. By the time anybody found us, we would be married, and have a family, and it would be too late! I would have chosen my own life, and you all could not say anything to change it!"

Sarah's heart hammered. "You have not actually married him yet, have you?"

"Well, no," admitted Rachel, her voice tinged with petulance. "He says we should wait until he is more settled before we move to that stage. Still, I believe the family part is covered!"

She patted her lower abdomen with pride. "I always knew I would get pregnant long before you did. This time it will be *my* child who bosses yours around, who tells yours what to do and how to think." Her mouth twisted into a grin. "You can act as midwife for me, and live vicariously through my pregnancy."

Sarah bit her tongue. She was hardly in a position to scold Rachel for her situation, considering her own state. She had never even told Reynald …

She suddenly looked up at Rachel, another thought muddling her already confused mind.

"I do not understand," she pressed, looking between Rachel's belly and her eyes. "If you were in love with Reynald, and had already won him over after my injury, why did you go after Denis? Were you seeking to make one or the other of them jealous?"

Rachel's eyebrows knitted. "Reynald? I tried to attract his interest, several times. He paid less attention to me than to a gnat. He was by your side day and night when you were first brought in with your stomach wound, even though you just lay there, unconscious. I tried everything. I held watch beside him, talking to him as sweetly as I could. I offered to give him massages. I suggested walks with him in the garden, to distract him from his worries. He was always courteous but insistent that he could not leave your side."

She chuckled at the memories. "Finally I told him that the room's air was addling his brain, and that he needed to go for a ride in the fresh outside breezes. That I was heading to Burbage and that he should go with me, to keep me safe."

Her eyes flashed with annoyance. "He told me in no uncertain terms to make the ride by myself."

A warmth returned to her cheeks, and she gave a toothy smile. "That was when I met up with Denis. He was far more receptive to my conversation."

Sarah looked at her sister in shock. "I thought that Reynald had been the one to chase after you? That this was his fault?"

Rachel laughed merrily at the thought. "Certainly it was his fault that I was out on my own! You should have heard his tone when he told me to ride without him. I imagine once I had been 'abducted' that he came after me all right – but he never found me! Denis has hidden our home where none could locate it. I have faith in him!"

Sarah sat back down against one of the wooden boxes, her mind in turmoil. How could she have been so completely wrong? She, who prided herself on her truth and honesty?

She realized in a blinding flash that her father was right. She had built a situation in her mind, and she had deliberately interpreted any news or evidence she heard to support that mindset. If she had been more open minded – if she had been less insecure and jealous – she might have been willing to ask more questions, to hear more answers.

She would have known the truth.

Rachel's mirth filled the room, and it was a few minutes before she had calmed herself enough to take the pot off the fire and place it to the side. "You never were good at sensing the emotions of others," she chuckled finally. "You were always better at telling others how to feel, or what to do. How could you possibly have thought that Reynald was interested in anybody but you? Could you not see it in his eyes?"

Sarah looked away, her face flushing. She had seen the emotion – and had deliberately assumed it was because of Rachel. She had felt so sure that Reynald could not love her, that he would fall victim to Rachel's charms. It was as if she was looking for the proof, and willing to interpret whatever signs she saw as that evidence.

A wave of exhaustion overcame her, and she moved over to the blankets, wearily laying down on them. Through her half-closed eyes she saw Rachel shrug, then pick disinterestedly at her stew.

Sarah rolled over and faced the roughly hewn back wall of the cave. She brought the image of Reynald's face up in her mind, and focused on it with all of her will.

He would find her. Somehow, he would figure out a way to find her.

Chapter 25

Sarah awoke to waves of nausea, and she stumbled through the morning gloom to a pot in the corner of the room. She emptied the contents of her stomach, her head spinning. Finally she began to feel better and sat back to look around her.

A voice tinged with sarcasm came from behind her. "Wow, am I seeing my big sister showing some fear? I do not think I have seen you like this since you were made by our parents to recite a psalm at the Christmas festival, all those years ago!"

Sarah wiped her mouth off with a nearby rag, sitting back against the side wall. The torches were guttering low, but light was trickling in from the opening high above. The dinginess of the room became more apparent with each passing moment.

She looked over wearily at her younger sister, who had propped herself up on one arm and was watching her steadily. Sarah met her gaze evenly.

"Do I have something to be afraid of, sister?" she asked quietly. "What is your plan here?"

Rachel's face creased into a frown. "My plan is for me to know," she snapped. "If you are not afraid, just why were you sick? You can hardly blame me – you did not touch a spoonful of my stew." Her gaze sharpened, and she rolled to a standing position. "Do not tell me that miss goody-two-shoes has finally spread her legs for some man?"

Sarah instinctively pressed herself against the back wall, bringing her legs in against her. Rachel's eyes flared first with shock, then with anger.

"I do not believe it! You just could not stand to have me bear the first grandchild for our parents – so you went and got yourself pregnant!" She stalked across the room towards Sarah. "Who is the father, then? Cedric? Simon? Reynald?"

Sarah flinched, but it was all Rachel needed. Her face grew cold. "Well, let us see how you like things when your bastard child grows up without a father, then," she snarled. "For once, I will be the treasured one in our family."

Sarah reined in her temper. She needed every facility under her control to get a handle on this situation. "Reynald has already dealt with Charles and Bruce," she pointed out calmly. "I hardly think Denis is going to pose much of a challenge for him."

Rachel's grin was immediate. "You do not know my Denis," she purred. "He is a Templar, after all! Plus, he is unimpeded by the twin pillars of honor and justice. He does whatever he wants. If things do not go his way, he twists the truth to achieve his desired solution. The ends justify the means, after all. Let us see how Reynald stands up to that."

She turned in a huff, hammering at the door to be let through. In a moment Sarah was left to herself.

Sarah wrapped her arms around her bent knees, pulling them close to herself. She felt as if the door closing behind Rachel's departing form was echoed by a door closing in her own heart. She had long since accepted Rachel's attacks on her personally. That was something Sarah could live with, could continue to support her sister through.

However, if Rachel was going to actively seek to cause harm to those she loved, to single *them* out for attack … that was a threshold crossing that seemed final.

After all Sarah had done for Rachel over the years, all of the sacrifices she had made, that Rachel could deliberately discuss harming those Sarah loved …

Sarah closed her eyes. Rachel had made her decision. There was nothing to be done but to accept it and to move forward.

Wearily, she got to her feet and moved toward the fire. She knew with every fiber of her being that Reynald would be coming for her. She stirred the flames into life and hunted through the boxes for safe food to eat, and water to boil. She was going to be sure to be ready to help him when he arrived.

Sarah kept herself busy through the day, doing exercises against the walls, organizing her food supplies, making sure to drink ample fluids. She listened carefully by the door, but could make out no sound to indicate if there were guards or what their routine was.

The light was fading from the room when there was noise at the door. Rachel entered the room, and Sarah spotted a guard who pulled the door shut again with a solid thunk. Rachel glanced over at Sarah, then at the row of supplies laid out along one wall.

"Nice to see you are settling in," she commented airily. She went over to a pile of hardened bread pieces, taking one with idle curiosity. "I guess I am on babysitting duty again tonight. Denis is out, so it is no great hardship for me."

Sarah turned her head to the side, ignoring her sister. She pressed the palms of her hands against each other, flexing first one arm, then the other. Her strength was slowly returning, hour by hour, and she focused on her efforts with grim determination.

Rachel chuckled. "Not talking to me, eh? This has got to be a first. I am so used to you telling me what to do. Surely there must be things you feel I have done wrong, which only you can fix."

Sarah forced herself not to rise to the bait. She moved on through her routine, counting to twenty before beginning the next set.

Rachel shrugged, grabbing a stick from a nearby wall and scratching out a solitaire board on the ground. She took a pile of beans from one of the boxes and laid them out, then jumped them over each other along the grid, humming a sailor's ditty to herself.

Sarah's heart dropped, but she forced herself to continue. She remembered so easily those many hours of playing with her sister, laughing, enjoying their time together. That it had come to this …

Rachel looked up suddenly, her face contorted with frustration. "How come you are so high and mighty, after all?" she shot out, as if she were continuing a tirade which had until now raged silently in her own mind. “You never even supported me when I needed you the most!”

Sarah shook her head in confusion, drawn in despite her resolution to remain silent. “What? When was it that I did not stand by you?”

Rachel turned to look fully at her sister. “When I told you that Dirk raped me! You did not even say a word!”

Sarah froze, her mind racing. “You never said any such thing,” she choked out. “You said you had slept with him, and that you had been drinking, as if that absolved you from any responsibility.”

“He was older than me!” Her sister sprung to her feet. “He should never have touched me!”

Sarah rose to her feet as well, staring at her sister in bafflement. “Yes, and you were old enough to know better!” she shot back. “You were in our home! You could have yelled for help! You did not raise any alarm when he touched you.”

She shook her head in shock. “If our situations had been reversed, and one of your suitors had come after me, I would have fought the blaggard tooth and nail. The thought of him touching me would repulse me!”

Rachel’s face grew dark and sullen. “I was drunk,” she insisted.

Sarah’s face grew firm. “If I was drunk, and your fiancé assaulted me, it would loosen my inhibitions all right – I would have punched him squarely in the nose, rather than trying to reason with him. I would have let loose with all that was holy, to mangle him to a pulp, to scratch his eyes out.”

She plowed ahead. The box was open, and could never be closed again. “If you were drunk at the time, you were certainly sober afterwards. You never thought it important to tell me the man I was going to pledge my entire life to was a cheating bastard?”

Rachel stared in anger at her older sister. “How could I tell you? I was embarrassed!”

Sarah’s heart constricted between steel bands. “Your embarrassment was so important that you would sentence me to a lifelong partnership with a man of such dishonor that he would *sleep with my sister*?"

She ran her hands through her hair, overwhelmed with raging emotions. "If it had been me, I would have told you immediately! I would have screamed, I would have yelled, I would have dragged you away from the traitorous whelp. I would never have let you near him again."

She took in a deep breath, her heart failing her. Somewhere within the woman before her lurked her little sister, the innocent blonde with pigtails, the one she had taught addition to, the one she had curled up with at night. Sarah's voice faltered. "I would have protected you; I would have defended you. No matter what embarrassment or shame I felt. It would have been nothing compared with my concern for you."

Rachel's voice was thick with venom. "Well, I am not you, am I," she snarled. "I knew you could not understand."

Sarah stared at her for a long moment, unable to think of anything to say in response. Finally she turned, went to her pile of rags, and curled up on it, face to the wall.

* * *

The room was nearly pitch dark; only the barest of flickers came from the settling embers in the fireplace. There was a quiet metallic noise from the door, the sound of the key turning in the lock. She was awake in an instant, her body tingling with adrenaline. Her fingers sought out a thick length of wood which she had secreted underneath her bedding. She had not been bothered so far – but she was not going to take any chances. The presence of her sister in the room seemed little protection against harm.

There was a soft creaking, and in a moment a dark figure moved carefully through the gloom. Sarah wrapped her fingers more tightly around her baton. He was only a few feet away from her. Just one more step …

A rasped whisper came through the night, so faint she could barely hear it. "Sarah?"

Sarah dropped her weapon immediately and clamored to her feet, relief sweeping over her. "Reynald," she exhaled with joy, her eyes glittering. He was at her side in a heartbeat, pulling her into a strong embrace. His mouth was against her ear, and his voice eased out, ragged with emotion.

"You are safe, thank God you are safe," he murmured. She held him tightly against her, losing herself in the safety of his arms. It was a few minutes before he pulled back slightly to look through the gloom at her, scanning her body for injuries.

Sarah glanced behind him, then back at his face. "Cedric? Is he seriously hurt?"

Reynald shook his head, leaning forward to kiss her tenderly on the forehead. "You are too much, my darling. He is fine; we found him only a few hours after the attack. Let us worry about you and your safety for now. I only have a few men with me; we hoped stealth would serve us best tonight."

He looked around the room again, getting his bearings. "Where is your sister?"

A groggy call eased from the other corner of the room. "Sarah?"

Reynald instinctively turned toward it. His voice came pitched slightly louder, to reach her ears.

"Rachel, do not worry. We are here to rescue you," he promised resolutely.

"No!" warned Sarah, fighting to keep her volume low. "We have to go … now!" She tugged at Reynald's arm.

It was like pulling on an oak tree. Reynald turned to her in confusion. "Surely we cannot leave your sister here?" he asked Sarah, his voice becoming harsh. "What are you thinking?"

Rachel climbed to her feet, her eyes glinting in the low firelight. "Reynald?" she called out, her voice growing louder with each passing second. "Reynald, it is you!" She cupped her hands around her mouth. "Wake up! Wake up you fools! We are under attack!"

Reynald drew his sword, then glanced between Rachel's fierce look of triumph and Sarah's desperation. Deciding in a heartbeat, he took hold of Sarah's arm and ran from the room, down the corridor, bringing her alongside with him.

The entrance was up ahead – Sarah could see the mouth of the cave silhouetted against the starry sky. She put on an extra burst of speed, and the pair ran through …

Rough hands grabbed at her from the side of the cave's mouth, yanking her hand out of Reynald's grasp. She cried out in panic, struggling to get free, but she was held in a strong grip. A knife was brought up to rest against her throat, and she froze in place.

She swung her gaze across the clearing, looking for Reynald. He was pressed up against the other side of the cave's mouth. Two men, each the size of a giant, held him firmly against the stone slab. He was straining with every ounce of strength to move towards her, but the men held him immobile.

A tall, muscular man with cropped, sandy brown hair stepped forward into the torchlight. He drew his sword and brought it forward to press steadily at Reynald's throat. Sarah shivered with fear, realizing suddenly how vulnerable they both were.

Reynald did not move or flinch. His eyes held the gaze of his attacker with an even fury.

"Denis. It has been a while," he commented quietly, his voice steel.

"Yes, it has," agreed Denis, his growl filling the clearing. "You have caused trouble far too many times for my liking." He called out over his shoulders. "You men out there. Drop your weapons, or Reynald and Sarah will be slain before your eyes. Do not doubt that I would do it. I would much rather see them dead than surrender to the likes of you."

There was a long pause, and then as Sarah's eyes adjusted to the lighting in the area, she realized there was a small group of men at the edge of the clearing. Cedric wore a bandage, and his eyes were blazing with frustration. Ethan and Elijah stood side by side, ready to spring in a heartbeat. Walter's muscles strained with the effort of holding back from a bull rush. Charles stood tall and proud, ready to lay his life on the line for his friend.

Every man there she knew and trusted with her life. All looked to Reynald for a sign, which he gave. Slowly, one by one, they let their swords fall.

Rachel came out of the cliff wall behind them, helping a man stagger along. The soldier held a cloth to his head; blood streamed down from beneath the compress.

The man stumbled toward his boss. "I am sorry, Denis," he gasped. "Reynald came at me unawares. It will not happen again."

"Indeed it will not," commented Denis dryly. With one sweep he removed his sword from Reynald's throat and ran the man through his chest, holding the sword hilt against his breastbone for a long moment. Then he smiled and withdrew, allowing the guard to slump to the ground, dead.

Reynald remained frozen in place, motionless in the grasp of his two captors, his eyes sharp on the knife held at Sarah's neck.

Denis wiping the blood from his blade on his pants. "I never could abide incompetence."

Sarah's eyes sought out Rachel's, and she pleaded with her sister. "Please, Rachel, there are only five of you now. Let us go. We can find some sort of a solution for you. Let us talk about it. Surely this is not the life you wish to lead."

Rachel scoffed. "Oh, now you will deign to talk with me, when you want to tell me how to run my life. Look at you! You are carrying a bastard child, and you are going to watch his father die. Of course you want to tell me how things should go – all to your benefit, of course!"

Reynald's gaze moved to Sarah in shock, his eyes widening. She took in a deep breath, then nodded quietly to him, confirming what Rachel had said. If he was going to die, he should know his line would not be forgotten. A look of tenderness eased through his face, replaced with a determined tenacity.

Rachel took a step forward, and Sarah's gaze moved back to watch her. Rachel stood there for a long moment, looking angrily into her sister's eyes.

"You always think your way is the right way. Well, not this time. This time I am going to do what I feel is right! Nobody will tell me what is proper for *my* child. I am the mother now! This is what I have chosen, and nobody can tell me otherwise."

Reynald glanced between Rachel and Denis, and a spark of hope lit in his eyes. He spoke into the silence, his voice pitched low but carrying easily across the area. "So, Denis, now you have a *woman* telling you what to do?"

Denis's face flushed crimson and he strode back to stand before Reynald. "Nobody tells *me* what to do!" he shouted with fury. "I am in charge, and what I say, goes!"

Rachel stiffened at this, and Denis laughed, his voice sharp. "Besides, out of the two sisters, I have by far gotten the better deal. Rachel has told me all about the wild things Sarah has done over the years."

Sarah filled with outrage. *She* was the one who was impetuous? She strained forward, the sharp bite of the dagger pressing at her throat. "Me?!" she cried out hoarsely. The whole situation had taken on an unreal, dreamlike quality.

Rachel wet her lips nervously, but Reynald watched Denis' growing emotional state with single-minded focus. His voice remained calm and even. "You insist that you are in charge. I know your logic. The only tenet you abide by is that might makes right. Are you claiming you are the best fighter here, then?"

Denis threw back his shoulders, scanning his eyes over his three remaining men with a sneer. "These men are perhaps capable enough, but they are certainly no match for me," he boasted proudly. "None here can conquer me."

Reynald waited for a heartbeat, then challenged quietly, "Are you truly a match for *me*?"

The world slowed to the quiet trickle of an autumn stream. She knew in her mind that Reynald was doing the right thing – the only thing which might save them. Even so, her heart screamed that there must be another way – anything but watching him fight this man. Rachel had said Denis was without honor – without mercy. That Reynald might fall to such a man …

Denis threw back his head and laughed, then stepped into the center of the clearing. He looked around at the ring of watchers, his grin growing.

"If I see a motion from any of you, the woman dies," he called out in warning. "I doubt any of your chivalric souls would dare risk that result." He looked back to his men and nodded. They both gave Reynald a solid push, throwing him forward onto his knees. One of the men tossed the sword far to the right of Reynald's dust-caked body. Then both moved to stand guard around Sarah, ensuring that nothing could interfere with the match.

Reynald pushed himself up to one knee, then turned back to gaze at Sarah. She held his look steadily, pouring all of her emotion into the moment. Nothing else mattered but the two of them.

A thick silence descended on the clearing. He smiled at her then, a wry smile that made her heart break.

An instant later, he was lunging sideways for his sword, rolling and coming up into a crouch. The fight was on.

Sarah held her breath as the men swept in with an attack, blocked, counter-blocked, spun, and attacked again. Both men were elite swordsmen, aware of every feint, ready for every turn of the blade. Again and again Sarah drew back in fear, certain that a sweep of the blade would contact Reynald, and each time she sighed in relief as he dodged the blow, countering with his own.

Reynald's moves were steady, sure, wearing down Denis with their persistence. Denis's attacks were more sudden, with a twisting dagger often coming in from the shadows as the main blade bounced harmlessly against Reynald's block.

Sarah saw movement out of the corner of her eye, and turned to watch Rachel sidle forward, her eyes fixated on the fight.

There was a sharp oath, and Sarah spun back to the combat. Reynald had stepped backward, and his left arm sported a four inch gash across the upper muscle. Blood was streaming from the wound, and Denis laughed with glee. "You did not see that coming, did you?" he challenged Reynald with a sneer. "You are going down, old friend."

Reynald's look darkened with resolve, and he rotated his blade more firmly in his right hand. He put the blade through a three quarter spin, ending with it facing behind him. He crouched there, waiting for the next attack.

Denis could not resist the opening. With a yell, he swung into an offensive, driving in on the injured man. Reynald turned and spun, dropping low under Denis's attack. Reynald drew his blade down at a diagonal, and as Denis twisted to dodge the attack, he lost his footing and went down hard. Reynald brought his blade up to press against Denis's throat.

"Let the woman go," ordered Reynald through gritted teeth, his blade not wavering. "Let her go, or you die."

"Noooo!" came a scream from Sarah's left. A blur moved past her, and suddenly a handful of dirt and rocks flew into Reynald's face. He staggered backward, wiping furiously at his eyes.

Denis was springing onto his feet and forward in one fluid motion, his sword driving straight toward Reynald's chest. Reynald moved by instinct. He dropped to one knee, Denis's sword barely missing his shoulder by inches. With his other hand, he drove his dagger into Denis's stomach, burying it to the hilt.

Denis's eyes flew open wide, and his sword went flying. He staggered backwards once … twice … and then his balance was lost. He toppled over backwards into the dirt and lay still.

Sarah's world blazed in joyful relief. Reynald was alive … Reynald was alive. A wave of happiness flooded through her as she watched him stand and stare down at the fallen man.

Reynald turned slowly, his gaze settling on the eyes of the man holding the dagger at her throat. Behind him, the row of companions lifted their own swords from the ground, coming up behind him to form a wall. Reynald's eyes were steady, piercing her captor with deadly promise.

"Release the lady now …"

Sarah's breath caught as her elation coalesced into pinpoint focus. She saw the tension ripple through the men before her, felt the subtle tightening of the arm which held the knife at her neck. Her captor gave a low, gutteral growl. She realized in an instant that the bandit would rather kill her, would rather die fighting than surrender to the law.

She reacted on instinct, moving as Cedric had taught her, in a sequence she had practiced hundreds of times in private since he had first shown her the move.

She flung her right arm up and slammed her head down hard to the right, momentarily trapping her captor's knife arm away from her skin. She knew she only had a heartbeat of surprise before his superior strength overpowered her again, and she spun, driving all of her energy and power and will to live in the second motion. Her booted foot slammed in hard against his kneecap …

He howled out in excruciating pain, and the dagger flew wide from his grasp. In seconds her friends were on the bandits, pulling her free, diving in to attack her guards. She stumbled away from the melee, giving the men room to work. There was a flurry of steel on steel, but the bandits were outnumbered and fell quickly. Her breath came in heaves as the last captor fell senseless to the dirt.

Reynald held his blade out to one side at the ready, giving a long, steady scan of the area. The other men spread out at the edges of the clearing, their eyes alert.

Finally relaxing, Reynald turned to Sarah. He took the distance between them slowly, carefully, as if the thinnest of ice lay beneath him and only the most attentive caution could keep them from danger. Even when he reached her, his posture held uncertainty. There was a long pause; his brow furrowed as if he was sorting through what to say.

Finally, he spoke in a low, hoarse voice.

"Are you hurt?"

Sarah glanced at the wound on his arm, still steadily streaming blood. "You would ask me that?" she responded with gentle warmth. She lay a hand tenderly against his cheek.

A glimpse of hope shimmered into his eyes, and she realized just how much she had hurt him with her wild imaginings.

She had been so wrong …

"Oh, Reynald, I have been a fool," she whispered, folding herself against him, wrapping her arms around his waist. He stiffened for a moment, as if he were afraid any movement might dispel the dream. Then with a long exhale he brought his own arms tightly around her, pressing his lips against her forehead, his eyes closing in relief.

They spent many long minutes simply holding each other, Sarah immersed in the serenity of his embrace. He was alive. He was hers.

Finally, Reynald pulled himself away, blinking as if waking up from a long sleep. His eyes sharpened and he looked around him, scanning the clearing. Rachel was nowhere to be seen. "Your sister …?"

Sarah shook her head. "Let her go. She is going to choose her own path, and she does not wish for me to be a part of it. I have done as much as I could do, all these years. It is time for her to walk alone, apparently."

Reynald kissed her tenderly on the forehead. "Then, if we have finished with your sister's distractions, I think we have some unfinished business of our own." He knelt before her, drew his signet ring from his pouch, and held it up in a silent offer.

Tears streamed from her eyes. She nodded quietly, putting her hand forward to Reynald, watching as he slid the ring onto her finger.

When he spoke, his voice was hoarse and raw. "Never doubt that I love you, and only you," he vowed to her softly. "I shall be forever faithful to you. I shall love no other."

Sarah pulled him back up to stand before her, and gazed with love into his eyes. "I trust in you," she promised in return. "I shall never allow my faith to waver again."

Chapter 26

Dawn was breaking as Sarah and Reynald arrived wearily at the keep. Word spread like wildfire throughout the complex, and by the time they had entered the main hall, everyone was gathered, cheering, and crying out. Sarah hugged her mother and father, reassuring them that she was fine and that Rachel had been unharmed. Someone pressed a mug of mead into her hand, and she gratefully took a sip.

Suddenly she felt Reynald go stiff beside her. Following his gaze, she saw a grey-haired woman enter the room, dressed in an elegantly embroidered burgundy tunic. She seemed sharp and alert, her eyes scanning the room before settling on Reynald. She strode forward toward him.

"There you are," she called out in a clipped voice. "So you are back at last." Her eyes scanned down to Sarah, looking her over critically. "This must be your bride to be."

Reynald's voice was even when he spoke. "Mother, this is Sarah. She is my fiancée. Sarah, meet my mother."

Sarah looked with interest at the woman who had caused so much turmoil. Suddenly, Abigail came running to wrap a slim arm around her mother's waist, beaming with joy.

"Sarah, can you believe it, my mother has forgiven me! She has invited me and Lloyd to come live at the keep. It is wonderful!"

Reynald's mother gave a dry smile. "I have heard a lot about you, Sarah," she commented. "Gertrude stopped by my home a few days ago, to catch me up on events. Hearing her talk about rebuilding her life made me think that perhaps I should give more thought to my own family." Her eyes moved back to meet with Reynald's. "It would please me to spend time with the two of you, once you settle in to your new life."

Reynald glanced at Sarah before responding. "We would welcome that," he stated. "We have not yet set a date for the wedding -"

Sarah took his hand. "Tomorrow," she announced, causing all eyes to turn to her in surprise. She smiled, tenderly looking up at Reynald. "It will be Saturday, after all, and everybody is here already. There is the full day to send out messengers and gather up friends who wish to attend." Her voice dropped lower, pitched for Reynald's ears only. "I do not wish to wait one more night …"

Reynald pulled her close into his arms, holding her tightly against him. "Tomorrow it is," he whispered gently into her ear, "and not one day longer."

* * *

Sunset drizzled crimson, tangerine, and golden hues across the sitting room as Sarah relaxed in Reynald's arms. It seemed surreal. Only a few weeks ago she was in this very room, turning away Simon, wondering what her future held. Now it seemed that her every wish in life had been fulfilled.

There was a gentle knock on the door, and her mother's head poked around the corner. "Sarah? Might I come in for a moment?"

Sarah drew up to sit beside Reynald. "Of course," she welcomed.

Her mother came in to sit across from them, looking between the two. "A messenger has just arrived from Gertrude. She has returned to the nunnery."

Reynald nodded. "I hear Charles will visit her regularly there, and do some service in atonement for his deeds."

"Indeed," agreed Mathilde. She hesitated for a moment. "And apparently there is another newcomer there as well."

Sarah wondered if she should feel surprise, or concern, or nervous anticipation, but instead there was simply a quiet distance in her heart. "Rachel?"

Her mother nodded somberly. “Apparently she has begged sanctuary from them. She wishes to reside at the nunnery, at least through the birth of her child, if not longer.”

Reynald pursed his lips, but said nothing, turning to look at Sarah.

Sarah searched through her heart, looking for traces of concern, or anxiety, or anger, but she found none. Rachel was under Gertrude’s stern care now. Her sister would spend time caring for women in dire straits, learning just how fortunate her own upbringing had been. As Rachel’s child grew within her, she would be reminded daily of the delicate young life which depended on her for its every sustenance.

Perhaps this would be the turning point, for Rachel to begin her new life.

Sarah nodded. “Thank you, mother. I appreciate knowing that,” she murmured at last.

Mathilde stood and moved forward to Sarah, offering a warm embrace, and then left the two of them alone again.

Reynald dusted a tender kiss along her forehead. “How do you feel about that?” he asked softly.

She gave him a half smile. “I would not throw the first stone,” she responded. “I can only hope that this new path is the one she was meant for.”

The pride in his gaze glowed through her, and she closed her eyes as he drew her against him.

* * *

Saturday dawned sunny and bright, and Sarah spent the morning washing and preparing with Polly and her mother. Her best church dress was laid out, and soon she was bedecked with red and pink roses. When she walked down into the main hall, she was amazed at the transformation. Overnight, the room had been turned into a garden of flower and decoration. The path to the chapel was lined with bouquets, and the chapel steps danced with colorful ribbons.

Every corner of the courtyard was crowded with familiar faces, and her father stepped up to take her arm. Sarah smiled at her many friends as she walked slowly across the cobblestones, nodding to Lily, Melissa, Bethany, Jack and all of her other friends as she went. Abigail and Lloyd stood with their baby; Kyle was alongside his friend, and Reynald's mother was alongside her daughter. Dorrie and Walter stood flanking the steps.

It seemed as if every person Sarah knew had managed to attend on short notice. Her heart swelled with pride.

Then, waiting by the priest on the top step, there was Reynald, standing tall and proud. Her father was tenderly passing over her hand into Reynald's firm grasp. She knew nothing else, heard nothing else, until they were pronounced man and wife, and she was in his arms, kissing him.

She looked up into Reynald's eyes, and her heart melted with joy. Nothing would part them ever again.

Dedication

To my mom, dad, siblings, and the family members who encouraged me to indulge myself in medieval fantasies. I spent many long car rides creating epic tales of sword-wielding heroines and the strong men who stood by their sides. Jenn, Uncle Blake, and Dad were awesome proofers.

To Peter and Elizabeth May, who patiently toured me around England, Scotland, and France on three separate occasions. Elizabeth offered valuable tips on creating authentic scenes. Visiting the Berkhamsted motte and bailey was priceless.

To Jody, Leslie, Liz, Sarah, and Jenny, my friends who enjoy my eclectic ways and provide great suggestions. Becky was my first ever web-fan and her enthusiasm kept me going!

To the editors at BellaOnline, who inspire me daily to reach for my dreams and to aim for the stars. Lisa, Cheryll, Jeanne, Lizzie, Moe, Terrie, Ian, and Jilly provided insightful feedback to help my polishing efforts.

To the Massachusetts Mensa Writing Group for their feedback and enthusiastic support. Lynn, Tom, Ruth, Carmen, Al, Dean, and Marjohn all offered detailed, helpful advice!

To the Geek Girls, with their unflagging support for my expanding list of projects and enterprises. Debi's design talents are amazing. I simply adore the covers she has created for me.

To the Academy of Knightly Arts for several years of in-depth training and combat experience with medieval swords and knives. I loved sparring with Nikki and Jo-Ann!

To B&R Stables who renewed my love of horseback riding and quiet forest trails.

To my son, James, whose insights into psychology help ground my characters in authentic behavior.

To Bob See, my partner in love for over 16 years and counting. He enthusiastically supports all of my new projects.

Glossary

Ale - A style of beer which is made from barley and does not use hops. Ale was the common drink in medieval days. In the 1300s, 92% of brewers were female, and the women were known as "alewives". It was common for a tavern to be run by a widow and her children.

Blade - The metal slicing part of the sword.

Chemise - In medieval days, most people had only a few outfits. They would not want to wash their heavy main dress every time they wore it, just as in modern times we don't wash our jackets after each wearing. In order to keep the sweaty skin away from the dress, women wore a light, white under-dress which could then be washed more regularly. This was often slept in as well.

Cider – A beverage made by pressing and fermenting apples. By default, cider in the middle ages was alcoholic.

Drinking - In general, medieval sanitation was poor. People who drank milk had to drink it "raw" - pasteurization was not well known before the 1700s. Water was often unsafe to drink. For these reasons, all ages of medieval folk drank liquid with alcohol in it. The alcohol served as a natural sanitizer. This was even true as recently as colonial American times.

Garderobe – an indoor toilet in a castle; usually simply a hole over a long drop to a ground-level sewer.

God's Teeth / God's Blood – Common oaths in the middle ages.

Grip - The part of the sword one holds, usually wrapped in leather or another substance to keep a firm grip in the wielder's hand.

Guard - The crossed top of the sword's hilt which keeps the enemy's sword from sliding down and chopping off the wielder's fingers.

Hilt - The entire handle of the sword; everything that is not blade.

Mead - A fermented beverage made from honey. Mead has been enjoyed for thousands of years and is mentioned in Beowulf.

Pommel - The bottom end of the sword, where the hilt ends.

Tip - The top end of the sword, where the blade comes to a point.

Wolf's Head – A term for a bandit. The Latin legal term *caput great lupinum* meant they could be hunted and killed as legally as any dangerous wolf or wild animal that threatened the area.

About Medieval Life

When many of us think of medieval times, we bring to mind a drab reality-documentary image. We imagine people scrounging around in the mud, eating dirt. The people were under five feet tall and barely survived to age thirty. These poor, unfortunate souls had rotted teeth and never bathed.

Then you have the opposite, Hollywood Technicolor extreme. In the romantic version of medieval times, men were always strong and chivalrous. Women were dainty and sat around staring out the window all day, waiting for their knight to come riding in. Everybody wore purple robes or green tights.

The truth, of course, lies somewhere in the middle.

Living in Medieval Times

The years in the early medieval ages held a warm, pleasant climate. Crops grew exceedingly well, and there was plenty of food. As a result, their average height was on par with modern times. It's amazing how much nutrition influences our health!

The abundance of food also had an effect on the longevity of people. Chaucer (born 1340) lived to be 60. Petrarch (born 1304) died a day shy of 70. Eleanor of Aquitaine (born 1122) was 82 when she died. People could and did lead long lives. The average age of someone who survived childhood was 65.

What about their living conditions? The Romans adored baths and set up many in Britain. When they left, the natives could not keep them going, and it is true they then bathed less. However, by the middle ages, with the crusades and interaction with the Muslims, there was a renewed interest both in hygiene and medicine. Returning soldiers and those who took pilgrimages brought back with them an interest in regular bathing and cleanliness. This spread across the culture.

While people during other periods of English history ate poorly, often due to war conditions or climatic changes, the middle ages were a time of relative bounty. Villagers would grow fresh fruit and vegetables behind their homes, and had an array of herbs for seasoning. The local baker would bake bread for the village - most homes did not hold an oven, only an open fire. Villagers had easy access to fish, chicken, geese, and eggs. Pork was enjoyed at special meals like Easter.

Upper classes of course had a much wider range of foods - all game animals (rabbits, deer, and so on) belonged to them. The wealthy ate peacocks, veal, lamb, and even bear. Meals for all classes could be flavorful and well enjoyed.

Medieval Marriage

Marriage choices were critical for both sons and daughters. Wealthy families would absolutely arrange for "proper" marriages for their children. This was about the transfer of land far more than a love match. Parents wanted to ensure their land went to a family worthy of ownership, one with the resources to defend it from attack. It was not only their own family members they were concerned with. Each block of land had on it both free men and serfs. These people all depended on the nobles – with their skill, connections, and soldiers – to keep them safe from bandits and harm.

Yes, villagers sometimes married for love. Even a few nobles would run off and follow their hearts. Even so, they would have first seriously considered the potentially catastrophic risks which could result from their actions.

Here is a modern example. Imagine you took over the family business which employed a hundred loyal workers. Those workers depend on your careful guidance of the company to ensure the income for their families. You might dream about running off to Bermuda and drinking martinis. But would you just sell your company to any random investor who came along? Would you risk all of those peoples' lives, people who had served you loyally for decades, to satisfy a whim of pleasure?

Medieval Women

In pagan days women held many rights and responsibilities. During the crusades, especially, with many men off at war, women ran the taverns, made the ale, and ran the government.

However, as men returned home and Christianity rose in power women were relegated to a more subservient role.

Still, women in medieval times were not meek and mild. That stereotype came in with the Victorian era, many centuries later. Back in medieval days, women had to be hearty and hard working. There were fields to tend, homes to maintain, and children to raise!

Women strove to be as healthy as they could because they faced a serious threat - a fifth of all women died during or just after childbirth. The church said that childbirth was the "pain of Eve" and instructed women to bear it without medicine or follow-up care. Of course, midwives did their best to skirt these rules, but childbirth still took an immense toll.

Childhood was rough in the middle ages – only 40% of children survived the gauntlet of illnesses to adulthood. A woman who reached her marriageable years was a sturdy woman indeed.

To summarize, in medieval days a person could live a long, happy life, even into their 80s – as long as they were of the sturdy stock that made it through the challenges of childhood. This was very much a time of 'survival of the fittest'. Medieval life quickly weeded out the weak and frail.

So medieval women were strong - very strong. They had to be. Still, would they fight?

Women and Weapons

Queen Boudicia, from Norwalk, was born around AD60 and personally led her troops against the Roman Empire, quite successfully. She had been flogged - and her daughters raped - spurring her to revenge. She was extremely intelligent and quite strategic. Her daughters rode in her chariot at her side.

Eleanor of Aquitaine, born in 1122, was brilliant and married first to a King of France and then to a King of England. She went on the Second Crusades as the leader of her troops - reportedly riding bare-breasted as an Amazon. At times she marched with her troops far ahead of her husband. When she divorced the King of France, she immediately married Henry II, who she passionately adored. He was eleven years her junior. When things went sour, Eleanor separated from him and actively led revolts against him.

Many historical accounts talk of women taking up arms to defend their villages and towns. Women would not passively let their children be slain or their homes burned. They were able and strong bodied from their daily work. They were well skilled with farm implements and knives, and used them with great talent against invaders.

Many of these defenses were successful, and the victories were celebrated as brave and proper, rather than dismissed as an unusual act for a woman. A mother was expected to defend her brood and to keep her home safe, just as a wolf mother protects her cubs.

Numerous women took their martial skills to a higher level. In 1301 a group of Italian women joined up to fight the crusade against the Turks. In 1348 at a tournament there were at least thirty women who participated, dressed as men.

This is not as unusual as you might think. In medieval times, all adults carried a knife at their belt for daily use in eating, chores, and defense. All knew how to use it. Being strong and safe was a necessary part of daily life.

Here is an interesting comparison. In modern times most women know how to drive, but few choose to invest themselves in the time and training to become race car drivers. In medieval times, most women knew how to defend themselves with a weapon. They had to. Few, though, actively sought the training to be swordswomen. Still, these women did exist, and did thrive as valued members of their communities.

So women in medieval times were far from shrinking violets. They were not mud-encrusted wretches huddling in straw huts. They were strong, sturdy, and well versed in the use of knives. Many ran taverns, and most handled the brewing of ale. Those who made it through childhood and childbirth could expect to enjoy long, rich lives.

I hope you enjoy my tales of authentic, inspiring heroines!

About the Author

Lisa Shea is a fervent fan of honor, loyalty, and chivalry. She brings to life worlds where men and women stand shoulder to shoulder, steady in their desire to make the world a better place for all.

While her heroines often wield a sword, they equally value the skilled use of their intelligence, wisdom, courage, and compassion.

Lisa has published ten medieval romance novels. She also has

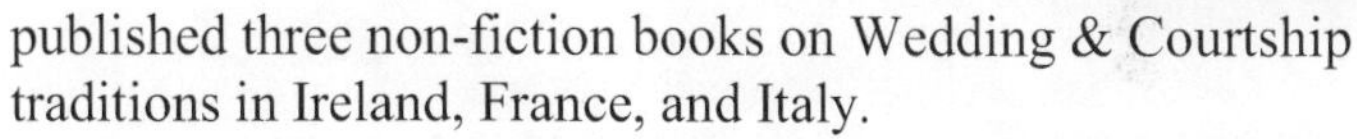

published three non-fiction books on Wedding & Courtship traditions in Ireland, France, and Italy.

Please visit Lisa at LisaShea.com to learn more about her background and interests. Feedback is always appreciated!

Lisa Shea's library of medieval romance novels:

Seeking the Truth
Knowing Yourself
A Sense of Duty
Creating Memories
Looking Back
Badge of Honor
Lady in Red
Finding Peace
Believing your Eyes
Trusting in Faith

Information on these novels can be found at

http://www.lisashea.com/medievalromance/

Each novel is a stand-alone story set in medieval England. These novels can be read in any order and have entirely separate casts of characters.

All proceeds from sales of these novels benefit battered women's shelters.

Made in the USA
Charleston, SC
12 April 2013